GIRL ON A DIAMOND PEDESTAL

BY
MAISEY YATES

Maisey Yates was an avid Mills & Boon Modern Romance reader before she began to write them. She still can't quite believe she's lucky enough to get to create her very own sexy alpha heroes and feisty heroines. Seeing her name on one of those lovely covers is a dream come true.

Maisey lives with her handsome, wonderful, nappy-changing husband and three small children across the street from her extremely supportive parents and the home she grew up in, in the wilds of Southern Oregon, USA. She enjoys the contrast of living in a place where you might wake up to find a bear on your back porch and then heading into the home office to write stories that take place in exotic urban locales.

To my mom, Peggy,
for always encouraging me to simply be me.

And many thanks to Robyn, Gabby, Nicola,
for giving me coaching on my Australian phrases.

CHAPTER ONE

BIRCH Manor was the last constant left. The only thing remaining in her life that had always been there. Everyone else, her mother, her piano teacher, her fans…they were gone. The house was all she had.

Until the bank took it, at least.

Noelle sighed and looked out the window, her stomach tightening as the glossy black Town Car drove through the open wrought-iron gates and around the circular drive, stopping in front of the door to the manor.

She moved away from the window and hoped her guest didn't notice the twitching curtains. It was too sad really, that she'd been reduced to this. Waiting for her home to be taken, watching for the financier coming to appraise the property. Waiting to be evicted. She had no idea where she would go.

The check she'd gotten last week had come with a handwritten note informing her that this would likely be the last royalty check for the foreseeable future. The company wasn't selling her old albums anymore, and several of her digital albums had been taken down from the big websites. No one wanted her music.

Not that the royalties had been amazing over the past year. Hardly anything really, enough to buy a latté on the odd occasion. Now she wouldn't even have that any more.

Suddenly she wanted the hot, frothy drink so badly she thought she might cry.

She was a sad case. Poor Noelle. She'd throw a pity party if she thought anyone would come. Well, the bank might if there was something to repossess. She laughed into the vast, empty entryway, then straightened her skirt and took her place in front of the door, not really sure why she was bothering to play hostess, only that it was reflexive. Her mother would have expected it of her. Demanded it.

Of course, her mother wasn't here.

Noelle sucked in a sharp breath and reached for the doorknob. Her fingers tightened around it, waiting for the knock, and as soon as it pierced the silence, she tugged the door open. Her heart skipped, spinning a downward spiral into her stomach as she took in the man standing before her.

Tall and broad, in a suit that was definitely not of the standard-issue, bank-employee variety, but quality, custom made and tailored to flatter his amazing, masculine physique.

His lips curved into a smile, not a warm one, but one that she felt down to her toes. His eyes were dark, deep like chocolate, but without any of the sweetness. Her stomach tightened, a strong, sharp craving overwhelming her.

For coffee. Still coffee.

"Ms. Birch?" He had a nice voice too, rich and luxuriant, just like the suit. Why couldn't it have been obnoxious? Nasal or high or something. But no, it was low and husky, smooth with a drop-dead-sexy Australian accent adding flavor to his words.

"Yes. Are you…" She changed tactics mid sentence, decided to go for something more forceful. "You're from the bank."

He stepped past her and into the house, his eyes sweeping the room, and her, in a dismissive manner. "Not exactly."

"Then why are you here?"

"I came in lieu of the assessor. I'm interesting in making an offer on the property."

"It's in foreclosure."

"I know. And I'm considering purchasing it before it goes to auction. I need to take a look and let the bank know what I intend to pay for it."

"Really? Why didn't I think of that? I would have given them…well, I think I might have five dollars in my bag over there." She gestured to the red purse hanging on its hook by the door. "Think they'd go for it?"

"Not likely." His answer was clipped, annoyed. Why was he annoyed? She hadn't barged into *his* home early on a Saturday morning. She was the one who got to be annoyed. It was her right.

"Too bad," she said, fighting to keep her tone light, flippant. Unaffected.

"From what I've seen of your loan information, you've been delinquent for months."

Delinquent. She hated that term. Like she was a criminal or something because she didn't have any money. Like she wouldn't have paid the mortgage if her bank balance ever managed to exceed double digits.

"I'm aware of why you're here—or, at least, I'm aware of what I did to make the bank take my house back." The words stuck in her throat. "I don't need a rundown from you."

"Good. Because I'm not here to give it."

"No. You're here to find out if you want to move into my home before the bank has even thrown me out onto the streets," she bit out. She never would have spoken to anyone that way a year ago. She would have been gracious, smiled, been faultless in every way. But that veneer had started eroding over the past year. She just felt angry now. Battered. Like she was dying slowly inside as life chipped away at her very last foothold.

She'd been trained never to show strain or fatigue, never, ever to give the tabloid media a reason to gossip about her. But the past year had been like hell on earth. A constant barrage of blows that never seemed to end. Every time she tried to stand up and dust herself off, something else would hit. And this seemed like the knock-out punch. Because what would she do without this last piece of security? Without this last link to everything she used to be?

Everything she would never be again.

"That's where you're wrong, Noelle," he said, his dark eyes locked with hers. She felt like he could see her—not just that he was looking at her, but that he truly saw *into* her, beneath her polished veneer to the cluttered mess beyond.

She wanted to hide. Not just from him, but from everything.

Isn't that what you've been doing for more than a year now?

Yes. Head down, trying to survive. Trying not to draw media attention. Too defeated to try and track her mother down. Because, as the lawyer she hadn't been able to afford had pointed out, the money had all been in her mother's name, so the battle would be long and expensive. It would devour the fortune that she was trying to win back. And if she didn't win…it would mean the kind of debt she could never crawl out of. It all seemed impossibly hopeless.

"Then do enlighten me, Mr…?"

"Grey." He extended his hand and she accepted the offer, his strong, masculine fingers curling around her slender, pale hand, engulfing it. Making her feel warm, too warm. "Ethan Grey."

Ethan felt a flash of attraction, of pure, raw need, race through him when his hand touched Noelle's soft skin. He ran through a litany of his very favorite swear words in his head. It had been too long since he'd gotten laid if a handshake had the power to get him hot.

Especially a handshake from this particular woman.

Maybe it's genetic?

He bit back a sound of disgust at that thought. He would never use that as an excuse. He was in control of his own actions. If he sinned, it was because he'd chosen it. And at least he was man enough to admit it. Unlike his father. Damien Grey hadn't been much of a role model in that respect.

Yes, she was beautiful, but mostly just fragile-looking with her delicate frame and pale skin. As if she didn't get outside enough. Everything about her was pale. White-blond hair, large, robin's-egg-blue eyes with long, thick lashes, darkened with the aid of makeup. She was like a porcelain doll, one that might break if handled too roughly.

The deep-red lipstick she was wearing was likely intended to give her more color, but all it did was show just how washed out the rest of her was. Pale and drawn, shadows beneath luminous blue eyes.

Even so, she was arresting. Her beauty was almost other-worldly.

She reminded him so much of her mother. That cold, self-possessed allure that made a man ache to see what was beneath all that control. The kind of woman who led men around on leashes, had them begging simply to be in her presence.

She had all of that, plus an air of vulnerability her mother hadn't had. It only added to her appeal. It made a man want to do more than simply possess. It made him want to protect.

"Nice to meet you," she mumbled, pulling her hand away.

He was relieved by the break in contact. "I don't think you really mean that."

She smiled, an expression that didn't reflect in her eyes. "No. You're right, but I'm too polite to say otherwise."

"I'm glad for your manners then," he said dryly.

"How is it I've misunderstood your motives, Mr. Grey?"

"I'm not planning on moving into your house."

She arched an eyebrow. "No?"

"No. I plan on expanding the house and making it a hotel property."

"What?"

She was small, maybe a foot shorter than his own height of six foot three. But there was nothing small about her presence. Even in her pale, diminished state she exuded a kind of force that demanded all eyes rest on her. Another similarity to her mother. At least from what he remembered of the woman. He'd been young the times he'd seen her, lingering near the gates to his childhood home, his father sneaking out to be with her like an adolescent boy. Leaving his wife and son behind so he could indulge in his forbidden passion.

Ethan clenched his hands into fists and forced his mind back to the present. He'd been over the past. Over and over it. Now was the time for action and he couldn't afford to be distracted. Not when the key to his plan was standing right in front of him.

"How can you do that?" she asked, not waiting for him to answer. "This house is two hundred years old. It's…it's a marvel of architecture and…and…it's my home." Her voice cracked on the last word.

He knew that this was the only home in her name. He wasn't sure what had happened to the penthouse in midtown Manhattan, or the townhouse in Paris. When the sprawling estate had come up as a home in foreclosure he'd acted immediately. It was opportunistic on his part, more than a carefully planned-out maneuver. But from the moment he'd walked in, he knew he'd made the right move.

Strange how largely she and her mother had factored into his life, while she seemed to have no clue who he was. He hadn't seen even a hint of recognition in her eyes, either on sight or at the sound of his name.

She was probably too dazzled by the brilliance of her own sparkle to look around and see anyone other than herself.

"I'm not planning on demolishing it, Noelle, merely expanding it. Adding a pool, maybe."

She flinched when he said that. It bothered her, him talking about changing the house. She was attached to it, that much was obvious. And that would prove useful to him.

"Great, well, I don't really want to be involved in the blueprint for this, so maybe I should leave and let you poke around for a while?"

"I don't believe I need to spend any time poking around. My mind is made up. It's a good investment and from where I'm standing it doesn't appear that I'll take a loss on it."

The expression in her eyes changed again. Anger, pure and real, joined the anguish. So much emotion in her. He couldn't summon up a single feeling in response. Too many years of shoving them aside. Of strangling the life out of his emotions whenever possible so he could move forward.

"So you can just buy it then? Like that? Without even

stopping to consider what it might do to your…to your monthly budget or anything like that?"

He laughed. It was only a sound. It didn't really express any of the things laughter usually did. "Not my main concern, no."

He could see the struggle in her, the emotions that made her body tremble even as she kept her face set into a firm, determined expression. She wasn't exactly what he'd imagined she might be. Pampered, yes. Clear prima donna tendencies, yes. But she was strong too. He was certain that beneath that brittle, fragile exterior was a backbone of steel. That only made her more interesting.

"Why is the house so important?" He was hoping it was important. Everything depended on it.

Because it all depended on her. On getting her to agree to his proposition. Revenge was sweet, but she would give it the bitter edge that he craved. That he needed in order to have satisfaction.

"*Why?* Why do you think?" she asked, her voice breaking again. "It's the only home I have. When the bank takes it, I won't get any money from the sale. I'll have nothing. Less than nothing. I have nowhere to go."

"Most single women don't live by themselves in a mansion that could easily house ten other families," he said.

Noelle fought to keep her cool, to keep from breaking down. From showing any weakness. She had been trained to look calm on the surface no matter what. If her mother tore into her before a show, telling her she wasn't beautiful anymore, that it was her fault ticket sales were down, she still had to go on stage. And she would keep every emotion locked in her, letting it escape through her fingertips. In the sound of the piano.

Her emotion didn't seem able to escape that way anymore. Now when she played it was dry, stilted. There was nothing behind it. Nothing but empty, technical skill.

She took a breath. "It's not a matter of downsizing, although that would have helped the electric bill." A bill she had done her very best to scale back. No lights during the day, no heat, the only source of warmth the fireplace in her bedroom so she didn't freeze at night. "I don't have anything," she said, shame creeping over her.

He arched one dark eyebrow, his expression cool, blank of any sort of caring or true interest. "How is that possible?"

The last thing she wanted to do was give him her big bad sob story. She'd found a lot of strength over the past year. Just getting up had been a struggle some days, but she'd done it. And she'd done it with no support. Asking for help now violated that sense of independence and pride. But she was staring homelessness in the face and she wasn't certain her pride came into it anymore.

"Everything's gone. Don't you know what happens to child stars when their parents manage everything? It's a story that gets repeated on entertainment news channels quite frequently."

She wasn't a child now, which was why she'd become so uninteresting to the public. Concert halls were half-empty when before she'd filled them. A nine-year-old girl playing original compositions on a massive grand piano was a spectacle. It was amazing. A woman doing the same thing lacked the wow factor.

Empty halls meant more pressure. More drills. More practice. Something was wrong and it was her fault. And then it had all stopped. The music quit playing in her head. She looked at a beautiful landscape, at people on the sidewalk, and she heard nothing. Once, it had all been enhanced by the soundtrack in her mind. Melodies that came about constantly, endlessly.

It was quiet now. Dead.

"They took everything," he said.

"My mother did." The betrayal was still like an open wound inside her, something she couldn't seem to reconcile or heal.

That got a slight reaction from him, a bit of real shock in his dark eyes. "And she's gotten away with it?"

"It's all in her name," she said. "Most of my money was earned before I turned eighteen and even after that I never bothered to change anything. I mean, why would I? She had always managed my finances and I trusted her. I have no contract saying any of it should have been mine, or that I earned it. So that's how I ended up with nothing." She paused for a moment and looked up at the ceiling. "Well, this house is in my name, so yay me."

The only person who knew about her mother was the lawyer she'd spoken to. She hadn't been able to bear the thought of telling anyone else. The fact that her own mother would do that to her. Her piano teacher had quit. Friends, people she'd toured with sometimes, were still busy making music. And she was alone.

In an old empty house with bills that she could never hope to pay. She'd been treading water until recently, working on a plan, some sort of solution…but now she was going under. And she knew she would drown before any sort of help came along.

Ethan knew he shouldn't really be shocked that Noelle's mother had betrayed her like that. A bitch like her didn't care who she hurt. She certainly hadn't cared about the pain she'd caused his mother. Not in the least.

But as much as he hated Noelle's mother for her part, it was his father Damien who had to pay for the sins of the past. And Noelle was in the perfect position to make that a reality.

He ignored the slight twinge of conscience he began to feel in his chest, spreading to his arms, making his fingertips feel numb. He didn't have time for a conscience. Noelle would get what she needed, and he would get exactly what he wanted.

Everyone would win.

Except for his father.

"Will you be touring again soon?" he asked.

Noelle had been touring since she was a child. He'd never been to see her, but he'd seen her name in the news frequently. She'd played at Carnegie Hall, she'd played for the Queen of England. She was a household name and had been for at least eleven years. And apparently, all of that touring had left her with nothing.

"I'm not touring anymore," she said tightly. "My label dropped me because I couldn't book venues. My publicist dropped me. My agent." She made a clicking sound with her tongue. "So, yeah, I'm pretty much done with music."

She looked down, lashes fanning over high cheekbones that seemed a bit more pronounced than they should be. She had that cabbage-soup-diet look about her, like she wasn't getting quite enough to eat. He couldn't imagine her turning down his proposition, not when he knew she needed it so badly.

And he was tempted, tempted to come out with it now.

But it was too soon.

He was a master of the business deal, and tomorrow, he would set in motion the most important deal of his life. He wouldn't allow impatience to ruin that.

"Come to my office tomorrow," he said. "I'll send a car for you around noon."

"Why? So we can discuss where in my hundred-year-old rose garden you're going to dig your inground pool?"

"Not exactly."

He had no intention of turning her home into a hotel. He had no intention of purchasing it at all. Sure, a hotel here would bring in money, but that money would be nothing compared to the satisfaction he would gain by executing vengeance against his father.

Noelle, and her home, were the key to that revenge.

CHAPTER TWO

ETHAN'S office building was warm. Noelle let it wash over her as she walked into the open, stately marble foyer and crossed to an elevator that took her to the top floor.

Even the elevator spoke of luxury. She ached for it. For gorgeous hotels with amazing views and thousand-thread-count sheets. For heat, and for lunch that consisted of more than instant noodles with little freeze-dried chunks of vegetables.

For a crowded auditorium and applause meant just for her.

"You really are pathetic," she said to the empty lift.

Yes, she really was. But knowing that didn't make the longing go away. Her life had never been easy, she knew that. Sometimes she'd wished for all of the fame, the practice, the shrill voice of her mother and the stern voice of her instructor to go away.

But now that they had, she was faced with some harsh realities she'd never dealt with before.

She sucked in a sharp breath as the elevator stopped. Her stomach turned over, her hands shook as if she was about to go out on stage. The kick of adrenaline was addictive. It was one of the many things she missed about her former life as a concert pianist.

This was different though. The familiar spike of adrenaline was infused with a warm, honeyed sensation that pooled in her stomach and made her body ache in places she'd never given a thought to.

She clenched her teeth and took a breath. *Focus.*

She walked from the lift to a reception area and gave her name to the man sitting behind the desk. While he searched for it in the computer, she picked one of her favorite pieces—not one of her own, but one of Mozart's—and began to run through the notes.

Pictured her fingers flying over the keys. Effortlessly, joyfully.

It was something she always did before a performance, to remind her of how prepared she was. That she was ready. That she wouldn't make a mistake.

"Just through that door there, Ms. Birch," the receptionist said, smiling brightly.

"Thank you," she replied, keeping her mind on the music as she walked to the door.

She tried to slow her breathing, keeping it in rhythm with the legato portion of the piece. *Slow and steady. Don't rush. Don't falter. Smooth.*

She opened the door and the notes fluttered from her head like startled birds. She wasn't prepared for whatever this meeting was, and there was no use pretending otherwise.

Because Ethan was more frightening than a theater filled with three thousand people. He was sitting behind a broad, neat desk, his large hands folded in front of him, his expression even harder than it had been yesterday at her house.

"Good morning," he said, unfolding his hands and putting them behind his head, the action so casual it was maddening. That he wasn't tense at all when she felt like a slight breeze could shatter her was beyond unfair.

"Morning," she said, refusing to lie and call it good. "I'm here for our mysterious meeting."

"Have a seat," he offered, gesturing to the chair in front of his desk.

"No." She wasn't going to put herself in that position. Him behind his big desk, her sitting there on the opposite side like a child about to be scolded.

Being meek and subservient didn't work. It didn't keep people with you. It only made you easier to deal with. And this past year she'd come to see that she'd been being thoroughly dealt with all of her life. That was one good result of having a bomb detonated in the middle of her existence. She wasn't going to play the pawn anymore.

A harsh lesson learned the hard way. But she *had* learned it. In some ways, without her gilded cage, she was stronger now than she'd ever been. Even if it didn't always feel like it.

A half smile curved his lips. She didn't like that. Because it wasn't an amused smile, it was something else. Something sort of dark beneath the surface of the expression. "No?"

"I'd prefer to stand," she said stiffly.

He inclined his head. "If you like."

He stood then, and she felt dwarfed. He was a foot taller than she was, and broad. More than that, he just seemed to fill the room with his presence. The something else that gave people whiplash as they passed him in the street, trying to get a look at him. Mad sex appeal or something. She stretched her neck and straightened her shoulders. It didn't help.

"I would say that this was business," he said. "That it's not personal. But that would be a lie."

She swallowed hard. "Would it?"

"Yes. I don't need the money your home would bring

in as a boutique hotel. I don't need the money that would come in from buying the family business, Grey's. But I don't want him to have it. And that's where you come in."

"Me?"

"It was a nice accident, seeing that your home was about to be foreclosed on. I thought I might be able to help you out. For a fee."

"A fee?"

"There is no such thing as a free lunch. Or, in your case, a free manor house situated a reasonable commuter distance from the city."

"You must realize that I don't have anything to give you," she said, her heart sinking into her stomach at the same moment that the back of her neck started to prickle. He must know she didn't have money. Which meant he must want something else. And that couldn't be anything good.

"You've never heard my name?" he asked.

"No," she said. "Should I have heard it?"

"I know yours. And not just because you're famous. Or, more accurately, I know your mother's name."

"How?"

"Do you know the name Damien Grey?"

"I…" She almost said no. But it was a name she knew, not the last name, but the first. A very familiar name. "Yes. Well, Damien, but…it could be a different Damien."

"I'm betting not. Damien Grey is my father, and for several years, he was your mother's lover."

As revelations went, it shouldn't have been shocking. It wasn't as though she'd believed her mother had been out having tea parties while Noelle spent nights alone in grand hotel suites before performances, but her mind had never gone there.

She did remember her mother talking about Damien,

though. Meeting him. Staying with him. She'd been eight, maybe, when that had started and she simply hadn't put the relationship in the right context.

"I always thought he was in the music industry," she said, realizing how stupid that sounded. She shook her head. "But what does this have to do with me? Or is it all part of drawing out the torture that has been the past year of my life? I'm not quite dead yet, want to land the fatal blow?"

"I have a proposition for you."

She gave him a pointed glare and drew on every shred of strength she'd been building in herself for the past year. "If this has anything to do with filling the position in your life that my mother filled in your father's, you can take your proposition and shove it up your—"

"I'd like you to be my wife."

She took a step back and sucked in air, choking on it, coughing and coughing while trying to catch her breath.

"Are you all right?" Ethan took a step toward her and she held up her hand, gesturing for him to stop. A gesture he ignored.

He put his hand on her back, his touch warm and…comforting, in some strange way. A connection. She hadn't had a connection with anyone in so long. She wondered if she ever truly had.

She cleared her throat and breathed deeply. "I'm fine now." She stepped away from him.

"Do you need something?"

She'd have to make a list.

Yesterday's craving came back to her in full force. "A latte?"

He nodded and walked back to his desk, pressing the intercom button on his phone. "Christophe, I need a latte." He looked back at Noelle. "How do you like it?"

"Vanilla. With whipped cream."

He repeated the instructions to Christophe then cut off the connection.

"It will be here soon," he said.

She wanted to cry, and it was the stupidest thing. Yet she couldn't stop the ache of emotion that tightened her throat. No, it wasn't emotion, she told herself. It was her recent choking experience. That was all. "Thank you."

"Now, shall I repeat my offer or will it send you into a fit again?"

She narrowed her eyes. "I choked. Although if it had been a fit, it wouldn't be overly surprising, would it?"

"Marriage in exchange for your home. Free and clear, not owned by the bank, but by you."

Well, wasn't that a bright shiny poison apple? *Take a bite, dearie.* "What's the catch? Why me?"

"I thought you might have a bigger stake in this than a stranger would. Think about your mother seeing you in the news, rising back to the top on my arm. The simple truth is, I need a wife to get the company. And if that wife was you, if you were a part of taking it from my father's grasping hands, well, it would be that much sweeter."

"That's...I don't know. I don't know if I can be involved in this. It's..."

"Let me simplify it. If you marry me, in name only, and divorce me once Grey's is transferred into my name, you get your house. And the rest of it doesn't need to matter to you."

"How can it not matter to me?" she asked.

He shrugged. "That's up to you. But how do you think it would be for your mother to see you in the paper, to see you back at the top? In circles she can't move in any more, not once you're in them. Because then they might find out what she did to you. Maybe you don't have legal recourse, but you can close her out of society. If I remember her correctly, that mattered a great deal to her."

Noelle tried to think through the pulse pounding in her temple. "Yes. It did. Does."

"Wouldn't it be nice to take a piece of that back from her?"

Yes. Yes it would. And no, she didn't think she was bigger than that. Because all her life, she'd been nothing more than her mother's ticket in. A chance for her to move in the circles she'd always dreamed of while Noelle did all the work to keep her there.

"How do I know I can trust you?" she asked.

"How do you know you can trust anyone?"

Noelle thought of her mother. Of finding out one day that the penthouse in Manhattan was empty…and so was her bank account. "I suppose you can't."

"Time. A blood relationship. Marriage vows. None of it can ensure you know someone. But you have nothing to lose. You can only gain. You don't have anything else for me to take."

Well, that wasn't entirely true, but she wasn't planning on announcing it anytime soon. "But this would…" She fought the blush creeping into her face. "Not a real marriage, right?"

"A real wedding. A legal marriage. But nothing more. Nothing permanent or physical."

"Oh." It sounded simple. Uncomplicated and…tempting. A chance not only to get her home back, but to have the bank stop calling and sending notices. A chance to show her mother she hadn't won.

"In the interest of us knowing each other better, I'm going to ask you some questions and you will answer me. Honestly."

Noelle blinked, the change of topic making her head spin. "Are you interviewing me for the position?"

"As any good businessman would."

Noelle shifted, uncomfortable beneath his assessing gaze.

"I know you've never been married," he said.

"No." She shook her head.

"Do you have a man in your life? A lover?"

She nearly laughed. Where would she have kept a lover? In her suitcase while they were on the road? Her mother would never have allowed such a thing. Sure, *she* got to make time for men, but she would never have permitted Noelle the same luxury. Would never have let her compromise her image like that. And now... Well, she wasn't about to bring a date back to her big empty house and tell him all about how washed-up she was over a cup of bargain-brand soda.

"Not at the moment," she replied dryly.

"Good. It would have to remain that way for the duration of the arrangement. For appearances."

"I think I can manage that."

An answering smile curved his lips. "Excellent."

"And I'll get my house?"

"And then some."

"What else?" she asked, hating that she cared. Hating that she was tempted.

"I would give you a settlement when we divorced. That's in addition to all the media attention you'll get as a result of our association. I attend a lot of events and as my fiancée, you would attend with me."

The longing that assaulted her was like a great, dark pit opening up inside. Empty and huge, waiting to be filled. Needing it.

Parties and people and cameras. Luxury. Things that

had been so absent from her life. A link to the girl she'd been, the things she'd had. This was a chance to have it again. She despised the weakness in her that wanted it. That needed it.

And yet she felt crushed by the desire for it.

There was a quiet knock on the door and Christophe came in, latte in hand. The wide-mouthed caramel-colored mug was like a vessel of life in her eyes. She hadn't bought coffee in weeks, months maybe. Not even for the machine at home.

She took it in her hands and let the heat from the ceramic seep into her palms. "Thank you," she murmured, her throat tight again.

Christophe smiled and made a hasty exit, as she imagined he was paid to do. Quiet efficiency.

She took a sip and was horrified when her eyes blurred with tears. She blinked hard as she swallowed the warm, comforting liquid, allowing it to soothe the pain in her chest.

She lowered the cup and looked fixedly at the swirl of thick cream on the top of her latte.

A flash of recognition mingled with the image of a headline in her mind. *He's offering you this. A way to escape. A way out.*

And a way to prove to your mother that she didn't win.

"So this would be a marriage as far as legalities go, but not…not permanent and not physical," she repeated.

"Exactly. No one, including my father, needs to know the personal aspects of the relationship. But it is imperative we make it down the aisle. I came close once, and it's going to take more than close to get what I want."

She nodded. Tried to picture it. Tried to picture getting married. Funny how she'd never really thought about it before. She'd played at weddings, celebrity weddings, weddings for royalty, but she'd never once thought of her own.

Her scope had always been so narrow. She'd lived and breathed piano. Performance, composition, practice, drills…she had dreamed music. It had been her all-consuming passion and drive. And when it had faltered, her mother had always been there to push her past it. To make sure that she didn't lose focus for even a moment.

It was good in a way. She didn't have a romantic fantasy tied to the thought of wedding. A wedding was…well, it was paper. Paper with performance added into the mix. And she did performance. At least she had done it. She'd done it well, too.

A kind of restless energy overtook her, starting in her fingertips, tingling up her arms and to her stomach. Why not do it? How was it really different than any other performance she'd given? She'd always projected a character on stage. Serene and sweet no matter what was going on inside of her. No matter if she'd been fighting with her mother or if she'd suffered a slap across the face at the other woman's hands ten minutes before show time. She just added another layer of powder and went out on stage, smile pasted on.

"It's a temporary arrangement. A business proposition. And I would pay you well."

"And we would be expected to…go out. Go to parties, that sort of thing." It shamed her that it mattered, almost more than the money. To be bathed in the glow of admiration again. Nothing felt like that. Nothing. It made her feel that she was a part of something, that she was important. That she was loved.

And she'd been so alone for so long. Hiding, hoping no one would find out what had happened.

"Yes. We would have to at least give the appearance of a courtship, even if it is a whirlwind one."

"Stranger things have happened, I suppose."

"Much stranger."

"Like a mother making off with her daughter's earnings?"

He nodded. "Or a father betraying his family to spend time with his mistress."

And this was a chance, for both of them, to make some of it right. And maybe she was making it more than it was because right now the latte was so warm and so comforting, and the caffeine was making her feel more awake and alive than she had in weeks but it seemed slightly poetic in nature.

They had both been manipulated. Betrayed in a way. They had both lost things they had earned, things that were theirs by right, at the hands of those who were supposed to love them.

They deserved to take those things back. They both deserved to win.

"You'll put this all in a…a contract, right?" She had learned the hard way that even her own mother couldn't be trusted, she wasn't about to put her trust in a man she'd only just met.

"We'll have a prenup. Of course it won't outline the specifics of the arrangement, as we don't want that made public. The house will be yours upon the signing of our marriage license, money after the divorce."

"You've thought this through."

A wicked grin curved his lips. "I'm making it up as I go along, but I've been told I'm pretty good at improvising."

"I would say so."

She wasn't. She was pretty crap at improvising, as it happened. The whole last year was proof of that.

"I've begun the paperwork with the bank to purchase the manor. I'll sign it over to you once we speak the vows."

"And the prenup?"

"My lawyer can have it ready by tomorrow."

She felt dizzy. Her life had been stagnant for so long, nothing to mark the passing of months but a new mortgage bill in the mail. Now suddenly things were changing. She felt like she might be able to see the light at the end of the tunnel.

And there had been nothing but damp, dank cold for so long.

"Good," she heard herself say. She felt as if she were hovering above the scene now, watching it all with a surreal kind of detachment.

It didn't seem real, that was for sure. But it felt hopeful in a really strange way.

That marriage to a man she didn't know or love seemed hopeful said a lot about the sad state of her affairs, that was for certain.

"I'll see you tomorrow then," he said.

"Your place or mine?" she asked, trying to force a laugh.

A dark light shone in his eyes. "I'd say yours, since it is the thing that brought us together."

CHAPTER THREE

ETHAN could hear the music as soon as he walked up to the door of the manor. It wasn't a classical piece. It wasn't a song at all. Repetition and scales, the same few notes over and over again with regimented perfection. A straight, staccato rhythm more like a military maneuver than anything related to music.

Strange. He hadn't associated that kind of discipline with her. But then, she looked so much like her mother it was hard for him not to think of their personalities being as identical as their features. Celine Birch was a cloud of perfume and gauzy clothing in his memory. Frothy and elegant, nice even. It had taken some time to realize what she was.

His father's mistress. No, more than that. The woman Damien Grey had loved above his family. The woman he hadn't even bothered to hide from his wife.

Ethan gritted his teeth and raised his hand, pounding on the door hard and fast. The strains of the piano continued, unbroken, unyielding. He turned the knob and the door opened. He followed the sounds of the piano, his footsteps echoing as he crossed the marble tiled entryway and walked into the formal sitting room.

There were no interior lights on, the opulent crystal chandelier hanging from the ceiling was dark. The only illumination came from the sun shining through two large windows.

And then there was Noelle, sitting at the piano, her eyes fixed on a point in front of her rather than down at her fingers, playing the notes over and over again. The sun was like golden fire in her hair, illuminating it, giving the impression of a halo. He wondered how it was possible for someone who looked so angelic to set fire to a man's blood without so much as a sultry glance.

She looked up and the music stopped abruptly, her too-large eyes overly wide in her face. "Ethan." She scrambled around to the other side of the glossy white grand piano.

"Am I early?" He knew he wasn't.

"I..." She looked around for as if searching for something. "I don't have a clock in here."

"What are you working on?"

She shook her head and tucked a strand of glossy hair behind her ear. "Nothing. Drills. Keeping up my dexterity."

"Do you practice every day?"

"Yes."

"I didn't think you were doing music anymore."

She shrugged. "I don't have anything else to do."

He walked over to the piano and ran his fingers over the sleek body. "I don't have a piano in my penthouse."

She frowned slightly. "Do you play?"

He chuckled. "No."

"Then why..." she trailed off, her mouth falling open. "Oh."

"You didn't imagine you would continue to live out here in the country did you? Especially not after we're married."

"I hadn't really...I hadn't really thought about it."

"I'll be installing you in a penthouse suite in one of my

hotels. All the better to garner the proper attention and establish ourselves as a real couple."

She winced over his choice of words. "Right."

"Is that a problem?"

She shook her head. "I'm used to moving around." Actually, the habit of moving around was so ingrained in her that staying in one place for so long had actually felt wrong in many ways. This past year, stuck out in the weeds all by herself, had been more surreal than a different city every night.

"I trust you'll find everything to your satisfaction."

Although the idea of running into her seemed extremely appealing.

"Great." She bit her lip and looked back at the piano.

"Do you need it in Manhattan?"

"I don't…it's a pain to move pianos. Hardly worth it."

"I'll buy you a new one and have it moved into the suite."

He said it so casually, like the purchase of a piano that would run him six figures meant absolutely nothing. There was a time when it had been the same for her. She'd had an allowance, provided by her mother, with the money from touring, merchandise and album sales, and she'd wanted for nothing.

There had been so much money then. Money she'd earned. Money that had somehow never been hers.

"I can't ask you to do that."

"It's nothing, Noelle. As you mentioned before, I have no shortage of resources at my disposal. You and I are working together and I see no reason why this partnership can't be beneficial for the both of us."

She frowned slightly. "I suppose."

Noelle wasn't certain what to do with such an accommodating offer. That he cared about her need to play the piano seemed strange. Her playing didn't benefit him. Now, her mother had always made certain there was a piano in every hotel suite they used. She couldn't skip practice, not for one afternoon. Being on tour was no excuse. She always got her hours in on the piano. It was her job, and she worked at it as faithfully as anyone who went to an office every day.

Or well beyond that point. It was her only input into the business that was her career. Her mother did the networking. She went to the parties, talked to booking agents, labels and made sure all the needs per her tour rider were in order. It was all about making sure that Noelle Birch—the business—was in order. It was never about her as a person.

But Ethan just seemed to be concerned with what she wanted, what might make her happy. It was strange. It made her feel warm inside, more even than yesterday's latte. She liked that even less than his wicked smiles. Because she knew better than to trust those feelings. Than to trust people who acted like they cared.

"Do you have the prenup?" she asked, stomach suddenly filled with a shivering sensation.

"Yes." He reached into his interior suit-jacket pocket and took out a folded stack of papers.

His fingers brushed against hers as he passed them to her. He was warm, like his office. She unfolded the papers and skimmed them, her heart accelerating when she got to the part about children and custody.

"But we don't need…"

"This is mostly a standard document. As far as even my lawyer is concerned this is a real marriage. My grandfather wanted me to have stability. The kind I lacked growing up, I think. Of course, I'm of the opinion that marriage doesn't necessarily bring that sort of stability. You can understand why."

"Haven't you tried just explaining to him?"

"You don't explain things to my grandfather. There's no point. He knows everything already. He's coming from a good place. And I don't mind following his rules—if only because I have such an easy time bending them," he grinned.

She kept on reading the prenup, her eyes widening when she saw the settlement she was entitled to in the event of a divorce. An event that they already had planned.

"Enough?" he asked.

She cleared her throat. "I…yes."

It was generous. Not enough that she'd never have to work again, but enough to keep her out of abject poverty, and with the full ownership of the manor in addition to the cash settlement it was all more than enough.

She could sell the manor, get a smaller apartment in town. She'd have enough to buy lattes and eat more than a cup of instant noodles for dinner.

It was enough that she couldn't say no. Even if the whole situation made her want to get in the shower and scrub her skin until she could wash away the film it had left on her. Her mother sleeping with his father, hurting his family that way. The idea of marrying just so she could keep her house…

Okay, so it might seem mercenary marrying for money, but it wasn't a real marriage. And why shouldn't she be a little bit mercenary? Everyone in her life had looked out for themselves, they'd used her to make their position in life better. What was wrong with her doing something for herself? And she wasn't using Ethan, she was helping him. They were helping each other. It was a very good rationalization, anyway.

"Once we leave here, you aren't backing out."

She shook her head. "I won't. I can't."

"Just remember, you stand to lose a lot more than I do."

"There's no way I could forget that." She bit her lip hard, trying to block out the feeling of hopelessness that was rising up in her, a feeling she had become far too familiar with. "Do you have a pen?" she asked, holding out her hand and hoping he didn't notice the slight tremble in her fingers.

"You don't have to sign it yet. We haven't even applied for the license. The actual wedding won't be for a while. We'll have to establish ourselves as a couple. For my grandfather's satisfaction."

"But I'm ready to sign." She was ready to move forward. Ready to commit one hundred percent.

"Good." He took the documents from her and put them back in his pocket. "Are you ready to come with me now?"

"Now?"

"Why wait?"

She looked around the living room, at the last connection to her former life. "No reason. It might take me a while to pack."

"I can wait."

It was the kind of opulence that felt like both a half-remembered dream and her due at the same time. The kind she had almost forgotten about, but longed for. She'd been reminded, with full and brutal force, just how much she missed it yesterday in Ethan's office, the warmth and glamour surrounding her like a comforting blanket.

And now, in the open, expansive suite, she just wanted to throw Ethan out the door and turn circles like the little girl she'd never truly been.

"Does it meet your standards?" he asked, resting his broad, dark hand on the white marble bar top.

She turned and forced a smile, trying to ignore the growing ball of emotion in her chest. "Perfectly."

"I can have a piano brought in tomorrow, does that work for you?"

"Yes, absolutely." A piano too. To go with the lush, amazing view of Central Park. And money. All fine and good to stand on principle and pretend it didn't matter… when you had some. But when you didn't…well, that was when you realized how important money was. It might not buy happiness, but it paid power bills, bought food and clothes. Those things made her pretty happy.

The knot inside her grew larger, made it hard to breathe. She felt…the whole thing just felt wrong, and yet she didn't think she could walk away. It wasn't like she was sleeping with him. That would make it all truly reprehensible.

But she still felt as if she was selling herself.

Haven't you always sold yourself?

What else was performance anyway? She had always been the product. It wasn't just her music. If her music had been all people wanted from her, it wouldn't have mattered that she was an adult now. That she was no longer a cute little cherub dwarfed by the grand piano she played.

This was just a different venue.

And she wasn't going to sleep with him.

Her body felt hot all over just thinking about it. She had zero experience when it came to men, and while in theory she knew about sex—all about it, since she had a pretty curious nature and she'd done a lot of…reading on the subject—she'd never had a chance to put her knowledge into practice. When would she have found the time? And her mother would have…

She closed that thought off. She didn't care anymore. She had once—she had cared so much. She'd wanted to please her mother, her instructor, her fans and her tutors more than anything in the world. To earn love by being talented and easy to deal with, to give and give.

She had nothing to show for it.

She didn't care what her mother would think of her now. And, considering her mother's personal life, it would be hypocritical for her even to have an opinion. So she could sleep with Ethan if she wanted to. She didn't have anyone around telling her what to do, what to wear and what to think. She could do what she liked, and that meant she didn't have to hide away, she didn't have to do drills every day and she didn't have to stay away from men.

A little tremor wracked her body. Sensual and shameful. Sensual because…well, Ethan just took her thoughts down that path. Shameful because, while in normal circumstances the idea might appeal, she wasn't out to sell her body in the interest of spiting her mother. No, things weren't as desperate as all that.

There was a quiet knock on the door and Ethan crossed behind her. She turned quickly. She wanted to make sure she could see him.

He opened the door without checking to verify who it was. "Yes?"

"Mr. Grey." An employee of the hotel, identified only by his highly polished name tag—his sharply tailored suit was as far from a hotel uniform as anything Noelle had ever seen—stood in the entryway. "When I heard you were here, I thought I would come and make sure that everything was—"

"Everything's fine, Thomas," Ethan said, moving to where Noelle was standing, his stance possessive. A clear sign that he was linking the two of them, proving to the employee just where things stood.

Of course, it was all for show. But he was as good as putting on a show as she had once been.

"Noelle will be staying here for the foreseeable future. Everything is to go to my account. Food and service, anything she wants."

She didn't—couldn't—believe that Ethan was truly giving her carte blanche to have whatever she wanted. All part of the show, she reminded herself. Because a man could hardly seem stingy in regards to his...whatever the world was meant to see her as at the moment.

A potential wife. A high-priced call girl.

Her heart thudded dully in her chest. They could see her as either, it wouldn't matter. Ethan would marry her in the end and that would put a bit of salve on her reputation. Of course, the reputation would blister again after the divorce, but that was the least of her worries. At the moment she had no reputation. Her star had fizzled out.

Ethan moved nearer to her, curling his arm around her waist, drawing her to his body. His fingers moved, idly, slowly, the touch feather light over her clothing. Yet it seemed to blaze a trail of fire that penetrated the thin fabric of her blouse, leaving smoldering embers in its wake that retained the heat long after the flame had moved on.

She tried to suppress the small shiver that raced up her spine, but she couldn't. Too much of her energy was focused on keeping her face neutral, keeping from conveying to Thomas that having a man's fingertips drifting over the line of her waist was anything more than a common occurrence.

"Yes, sir." Thomas nodded. "And will you be staying here as well? In the interest of providing you with the best service."

Yeah, right. More like in the interest of being nosy.

Ethan's fingers drifted further up her body, to her ribs, curling around, barely brushing the underside of her breast. She stiffened, not allowing the gasp that had climbed into her throat to escape, not allowing her face to betray her shock.

"I'll call down in the morning for room service when I'm here. Rest assured, I'll be certain my needs are met while I'm staying."

Her face was hot, it felt like the blood beneath it was boiling, pulsing as it rushed through her veins and lit her skin like a beacon. She sucked in a breath. "Or I will." There. This was a game. That's all it was. And she wasn't about to be bested.

She didn't need heaps of—or any—sexual experience in order to play the part.

Ethan caught her chin between his thumb and forefinger and tilted her face up so that she had to meet his liquid black gaze. "I have no doubt about that. In fact, I have a feeling I'll be requiring very little in the way of hotel room service."

Her pulse was pounding in her temples now, but she ignored it. Instead of shrinking away from him, as her body was screaming at her to do, she curled herself into him, putting her palm flat on his chest.

It was solid, well-muscled. She could feel the definition of his body beneath the layers of his crisp dress shirt and suit jacket. He didn't have the body of a man who spent all his time behind a desk.

He had the body of a man who worked out. Shirtless. Maybe he swam? Water sluicing over all that enticing, golden skin, muscles shifting and bunching, tensing and relaxing as he moved…

She chastised her imagination big-time for that unnecessary foray into fantasy.

Understandably, their little sex farce brought sex to mind, but that didn't mean she was allowed to indulge in thoughts like that.

No, she was allowed to. If she wanted to. Which she didn't. Because this thing with Ethan was a business transaction. And that meant sex and fantasy had no place in it. She had to remember that.

She pressed her palm more firmly against him, proving to herself that he was just a man. A person. A body. Nothing to get excited about. "I'll make sure you have whatever you need," she said, fighting to keep the tremor out of her voice.

Thomas, the nosy employee, forced a smile. "Excellent, sir, then if everything is to your liking…?"

"Yes, we're fine for now."

"I'll leave you then."

When he turned and left, Noelle let out a gust of breath and tried to extricate herself from Ethan's hold without flailing.

"I think the show is over," she said, gritting her teeth when he continued to hold onto her.

"Is it?" he released her. "Too bad. I enjoyed that very much."

"It was beyond thrilling," she said, her smile false, very purposefully false so he would know just how fake the sentiment was. She had a feeling he wasn't being sincere. Just trying to see if he could agitate her.

"You surprise me sometimes."

"Do I?" she asked, her teeth locked tightly together.

"The day we met you seemed very…pale."

"I was about to lose my home, and you were scoping it out and making changes before my rear end had even hit the gutter."

"True enough."

Pale. What a strange way to describe her. Or maybe not. *Pale* sounded weak, washed-out. As if something had more potential and yet wasn't reaching it. Her stomach sank a bit. That was her. She couldn't even argue.

She was beginning to find that lost potential now though. She just had to get her life back on track. Get some resources so that she had a square one to start from. Maybe she could play again. Maybe the music would come back to her. If she played this opportunity right, she would have a chance.

Without it, she would lose the only asset she possessed. She would be on her own again, with nothing. No job experience, and not a whole lot of real-life experience.

"A year ago I never would have had the courage to do this," she said. "But, way back then, I didn't recognize a very important truth."

"What's that, beautiful?"

Her stomach tightened when he said that. *Beautiful.* She used to feel beautiful sometimes. She wanted to feel beautiful again.

It's up to you to feel beautiful though. Everyone else could just be lying.

Yes, it was up to her.

"I learned that you can't count on anyone. The only person I can trust to hold my best interests in high regard is me. If I want to change things, I have to do it, because no one else will do it for me."

"A hard lesson to learn, but an important one," he said.

"Very. So I'm taking care of me. Of my best interests."

"Don't forget my best interests. Don't forget your end of the deal."

"I won't."

"Good." He leaned in, his scent teasing her sense. The only man she'd had any exposure to was her piano teacher, and he had smelled of hair grease and heavy cologne. Ethan smelled like soap, clean skin and a little bit of something unique that was simply…him. A smell that made her want to lean in to him, to lean on his strength.

No. The only strength she could trust was her own.

Of course, it would be better if she could find a decent amount of strength.

She swallowed heavily and took a step back. He took a step toward her and she stopped, rooted to the spot on the plush carpet.

"I'm glad you're intent on playing your part, Noelle. Because tonight," he lifted his hand and skimmed her cheek with his thumb, brushing a lock of her pale gold hair from her shoulder, "I'm going to show the world that you're mine."

CHAPTER FOUR

I'm not yours. I'm not anyone's.

Her words echoed in her head as she contorted her arm in order to pull the zipper up on the tiny black cocktail dress that Ethan had had sent to her room an hour earlier.

Her words were feeble because hey, power, he had it. But she didn't belong to him. That was how her mother had seen her, too. A thing she could own. A thing she could sell. It was a good thing she'd had musical abilities or there was no telling what her mother would have used her for.

She shuddered and bent over, lifting a foot up and tugging on one of the glittering, beaded high heels, also provided by Ethan. Or Ethan's personal shopper or assistant. He didn't exactly seem the type to go and pick up a pair of gorgeous, sparkly shoes.

She bent and started pulling on the other shoe, lost her balance and wobbled sideways, catching herself on the couch but still tumbling to the floor. She let a curse slip through her lips and then laughed.

"Not quite ready yet?"

She turned sharply at the sound of that rich, oh-so-sexy voice. "You didn't knock. Did you knock?"

"It's my hotel," he said, shrugging broad shoulders and walking over to the bar. From her vantage point on the ground he looked even taller, and slightly more infuriating than normal since he'd just caught her at a disadvantage.

"It's my room," she said.

A half grin tugged at the corner of his mouth. "I'm paying for it." He picked up a bottle of Scotch and poured himself just enough to fill the bottom portion of the glass. "Drink?"

"Soda?" she asked.

He raised his eyebrows. "Soda?"

"I have a one-drink limit if I'm going out in public. My mother's rule, but in cases like this, I've always found it to be a good one."

"Have you?" he opened the fridge that was set into the bar and produced a little glass bottle of lemon-lime soda.

"I've seen too many starlets sprawled out on the floor at a big party after too much heavy drinking."

He looked down at her, his lips curving upward. "Sprawled on the floor, eh?"

She pushed her shoe on the rest of the way and pulled herself up, tugging the hem of her dress down. "A clumsy moment isn't the same as getting completely drunk and making an ass out of yourself in public."

"Relax. Have a soda, it'll calm your nerves. Well, it won't, but here you go." He picked up the bottle and walked over to her, putting the cool glass in her hand.

She was surprised that it still felt cold. After being in his hand she'd half expected it to be hot. From him, his skin. And good grief, but he was handsome.

Rugged and polished at the same time, totally put together while maintaining a slightly dangerous edge. It was the glimmer in his brown eyes, the sort of devilish look that told a woman he knew how to be bad at just the right moments....

And here she was turning Ethan Grey into some kind

of simplistic fantasy. She was too innocent when it came to men and she knew it. It was too easy to imagine she could handle him when she knew nothing could be further from the truth. When it came to sexual games, she couldn't compete with him.

But at least she'd be comfortable at the party. At least there she'd be in her element. More than she'd been since her world had crashed, burned and crumbled at her feet.

"Thank you," she said, suddenly feeling very thirsty. As if she'd swallowed sawdust.

Ethan pushed his dark hair off his forehead, leaving it disheveled. Her fingers itched to put it back in place. She gripped the bottle tighter.

"Just about ready then?" he asked.

"Um… Yes. Ready."

If she just thought about the party, and not how it would feel to run her fingers through Ethan's hair, she just might make it through the night.

Ethan watched Noelle's eyes as they entered the grand ballroom, all decked out for the kind of pretentious party he didn't care a fig about. Her eyes were lit up, like everything else in the room. It was the brightest he'd seen her since the day he'd first met her, pale and drained in the foyer of her home.

This was the sort of party his mother had lived for. He remembered her looking the same way, getting ready to go somewhere, getting out of the house. It was the only thing that had made her smile. When she could go to an event and shine. When she could bask in the glow of her dimming fame and receive some form of adoration. The adoration he'd given her had never seemed to matter.

And his father…he had been too consumed with chasing after another woman. Lavishing his affection on her.

Making an ass of himself and embarrassing all of them because he couldn't control his libido. He'd never seen how being easy was supposed to make a man more virile, more of a man. In his estimation, control counted for a lot more.

And Damien Grey had never possessed any sort of control when it came to women. But Ethan was different. When it came to relationships, he was in charge. It began and ended when he wanted it to, and if he didn't have the time to invest in a relationship, he simply didn't.

Of course, now he was paying for the long bout of celibacy.

"Like it?" he asked, his throat tight.

Her arm was draped through his, her hips brushing against his as she walked. Every stroke of her soft curves was like getting licked by a flame. He had thought her insipid that first day...but tonight he was seeing the real woman.

She was beautiful, perfectly made-up with her blond hair pinned into a low bun and the fitted black dress skimming her curves. He'd just about swallowed his tongue walking into the room and seeing her sprawled on the floor, long shapely legs exposed up to the tops of creamy, toned thighs.

He couldn't remember the last time the sight of a woman's legs had gotten him so hot.

Disgust rolled through him. Was he really letting her get to him so easily? Just because she had feminine curves and a hot pair of legs? She was also the daughter of the woman who had torn his life apart. There should be no attraction there. He should look at her and see Celine Birch. And yet he didn't.

Attraction or not, he wouldn't act on it. He wasn't his

father. He thought with the brain in his head, not the one in his pants.

"It's lovely. Amazing. Whose party is it?"

He realized he hadn't told her. He used that much-needed distraction to get his body back under control. "Birthday party. One of the big important socialite types."

"Which one?"

"Sylvie Ames."

"Oh, I played at one of Sylvie's birthdays. Her sweet sixteen. I remember it." Her cheeks flushed pink and she seemed to shrink a little bit beside him.

"When was that?"

"More than ten years ago."

"How old were you?" She seemed too young to have been doing anything on a grand scale ten years ago. Or even three years ago.

"I was eleven." She *had* been too young. He'd known she'd been a famous child, had even had a vague concept of who she was when his father had been sleeping with Celine, her mother. But it hadn't really struck him until that moment just how vulnerable she would have been.

"That's quite impressive," he said. Scanning the crowd, trying to keep his mind on picking out the possible paparazzi that might be sprinkled throughout. He needed to get his picture in the papers. That was the whole point of tonight, after all. Not to think of Noelle, in front of so many people at such a young age. Exposed to all manner of criticism.

He shouldn't care. But he found that he did.

"Oh yeah, fabulous. I've burned through the career of the lifetime and hit the point of redundancy at twenty-two. Hooray for me."

"Why is it you think you're redundant?" He broke from looking into the knot of people and turned his focus on her.

"Well, let's see. I'm broke. Instant noodles is fine dining in my home and…oh yeah, I just took a position as a man's fake future bride in order to keep myself from having to move into a cardboard box."

"Honestly, I will never be able to fathom women's moods."

Her eyebrows snapped together. "What does that mean?"

"You were fine a moment ago."

"Fine before I found out…" She looked around furtively. "Fine until I found out I was here, at this party, on charity when I was a performer at a party for the same person once. A highly valued one. If it weren't for you the only way I'd be allowed in here would be if I was serving drinks."

"Jealousy, or inadequacy?"

Noelle felt unreasonable anger at Ethan rise up in her. "Why not both?"

He grabbed onto her arm and turned her so that she was facing him, not caring that the wait staff and guests were having to move carefully around them in the crowded space. "I'll tell you something, Ms. Birch. You're here with me. And that means it's not you who should be feeling jealous."

"High opinion of yourself."

He snorted. "You think I'm full of myself? Nah. I'm just realistic. I've got more than a billion dollars. I'm talking sitting in my bank account, that's discounting assets. My family on my father's side is old money, made even richer by the success they've had with their resort chain. And my mother is a former A-list movie star with connections most people can only dream of. Half the women in here would give their favorite handbags to be with me and it has absolutely nothing to do with who I am as person, but what I could give them. But they aren't with me. You are."

It didn't really make her feel better, his little speech. After all, he wasn't here with her because he cared for her. He'd sort of taken her in, like a stray cat. A stray cat who had to earn her milk and catnip by posing as his fiancée. But that was a whole different ball game to being the woman he desired.

But his speech did resonate with her. People wanted him because of what he had, because of his influence, and just like her, if it was all gone tomorrow, his popularity would be too.

And how empty was that? No wonder he was willing to get married to inherit the resort chain. He had to get everything he could to cling to the things that made him special.

It was relatable on a bone-deep level. It was what she wanted too. She was trying to get what she needed back. The things that made people look at her, acknowledge her.

If she couldn't have the fame and the glory she'd accept just not being homeless. She wasn't feeling particularly picky.

"I know all about that, Ethan," she said, taking a glass of champagne from a passing waiter's tray. The time to have a drink was now.

"Do you?"

"Look around us. Look at all the friends I have. Didn't you see my support crew rallying around me back at the house that day you first came? People ready to hold a bake sale to help me hold onto my home? Oh, no, there was no one. Because *I'm* no one. At least as far as everyone else is concerned."

Ethan looked at her, his dark eyes locking with hers. He pressed his palm to her lower back, dipped his head low. Any of the people around them would be forgiven for thinking that he was going to pull her to him and kiss her right there in front of everybody. She didn't think that. She didn't. It certainly wasn't why her lips were dry and her pulse was pounding.

"Let me tell you something, Noelle. It's these people—anyone who believes that. They're the ones who don't matter."

She swallowed hard, her eyes stinging with a sheen of moisture, threatening to turn into a source of real embarrassment. She pulled away from him and looked at the stage. There was a piano there. She wondered who was playing tonight.

Her hands itched all of a sudden. Flexed as she thought of playing a slow, smooth song

Because she couldn't look at Ethan. And she couldn't think about what he'd just said. It was contrary to everything she'd ever been taught about life. About what was important.

And he was just trying to make her feel better, because who wanted a cranky-looking woman on their arm all night?

A woman, a very young woman in a long red dress, came floating out onto the stage and sat in front of the piano, a string quartet sitting down the stage from her. The first strains of the music started to filter through the room and Noelle closed her eyes. Let them fill her with longing, with an ache that she was afraid would never go away.

"Care to dance?"

She opened her eyes and looked at Ethan, his eyes hot and intent on her. She cleared her throat. "You dance?"

"My mother insisted I learn. And anyway, I found it quite instrumental in picking up women back in the days before my bank balance was quite this healthy. Back in the days when I had to rely on charm and skill to get a date."

She looked back at the stage, at the performers. She'd always been the one up there. Separate and removed. The mood of the room. A part of the parties, an integral part, but never in them.

"For the press?"

His lips curved up slightly. "Yeah, of course."

She accepted his offered hand. It was hotter than she'd imagined it would be, his palm a bit rougher. He led her to the dance floor and her heart started tripping on itself. She'd never danced with a man before. She'd never danced. Not even at her own CD-release parties. But she'd even performed at those, even then more the entertainment than the guest of honor. And dancing wasn't essential to piano, which meant it was a skill she'd never acquired.

"I don't really know how to dance," she said, when they stopped at the edge of the dance floor and he pulled her gently into his arms.

"But I do. And you can let me lead." He laced his fingers through hers and wrapped his other arm around her waist. "Put your hand on my shoulder," he said, his voice soft, enticing.

She obeyed the instruction and immediately had to fight the urge to slide her hand, palm flat, down to his hard-muscled chest. She knew it was muscular because her breasts were crushed against it, her heart raging, and she was certain he could feel it.

She looked back up at the stage as Ethan moved back. She felt it all flow through her, the music and his movements, and her feet seemed to obey the prompting from Ethan's body. Everything just seemed to work.

"So tell me, why don't you know how to dance?"

"No time," she said, her words short and breathless, not from the exertion of dancing, but from being in such close proximity to a man. To this man.

"Ah, right. The drills."

"Yeah, the drills. They took up—take up—a lot of time."

"I see."

"A person can't be great at everything. You can be great at one thing, if you work at it. If you want it badly enough." She repeated the words of her former piano teacher, slightly shocked at how quickly the words rolled off her tongue, even after all this time.

"I don't accept that," he said, pressing his hand more firmly against her lower back, moving the lower part of her body closer to his. It made her tingle, made her uncomfortable…aware of her breasts. It was the strangest thing. Not completely unpleasant.

"Doesn't matter whether you accept it, it's true. It takes hours and hours of dedicated practice to claim proficiency at anything. It takes true commitment."

"Hmm, commitment I'm not so good with."

Her pulse pounded harder. He flexed his fingers and the slight motion against her back made a shock of sensation skitter through her veins, lighting up every last part of her body, from her head to her toes and every inch in between.

"Are you sure? Because you asked me to marry you only twenty-four hours after meeting me."

"Commitment with a catch I can deal with. Commitment with a defined end date, I actually think that's quite perfect. But then, that's why I don't make commitments. Because I know I wouldn't want to keep them."

"Well, then your proficiency must be in something other than relationships."

He smirked. "I have a major in business with a pretty accomplished minor in bedroom skills. And I only claim a minor because you insist a person can't have a double major in life."

She felt her face get hot, her blood pounding in her temples. She didn't know how he could say things like that so casually, like it didn't mean anything. As if it didn't throw his mind straight into the bedroom with all kinds of sweaty, half-formed visions.

She'd watched her share of late-night cable when she'd been alone in her hotel room, so she knew what kinds of things he was talking about. And it was making her feel weak and shaky all over.

"What about you? What's your view on commitment?"

"I majored in piano," she said, forcing a smile. "Figuratively speaking, of course."

"Yeah, I got that. I see what you were doing there."

"You're making fun of me," she said. But he wasn't doing it in a cruel way. He was teasing her. She wasn't sure if anyone had ever really teased her like that. If anyone had engaged her in conversation quite like this. Intimate. Sharing. Strange.

"A little bit."

He turned away from her and she couldn't help noticing how striking his face was in profile. Strong nose and square jaw. He was almost too perfect to be real. He was like a man chiseled from rock, only infused with breath and warmth. And a glint in his eye that spoke of sin and pleasure.

"Over there," he said, inclining his head slightly. "That's Anita Blaire, she's the lead writer for the society pages."

Noelle turned her head slightly and saw a woman craning her neck to get a look at them.

Ethan released his hold on her hand and placed his palm on her hip, sliding it around slowly until both of his hands were rested on the indent in her spine, just above her bottom. He moved his thumb slightly, slowly, his touch edging near intimate territory.

She stiffened, her heart pounding so hard she was afraid she was going to pass out. She swallowed, barely able to finish the job thanks to her suddenly dry throat.

"Relax," he whispered. "Lean into me."

She did her best to relax but her muscles were locked up, tense. Not with fear, but with anticipation. She didn't know what he might do next. Where he would touch her. It made her hot and shivery all over. Like having a fever, one that burned from deep inside her core.

"How's this?" she asked, her voice a little bit thin, shaky.

"Better," he whispered, his lips brushing her temple, the slightly intimate caress making her stomach tighten with raw, sexual need. It was different like this. In the arms of a real man, instead of just the hazy fantasy of a dream lover's caress. Her ideas of desire were all viewed through a Vaseline-smeared lens in her mind's eye. But this wasn't obscured or blurred, it was sharp and clear. Almost painful in its intensity.

And he hadn't even kissed her.

Would he? Eventually. He would have to eventually because he would have to do the kiss-the-bride thing at the wedding. And now her palms were sweaty. She tightened her grip on his shoulders.

He angled his head and his lips skimmed the line of her jaw. She blew out a shocked breath and dug her fingernails into his shoulders, just to get that extra hold, because she felt as if she might melt into a puddle of Noelle at his feet. Wouldn't that be a good picture for the society pages?

He pressed his lips more firmly to her skin, just beneath her ear. She shuddered when he brushed the tip of his tongue over the tender skin. She'd never even known to fantasize about such a simple, sensual thing. Even if she had, she wouldn't have known the effect it would have on her.

"You taste like vanilla," he said, his voice soft and husky, his breath touching her neck, making goosebumps spread over her.

She pulled her head back so she could look at him, at his dark eyes, so intent on hers. Was he going to kiss her now? Like, really kiss her?

He looked away from her, back in the direction of Anita. "I think we've caught her attention," he said.

The shroud of arousal that had cocooned them just a moment before broke and Noelle became conscious again of the noise in the room. The buzz of conversation, the music, the fact that there were other people there, in the ballroom, in the world.

"Oh," she cleared her throat, "yes."

"Ready to go and be social?"

No. She was ready to go and crawl under a rock and hide for ten years, thank you very much, because she'd made an idiot of herself over the brief brush of his lips on her skin. The worst thing was, she was still wishing he'd done more.

"Of course," she said, her voice brittle.

"Come on then, sweetheart, let's spread the good news of our new-found love."

CHAPTER FIVE

TOTAL bliss. She was warm. And comfy. Happy even. Cocooned in the thousand-thread-count sheets in a luxury hotel. And room service was on its way up with coffee.

Noelle snuggled down deeper into the bedding and sighed. For a few moments her mind was blank, and then last night came rushing through it. Not just her mind, her body. She could feel him again, his large, warm hands on her hips, his lips against her jaw.

She flung her arm over her eyes and growled into the empty room. She didn't want to be dealing with this at the moment. And definitely not with him. She had to keep it in the realm of business transaction or it was just...wrong.

There was a heavy knock on the door and she tugged the covers up to her throat. "Come in."

"Morning." He brought coffee, but he wasn't room service. Ethan strode in, looking amazing and not at all like they'd stayed at a party until the early hours of the morning.

He was wearing a dark suit and a white shirt that was open at the collar. She could see just a hint of dark chest hair when he moved and the shirt gaped a bit...and she was staring. And it was probably obvious. She looked out the window.

"So you aren't...I was expecting room service."

"I intercepted them. Said I wanted to wish my darling Noelle a good morning in a way only I could."

She felt her face get hot. "You do have a flair for drama."

He chuckled. "I wouldn't say that. But I do want this to work. And in order for that to happen, everyone around me has to believe that you've done a real number on me."

"Do they?" She couldn't really imagine doing a number on a man. Not when his presence made her feel hot and sort of uncomfortable. But not in a bad way, really. Actually, it was the most pleasant discomfort she'd ever felt before.

"So, what's on the agenda for today?" He looked surprised by her question. "What?" She shrugged. "I'm sort of…working for you now. Kind of my job to be at your beck and call."

His facial expression shifted, a subtle change, his lips parting slightly, a dark and dangerous light illuminating his brown eyes. The intensity of his focus only made that discomfort spread through her a little more, from her tightened stomach and pounding heart down to her limbs, to the apex of her thighs.

"Now that is a very interesting and tempting thought, Noelle."

Noelle felt heat creep from her breasts up her throat and into her face. She knew she was pink everywhere. She was usually so pale, her skin always gave her away.

Because she knew what he was thinking. It was the same thing she was thinking. Her mind was back on last night, on what it had felt like to be in his arms. And now here she was, in bed, and it all seemed easy…as if everything might be simpler if she just scooted over and made room for him next to her.

She gulped a too-hot mouthful of coffee and swung her

legs over the side of the bed. The briefness of her nightie was now the least of her worries.

"Not what I meant, Ethan."

"I don't have designs on your womanly virtue," he said, his tone heavy with sarcasm. "Promise. Much too complicated at this stage in the game."

"Agreed," she said, ignoring the heat in her cheeks. *Womanly virtue.* Good grief. If only that wasn't so close to the truth—not that she counted it as a virtue. More like a somewhat telling commentary on just how thoroughly her life had been managed from moment one.

No boyfriends. Not even a hint of teenage rebellion. She'd been too busy. And she'd believed so strongly in everything her mother had asked of her, had wanted to repay her for the years of travel and lessons by doing well.

By doing what she'd been asked, or rather ordered, to do. And now she *was* paying for it, since she didn't know the first thing about real life. She knew about glitz and glamour, but not how to make the money to achieve it for herself. She knew about air kisses and fake praise, but not about real relationships. Real kisses. Ethan had come the closest.

She shivered at the memory.

"Come to work with me?"

"Um…sure." It wasn't at all what she'd had in mind, but then, she wasn't really certain *what* she'd had in mind. "I'm not going to be spending every waking minute with you, am I?"

"I don't know, what would you do if you were head over heels in love? In love enough to get engaged only a couple of weeks after meeting someone?"

She laughed as she edged over to the bathroom, conscious of her semi-dressed state. "I have no idea."

"I don't either, but I imagine that we very much would spend every waking, and non-waking, moment together."

His eyes, so hot on her, felt like an intimate caress. One that made her burn inside. She crossed her arms over her breasts to disguise her nipples, beaded tight against the filmy fabric with no bra to help hide the effect he was having on her.

"In any case, going to work with you today might be… fun."

Ethan gritted his teeth and fought hard against the razor-sharp edge of arousal that was digging into him, cutting into his control. She was barely covered up by a silky, bright-blue confection that looked as though it was designed for the sole purpose of driving a man to an early grave. Or at least to the hospital to see a doctor about an erection lasting longer than four hours…

She wasn't just an easy tumble though. This wasn't about sex, and it sure wasn't about using her body. He didn't need her body. He could have his pick of any woman he wanted. He wasn't about to let her control him, not about to let himself believe the attraction to her was special in any way beyond what was normal. He'd let it make an idiot of him last night. He'd flirted with her. Nearly kissed her.

He just hadn't had sex in so long that his body was trying to convince him she was special. She wasn't. She was just another blonde. Blondes he'd had. Lots of them.

But her legs. So long and shapely, and her figure, petite and luscious, pert round breasts that called out to him. To touch. To taste. He had a feeling that even if he'd satisfied his libido last week—hell, last *night*—he'd feel the same way.

Feel some sort of sick craving to possess her in every way. To make sure the deal went through? No, not even he would stoop that low. This wasn't about her; not about hurting her anyway. It wasn't even about hurting her mother, not on his part, anyway. It was about showing his father that going through life using people as rungs on the ladder of success and satisfaction didn't work.

About making sure Damien Grey wouldn't get rewarded for it.

"Maybe you should go get dressed."

Her cheeks turned pink, a deep rose that betrayed her embarrassment. That was a novelty, one he wasn't sure how he felt about. A woman who blushed like that over something so simple, that wasn't really his thing. And yet for some reason, it made his body harder, more tense, more aroused.

This was a business deal, in a way, and he had to remember that. But he worked with women every day without experiencing this problem. Of course, the women he worked with didn't come into the boardroom wearing silky lingerie.

He ground his teeth together and tightened his hands into fists, channeling his tension into his screaming tendons. He had to get a grip. On his libido or his body, he didn't really care, but the attraction to Noelle had to be managed.

"Right." She slunk off to the bathroom, and he let out a breath he hadn't been conscious of holding.

The office was safe at least. It would give him a chance to remember why he was doing this. Give his body a chance to calm down. Because he had a goal and he wasn't about to let an errant attraction distract him from reaching it.

More importantly, he wasn't about to give in to temptation, to let his body have the control when he despised men who behaved like having testosterone meant they couldn't be their own masters.

He'd watched his father do it, time and again. Disregarding the feelings of his wife, his children, and for what? For the pursuit of his own selfish pleasure. Casting off every last piece of his honor, his commitments, to chase after a woman who, in the end, wouldn't even stay with him.

He looked at the closed bathroom door and tried not to imagine Noelle's nightgown slithering over her curves and pooling onto the floor.

He wasn't his father. And while she wasn't her mother, she was the one woman who was patently off limits.

"You do have a nice office." Noelle leaned back in his office chair, her long legs stretched out in front of her, black tights covering all that tempting, creamy skin, but doing nothing to disguise the shape.

Turned out she was just as sexy when she was fully dressed. Which he'd known after last night, but when he'd invited her to the office he'd imagined she'd put on something more business-casual. He had discovered that ex-performers didn't have much in the way of business-casual. What she did have was a brief, black dress, black tights and a pair of gold high heels that glowed from fifty paces away.

And all that pale blond hair, hanging loose around her face like a halo…she was just impossible to put in a corner and ignore. And that was problematic on many, many levels.

"Gets the job done anyway," he said.

"Is there something I can do?" She straightened, crossing her legs at the ankles. It did not help make her look any more demure.

"You can get out of my chair."

She turned crimson and popped up. "Okay, done. Anything else?"

"You want to work?"

"Well, I'm here." She shrugged. "It seems like I ought to do something. Won't people think it's funny I'm just hanging out?"

"I don't think anyone thinks it's funny at all. I think they assume we're in here not working."

"Oh. Really?"

"Really. Did you see the paper this morning?"

"No, I didn't have the chance to grab it."

"We're the new hot couple, you know."

"Can I see?"

He rounded the desk and leaned over, typing in the web address for the newspaper they'd been featured in. "There you are."

She leaned in next to him, that sweet vanilla scent teasing his senses, making his body harden with tension and arousal.

A small smile curved her lips. "They know my name."

"You sound surprised."

"No one's missed me much over the past year. Which I actually consider kind of a blessing. I haven't really been keen on sharing my downfall with the world."

"What? That your mother stole your money?"

"That she abandoned me because she knew she'd gotten everything she could out of me. Because my sales—album sales, ticket sales—were dwindling to nothing."

"So what have you been doing then, this past year?"

She shrugged again, her blue eyes fixed on a point somewhere behind him. "Nothing."

"Nothing?"

She looked at him, pale eyes filled with anger now. "Maybe I haven't done the best I could with my time. But

I didn't really know what to do. I only know how to do one thing." She looked away. "My mother made sure I only knew one thing. I tried to…I tried to talk to my old booking agent. Tried to see about playing venues I used to play. I called my label and asked them if they wanted to release a greatest hits album. Turns out, they don't think I have any." She laughed, a hollow, bitter sound that made his chest ache. "So in that sense, I did something. But I just…I didn't know what else to do when all of that was shot down."

"What about playing piano bars and things like that?"

"Ironically, that's the kind of thing I am a bit too famous for, and I don't mean that in a snobbish way, I mean…I didn't want that to show up in tabloids."

"That's not really a great excuse, Noelle. You basically just sat there and let everything fall apart."

"No. No I did not. Everything was wrecked, utterly wrecked by my mother. She smashed everything to pieces—I didn't let it fall apart. And yes, maybe I could have done something, maybe I should have, but every night I've gone to bed hoping…hoping that somehow in the morning it would be fixed. That things would go back to normal. I tried to force it to go back to normal." She looked at him, blue eyes intent on his, an impact he felt all the way through his body. "Now…now I don't even want things to go back to normal. But I just…I felt burned out. I was just so tired. This, having a chance to hold onto something, this at least makes me feel like I can fight. Like I have something to fight with."

His chest felt strange. As if it had gotten smaller, or his heart had gotten larger. He didn't like it. "You could learn something else."

Her frame slumped. "I don't know if I have the energy anymore. To devote myself to mastering something other than music, I mean. I've done that. Practicing, improving, every day without stopping since I was a child. It didn't really get me anywhere, did it?"

He didn't know why he felt compelled to try and offer her...something. Comfort maybe? He only knew that he did. "Very few people live their lives that way, Noelle. With drills and practice for eight hours a day, in addition to performing and promoting and traveling."

"Are you telling me you work any less hard?" she asked.

"No, I work a lot. But I choose to. There are plenty of people who go nine to five, five days a week."

She looked down, her throat working. "What if I can't do anything else?"

Everything about his carefully laid plan, her being in the office, her being anywhere near him, suddenly felt wrong. Like he was joining in the queue of people who'd used her.

A bit too late to feel that way.

Much too late. And she was walking in with her eyes open.

"Of course you can. Here," he slapped his palm on the leather back of the chair, "get in the chair."

She sat back down, her expression confused. Damn, but she made him feel every inch the Big Bad Wolf to her Little Red Riding Hood. He didn't really like the feeling.

He shoved his conscience to one side. He'd deal with it later. "Do you type?"

She grimaced. "Not really. Not fast."

"Well, you're going to learn." He pulled out a stack of papers he'd set aside for his PA. "I want you to enter this into the computer. These are specs for different building plans. If you enter the numbers in these cells, the computer will do the math for you. You just enter it in."

"I can do that."

"Okay, do that. I'm going to go down the hall and make some phone calls, and I'll be back to check on you." Distance was definitely necessary.

He walked out of the office and closed the door behind him, his chest still tight. He didn't know why it mattered, but he wanted to show Noelle that she could do something. Something other than doing drills every day for a career that had crumbled to nothing right in front of her.

More than that, he didn't like what he saw in her eyes. That look that said she saw herself as a failure. He'd watched his mother go through that. Watched her pin her self-worth on the perception of a fickle public.

There was no happiness there.

When and how had he started comparing her to his mother? He ought to be comparing her to her own. Actually, the truth of it was, he shouldn't be putting this much thought into her either way. She was just the means to an end, and he was the same to her.

This wasn't personal. Not between the two of them.

He ignored the kick in his gut that said otherwise.

The sense of accomplishment that filled Noelle when she moved the last piece of paper to her finished stack was silly, and she knew it. It had been an easy job, one that she was sure anyone with fingers could do, and yet, it was more than she'd pushed herself to do recently.

She'd been so determined to live in the past. All the time she spent still doing drills she could have used to learn any number of job skills. She simply hadn't. Part of her hadn't believed she could. But Ethan had believed in her. Enough to leave her in his office on her own, to trust her to do the work.

The door to the office opened and Ethan walked in. "I

did it," she said, not quite able to wipe the idiot grin off of her face.

"Good," he said, not half as thrilled as she was.

"Thank you."

The corners of his mouth turned down. "It's nothing. My PA will be happy that she doesn't have to do that today."

"It was something to me."

His eyebrows locked together. "You can do things, Noelle. You aren't stupid. You aren't handicapped in any way. You can do whatever you like. Don't leave it up to the public to decide how much you're worth."

Did she do that? She supposed she had. She'd been so worried about what people might think…that was one reason she hadn't gone and gotten a job. That and the lingering hope that someday she'd be able to fix things.

But she hadn't fixed it yet. And she'd let things get too bad. So much of this had become her fault.

"You're right."

"Yeah, well, of course," he said.

"Really. I could have done something. I didn't."

"Well you can do data entry for me if you like. It's boring, but my PA thinks so too, so she'll be glad to do other things."

Noelle felt her throat tighten and then she just felt silly. Getting emotional over a desk job.

"Thank you."

"It will allow you to be around the office more, which will be good as far as setting the stage for our wedding."

She swallowed. "Yes, it will."

"No working late, though. I plan on keeping you very busy at night."

CHAPTER SIX

KEEPING her busy at night turned out to mean something very different from what she'd immediately thought. She was slightly embarrassed to admit, even to herself, exactly what her first thoughts had been.

But what he actually meant turned out to be something far beyond what she'd imagined.

"Australia?" she asked the next morning when Ethan stopped by. It was good for the staff to see him there, he said. Even better if they just thought he was leaving early after a night of unbridled passion.

"Yeah. I need you to come and meet my family, and in order to do that you have to come to my family's home. Not my parents' home. My grandparents' home. I spent a lot of time there growing up."

"That's…that's really nice." She frowned. "I really don't like the idea of lying to your grandparents."

"I'm sure my grandfather half expects this. He's controlling as hell, but I actually think he means well. He knows I'll do the right thing, or at least the thing he asks of me. Which is more than he's ever got from his own son."

Ethan made it sound as if his parents were a lost cause, but at least he had his grandparents. She didn't have that. Her father, an investment banker from Switzerland according to her mother, had left before her first birthday. And her mother's antics had alienated Noelle's grandparents long before she was born.

She couldn't help wondering what it would be like to have that stability. Any stability.

"Do they…do they know about my mother and your father?"

"Odds are they do. He wasn't exactly discreet."

"Ethan, I'm…"

"Don't."

She stopped the apology from tumbling out and tried not to be too hurt by the hard tone of his voice. She cleared her throat. "But your grandfather…he's good to you?"

Ethan shrugged. "Yeah. He's tough, but that's probably a good thing."

Do it again, Noelle. You're getting sloppy. Why was her mother's voice still so loud? Just the memory of it made her hands ache. She remembered doing scales for hours, so long that she could hardly feel her fingers anymore, so that the action seemed disconnected from her body, divorced from conscious thought.

"Too tough isn't always good," she said, flexing her fingers to try and relieve the phantom pains.

"Too easy isn't good either. No discipline? No control? Makes for a pretty worthless excuse for a human being."

The venom in his tone surprised her. "And too much turns you into a machine repeating the same drills on the piano eight hours a day."

"It's a rare person who has too much discipline, Noelle. But you might fit under the heading."

"You too, Ethan?"

He turned to face her, his dark eyes molten, hot, burning straight into her. "That remains to be seen, I think. Be prepared for my grandmother to grill you, by the way."

She let out the breath she'd been holding and tried to smile. "This is going to be quite the dinner party."

"This may be why I haven't married yet." He chuckled darkly. "My family is far too dysfunctional to inflict on anyone else. Of course, it may be me. If they're as bad as all that, I can't be much better."

"You seem nice to me."

"Well, that's the thing, Noelle, you don't really know me. If you did, you might feel differently. And you aren't marrying me, not really. Not forever." The look that flashed in his dark eyes was strange, pain-filled. It made Noelle's stomach tighten.

"It's all right, you don't know me either."

"It's probably why we get on so well."

She laughed. "Is this your definition of getting on well?"

"We're both still standing." Ethan cocked his head to the side, his expression intense. She could feel his gaze, almost like a physical touch as he looked at her body. Her breasts. She was certain he was looking there because she could feel it. "For now." The air in the room seemed to thicken, a strange electric feeling arching between them as he took a step towards her. Only one step. No more. And she had the feeling that if there was going to be anything more, she would have to make the next move.

Her feet seemed to be rooted to the spot.

"I guess we'll get to know each other in Australia," she said. "Although I think it's kind of a raw deal, you hiring me and then making me ask my boss for vacation time."

"I'll keep you busy," he said, his voice rough. "And yeah, we may get to know each other a little better."

"We won't actually be staying with my grandparents." Ethan turned to look at her as he navigated the busy

Brisbane expressway and took an exit that led off into one of the suburbs.

She could swear that Ethan's accent had thickened the moment they'd landed in his home country. And she liked it. A little bit more than she should. But it was fascinating, being alone with a man like this. It was something she'd never really experienced before. Well, discounting her piano instructor.

"Where will we be staying?"

"One of my hotels. On the beach. I think you'll like it."

"How long have you owned it?"

"It's been there for years, but I bought it and had some renovation done on it about six years back."

"I've been here before," she said, looking out the window at the passing scenery. "I didn't get to see anything. Just the roadway from the airport to the hotel, to the theater, then back to the airport. We went to Sydney after. I didn't get to see much of it either."

"You never went sightseeing when you traveled?"

She bit her lip. "When we were in Europe we did a bit of it, as part of my schooling. I had a good tutor. He made sure I finished my studies early. I graduated at fifteen, so I was able to practice my music more."

"Have you ever concentrated on anything but your music?"

"I've just been concentrating on breathing this past year," she said, watching the deep green eucalyptus trees blur together into a continuous smear of color. "And before that, just breathing and playing. I want to do more than that now."

"Data entry?"

She shot him her deadliest glare, which, she knew, wasn't very deadly. She'd been told she looked like a Kewpie doll more than once. Not very threatening.

"Something more than that maybe even. But it's a good start."

The car pulled up to a massive, wrought-iron gate and Ethan leaned out the car window and punched in a series of numbers. "Gated community," he said. "Nothing but the best, you know."

"I think it's nice." The car wound up a long, winding hill and she knew that Ethan's grandparents' house was certain to have billion-dollar views.

"It's a bit pretentious, actually, but don't tell my grandmother I said that."

"I wouldn't."

He turned to her, sliding his hand across the expanse of seat between them. He laced his fingers through hers, his thumb drifting over the back of her hand. She felt goosebumps raise up on her arms. He hadn't touched her for a long time. Only a few days, actually, and yet…it felt like a really long time.

"I'm going to introduce you to my grandparents and get the family ring from my grandfather after dinner, let him know my intentions and all that."

Her heart slammed against her breast. She nodded, trying to pretend she was unaffected.

"And then I'll give it to you after we leave. We'll have to come up with a nice story for my grandmother because she'll want all the gory details. Women always do."

"Yes. True." Her stomach tightened, a sick feeling spreading through her. "I…I don't know how I feel using your family heirloom ring when it's…when we're lying."

"So? I'll return the ring when our marriage fails. What difference does it make?"

"None, I guess." Except it kind of did. "Why didn't your mother end up with the ring?"

"It wasn't new. She doesn't really like antiques." The

corner of his mouth curved up slightly. "She likes really modern stuff. Spot-on trend. And my grandmother never would have let her put it into a new setting."

"Family traditions shouldn't be broken. I mean, I don't think. We didn't really have any."

It was no use feeling wistful about it. She'd spent so long just wishing things were different. From the moment she'd realized her life wasn't like other girls', she'd wanted something else. More. A connection with her mother that wasn't based on her career.

But that hadn't happened. It had always been about Noelle's career for her mother. About what she could do, what she could get thanks to Noelle's talents. Noelle accepted it now, more or less. Anyway, the charming revelations Ethan had uncovered about her mother made her realize Celine wasn't the kind of woman she wanted a relationship with anyway.

No, she wasn't going to waste time being pouty about what she had and what she didn't have. Not anymore. She was going to take the money, and she was going to get on with her life. She would take her new office skills, or her rediscovered favor with the media, and she would make something of herself, and manage her own money. Without her teacher. Without her mother. Without Ethan.

She was done being played like a puppet. She was in charge now.

"Mine have more to do with status than sentimentality. My mother is new money, you see, so she doesn't understand how special it is to have things that have been passed down. Or so I've heard," he said, his words cut short as they passed through another gate and onto the grounds of an opulent estate with lush, manicured grounds and three fountains stationed right out front, seemingly for the sole purpose of trumpeting that the people who owned the house had money. Bags of it.

Ethan pulled the car through and parked it in the drive. "My grandparents have valet service," he explained dryly.

He got out and rounded to her side, opening the door for her. "Full service," she replied, standing to find herself just about breast to chest with him.

"I'm a full-service kind of guy," he said, his eyes seeming darker, his voice rougher. She wished she knew what he was thinking whenever that happened. Why it seemed like one part attraction, one part anger, and complete confusion.

Her fingers twitched with the urge to reach out and put her hand to his stubbled cheek, to find out how rough it would be beneath her palm. She wanted to. Badly. But she wouldn't. That part wasn't really confusing. But it was crossing boundaries she wasn't here to cross.

No show without an audience. No touching unless someone was around to witness it. Otherwise it would just be a personal indulgence and she wasn't about to go there.

"I have no doubt," she said, turning away from him. "Ready?"

She started playing Vivaldi's *Four Seasons* in her head, imaging her fingers moving over the keys. Finding her balance, her center and her tempo. "Ready."

"Then let's meet my family."

As always, a family dinner was a formal affair at his grandparents' home. He'd always found it part of their upper-crust, slightly stiff charm. They weren't perfect, and they were hardly suburban normal, but life with Nathaniel and Ariana Grey had been much more functional than life with his parents.

And after his mother's breakdown, this was where he'd

spent most of his time. His father had been too busy, his mother too ill. And as controlling as his grandfather could be, at least he cared.

When it came down to it, he wasn't overly thrilled about lying to them, any more than Noelle was. But no matter how stern his grandfather pretended to be, he'd never had it in him to cut off his only son.

But Ethan had what it took. No question.

He took Noelle's hand in his beneath the table. A subtle gesture, not one of open ownership. The kind that had the appearance of being only for them, something intimate and special, but was really for the benefit of everyone else. The art of performance.

Still, even if it was a gesture meant for everyone else, the feeling of her silky-smooth skin beneath his palm sent shocks of pleasure through him, desire tightening his gut, making his blood hot.

Noelle Birch was slowly driving him crazy. How else could he be getting hard from holding hands, of all things? Hand-holding hadn't gotten him hard when he was fourteen. He had no excuse for the reaction now.

His grandfather's eyes were fixed on Noelle, and Ethan knew Nathaniel had made the connection. Fifteen years might have passed since the affair between Celine and his father had ended, but no one had forgotten.

"How long have you been seeing each other?" Ariana smiled at them both and he wondered whether his grandmother actually hadn't recognized Noelle. Maybe her manners were simply so polished that nothing could tarnish them.

Noelle looked at him, her blue eyes slightly panicked.

"A few months," he said. "Quietly."

"Must have been," his grandfather said. "I haven't seen anything about it in the news."

"I don't always rate the papers," he replied.

"But she would." Nathaniel dipped his head in Noelle's direction.

Noelle cleared her throat and shifted in her seat. "Not always."

"So, Noelle, you used to travel quite a bit." Nathaniel's focus was on her now. "What are you doing with your career these days?"

Noelle shifted in her seat, her fingers tightening around his for a moment. "I'm on hiatus."

A laugh stuck in Ethan's throat.

"Good." Nathaniel nodded. "A woman needs to focus on things beyond a career."

"If she wants to, I suppose," Noelle replied.

The laugh escaped this time. "You'll find Noelle holds to her own opinions," Ethan smiled wryly.

"Good," his grandfather returned. "Doesn't do any good for a woman, or a man, to have nothing outside of a relationship." The look he gave Ethan was pointed.

"No," Ethan said. "It doesn't."

"Drink, Ethan?"

Ethan nodded and stood from the table, leaning in to drop a kiss on Noelle's cheek. He paused just before his lips brushed her skin, her scent halting him for a moment, just a moment, long enough to savor it, to let it fill him. He couldn't define what it was she smelled like, because it was so unique to her.

Her posture went rigid and she turned her head slightly, like she was anticipating the touch of his lips, but dreading it. He cocked his head to the side and skimmed his lips over her jawbone, just beneath her ear.

"I'll be back in a moment," he whispered, trying to ignore the fierce tightening of his stomach.

He followed his grandfather down the hall, dark and

carpeted with a threadbare Aubusson that spoke of age and money, into his study and shut the door. He crossed to the bar and took out two glasses, one for him, one for the old man, and a bottle of whiskey. He added three fingers of the liquor to the glasses and handed one to his grandfather, raising the other to his lips.

"What exactly are you playing at here, Ethan? Noelle Birch? Am I expected to believe this is a happy coincidence?"

Ethan shrugged and took a swallow of his whiskey. "Don't know if I'd call it happy."

"I'm certain I wouldn't call it a coincidence. I know you far too well for that."

"Maybe I'm in love."

"Are you marrying her?"

He nodded once. It was the truth in the strictest sense. He was simply leaving out his plans for what came after the vows. "That's the plan."

"And you'll be faithful to her?"

Ethan set his glass down on the bar top. "I'm not like my father. If I make a commitment, I honor it. I take care of what's mine."

"Now, that I trust. You know if I do pass the company straight to you what a slight it will be to Damien. Your father has been waiting for this all of his life."

"I'm completely aware." He was counting on it.

"He's my son, Ethan, but I'm not proud of what he's become. I want to make sure you do better for yourself. I want you settled before you get wrapped up in running a corporation like Grey's."

"No offense intended, but the one I run now is larger than Grey's."

His grandfather nodded. "True enough. Which begs the question why you want Grey's so badly."

Revenge was the easy answer, one that didn't seem quite right in this scenario. But there were other reasons, more complex. Ones he didn't like to dwell on. Those reasons took him back to being a boy, a boy with nothing. Of no importance to his parents. Barely worth a second glance if they passed him in the hall of their large family mansion.

"Because what you have is never enough," Ethan said. "That's how it is for businessmen. You know that. You always need more."

"I don't really know what it is you're doing here, Ethan." Nathaniel let out a sigh. "Maybe I don't want to know. I just want you to be happy. Stable."

"I'm stable. I know that my marriage to Noelle will make me very happy." If not for the reasons marriages usually made people happy. If they ever did.

"I hope so. I assume you will want your grandmother's ring?"

This was a huge part of making it all look real. "Yes."

"I'll go and get it from the safe."

Ethan ignored the slow burn of guilt that mingled with the alcohol in his gut. Everything was working out now, just as he'd planned. The ring was another piece of the puzzle.

He downed the last of his whiskey, letting the fire overtake the uncomfortable emotion that was swirling in his stomach. Everything was starting to fall into place, and guilt had no part in it.

"You're tense," Noelle commented.

They were about five minutes into the drive from his grandparents' house and he hadn't spoken a word. His hands were locked tightly around the steering wheel, the muscles on his forearms corded, showing his strain.

"Not at all," he replied, teeth gritted.

"You're a bad liar."

He tossed her a quick glance. "I'm not."

"You are."

"I'm not trying to lie."

"Well, then you're a bad liar when you aren't trying to be a good one. You aren't fine, even I can see that, and I'm not really an authority on reading people. You can use my mother as exhibit A on that one."

He hunched slightly and shifted his hands lower on the wheel. "It doesn't thrill me to lie to my grandparents."

She swallowed. "I'm with you. Your grandmother is... she's very kind."

"She always is. She's so stable. Calm."

"Not like my mother at all."

"Or mine."

"Want to tell me about her?"

He leaned his head back against the seat. "Not in the least. You?"

"Don't you already know about her?"

"I know what I saw. She was beautiful. Charming. She had my father under a spell. What did you see when you looked at her?"

Noelle bit her lip. "All of that. She could play this kind of sweet beauty, act a little bit naive so that she could get away with being demanding. But that was an act. She was smart. Smarter than I am, obviously. She used me to make money, and I can't seem to manage that."

"She was dishonest, you weren't. That's not smarter. That's cheating."

"Then what are we doing right now?"

"We're cheating too. But it's for a good cause. Trust me."

She wished she could.

They were quiet again until he turned the car down a winding road that led toward the beach. Noelle unrolled her window and let the salt air and the sound of waves on the sand fill up the interior of the car. It was preferable to that ear-ringing silence.

Ethan pulled the car up to the front of the hotel and left it, keys in the ignition. He got out, slamming the door behind him, not bothering to come around for her door this time. She sat with her hands in her lap for a moment before opening her own door and following him in to the opulent lobby.

Her stomach tightened as she hurried to catch up with him, her high heels clicking on the black marble floors. She looked up at the high ceiling, at the five levels of rooms, each with a balcony that overlooked the massive lobby, ornate carvings on the hand rails with vines growing over them. Like a ruined city that still glittered with riches.

She'd been here before. Stayed here with her mother whenever she performed in Brisbane. It brought so many things back. Every time they'd come, she'd practically been frog-marched through the lobby on her way to the many-roomed suite at the top floor, and, jet lag not even accounted for, had been settled in front of the piano to practice within five minutes of her arrival.

And her mother had gone out, as she always did. To network or whatever it was she called it. And she'd been alone.

"We're staying in the room with the piano, aren't we?"

Ethan stopped dead in his tracks and turned, his dark eyebrows locked together, the heavy tension still radiating from his body. "Yes."

"I've been here. We came to Brisbane quite a bit for a few years and we always stayed here."

There was a strange light in his eyes, something cold. Dark. "Is that so?"

"Yes. I mean, I like it…it's…nice."

"If you'd like to stay somewhere else…?"

She shook her head. "No. It's fine."

She followed him over to the side of the lobby that had a stone wall and water running closely down the side of it. There was a line of elevators with golden doors, the water routed well around them so that people could step inside without fear of getting their designer clothing wet.

"When did you buy this hotel?" she asked, stepping inside the lift behind him.

"A few years ago. The first of my grandfather's hotels that he surrendered to me. My father used to manage it." He spat the last words out as if they tasted bitter.

"I don't even know who my father is."

He turned to her, his eyes hardened into black ice. "There are times when I wish I didn't know who mine was."

It was difficult to hold his gaze when he looked like that, when the remnants of his charming facade fell away and he was all hard, angry male. But she managed it. She'd spent a long time being submissive, doing as she was told and cowering in fear. She didn't want to do it anymore.

"Why?"

"I think he was quite like your mother in many ways. A cheat."

"Aren't we a pair, Ethan? Probably a good thing we aren't getting married for real."

He grunted in what, she assumed, was agreement.

The doors to the elevator slid open after a moment and revealed an opulent gilded entryway, glowing with gold and cluttered with ornate carvings. She couldn't hold back a laugh as Ethan punched in the key code. She was glad to find a reason, any reason, to laugh. To break some of the tension in her. Tension brought on by being here again. Tension from being near Ethan.

"What?" he asked, pushing open the door.

"This whole hotel is so very not you."

"How do you figure?" he asked, holding the door open for her and letting her enter the room first. He must have calmed down because that reflexive chivalry of his had returned.

"You don't strike me as a man who does ornate. Your hotel in New York is much more in keeping with how I see your style."

"Hotels aren't about me. They're about the people who patronize them."

"True." She knew all about that. When she composed music she had to keep in mind what people would want to hear, and yet...pieces of her soul were always there.

She wished that her gift hadn't gone. That aspect of music...it had been so much in her. Woven through her being. To look at the scenery, this gorgeous hotel, and not hear a soundtrack to it was still painful. She didn't know if she'd ever get used to that resounding silence always filling her head now.

It made her body feel foreign to her. Wrong. All of her, every bit, felt wrong. Like being caught off guard by a change in tempo and not quite being able to find the rhythm again, stumbling over notes, breaking the melody so that it was an unrecognizable jumble. It was such a hellish nothing.

She meandered across the plush living area, her fingers drifting over the keys of the piano reflexively as she passed it by on her way to the exterior balcony. She needed air. Space. If only she could escape from herself. Just for a moment.

She opened the sliding door and stepped outside, the cool air from the ocean raising goosebumps on her arms. At least out here she could breathe better. She hadn't gone out on the balcony the previous times she'd stayed here. She'd looked out the windows at the view, had thought about stepping out, but there hadn't been time.

She frowned. Why? It would only have taken a moment. What else had she missed? Small things. Simple things. An ocean breeze. Having friends. Being kissed.

She closed her eyes and relished the feel of the damp wind on her cheeks.

As much as she wanted to blame everything on her mother, she'd been guilty of having tunnel vision. Her mother had pushed it, supported it, but it had been in her. That drive. That obsession. The need to be better, the best. To push a bit harder each and every day.

Was it any wonder it had all deserted her?

She opened her eyes, watched the waves, the whitecaps glowing in the moonlight as they crashed over the shore. Ebbing and surging, soft and hard, fast and slow. Like music. Something she'd never stopped to look at before, not really. She felt a low hum vibrate in her throat and a couple of notes spilled out. A piece of music. Not one she'd heard before. Her heart thundered hard, adrenaline surging through her. It was the first time in a couple of years there had been something, a sound, a note. Anything.

"Thought the night called for champagne. Alcohol of any kind, really."

She turned at the sound of Ethan's voice and saw him standing in the doorway, two flutes of bubbly in hand, his shirt unbuttoned halfway, his feet bare, dark hair tousled like a woman had just run her fingers through it.

Now, this was very, very different than her stay last

time. She swallowed, but despite the moisture in the air, her throat felt dry.

"I won't say no to that."

He walked to where she was standing, looking like every woman's secret fantasy, his dark eyes locked with hers. He handed her a glass and leaned over the railing, touching the edge of his flute to hers. "Cheers."

She lifted hers in mock salute. "Cheers indeed." She took small sip of the bubbly liquid, then cursed it, because champagne wasn't going to help her dry throat. She turned her focus back on the waves. "It must be nice. Having your own success. Having all of this." She gestured to the view.

He shrugged and leaned against the railing. "I don't mind it."

"You still want more, though? Enough to lie to your grandparents?" He shot her warning look. "I'm not judging. I'm involved in this too, aren't I? I'm just asking."

A muscle in his cheek ticked. "It's not about having more. It's about keeping my father from getting it."

"I don't understand why your grandfather would pass it on to him if he was that incompetent."

"It's not about his incompetence, though I guarantee you I'm twice the businessman he is. It's about principles. You can't just treat people like they're there to serve you, with no regard for how they feel, and then get rewarded for it. I won't see it happen."

"Ethan…"

"I won't watch him win, Noelle. Not after the way he treated my mother. It goes beyond the fact that he was unfaithful to her. He took her money, you know. Like your mother did to you. When his father wouldn't give him what he thought he needed to expand his business interests, he siphoned it off of my mother while he was screwing other women behind her back. Or worse, in plain view. Everyone knew how little he respected her." He took a drink of his champagne. "My mother's not perfect, but she didn't deserve that."

Noelle's throat felt tight. "No one does. I…I'm sorry."

He laughed. Cold. Humorless. "Now isn't that ironic? You, apologizing. I thought I told you not to do that."

"Fine. Then I won't. But I am sorry your mother was hurt. But will this…I mean…will it fix anything?"

He knocked back the rest of the champagne and backed away from the railing. "I'm going to bed."

"Instead of talking to me?"

"I didn't ask you to marry me for psychotherapy or companionship, Noelle. I won't start pretending now."

He turned and left the balcony, left her standing there with her heart pounding in her chest, a sick feeling rolling in her stomach. This was pretend, he was right. And it wasn't about getting to know each other, or caring, or anything real.

So why had it started to feel like it was?

CHAPTER SEVEN

It was sort of nice to have a reprieve from Ethan's presence. Noelle spent the day in and around the hotel, trawling the little shops and indulging in a Vienna coffee at a café near the beach. It was decadent in so many ways. No one telling her what to do, and no pressing, horrible worries.

The bubble bath afterwards had been a major highlight too. Relaxing, which was nothing like being with Ethan. Warm and sensual too, which *was* a bit like being with Ethan.

She swore out loud in the empty hotel suite and embraced the rush of satisfaction it gave her. Her mother had used whatever language she wanted, whenever she felt like it, but Noelle had always been bound to protect her image of being a sweet, eternal child. Nothing even remotely adult or scandalous could be associated with her.

In the end, it hadn't helped. She'd grown up. She'd gotten uninteresting.

She flopped onto the couch and put her feet on the coffee table. This was familiar. Nights spent alone in a hotel room. She'd always cherished the time. Time simply to be herself. To eat a chocolate bar and watch a movie showing her what she was missing, locked up in her ivory tower while the rest of the world lived.

She took a bite of her chocolate bar. She was reliving

old times in a way. But there would be no sexy movies. Being around Ethan was messing with her head and she didn't need to encourage her suddenly perky hormones.

The door to the suite opened and Noelle scrambled to get her robe into place so that everything was covered.

"Hi." He walked in and stripped his black tie off in one fluid motion, casting the strip of silk to the floor. It was like something from a cologne commercial—or one of her late-night movie indulgences. The gorgeous man returning home after a long hard day to sweep his woman off her feet and into bed…

"Hi," she replied, hopping up from the couch, holding the lapels of her robe tighter now.

"Good day?"

"I did more data entry. And had coffee."

"All good then?"

"I suppose."

"We've rated the papers over here. Pictures of us getting off my private plane are everywhere."

She took a step toward him. "Do you have them with you?"

"You like being in the news, don't you?"

She shrugged, slightly embarrassed by her enthusiastic reaction. "I got used to it. To watching it. Seeing what people said, what they thought. Good and bad, it all sort of…validated me."

He reached into his laptop bag and pulled out a folded paper. "Enjoy."

She took the newspaper from his hand and opened it slowly, her heart pounding as she looked at the pictures, at the headlines.

Ethan Grey returns home with new squeeze, pianist Noelle Birch, in tow. Meeting the grandparents?

"That's…cool," she said.

"Cool?"

"To get in the pubic eye again like this…like we talked about. But it's more than just showing my mother up. You don't know what this might mean for me."

He didn't smile. His face didn't seem to change at all. But something in his eyes looked different. Darker. "I have an idea."

"You don't approve of my enjoyment of fame?" His silence was its own kind of answer. "My life…the life I had before, it was…It's hard to explain. Parts of it were brutally hard. And yet, there were things that I loved. I loved to play in front of a crowd. I loved it when I would hear the beginning notes of a new song in my head. And I loved when people recognized me. When they were excited to see me. Like they cared or something."

He shook his head, his expression suddenly fierce. "That's not real. None of it is."

"It feels real," she said softly, looking down at the picture.

"Trust me, it's not. Ask my mum how real it is. She was an A-lister for a while. Invited to every party, cast in all the big movies. The public built her up and then forgot about her overnight while she poured everything she had into a husband who acted like she wasn't alive half the time. There's no happiness in seeking the approval of the people. Because maybe they'll give it, but only for a while. And when they take it away, it's a cruel reality."

"Yeah, I'm sort of living that reality, Ethan. I'm aware of how much it sucks."

"All right, Noelle, today your picture's in the paper. What about tomorrow?"

She didn't really want to think about tomorrow. She was safe now. Safe and warm, and feeling pretty happy to be back in the public eye in a positive way. But that attitude was what had gotten her into trouble in the first place. She might be enjoying these snatches of happiness right now—enjoying them too much to see something bad around the corner, something like her mother running off with all her money.

"I don't know."

"No one should have the power to decide how you feel about yourself, Noelle, good or bad. Give yourself that power."

"I suppose it's easy for you."

He shrugged. "I've never cared what other people thought. As long as I'm getting where I want to go, I don't care what other people think of my methods. When you're successful there will always be people waiting to watch you fail. They don't matter."

Ethan's heart was pounding heavily in his chest, a strange, protective sort of anger pumping through him, hot and fast. Reckless. There was no reason he should care, none at all, about the way Noelle saw herself. About the look on her face when she'd seen her picture in the paper.

But it reminded him too much, far too much, of how his mother had reacted to reviews, good and bad, about how she'd been disappointed when the paparazzi had stopped following her. About how thoroughly demolished she'd been when the press had gleefully dissected Damien Grey's appearance with Celine Birch at a major Hollywood industry event, leaving his wife, the movie star, at home.

The constant bitter regret, the desperate wishing that she'd never moved away from California, never sacrificed her figure to give birth to a son who didn't bring her happiness anyway.

Terrible memories of trying to revive her after she'd swallowed a whole bottle of pills.

Putting Noelle in that spot made his gut tighten so hard he couldn't move. Couldn't breathe.

He didn't know why he was doing this, why he was putting her in that place. Why he was feeling things for her.

All he knew was that he wanted to touch her, to comfort her in some way. But the minute he did that, the minute his hands touched her smooth, silken skin, it would be over for him. He would take her in his arms. Kiss her. Seduce her.

No. He wouldn't. He would be in control. Just as he always was. She wasn't different. She wasn't special. He tightened his jaw, clenched his teeth, tried to stop his body's intense reaction to the thought of what it would be like to seduce her.

So sweet. For a moment.

It would almost be worth it.

"What?" she asked, her voice breathless, her breasts rising and falling sharply. She knew. And she was just as affected as he was.

"We'll have more public appearances to make over the coming weeks," he said, his eyes fixed on her full, pale lips. "We have to be sure we're comfortable touching each other."

He took a step toward her, his body urging him on, his mind screaming at him to pull back. He would. He would pull away before it was too late. Just not yet.

Not quite yet.

He put his hand on her cheek, shocked to see how unsteady it was. She was soft, softer even than he'd imagined she would be. And the need to do more, touch more, was so strong it made his body shudder.

"Comfortable?" she asked, her words hushed, her blue eyes wide.

"Not even a little bit. You?"

She shook her head.

"Then we'll have to change that," he said.

He dipped his head and closed the gap between them, pleasure bursting in his stomach, heating him to boiling point, his whole body instantly hard with desire. She tasted sweet, her kiss better than any wine he could remember. And far outstripping any other kiss he'd experienced. He couldn't remember being affected this strongly by the simple touch of lips against his, not even when he'd been a teenage virgin.

A soft sound escaped her mouth and he devoured it, taking the chance to dip his tongue inside, to taste her a bit more thoroughly. Just a taste.

But a taste could never be enough. Not when it made him crave more. Everything.

He raised his other hand and allowed himself to rest it on the indent of her waist, another step into temptation. Another concession. But he would pull away in time. Before it got out of control. There was no 'out of control' for him, he always had it. Always had the power.

She touched the tip of her tongue to his and need shocked him, like a lightning bolt from the point where she made contact straight to his groin.

He couldn't breathe. But it was all right. He would gladly drown in her. In the passion that poured from her and filled him, pushing at the bonds of his control, cracking it, threatening to shatter it.

Was this what his father felt when he was with his mistresses? A pull, a need that felt essential as air?

The thought was a bucket of ice water to his overheated libido. He pulled away from her, his throat tight, his lungs burning with the need to draw a breath he couldn't quite manage to pull in.

"That's enough, I think," he said, his voice rough.

She looked dazed, dizzy. A lot like he felt. "I..."

"Don't worry about the press," he said. "I've got work to do, so I'm going to go to my room now."

He turned without looking at her again. Because if he did, if the look in her eyes reflected the longing he felt, if he caught her scent, he would be lost again.

He couldn't afford that. It was a matter of keeping his focus. And it was a matter of pride. He wouldn't lose either.

Notes moved through her. Music, a melody, vague and unstructured. Noelle turned over in bed, felt the cool sheets against her bare legs. The chill didn't last long. As soon as her thoughts came into sharper focus, she remembered the kiss.

Ethan's lips moving over hers, so expertly. So sensually.

Her first kiss. And it had been...it had been so much more than she'd imagined it could be. All fire and need. Exciting. Terrifying. It had brought something out in her that she hadn't felt before, something she hadn't realized lived in her.

She sat up and swung her legs over the side of the bed, her toes digging into the plush carpet. She could feel it swelling in her, moving through her. It made her ache. Or rather, it added to the ache that was already centered in her chest. An ache that was physical as well as emotional.

It was as if everything was changing, shifting beneath her feet. Not like the cold shock of change that had happened when her mother had disappeared with her money, but something else, something more subtle, but even more dangerous in some ways.

She was starting to feel changed, rather than simply feeling that her life had changed around her. She felt more power. More control. And less, at the same time. She wasn't sure how that worked exactly.

She closed her eyes again, found the melody she'd heard in her sleep. Vague still, but present. Inspiration that felt familiar, like something she used to feel before. She stood, excitement flooding her, and walked through her room, out into the main area of the hotel suite. It was automatic, sitting at the piano, her fingers resting lightly on the keys.

She could still feel Ethan's lips on hers, the hot press of his hand on her waist.

She pressed one key down. Low. Soft and tentative at first. Then she added another. Several joined together, the strains harmonizing, creating a haunting dissonance that filled the room, that reflected the feelings swirling inside of her. Minor. Confused. A little bit sad.

"What are you doing?"

She halted her movements and looked up. Ethan was there, wearing only a pair of jeans resting dangerously low on his hips, revealing lines that led to a part of his body she definitely shouldn't be thinking about. She shifted her eyes up and it was really no better. His chest was art, his abs a sculpture. Every inch of his body was well-defined, dusted with just the right amount of dark hair. Sexy beyond all reason.

"Playing." She forced the word out around the lump in her throat.

"Not a drill."

"No."

He walked closer to her, resting his forearm on the closed top of the shiny black grand. "Not a piece I recognize either."

"Original," she said. And as she said it, she realized it was. It was a song. And it had come from her.

Her stomach tightened.

"I liked it. What was it?"

"I don't know," she replied. Because it was true. She wasn't sure what she felt. What she wanted.

He circled her, moved so that he was standing behind her. He stretched one arm forward, brushing her bare shoulder as he did, resting his fingers on the keys, pressing a few of the them.

"Why not?" he asked, his breath fanning over her cheek.

"Because I'm not sure what I want. Where I'm going. But I want to. I think that's what the song really is. It's longing."

"What is it you long for, Noelle? Fame?"

"I thought so," she whispered. "I'm not sure now."

"Something else?" He put his hand on her shoulder and brushed her hair to one side, exposing her neck, his skin hot against hers.

"Maybe." She sucked in a sharp breath.

"Something with a little bit more…immediate gratification?"

His lips were near her ear, brushing against her, his voice soft, husky, an invitation to sin. She wanted to accept. Regardless of the consequences, in that moment, she wanted to turn and press her mouth to his. To have another taste of the passion she'd been introduced to earlier.

But she didn't think she could take that step. What if he pulled away? What if he didn't want her? She wasn't sure she could handle more rejection, even if it was only physical rejection.

He moved his hand over the back of her neck, the tips of his fingers gliding over her skin. She shivered, her nipples tightening, arousal trickling through her, thick and sweet like honey, making her ache for more.

She knew exactly what it was her body wanted. And she also knew that Ethan could give it to her. It was the other stuff, the heart-pounding, stomach-tightening emotion that frightened her.

The touch of his lips against the curve of her neck made the butterflies in her stomach disperse, letting desire take over. There was no place for fear, not when his touch made her feel so good. So warm.

He kissed her again, a featherlight touch on her shoulder that echoed all through her body. She leaned into him, against his hard body, his bare chest hot against her back. He gripped her shoulders, his hold keeping her from melting into a puddle and sliding down the piano bench.

He moved one hand to her shoulder and brushed the strap of her silky top aside.

"I just want to see," he said, his voice tight. He moved her other strap aside and she felt her top fall, revealing her breasts. The only light in the room was the silver glow of the moon pouring through the window.

Ethan's unsteady breathing, the slight tremble in his hand as he slid his fingertips down her arm, made her feel powerful, made her feel confident in a way she never had before.

"You're more beautiful than I imagined. And I imagined you would be stunning."

She tried to ignore the tightening in her throat, tried to focus only on the desire that was coursing through her. The physical. She didn't want anything else. Didn't need it. She just wanted him to touch her. She didn't know what she wanted after that, wasn't sure if she was ready for more, but if he would just touch her...

"I need to touch you."

"Yes," she breathed.

Permission seemed to be what he'd been waiting for, because the moment the word left her lips, he moved his hands to her breasts, cupping her sensitive flesh, skimming his thumbs over her hardened nipples.

"Oh, Ethan…" She let her head fall back against his stomach and focused on nothing. Nothing beyond the sharp, overwhelming darts of pleasure that were piercing her body, making her ache for more.

She could feel the evidence of his desire, hard and hot behind her. It made her wish she knew what to do, made her wish she had some experience with men so that she'd know how to please him, make him feel even half of what he made her feel with the slightest stroke of his hands on her skin.

He kissed her neck again, more firmly this time. She angled her head and pressed her mouth to his. Passion and fire exploded between them, the heat tangible, enough to burn her inside and out. And she liked it. A lot.

His tongue slid over hers, and she met him, thrust for thrust, tasting him, devouring him as he continue to tease her breasts with his talented hands.

She turned around, still on the bench, rising up on her knees and winding her arms around his neck. He braced his hands on her hips, holding her to him, her bare breasts pressed tightly against his chest.

He nipped her lip, and the shock of the pain, slight but intense, made her heart pound faster, made her internal muscles tighten. She pulled her lips away from his, trying to catch her breath. He kissed her throat, her collarbone.

More. She begged him silently. She wasn't ready to ask out loud. She didn't think she could. But she wanted it. Wanted his mouth on her breasts. She wanted him…all of him.

"Oh, Ethan…" His name seemed like the only thing she could say. Because it was all that filled her mind.

He froze, his hands tight on her still. He pulled his

mouth away from her. His chest was rising and falling sharply, his dark eyes unreadable in the dim light.

He shook his head. "This shouldn't have happened. This can't happen."

The rejection cut into her, clearing the fog of arousal quickly and brutally. "What?"

"Not now. Not with you." He pulled his hands away from her and she wobbled on the bench, bracing herself on the piano keys. The sound of incompatible notes was horrible and far too loud, jarring her the rest of the way back into reality.

"Not with…"

He turned away from her and walked back into his room, shutting the door behind him.

She could only sit there, stunned, not so much by her own behavior, but by his. He wanted her, she knew he did. No matter what he'd said.

Not with you.

Because of whose daughter she was? Or because she wasn't sexy enough? Or for some other reason he'd chosen to invent? She curled her hands into fists and fought the urge to pound them on the piano keys. To make so much noise that he wouldn't be able just to walk into his room and shut her out.

She was angry, embarrassed. But not destroyed. It was funny, she'd felt changed earlier, and now she realized that she really was. Because the old Noelle would have curled up in a ball and hidden after suffering something like that. Or she would have frozen, pretending things would some-how magically get fixed.

But she wasn't hiding now. She had a house to get back. She was strong enough to get through this, and she wasn't going to let something like errant attraction—or rejec-tion—stop her from achieving her goal.

If Ethan didn't want her, that was fine. She would deal with it. And she wouldn't make the mistake of giving in to desire again.

CHAPTER EIGHT

NOELLE had been like a living flame to the touch. Her skin so soft, her breasts the perfect weight in his hands. It had been hell to leave her. Hell to turn away from her when he'd wanted nothing more than to lift her onto the piano and settle between her thighs. To lose himself in her body.

Twelve hours later and he was still so turned on, his teeth ached. And it was the wrong time to be so distracted. And she was absolutely the wrong woman.

It was like a cosmic joke that his body responded to her. Actually, *responded* wasn't a strong enough word—a response was expected between a man and a woman. No, this was…combustion. And it made him feel on edge and out of control, both things he hated.

He gritted his teeth and tried to fight the arousal that still pounded through him. Part of him didn't want to fight it. Part of him wanted to embrace it. To sink back into the dark sensuality that Noelle seemed able to create around them with such ease.

No. Not happening. This was complicated enough without adding sex to the mix. He could control his desire for her, and he *would* control it.

He walked out of his bedroom and into the main area of the hotel suite. It was empty, and he wondered if Noelle was still in her room. And if she was wearing that same, brief nightgown she'd been wearing the night before. She seemed to have a collection.

He could feel his body hardening, his erection pushing against the seam of his jeans, and he tried to reroute his thoughts. Spreadsheets. Spreadsheets and the falling value of real estate. That wasn't sexy at all.

But Noelle still was, and he couldn't shake the image of her from his mind.

He stepped down to the piano and looked outside. She was out there on the balcony, a stack of documents on the table in front of her, alongside a cup of coffee—a vanilla latte, he assumed—and the laptop he'd packed for her.

He slid open the glass door and walked out into the warm coastal morning, relishing the slight bite of the salt air in his throat when he breathed in. Relishing even more the scent of her as it caught in the breeze and teased his senses.

"Working?" He looked at her intently, taking everything in. The way her brows knit together with concentration, the way her fingers moved over the keyboard as they had over the keys of the piano the night before...

Just thinking about the night before made his erection throb.

"Yes," she replied, not looking at him. Her posture was still, her manner cool enough to cut through the Brisbane temperatures. A pink flush spread from her cheeks down her neck. He was starting to wonder whether she actually wasn't that experienced with men—an idea that completely contradicted what he knew about her mother, and what he'd imagined it would have been like for her growing up.

But that blush. Those eager, honest responses...

No. He wasn't letting his thoughts go there again. *That way madness lies.*

"I appreciate it, but you don't have to. I can do that. Or it can wait until we're back in the States."

She kept her eyes fixed, very decidedly, on the computer screen. "No. It's nothing. I mean it's something. It's part of my job, right?"

"Not really."

"You told me that…"

"Yeah, I said you could do it, and you can, but it's not what I need from you."

The flush on her face darkened, and she turned to face him. "Oh. And what exactly is it that you…need from me?"

A few days in his bed. Uninterrupted. Room service brought to the door so they could just forget the world. Just for a while. That idea was more tempting than it ought to be.

Unsatisfied desire made his tone a little rougher than he intended. "What we discussed in the beginning. My priorities haven't changed. I assume yours haven't either."

She looked away again. "No."

"Good." He sat down in the chair across from her. "Last night…"

"I know what it was."

"You do?" Because he was starting to wonder whether he knew. And he knew.

"There's tension between us. We'd be lying if we pretended there wasn't. So it was a…tension…relieving… thing."

"Oh yes, I feel much less tense," he said, fighting the urge to reach back and work the knotted muscles on his shoulders.

"So do I."

"Liar."

She turned to face him again. "You were the one who… stopped it."

"It was the right thing to do, Noelle."

"I know."

"You know?"

She nodded. "Of course. Sex complicates things. And sex between the two of us would get more complicated than things have a right to be. I'm glad one of us was thinking straight. I just want to get through this and get what I need. My house. That's all I really want from you."

It wasn't all she'd wanted from him last night. He was sure of that. She'd been with him every step of the way, no doubt. And today, if not for the blush, he would've assumed she didn't remember that it had happened at all.

"And don't worry, I'll be able to put on a show for the press. What happened happened, and it doesn't change anything. It certainly doesn't change my expectations."

"It doesn't?" Because his body's expectations now seemed radically altered.

"Even if it did, I would do my part. I've always been a good actress."

"You were a musician, you weren't an actress."

She looked past him, her blue eyes unfocused. "Sure I was. I would spend the whole day rehearsing, until the sides of my thumbs bled from scraping against the edges of the piano keys. The whole time my mother would scream at me to do it better. Cleaner. More precise. My teacher would pace the floor and try to run interference between the two of us. When I was a teenager I started yelling back. I would get slapped. And then, after all that, I would go on stage. And I would smile and I would play like I didn't have any troubles. I *am* an actress, Ethan. Better than most you'll find in Hollywood."

She stood up and closed the laptop. "I need to shower."

He grabbed her wrist and held her still for a moment, his stomach tight, sick. "Clearly, the affair with my father was the least of your mother's sins." She looked away from him and he took her chin between this thumb and forefinger, directing her attention back to him. "What happened to you wasn't right. It wasn't normal. You don't have to live that way."

He wasn't so dumb that he hadn't realized Noelle wasn't her mother. It had become obvious after only a few days in her company. But he'd never imagined it could have been like that for her. Had never fathomed just how much she'd been controlled.

Noelle nodded slowly. "I know that's not how it's supposed to be. But I'm not really sure how I *am* supposed to live."

She left the terrace and went back inside the suite, sliding the door closed behind her.

"What was one thing you weren't allowed to do?"

Noelle jumped when Ethan strode into the main area of the suite, and her heart leapt up into her throat. After last night, being around him was… She wanted to turn and run from him or climb him like he was a tree. Which instinct was stronger greatly depended on the moment.

"When I was younger?"

He nodded. "Yes. What was one thing that your mother wouldn't let you do? Something frivolous that has nothing to do with piano-playing or performing or milking you for cash."

A whole lot of things rushed through her head. Shopping. Movies. Dating.

That thought reminded her of last night. Made her body hot all over. The way he'd touched her, the things he'd made her feel…amazing didn't even begin to cover it. But then he'd rejected her. *Her.* Not just sex, but her specifically.

She wished she knew why. She also wished she didn't.
And she wished he wasn't so determined to make it up to
her. Because she was certain that's what this was: a Band-
Aid for the boo-boo he'd inflicted by turning away from
her.

He would need a much bigger Band-Aid than a day out
to erase the sting of that humiliation. Yet, perversely, she
still wanted to be with him. To be near him. To spend the
day with him.

"Nothing," she said.

"There was nothing you weren't allowed to do?"

"No. I mean…I was never allowed to just do nothing.
Even now, I practice all the time. And what for? For con-
certs I'll never give? I was never allowed to have a day that
was just mine. If we ever shopped it was for my mother,
wherever we ate, that was for her too. We never went to
the beach because she hated getting sand in her shoes."

"Then that's what we're doing today."

"What?"

"Nothing. Nothing and everything. Whatever you
want."

That conjured up images of his hands on her body, his
lips against hers. Why she still wanted that after he'd made
it very clear he didn't was beyond her. Silence filled the
room along with a tension so thick she was pretty sure she
could eat it with a spoon.

"Ethan," she said slowly. "Why are you doing this?"

"Because I want to. Because maybe I need to do nothing too." He looked as confused by that as she felt.

"So we'll do nothing then."

"Sounds like a plan."

Noelle looked down at her vanilla ice cream melting
steadily in the sun. She'd been sitting in front of the ocean,

watching the waves crawl up the shore, then recede, while she indulged in her frozen treat.

Ethan had gone off to take a call, and she finally felt like she could breathe.

The whole day had been…well, it had almost been fun. And would have had zero value as far as her mother was concerned. They'd taken a walk through a historic beach town, eaten lunch at a small fish and chip shack, then got ice cream at a shop right on the ocean.

Perfection. Not exactly relaxing the way she'd hoped it might be, but being near Ethan just wasn't. It ramped her up, made her feel like she was on high alert, made her skin feel extra sensitive, like her blood was flowing closer to the surface. Like everything was more real and more fantastic all at the same time.

"I'll take some of that ice cream." Ethan returned holding two water bottles, looking sexier than any man should in a pair of sandals and some board shorts. He sat next to her and she fought the urge to move closer. Or scoot away. She wasn't sure which she wanted more. So she stayed where she was.

"You had yours. You ate it too fast," she said, licking a drip from the side of the cone.

"And yours is melting. You need help."

She laughed. "I assure you, I don't." She lapped at another drip.

"While I love watching you do that, my professional opinion remains the same." He smiled and she had a vision of the charming playboy she was certain he could be. But behind that, deeper, there was a flicker of heat in his eyes that went beyond simple flirtation.

"I…"

He leaned in and her heart stopped. He was so close

to her, close enough that if she just dipped her head, she could brush her lips against his.

He moved first, angling his head, but not the way she'd been anticipating. He took a long lick of her ice cream cone before leaning back again. "Thanks," he said, his voice rough.

Her hand was shaking from anticipation. From the fact that watching his tongue sliding over the ice cream had actually been pretty hot. She didn't know herself right now.

No. That wasn't true. She was getting to know herself. A sexual encounter on a piano bench and an ice cream cone on the beach at a time. It was like finding out there was a whole different side to herself when she'd always thought there had only been one. She'd been all about the piano. All about performing. But this was living. Real living.

"This has been...this has been great. Thank you," she said, still trying to catch her breath from the sexual shock of watching him lick her ice cream cone. "Sorry I unloaded on you earlier. About my mother."

"We all need to let it out sometimes."

"We both lost the parent lottery, didn't we?"

"Seems so."

"Will you be happy when you get the resorts? I mean, will that be it? Will you win?"

"Is that a trick question?" he asked.

She shook her head. "Not a trick. I'm really wondering. Because I want my...I want my life back, Ethan. Not exactly like it was. I want beach days. But I also want to perform. I want the recognition, the hard work, the reward. The money. I don't...I don't know what to do without it, and I have to believe that if you have a goal like that, when you reach it you'll be satisfied."

Ethan looked toward the sun glinting off the crystal-line waves, his brow furrowing. "I don't know the answer to that. I don't really care. I'm more than happy to keep fighting for the next thing. Bigger and better."

"That sounds…exhausting."

"More exhausting than doing piano drills for the rest of your life?"

"Infinitely more."

"There's not really anything more to life, Noelle. You keep going, you get more. I doubt you'll be satisfied just playing again. How many people do you need in the auditorium, and after you fill up a large one, won't you need a stadium? That's how it works."

"I don't…" Noelle's voice trailed off. She didn't like what he was saying. Because it was frighteningly close to what she feared might be the truth. That there would be no satisfaction in 'reclaiming' her career. That she would get back to that life and find it as empty as the one she was living now. "I don't believe it. I won't need more. I'll be happy sitting at the piano, playing."

"Maybe you think sitting at the piano will satisfy you. But then, you do know how to have fun on a piano bench, don't you?"

His words hit her like a physical blow, the sudden venom in his tone shocking her. She stood, brushing sand off the back of her shorts. "Why would…why would you say that to me?"

"Noelle—"

"I want to go. Today was…fun. And it was neat to kind of play hooky from life. But we both have a plan. And hanging out on the beach just isn't in it."

He nodded. "Not for either of us."

"I don't think hanging out on piano benches is in it for us either." She turned and headed back to the path that led to the teeming boardwalk area. A little noise would be good. A little something to keep her mind off the raw wound in her chest.

How could he say that? As if she let men touch her like that all the time? Though, he might think she did.

Well, so what if she did? She knew *he* was an epic playboy, and if she wanted to get off with men on piano benches every other night of the week that was her business. Not her mother's and not Ethan's. Hers.

She whipped around and was not that surprised to find Ethan only a couple of paces behind her. "You know what, Ethan? It's none of your business what I do in my spare time. Beyond this little charade of ours, my life is none of your business. I could have had sex with a hundred guys, and guess what? Not your job to judge. I'm the one who has to live my life. The one who has to live with me. So… there."

She turned again and walked away, her heart pounding hard in her head, her entire body shaking. It was true, and she hadn't even realized it until she'd said it.

She had to live her life. No one else. Why had she always taken the path other people put her on? Why was she still doing her drills for hours every day?

It was *her life*. No matter how much her mother had wanted to treat it as her own, no matter how much her instructor had fed his ego on her success. They had had no right.

She was angry now. Not just about her situation, but for herself. For everything she'd accepted, her whole life, because she'd believed that her only option was to do as she was told.

Ethan's firm grasp on her arm stopped her in her tracks. He didn't seem at all concerned by the people walking by, craning their necks to see if there was going to be a huge fight between them.

"You're right, Noelle, it's not my job to judge you. And I don't. My comment was out of line." His dark eyes blazed with an intensity that stood in direct opposition to his apologetic words.

"Really?"

"Really."

"I...you apologized," she said.

"Yeah."

"I don't think anyone has ever apologized to me."

"I'm a confident guy, Noelle, and that means my ego can take it when I have to admit I'm wrong. That *was* wrong. It isn't my business how many men you've slept with, or intend to sleep with. It was my sexual frustration talking there. A bit of jealousy, which, I'll be honest, is unfamiliar to me."

"The...jealousy or the sexual frustration?"

"Both."

"Oh." She looked around at the people, moving around them now as though they didn't exist, no more interesting than the pylons that divided the boardwalk from the sand.

"You sound shocked."

"I don't think I've ever aroused either emotion in a man before. So, yes, I am a bit shocked. Maybe as shocked as you are."

"Not possible. I'm sure you make men feel like this all the time."

He looked at her, his dark eyes intense, his jaw shifting as he tightened it, his Adam's apple bobbing.

"I...I doubt it."

He stepped closer, the hand on her arm gliding up to her shoulder, around to the back of her neck, his thumb moving over her skin, fingers sifting through her hair.

"I don't. Not for a moment. You really are beautiful."

"Ethan, I thought we decided that...it's a bad idea." She

hated that. Why was it a bad idea? Ethan felt good. And warm, so warm. Everything had been frozen over for so long, dead and dry. Ethan was like the sun.

She wanted to bathe in his warmth, in the promise of new things that seemed to come every time he touched her.

But it was a bad idea. They'd decided that. She'd agreed.

She moved closer to him, her heart pounding. His hand was still on her neck, massaging her, spreading heat and fire through her.

She didn't want to move away. Didn't want to break her connection with him. It was her life. And she had to live it.

She wanted a little bit of Ethan in it. For as long as she could have it. Because he made her angry and happy and he turned her on. He made her *feel*, when for so long she'd simply been existing. He made her aware of things—needs, desires she'd never been mindful of before.

It was like finding a new dimension to life. And that was more than just the beach and sand and ice cream. It was deeper, it made everything seem as if it had broader scope, more depth.

She didn't want to run from that. She wanted to dive into it head-first.

She stood up on her toes and leaned in, brushing his mouth with hers, her entire body trembling as she increased the pressure of the kiss, as the shock of his flesh on hers fired through her, charging her like a bolt of electricity.

It didn't satisfy her. Not even close. She felt like he was water and she had been lost in the desert. She felt insatiable. She touched her tongue to the seam of his lips, explored the shape of his mouth, tasted his skin.

They hadn't kissed enough last night. He'd done the

touching, he'd done the pleasuring. But she wanted more than that. She wanted it all.

A short groan vibrated in his chest, and he locked his arm around her waist, pulling her to him, holding her against his hard, well-muscled body. She arched into him, could feel the heavy weight of his erection against her stomach.

And that was when she realized they were standing on the boardwalk, in broad daylight.

She pulled away from him, blinking hard. Pushing shaking fingers through her hair, she looked around, trying to see if they'd caught everyone's attention. No, there were one or two people in line for ice cream who hadn't noticed them. Great.

"I...for someone who was trained not to draw the wrong kind of attention, I seem to be doing a pretty bad job at... not drawing the wrong kind of attention."

"You kissed me," he said.

"Not...not *your* attention. People are staring," she hissed, lowering her face and walking back toward the hotel.

"Isn't that the idea? We are supposed to be an engaged couple."

"That wasn't the idea...just now. For me I mean."

"I see, then what was it?"

She stopped and put her hands on her hips. "If you were a gentleman, you wouldn't ask."

"I didn't say I was a gentleman."

"No. I guess you didn't."

"You're right." He sighed. "This is a bad idea."

A bolt of panic hit her in the chest. "Not the whole deal, just the kissing, right? Because I need this, Ethan. I need my house. I can't lose it."

He frowned and reached his hand out, brushing his

thumb over her cheek. "Your cheeks are pink. You need sunblock."

"Please tell me you don't mean the whole deal," she repeated.

"I think it's all a bad idea, Noelle. But I'm not backing out of it. We have a deal, and we'll stick to that. But it's a business deal, don't forget that."

"I...I won't." Of course, if she really felt like it was a business deal her heart probably wouldn't be beating so erratically, and her lips wouldn't still be stinging from the kiss. "We should probably go."

They were still standing in the middle of the crowded boardwalk, but even with so many people everywhere, she felt as if they were the only two people on the planet. At least, the only two who mattered. She wasn't sure what that meant, or why he could make her so mad, and then make her want him, then make her nearly melt inside with the things that he said, all in the space of a few moments.

"Yeah, I've got some work to do this evening," Ethan replied.

"Oh. Good." That meant they wouldn't have time to spend together and maybe she could figure out what was happening inside her. Newfound feelings, along with life-changing revelations, needed to be examined after all. "I mean...I'll have a chance to play around with that song I started working on last night."

A spark crackled between them. The shared memory of what had interrupted her songwriting. His lips on her throat, his hands on her breasts...

"You should wear this." He reached into the pocket of his shorts, took out a small velvet box and handed it to her without opening it. She curled her fingers around it, holding it firmly closed like there was a great hairy spider inside, instead of what she knew was a giant heirloom engagement ring. Actually, at that moment, the ring seemed scarier than a spider.

"You going to open it?"

"Later," she said. Not now. Not on the boardwalk with people all around. Not while she felt scrubbed raw from everything that had happened over the past week.

He nodded once. "We'll fly back to the States tomorrow. Things will settle down. Get back to normal."

She nodded in agreement and tightened her hold on the box. She didn't ask him what he meant by normal, because she was starting to wonder whether she'd ever experienced normal. This wasn't normal. Kissing a man in public, then screaming at him, then having him give her a ring. Marrying him for a house. No, this wasn't normal.

And what she felt for Ethan had even less to do with normal than their marriage farce did.

She'd been expecting that performing, playing for crowds again, being famous and staying in posh hotels would make her feel like herself again. Now she wondered if that had ever been the case. She was starting to wonder if she'd ever figure out what it was she wanted.

She looked at Ethan's strong profile and tried to ignore the tightening in her stomach. All right, so there was one thing she wanted. But it was the one desire she should probably ignore.

Ethan had been wrong about New York bringing normality back. Waking up in the soft, luxurious bed was still too good to be *her* normal. Having Ethan to talk to every day, even if it was about mundane things, was better than normal too.

It was like having a companion, if not almost a friend. Someone to share things with. The details of her day. Three days a week she went to work with him and shadowed his assistant, learning different, somewhat menial office tasks. But she made a mean pot of coffee now and her typing was getting a lot faster than it had been that first day.

And yesterday, Ethan hadn't come by the suite to pick her up in his car, so she'd simply called his assistant and asked her to come and share a cab. It felt…good. As if she was building a life. A *real* life—*her* life—not just the broken remains of a life that had never been hers in the first place.

Ethan was due to arrive, and she was pacing, trying to shake off her nervous energy, fairly certain it was futile. Even after a month with him, even though it had been three weeks since he'd kissed her, she just couldn't relax around him.

She crossed the room to the piano and slid her fingers across the length of the keyboard. Excitement fired through her veins, her stomach tightened in that way that it did when Ethan touched her. Desire. A thrill. She'd been working on the song that had grabbed hold of her in Brisbane, but it hadn't progressed easily. It was still harder to write music now than it had been.

She sat down on the bench and put her hands into position, flexing her fingers for a moment before pushing down on middle C. She added E and G and let the chord fill the empty room, let it fill her.

Then she followed the feeling. She saw Ethan, remembered how he had stood behind her that night back in Australia. How he'd touched her. She hadn't let herself think of it, if at all possible, since their return to New York. But she opened her mind up to it now.

It was easy to put the feeling into her music, effortless. This wasn't like the songs she'd written a year or more ago. Those songs had been born out of technical ability, mostly because she'd had to tame her creativity to make her teacher happy with the structure of a piece.

But this one held her. Her as she was, not beaten into submission, into a shape and form that her teacher deemed salable. Here and now, she was pouring out her feelings, dissonant and minor, filling the room. Uncertain but powerful, deep and all-consuming.

It didn't empty her of the emotion, but made it stronger, growing inside of her, flowing from her fingertips.

She didn't know how long she played, how many times she went through the piece so she could cement it in her mind. When she stopped she sat frozen, before letting it all overtake her.

She felt one tear slip down her cheek, then another. She put her hand over her mouth to cut off the sharp sound that was trying to escape. And then she stopped. She let it all happen, because she'd never done that before. She'd been trying to hold on. To her past, to a life she wasn't certain she would have chosen for herself, but one that she'd been comfortable with.

And she'd never let herself truly grieve the loss of it. She'd never moved on. She'd cut off everything inside of her instead, and she'd lost her music. Not the crowded auditoriums and the CDs, but the music that had always lived in her, coloring the way she saw and heard the world.

It had been quiet in her when before it had always been filled with a rich, layered sound. Music.

She was finding it again. But different. On her terms.

"Are you all right?"

She turned around on the bench and wiped her cheeks, trying to hide the evidence of her crying jag. "I'm great."

"You don't look great." Ethan, who did look great in his custom-made suit, stepped further into the room.

"Gee thanks, Ethan."

"Why were you crying?"

"I have a song," she said. And it sounded lame. It made sense in her head, but she imagined that Ethan probably wouldn't get it.

"Did you finish the one you started back in Australia?" he asked, his voice rough. That pesky, shared memory again. She knew he was thinking exactly what she was thinking.

"Kind of. It was sort of a take-off from that. But it was… different too. I think I might really have something though. It's been such a long time since… I've been able to do drills, songs I knew, but there was nothing new and…that made me feel like part of me had been cut off. Music has always been in me. That's how it all started. I was com-posing music from such an early age and…my mother saw potential that needed to be capitalized on."

"So it was lessons for you then?"

"With the very best instructor. Neil was—is—a genius. He was my support system until…until my mom ran off with all the money and it was clear I couldn't…pay him anymore."

"After so many years?"

"He gave up everything, every other pupil, for me. And it turned out my mother hadn't paid him in two years. In the end, he just couldn't stay anymore. I mean, after so many years of training it isn't like I needed a teacher, but he was a coach. A mentor. The closest thing I had to a friend. He understood me. My mother was with me nearly twenty-four hours a day, traveling with me, making sure I did what I had to do to keep the money coming in. To keep the spotlight on us. But she never really tried to know me."

Ethan moved to the piano, his palm flat on the glossy black surface. "It was her loss, Noelle."

Noelle's throat tightened. "You do know how to say some nice things, Ethan."

"It's a gift."

He looked down at her hand. "You still aren't wearing the ring."

"I don't… No. I can get it. It's the bathroom." Still in the box.

"You've got to put it on eventually. I'm planning an engagement party for us, you know. And we still don't look engaged."

She swallowed. "That won't work."

He leaned in and her breathing stalled. "No. It won't." He turned and walked from the room. Normally, the distance between them would let her breathe a bit easier, but not now. Because she knew what was coming next.

He returned with that blasted box in his hands, the one that had stayed closed since he first handed it to her on the boardwalk.

She stood up from the piano bench and locked her hands in front of her, trying to keep them from trembling. Trying to keep her expression neutral. It didn't mean anything. This was part of the show. The problem wasn't the ring, it was the importance she'd assigned to it. She just had to remember that it was just a prop.

He didn't get down on one knee, not that she'd thought he would, but she was relieved anyway. He held the box out, and this time, he opened it.

She could only stare at the ring, an antique platinum band with a large, square-cut diamond at the center. She didn't want to touch it. Didn't want to take the final step of putting it on her left hand. It was all well and good to say she was marrying him to get her house, but this made it so much more real. It forced her to face what she was doing.

"Wear my ring, Noelle?"

She lifted her hand, and there was no disguising the trembling in her fingers as she plucked the ring from its satin nest and slid it on. She made a fist, acutely aware of the thick band digging into the sides of her fingers.

"It's lovely," she said, trying to swallow around her heart, which seemed to have taken up permanent residence in her throat.

His Adam's apple bobbed and he took a step back. "It will be over soon."

She was supposed to feel relieved by that, but she didn't. She felt a little bit sick. "I know."

"I'll be pretty busy the rest of this week, but we'll get an engagement announcement in the paper. Party's on Friday."

She nodded. "Okay. I'll see you then." Five whole days without seeing Ethan. She should have felt relieved by that too. A chance to have space. A chance to get her thoughts in order.

But the stupid thing was, she missed him already.

CHAPTER NINE

It had been five days since he'd seen Noelle by the time the engagement party rolled around. Five days since she'd put his ring on her finger. It had been twenty-six days since he'd kissed her. Not that he was counting.

He shouldn't be counting anyway. Hard not to though, when just the thought of her was enough to tie him in knots. He couldn't remember ever wanting a woman more. Worse, he hadn't been able to force himself to look at another woman since the first day he'd seen Noelle.

It didn't change the fact that she was off limits. It was a joke, considering he had to hold and caress her like a lover for the entire evening.

He pulled Noelle closer as they walked into the hotel ballroom. He could feel her vibrating with energy beside him. Something in her was different, changed. She was alive. Not like the time they'd gone to see his grandparents, not like their first public appearance.

But then, this was about her.

He looked at her, at her broad smile and shining blue eyes. She was wearing red lipstick again, but this time, it made her glow with color, not appear more pale. It matched her scarlet dress, so bright against her alabaster skin, skimming her slender curves, flowing down over her body like a glimmering scarlet waterfall that caught the light with every step she took.

This party was about her. It was *for* her in a way. Everyone in the room was looking, and she was soaking it in like rays from the sun.

He recognized this, because it was what his mother had done. His mother, who was never satisfied, always needing more. Never getting enough from her family, from the ones who loved her. And there had been a time when it had become too much...when his father had twisted the knife too far.

He swallowed and tightened his hold on Noelle. He didn't think she would reach the lows his mother had. But the similarities were eerie enough. Strange that he'd initially been so determined to compare her with her mother, the woman who had caused so much pain in his life, and had ended up identifying her much more closely with his own.

"Noelle Birch!" Sylvie Ames, professional shopper and born socialite, approached them with a broad smile on her face.

He felt Noelle stiffen beside him. Going to Sylvie's party had been a pretty big source of stress for her, and he didn't know how she would feel actually having to talk to the woman.

"Sylvie," Noelle said, her voice soft, measured.

"I was wondering where you'd been, and now here you are, resurfaced with Mr. Ethan Grey. Now that's impressive! I was sorry I didn't get a chance to talk to you at my birthday party."

"Oh, I didn't mind. There were so many people."

"I always enjoyed your music. Do you have another album coming out soon? I'd love to have you play at a little soiree I'm planning for next month."

He felt Noelle relax beneath his hand as she exchanged dates and times and availability with Sylvie. Sylvie gave them both air kisses before sashaying away.

"Sounds like you have a gig," he said.

"I...yes," she said, sounding a little bit shocked. "I didn't think anyone would remember me."

"Why wouldn't they, Noelle? You've always been talented. You're bound to get more talented as time goes on, not less."

"It's not all talent, Ethan. It's about connections and marketability. A kid at a massive piano, barely able to reach the pedals, playing like an adult, people pay to see that. These days I've sort of outgrown my usefulness to the public."

"Who told you that?"

"No points for guessing, Ethan," she sighed, her voice resigned.

"Your mother. She's a right peach, Noelle. I think you should just assume everything she's ever told you is a load of crap. But that's just my thought on it."

"It's not that simple though. I really trusted her, all of my life. Didn't you trust your dad a little longer than you should have?"

He nodded, his lip curling at the thought of his old man. "I don't know. I don't know if I ever trusted him. But it was clear early on...he always spent more time with his mistresses than he did with us. I've lost count of how many times I saw a woman in a minidress leaving his office, still putting her shoes back on. I was young, but I wasn't stupid."

"Ethan, that's—"

He couldn't listen to an apology. Not from her. "It's nothing," he lied. "And once I have the resorts, there will be some justice. You can't just…treat people with such disregard and expect there to be no consequences."

Noelle offered a sparkling smile to a passing guest, one that rang false. "Well, that's what my mother's done. She took everything."

"She didn't take your talent."

"She took the music for a while."

"But it's back."

She frowned slightly. "It is. In some ways it's a bit more frightening than it being gone."

They were interrupted again by a line of well-wishers and fans of Noelle. The fact that her name was in the papers again seemed to have reminded everyone of who she was, of the fact that she had been out of the public eye for so long.

She did a good job glossing over the details of the past year. She claimed it had been a resting period. She was very like his mother in that way too. Able to hide failures beneath bright laughter and smooth little lies. On vacation. A hiatus. Suffering from exhaustion. Words his mother used instead of *no one will hire me* and *addicted to pills*.

But he didn't truly believe Noelle's career was over. She was beautiful and, without her nerves in play, she worked the crowd like magic. When she played it was like someone had reached into him and grabbed his heart, squeezing it tight.

She touched him with her music on a visceral level. And he couldn't be the only one. She had a gift, one that went beyond the novelty appeal of a small child at a big piano.

Ethan had no doubt she would regain that indefinable thing she needed to go on. The adoration of the crowd, her photo in the tabloids.

And he would have Grey's Resorts. A chance to watch his father's world broken into pieces, as Damien Grey had broken so many others. Maybe somewhere in that he would find some kind of satisfaction. Bloody perfect.

But those goals, goals that had obsessed him since he'd been a teenager, seemed strangely insignificant when he thought of his encounters with Noelle. And not just the moment in the hotel room, but the kiss on the boardwalk. Something so small, really. Something that wouldn't have mattered with any other woman.

The kiss was just a prelude, usually. It was never a main event in and of itself. Kissing Noelle was different. Suddenly, he wanted to kiss her more than he wanted his next breath.

Of course, the point of the party was to flaunt their relationship and promote their upcoming marriage, so maybe taking her into the garden to make out wouldn't be the most inappropriate thing.

He was strongly considering it when Sylvie approached them again, a much older man in tow. "Noelle, will you please play something? I know it's your party, but you're so amazing, and I was just telling Jacques how good you are. He's never had the pleasure of hearing you play live."

Jacques inclined his head. "I am a fan. It would be an honor."

Noelle looked at Ethan, her eyes bright with nerves and excitement. "Do you suppose the band would mind if I played something, just for a moment?"

Ethan shook his head, his body tight with frustration. "It's your party."

He watched as she wove through the crowd, a bright spot amid the sea of customary New York black. Golden hair, pale skin, silken red dress. She was a force of color and light that was impossible to ignore as she made her way to the stage.

And once she was there, sitting behind the piano, she commanded every eye in the room to watch her.

She put her hands on the piano and he swore he felt her fingertips on his body. Long, elegant fingers caressing the keys, easy to imagine them on his skin. She started playing a piece he recognized, one he'd heard in department stores many times. Something from one of her old albums, he assumed. But actually hearing it in person, watching her perform it, was a totally new experience.

It was so fluid. Smooth. Pure perfection.

And he felt as if it was only for him. Not for anyone else in the room. His chest tightened, breathing became a little harder as arousal assaulted him, flooded him.

Each note was a caress, the flow and rhythm of the song like making love, hard and fast then slow and sweet. Everything he wanted to do with her, everything he dreamed of, put out in the open, forcing him to confront it.

She lifted her head and looked into the crowd, looked at him. Her eyes locked with his as she continued to play, her entire body moving with the effort she put into playing, every part of her involved in her performance.

She would move like that in bed. Perfection. With passion, with all of herself.

He tightened his jaw, and the strain on his muscles was a welcome distraction from the desire that was pounding through him. The last thing he needed was for some photog to snap a picture of him sporting a hard-on over his fiancée's performance.

Of course, it would lend authenticity to the whole thing.

He frowned. He didn't like thinking of it that way. Didn't want to bring the agreement into this, because this was real. His desire for her felt more real than anything in his recent memory. His past affairs had all gone hazy thanks to the passage of time, but he truly didn't think he'd ever been so aroused by a woman who was more than a hundred feet away.

He wasn't the only one enthralled by her. Everyone was mesmerized, savoring every note, existing for the next. *Captive audience* didn't even begin to describe it.

She had brought everyone in to her for a moment, let them all feel what was inside her. And, as the last note faded in the ballroom, the emotion lingered. At least it lingered in him. Everyone around him was applauding and he found that he couldn't. He wanted more. To hear more. To feel more.

But he couldn't have more. He wouldn't. Only this small indulgence. This window into her, into himself.

"She's amazing." This came from Jacques. The Frenchman was watching Noelle, his dark eyes shining, his mouth curved into a smile. Ethan wanted to hit him.

Unexpected and a little bit cavemanish. And yet, he was unrepentant.

"And she's mine," Ethan said, walking away from Sylvie and Jacques, weaving through the crowd and up to the stage, just in time to take Noelle's hand as she descended the steps.

"Was it okay?" she asked.

"Amazing." He bent his head and kissed her. Just part of the show. A necessary act that had no place lighting his body on fire.

When they parted, he was still having trouble breathing, his body tight with need.

"Amazing," she whispered.

"Let's hope this party ends soon," he said, his voice rough. Because he needed distance. He needed to send her back to her suite and he needed to get home to a very cold shower.

Walking away was the only option. But for the first time, he wondered if he had the strength to do it.

The kiss at the party had changed something. Or maybe it wasn't the kiss, maybe it was the performance. Or maybe it was both. Either way, the moment Ethan's lips had touched hers Noelle had made a decision.

She was going to have Ethan Grey. For a night, a few weeks, whatever, she was going to have what she wanted. With him.

Tonight she'd played. For her. And for everyone else. Without permission. And it had been amazing. The best feeling she could remember ever having on stage. It made her want more. Not just from Ethan, but from life. Why look ahead to the day she would get the house, shutting out everything else on the way? There was too much living to do between now and then.

She'd spent her whole life with tunnel vision. Play the piano. Be famous. Be brilliant. Everything else shut down and ignored.

But since meeting Ethan she'd discovered other things. Data entry and desire and a day at the beach. And she wanted more of that. Tonight, she was determined to have it.

Ethan stopped at the door of the hotel room. "I'll see you tomorrow."

"Wait." Good or bad, it was out of her mouth now. All she could do was commit and go forward. Or change the subject. Tell him he had lint on his coat? No. This wasn't the time to lose her nerve, or to worry about what he might think. It didn't matter. She couldn't be scared forever. And she wouldn't be scared now.

His eyes were nearly black in the shadow of the hall. "That might not be the best idea."

"I want to…play for you. The song I started in Australia. I want you to hear it."

He hesitated, his hands curled into fists, a muscle in his jaw shifting.

"Ethan…"

He took one step into the room. The tense lines in his body, the pronounced tendons in the backs of his hands, were proof of just how tightly he was hanging on to his control and told her that he knew what she was really asking.

And that by coming in, he hadn't committed to saying yes.

The risk of rejection was high. A little bit scary. But a lot worth it. Because Ethan did want her. And it was their connection, one that had nothing to do with the two of them but everything to do with their parents, that held him back. Maybe it should hold her back too. But she had never felt like her mother's actions, away from the cloistered life of music, had included her in any way.

She felt separate from their parents' history, separate in a way Ethan couldn't because of how it had affected his family. But maybe if he saw her, if he knew that she was nothing like her mother. Maybe then he would want to want her.

Ethan walked to the couch, his eyes trained on her as he worked the knot on his black silk tie. Her senses felt heightened. She could hear the slide of fabric over fabric as he tugged at it, could feel her heartbeat through her entire body. She could taste something in the air between them. Foreign and exciting. Tantalizing.

Maybe he had committed to her unspoken question. If it was even a question. It felt more like a command.

She moved to the piano, trying to imagine that there was a crowd, trying hard to hold on to her nerve. That crowd back at the party had been much easier to deal with. Even then she had felt Ethan watching her, had been compelled to turn and look at him. But it was easier to do with so many other people there. An audience of one was always much harder to perform for.

Because the more people there were, the more they blurred into an indistinguishable mass. When there were fewer of them, it suddenly became personal.

But rather than shutting Ethan out, she thought of just how he made her feel. She took a deep breath, put her hands on the keys and started playing. Slowly at first. She thought about ice cream and the beach. Ethan's hands on her body. His lips on hers. She didn't think about the future or about anything other than the immediate feelings Ethan gave her.

Lust, excitement. Happiness.

She shut everything out, everything except Ethan, and she played. Played for herself, to imprint the memories of what they'd shared inside her, to put it out there, the way some people would write in a diary. She wrote it into the song.

One she would be able to play whenever she wanted. Whenever she missed Ethan after all of this was done. Something to bring back the memories, clear and sharp, of what it had been like to be with him.

To simply share a conversation with him. A moment of pleasure.

Everything built to a crescendo, the rise of the music intense, exciting, mirroring how she felt now. The need for him. The fear he would say no. The fear he might say yes.

And then she stopped. It was quiet in the room, except for the sound of her uneven breathing. She took her shaking fingers from the keys and turned to him.

"That can't be the end," he said softly.

She shook her head and stood up, rounding the piano bench and moving towards the couch. "It's not. But I…I don't know how it ends. I was hoping you could show me."

The air was thick between them. Ethan sat unmoving, gripping the arm of the couch. She took another step toward him and his chest rose sharply, his fingers tightening their hold on the fabric.

"How do you want it to end, Noelle?" he asked, his voice tight, rough. Like each word took supreme effort to speak.

"I'd like to start where things left off that night in Australia. And I'd like them to end where they should have ended then."

"It should have ended before it started that night."

"But it didn't."

He swallowed, his Adam's apple dipping with the motion. "No. It didn't."

She took another step, stopping when she was right in front of him, her legs touching his. "So it's too late for that. We can ignore it, and neither of us is doing a great job of that, or we can see what it would be like. You and me."

She lifted her foot from the floor and rested her knee on the couch, next to his thigh. He lifted his hand and caught her wrist. "No matter what happens here, there will never be 'you and me.' I don't say that to hurt you, just to warn you. I'm not the kind of man who does forever. I don't even do long-term." He let go of her wrist and traced the line of her arm with his finger, up past her shoulder, the curve of her neck, along her jaw. He touched her lips, the contact soft. Erotic. "But what I do, I do well."

"That's all I'm asking from you, Ethan. Nothing more. I don't have any idea what I'm going to do when all of this is over, but that's not what I'm thinking about. Not now. For once I just want to…live. Right in the moment. To enjoy every last bit of now. To enjoy wanting you. The rest of it doesn't matter. Not right now."

She lifted her other foot off the floor, resting her knee beside his other thigh. He curved his arm around her body and placed his hand on her lower back, the heat of his flesh through her thin silk dress warming her, spreading sweet heat through her body, pooling in her belly, flowing out to her limbs, making them feel heavy.

He captured her mouth with his, their breathing mixing together, harsh and uneven. He slid his other hand down her thigh, gripping the skirt of her dress and tugging it upward, pushing slick silk up around her hips.

His hand met the bare skin of her buttocks. She'd gone with the filmy-fabric-friendly option of a thong when she'd dressed tonight. She was glad she had now. Even more so when a harsh groan escaped his lips and he squeezed her gently.

She gasped when he dipped his finger beneath her underwear, teasing her lightly, sliding over damp flesh.

He pulled his lips away from hers, pressed them to her neck. "How do you want this?" he asked. "I want you to set the tempo. Show me what you like. Show me how you think the song ends."

She put her hands on his shoulders and tilted her hips, a sharp whimper escaping her lips when the movement pushed his fingers forward, the tips grazing the sensitive bundle of nerves at the apex of her thighs.

"Good," he said, his voice hoarse.

She repeated the motion, pleasure streaking through her like fire. She tilted her head down and rested it on his shoulder as she continued to move over his hand. He dipped one finger inside her and all the tension that had been building in her broke, unraveling, spiraling through her in waves of sweet satisfaction, so acute it was almost painful.

She leaned against him, her entire body limp, weak. Her dress was clinging to her damp skin, her hair sticking to her neck. And he didn't seem to mind. He wrapped his arms around her and held her on his lap, his lips by her ear.

"I wondered if you would be as passionate about making love as you are about playing the piano. I think that question was just answered."

"For me too," she said softly. "I had no idea…"

He kissed her again, his mouth hungry, devouring. And she felt an answering hunger in her own body, arousal building even faster than before. Now she knew what he could make her feel, knew how powerful it was, how amazing it felt. And she knew he could make her feel that way again.

He put his hand on her bottom and stood, supporting her weight with one arm. She locked her legs around his lean hips, the hard length of his erection pressed against her clitoris. Every step he took sent waves of bliss through her, renewed her need for him.

He pushed open the door to her bedroom and walked to the bed, bringing them both gently down onto the mattress, his body covering hers. She arched against him, pressing her breasts against his chest. He reached around and unzipped her dress, tugging it down, baring her breasts. His eyes glittered in the dim light of the bedroom.

"You're even more beautiful than I remembered. And I didn't think that was possible. I thought for sure I must have imagined that you were this perfect."

Her throat tightened, emotion building in her. Emotion she didn't want to deal with. Not now. Not when she simply wanted to live in this glorious moment.

"I remember you being pretty perfect too," she said, ignoring the persistent ache in chest. "You might want to refresh my memory."

He pushed himself up with one arm and shrugged his jacket off, pulling his undone tie over his shoulders and casting it to the floor. She watched, every bit of her completely enthralled, as he unbuttoned his white dress shirt, revealing teasing glimpses of perfect, muscular chest and abs that had not come to him by accident.

He let the shirt fall from his body and started working at his belt. Her mouth went cotton-dry, her eyes fixed on him. She didn't want to miss anything, not one second. This was her moment—their moment—and she was savoring it.

Ethan let his belt fall open and undid the fastening on his slacks, tugging his pants and underwear off in one fluid motion.

She rose up onto her knees, letting her dress fall around her body. She'd expected to feel nervous or unsure, but she didn't, she knew just what she wanted. She moved forward and gripped his erection, the flesh hot and smooth, different than she'd imagined. When she squeezed him, his head fell back, a raw sound of satisfaction rushing from him.

She leaned in and flicked her tongue over the head of his shaft, a sharp sensation of desire and power racing through her when he reached out to grab her shoulder, like he needed something to brace himself against, as she had earlier.

"You want me," she said, feeling a little bit shocked by the revelation. Not just that he wanted her in a vague, sexual sense, but that he wanted her in the way she wanted him. In that knees-buckling, body-shaking sort of way.

"More than my next breath," he panted.

He moved back onto the bed, his hands moving over her curves as he bent her backward. She stretched out beneath him as he cupped her breast, his thumb skimming her nipple. He dipped his head and tasted her, pulling the hardened tip between his lips.

She arched, her hips lifting from the bed, and he took advantage, tugging her thong down her legs. She kicked it off the rest of the way, not feeling even a moment's embarrassment over being naked with him. There was no room for embarrassment. There wasn't room for anything other than the fierce need she felt to have more of him.

To feel the rush of orgasm with his body joined to hers. To give him the kind of pleasure he'd already given her.

He reached over to the side table and fumbled around for a moment before pulling out a condom. "Oh good," he said. "I don't have to fire anyone today."

"Don't tell me you knew this would happen."

"No. But my suites are always supposed to be stocked with basic amenities."

"You really are all about full service."

He smiled and pressed a kiss to her neck, then nipped her lightly, immediately following it up with a pass of his tongue. "I told you I was all about service." He moved his hand down in between her thighs, stroking her, heightening her arousal.

"I believe it," she whispered.

"Ready?" He tore the condom packet open and rolled the protection onto his length quickly before moving back over her.

"I've been ready for a long time," she said. She put her hands on his shoulders, held onto him as he pushed into her.

It didn't hurt, not in the dramatic way it seemed to in some of the books she'd read. But she was thankful that he went slowly, that he gave her a chance to adjust to him, time to savor her first moments of full intimacy with him.

He flexed his hips and buried himself to the hilt, his muscles locking in place, his breath coming out in harsh, short bursts. "Are you all right?"

"Great," she replied. "I'm great."

He looked at her, and for a moment she saw darkness in his eyes, a sadness that stole the air from her lungs. She put her hand on his cheeks and kissed his lips.

"Please, Ethan," she said.

His answer was the short thrust of his hips, a movement that sent a sharp burst of pleasure through her. He moved in her, building her desire, low and intense in her pelvis, deeper than the first time. Stronger, which she hadn't even imagined possible.

She could feel his control slipping, as each movement became less measured, less controlled. All of that will-power he carried like a millstone around his neck seemed to fall away, leaving only the man, without his civility, without the trappings of modern society.

Now, in this moment, he was simply a man, and she was a woman—his woman. And she reveled in it, moving with him, against him. She felt she was drowning, not just in pleasure, in emotion. In the connection she felt with him. As if he was truly a part of her.

She felt whole, and she felt herself splintering into pieces at the same time, her orgasm rushing up, tangling with the tide of emotion that was crashing inside of her. Ethan stiffened above her, her name on his lips as he found his own release.

This time, it was her turn to hold him, his head resting on her chest, his breath cool on her sweat-slicked skin. Silence filled the room, but it wasn't awkward. It made the

CHAPTER TEN

NOELLE stretched, smiling when she felt a couple little aches in some very intimate places. Oh yes, Ethan had been amazing. Over and over again.

She had been well and truly introduced to sex.

Her smiled faded a little as she recognized a new ache, right around her heart. She was also being introduced to something else, something big and new. Emotions, a connection she'd never felt with anyone before.

She didn't know what to call it. Or maybe she was too scared to call it anything.

Ethan saw her. More than that, he *wanted* to see her. Who she really was, not the veneer. No one, not her mother, not her piano teacher, not the flighty acquaintances who had sometimes called themselves her friends had ever bothered to do that.

"Good morning." Ethan came into the bedroom holding a tray with coffee and muffins. He wasn't wearing much more than a smile, his broad chest bare, powerful thighs on display. Only a very brief pair of briefs covered him. She wished he hadn't put them on.

"You are every woman's fantasy," she smiled, sitting up.

"In my spare time." He sat on the bed with her, rais-

No. That wouldn't happen. He wouldn't do that to her. They would have their affair, and they would both move on.

Even if there was a small, insidious part of himself that wished things could be different. They couldn't be. And he would have to accept it.

ing a mug of hot coffee to his lips, his eyes trained on her. "You're most definitely my fantasy."

"I probably have makeup smeared down my face."

"There's a certain debauched charm in that look."

"Yeah, I bet."

"You got a call."

"I did?"

"Yes, Jacques D'ambois left a message on my phone for you."

"The man that was at the engagement thing with Sylvie last night?"

"The same."

She frowned and took a bite of chocolate muffin. "I wonder what he wants."

"If he wants to seduce you, tell him he's about twelve hours too late." Ethan said it as a joke, but there was a hint of seriousness in his words.

"No worries there, Ethan. I'll call him after breakfast. And I'll be sure to let him know I'm no longer in need of seducing."

"Now that the big engagement party is out of the way, we need to move on to the planning of the actual wedding."

"Oh yes, that." Her heart sank a little. Now it seemed… it seemed much more complicated, this whole wedding thing.

"Don't look like that, Noelle. This," he indicated the bed, "has to stay separate from the business arrangement we have. The wedding is still a business arrangement."

"No, no, I know! I just…well, all right, it seems a bit more personal now, I can't lie. But I get it, Ethan, I do. I don't want a real marriage anyway." Did she? She didn't think she did. Marriage was….well, her mother had never been married to her father. And it seemed that to Ethan's father, marriage vows had been merely a suggestion. A suggestion he hadn't taken. What was the point of it?

"You don't?"

"No. Not now. Maybe someday."

"Marriage is a crock anyway."

"You think so?"

"What is it, really, Noelle? So, we're getting married. And what do we have to do to get married? Love each other? Make vows we'll keep? No. We just have to sign a legal form. Marriage never made my parents happy. It gave them both a new kind of status, and that was the point for them. My mother was able to spend my father's money, my father had a beautiful trophy wife who walked red carpets and had her name up in lights. Until she didn't, of course. And then he cared a lot less for her. Which was when he started finding other women."

"That's...well, that's bad." Noelle looked down at her coffee. "Love is real though," she said softly. "Isn't it?" She wanted to believe it was. That maybe someday... She ignored the sudden, deep tightening in her stomach, a kind of grief at the thought of a future without Ethan.

Ethan stared at a point beyond her. "I think so. I think it's pretty sadistic though, to be honest with you. I think my mother loves my father, still, in spite of all he's done to her. I think my father loved your mother. Even though he was married to mine. When my mother stopped getting invited to Hollywood events, he stopped bothering to take her out in public. That was when he started going with Celine Birch. When he let the world know he didn't care enough for my mother to even try and shield her from his affair."

Ethan's lips curled. "I remember there was this big premiere my mother was desperate to go to, and your mother got invited. The next day it was all over the tabloids how Celine and my father had been all over each other."

"Oh. That's awful."

"There's more. There's a reason I can't...there's a reason I have to do this, Noelle." He still didn't look at her, his expression fixed, his dark eyes blank. "I came home from school that day, and, of course, all the kids had already seen the news. They were taunting me. And when I came home it was so quiet. The television wasn't on, and she always had it on. I went to look for her. She was face down on the bathroom floor. I was fifteen, but I had learned some CPR in school. Thankfully the ambulance came quickly, because my skills weren't really up to the task. It was the paramedics who found her pills. They were the ones who figured out she'd done it to herself."

"Oh, Ethan..."

"That's love, Noelle. That's what it does. It's one person trying and trying and never being able to be enough. I don't want to be a part of it. And I sure as hell can't let my father come out of it unscathed."

Sickness weighed her down, enveloped her being. "I can't believe they were both so selfish...I can't believe..."

"It was a long time ago. And I'm not seeking any kind of sympathy. But now you understand why I feel the way I do, not just about love, but about my father getting his hands on Grey's."

"I understand."

He was silent then and she knew he was done talking about his mother.

"So, the wedding, when is it?" she asked.

"I thought we might keep it low-key. Elope even. At this point, the scale of the wedding doesn't matter. Only that there is one."

"That's...good." A rush of relief flooded her. She didn't

want to do the white and the cathedral and the priest. Elvis and the Vegas strip would be much more appropriate. It would be easier. It wouldn't be so likely to trick her raw emotions into thinking it was anything more than what it was.

"Great. I'll see about arranging all the legalities."

She blew out a breath. "And they say romance is dead."

Ethan looked at her, his dark eyes blazing. "I'll show you romance, Noelle. It'll just be separate from this."

He turned and walked out of the room and she couldn't help but watch his butt, barely covered by skin-tight black briefs. He was so hot. And what they had might not be the epitome of love and flowers but it made her feel alive.

More alive than she'd ever felt.

That had to count for something. That had to make it worth it. Whatever it was.

"Keep telling yourself that," she said into the empty room.

She could angst about Ethan later. For now, she would get dressed and give Jacques a call.

An audition. She had an audition.

Auditions are beneath her. She's Noelle Birch.

Her mother's words rang in her head. Words that seemed meaningless when she hadn't had a job in forever. Auditions most certainly weren't beneath her. That attitude, fuelled not by snobbery but by a genuine desire to avoid the public discovering that she was a falling star rather than a rising one, was what had kept her down for the past year.

She was over it now. Over just sitting around and letting life happen to her.

Ethan walked into the large sitting area of the penthouse. He was wearing black slacks and a white button-up shirt, open at the collar. His hair was wet from the shower. He looked delicious. And all she wanted to do was take that perfectly tailored outfit off of his body so she could taste all of his fresh clean skin.

"Busy this weekend?" he asked.

Not busy until next weekend. "This weekend? As in... tomorrow? No." She lifted her coffee cup to her lips and tried to look casual. She didn't want to tell him about the audition. It was too new. And what if she screwed it up? What if Jacques ended up not wanting her to play either?

"Good. We're getting married."

She snorted into the hot liquid and it sloshed over the side of the cup. "A little warning please."

"I told you I was going to arrange it. I think after the engagement party it will be romantic if we simply elope, don't you?"

"You mean less of a hassle for us?"

"Yes, that's exactly what I mean, but I'm spinning the headline."

"Right."

"We just have to get through this part, Noelle. A few weeks of marriage, a few signed papers. And then you're free. I'm free. We'll both have what we want."

Money. The audition. A chance at starting over, at grasping the fame she used to have. The luxury. She'd thought she'd find that with Ethan, and she had.

It didn't really make her happy though, and she wasn't sure why. She didn't want to think about why.

"Great. Yes. Yay for met goals and all of that."

"When I put my mind to something, it gets done."

"Yeah, I uh...remember that. From last night." She felt her face get hot and she cursed her pale skin, knowing she was wearing her embarrassment like a neon sign.

* * *

Ethan's stomach tightened. Noelle's face was flushed and she looked perfect. Perfect to take to bed and spend hours kissing, tasting, making love to. But he couldn't afford that. He couldn't afford the strange kind of attachment he felt for her.

He'd made the decision sometime during his shower as he'd dealt with a hard-on that refused to quit. She was sexy, no doubt. Compelling and amazing in bed. But he didn't have time for a lover, especially not a lover who had such a strong effect on him. Not after Grey's was signed over to him.

This relationship was on a very tight timetable. As soon as the ink hit the signature line on the divorce decree, that was the end. Because a new contract would take priority then, and Noelle…well, she would be taken care of, at least. He would make sure of that.

He breathed in deeply, trying to loosen the feeling in his gut. It felt as if someone had reached a hand inside of him and grabbed his stomach in their fist.

"I would love to push you back against the wall right now and go in for some hard and fast," he said, arousal and the general direction of his thoughts making his voice rough. "But I think you might need some recovery time. And we have a plane to catch."

Noelle looked uncomfortable with his choice of words, and he didn't really blame her. He was being an ass because he wanted her, and he was contemplating never having her again at the same time his body throbbed with need of her.

"A plane?" she asked, pale eyebrows arched.

"Oh yeah, we really are getting married in Vegas."

"Are you kidding me?"

"No. How tacky would you like it?"

He was rewarded with a smile. Maybe, just maybe things could get back on good footing. Maybe they could have the next month together. Sating their desire for each other, and hanging out as companions. Because whether they were in bed or not, he simply liked having her around.

Bloody hell, that was complicated.

"Maybe not Elvis-tacky, but I feel like a leopard-print wedding dress might be pretty awesome."

"Are you joking?"

She rolled her eyes. "Well, I can't wear white, Ethan, and don't pretend you don't know why. You were there last night."

"I'll never forget it." That part he said with absolute sincerity. Because he knew for a fact that he would never forget Noelle.

He knew it with a certainty he couldn't recall ever feeling before. No matter how many women came after her, no matter how much time passed, the memory of her silken skin beneath his fingertips would linger. And it would always make him burn.

He wondered if she would think of him like that. Or if he would fade in her mind. That seemed to be the way most people felt about him.

He closed off that train of thought, tried to get his breathing steady.

"Right. Well, I guess we both need to pack."

Their quick flight to Las Vegas had already appeared on some entertainment news websites by the time Ethan's private plane had touched down in Nevada. Speculation about a wedding was already rampant, of course, because in Vegas, gambling or a quickie wedding was usually on the docket.

Either way, it was newsworthy.

Noelle looked pale, her blue eyes large in her face as he took out the keycard to the hotel suite and unlocked the

door. They were staying in one of Grey's most famous resorts, a den of sin and sex that was infamous even on the
strip, adding to the irony of his grandfather's insistence
on him marrying, being a family man before he took over
the company.

"You all right?" Ethan asked.

Noelle looked up from the smartphone. "Just reeling.
The speculation is intense. Frighteningly accurate."

He took the phone out of her hands. "In what way?"

"Just that we came here to get married."

"Nothing about a leopard-print wedding dress?"

She laughed, a high, kind of unnatural sound. "Uh, no."

He took her hand in his, her skin so soft and tempting
it made him ache. "Are you okay, really?"

"Do I look that bad?"

"You look nervous."

"We're getting married tomorrow. And I know it's not
married married, and I know it shouldn't matter. But it's
kind of overwhelming."

He wanted to kiss her. But he also felt as if resisting the
impulse was important. He needed to get a grip on this…
thing between them. Not that he wasn't going to sleep with
her again. He planned on it. But he needed to be in control. To rid himself of that shaky, wild feeling that overtook him when her tongue touched his.

That sensation of being a teenage virgin that he couldn't
quite seem to shake. Well, he *was* shaking it.

He pushed open the door to the hotel suite.

"Wow," Noelle said, walking into the room, her eyes
fixed on the crystal chandelier hanging low in the center
of the massive entryway. "This is…"

"You said you wanted tacky."

"Eek."

She walked over to the transparent bar, built from thick

Plexiglas and fashioned into a kind of art-deco piece that seemed to transcend style. And taste. The walls were glossy too, and they seemed to be made from some kind of opaque, frosted glass. It was all extremely expensive, from the plush carpets to the rich drapes, it was just lacking in any kind of restraint.

"This place makes a killing," he said. "Just so you know."

"Well, it is kind of fun. And hey, why not? It goes with the fake wedding."

"We could have the reception here," he suggested dryly.

"Oh no, please tell me we're not really having a reception."

"No. That's the point of eloping."

"You're right. Let's do it now."

"Now?"

"Yes." She looked determined, a glint in her blue eyes. Startling and arousing. "Marry me now. Why wait until tomorrow? There are twenty-four-hour chapels and very loose laws about obtaining licenses in this state, and I say we make the most of it."

"You seem to know a lot about it. Is there anything you need to tell me?"

"No quickie marriages in my past, but time spent playing the Vegas Strip? Oh yeah. I did shows here for a year when I was nine."

"You're sort of amazing, do you know that?" he asked.

Her cheeks darkened. "I never really thought so, but, thank you."

"I say we go find a chapel," he said.

The sooner they got the marriage out of the way, the sooner everything could be finished. All the loose ends tied up. All the paperwork signed. Grey's Resorts moved into his name. And he would have the satisfaction of seeing his father's face as he confronted him with everything he would never have.

So why was the wedding night all he could think about?

CHAPTER ELEVEN

ETHAN wore jeans and a tight black T-shirt. And Noelle had managed to find a leopard-print skirt and black tank top in the gift shop on their way to the nearest chapel.

The car ride was silent until they pulled in to the parking lot. The white chapel, framed with neon lighting, was like a beacon amongst all the color of the strip. Bold letters boasted they had low waits and good rates.

Noelle snickered. All of it was simply too absurd, too wondrously insane not to be enjoyed.

"What?" Ethan asked.

"This is the funniest, craziest thing I've ever done."

"Ranks up there for me too."

He got out of the limo and rounded the shiny black beast of a car, opening her door for her.

"Such a gentleman," she said. "No wonder I said yes."

"And I'm paying you a lot of money."

Her stomach tightened. "Yeah. And that." She didn't want a reminder of that. Not now.

She followed him through the double doors and into the little building. It was much more sedate than its exterior implied.

"You're Noelle Birch!" The girl standing behind the counter, her hair dyed blue-black and cropped short, her arms decorated with tattoos, looked at Noelle with wide eyes.

"Uh…yes. I am."

"Wow. I have all your CDs. I begged my mom to let me take piano lessons because of you."

"Oh…wow. That's…a really great compliment. Thank you."

"I kind of suck. I mean, I don't suck, but I play here for weddings, so how good can I be, right?"

Noelle looked over at Ethan, then back at her fan. "I don't play much of anywhere anymore myself."

"Getting married though, huh?"

"Yes. Yes I am."

"We'll take the paperwork," Ethan said.

"Right!" The girl bent down behind the counter and popped back up with a clipboard. "Just sign and date. Do you want Elvis? He's extra."

"No," she and Ethan answered in unison.

"Somehow, I didn't figure you would. I'm Tara, by the way."

"Hi, Tara. Nice to meet you," Noelle said.

"Thanks."

Noelle exchanged an awkward smile with Tara while Ethan quickly filled the form out before passing it to her. Her fingers shook as she gripped the pen, and her writing reflected that.

She signed it and Ethan added a check to the papers before passing it back.

"Sweet. That's one way to get your autograph," Tara said.

"I could…sign something…else."

Tara produced a blank sheet of paper and Noelle signed it while Ethan stood next to her, his impatience apparent.

"We'll just take the next available officiant," Ethan said. "If he happens to be Elvis I'm all right with that."

"Nah, I think Janine is free. Just a sec."

Tara disappeared behind a purple curtain and Noelle looked over at Ethan. "You were the one who wanted to get married in Vegas," she said.

"I wanted no fuss."

"This is no fuss. There aren't five hundred people here, are there?"

"No."

"Will your grandparents be upset that they weren't invited?"

He frowned. "It's better they aren't here. I don't really want them getting too attached to this. To us."

She tried to ignore the sharp stab of hurt his comment left behind. He'd said the wedding was separate from their personal stuff. So she shouldn't go getting weepy and hurt now.

"No. No of course not," she said quickly.

Tara appeared again, a smile on her face as she rounded the counter. "This way." She gestured to a long hallway and led them through the second door. "I'd ask if you wanted to pay for a pianist but…I'm pretty sure you don't want to hear me play. We have one of your CDs here though. I'll put it on. And congratulations!"

Ethan looked up at the domed ceiling and Noelle followed his gaze. There was a poor reproduction of the Sistine Chapel's mural painted there.

"This is depressing," Ethan said.

Music floated in over the speakers. Very familiar music. "Not as depressing as that," Noelle frowned.

"It's nice."

"Thanks, Ethan." She smiled as the familiar notes continued. "It's funny because when I'm nervous I go over pieces in my head, imagine how I play them. Fast. Slow. Soft. Loud. It helps get me focused. Now my music is playing for me."

"Have you done that since I've known you?"

"Yes. Lots."

"I make you nervous?"

"Sometimes. Mostly you just make me excited," she admitted, the words spilling out in a rush.

He studied her face, his dark eyes filled with intensity. "Noelle…"

A woman with a very similar look to Tara walked in, Tara trailing behind, acting as a witness. "Hi there, you must be Ethan and Noelle. Are you ready to do this?"

Noelle looked at Ethan again and her heart slammed against her breastbone. She was ready. And that was scary. Because here they were in the world's tackiest place to get married. Ethan looked like he was headed to the gallows and they had an officiant with a nose ring. And yet, it felt right.

If it had been a huge wedding with a big white gown and a harpist, she might expect that. Might expect to be lured in by the fantasy. But there was no fantasy here. Only a stained green carpet and fake flowers woven through tacky white lattice.

And it felt momentous. And amazing. And it shouldn't.

Janine gave the most informal, straightforward version of marriage vows Noelle had ever heard. Nothing florid or personal, just the legal stuff.

"Do you have rings?" Janine asked.

"Oh…" Noelle felt stupid for wishing she had a ring for Ethan. The wedding didn't mean anything, and a ring would mean even less. But for some reason, the image of a thin gold band on Ethan's left hand made her feel short of breath.

"I do." Ethan reached into his pocket and took out a small box. He opened it slowly, the glitter of the large center stone catching in the overhead lighting.

"Ethan…"

He took her hand in his and pulled the ring from its silken nest, sliding it gently onto her finger. "A woman as unique and special as you deserves something equally special."

It was both of those things. A band that was shaped to fit her unique engagement ring, diamonds encircling the platinum, the precious metal fashioned into vines, the stone like glittering flowers.

"I don't know…I didn't know." This was a ring beyond her expectation or imagination.

It locked together perfectly with the engagement ring. A perfect set. A perfect couple. Unlike them.

"And now, by the power vested in me by the State of Nevada, I pronounce you husband and wife. You can kiss now," Janine said.

Ethan didn't hesitate. And for that she was grateful. He pulled her into his arms, his kiss starving, devouring. And she was right there with him. She was dizzy with her desire for him, with the need to do so much more than kiss him. She hadn't realized just how much a day without physical contact had worn on her.

He slowed the kiss down, the movements of his mouth less ravenous but still deep, his tongue stroking over hers. When he started to move away, he paused, pressing another kiss to the side of her lips, then the other side.

She really did melt then, his strong arms the only thing keeping her from sliding to the floor.

"Wow," she breathed.

Then Ethan laughed, a smile curving those talented lips of his. "Glad you feel that way."

Janine fanned herself with her notes. "I'm with her. Wow."

"You're universally appreciated," Noelle smiled at Ethan.

Ethan forced a tight smile in return. "Is that it?"

"Yes. You're married. Mr. and Mrs...." she checked her notes, "Grey."

"All right then." Ethan took her hand in his. "Thank you."

"Don't forget your marriage license." She handed Ethan the documents they'd signed earlier, which now boasted both Janine's and Tara's signatures too. "All legal now."

Ethan took the license from Janine and folded it carefully. It was done. The marriage was legal. It was the last thing he needed to get his grandfather to sign the resorts over to him. But he didn't feel particularly accomplished. His long-range goal seemed hazy, blotted out by the desire that was pounding through him.

He'd expected a few hours to give him dominion over the need he felt for Noelle, but it didn't seem to be working that way.

It'll burn out. You know it will. It always does.

Lust was like that. Hot and bright at first, but it burned out quickly. There was no real fuel to sustain the blaze. Just a brilliant flash, spectacular for a moment, then growing cold after that first real explosion.

This was lasting a bit longer. Probably because Noelle had been a virgin. And because he'd spent so much time with her. He genuinely liked her, felt a connection with her. But that seemed natural. Normal, really.

Not that anything about the pure, liquid desire rushing through his veins seemed natural or normal.

Later. After tonight. After he made love to Noelle, he would call his grandfather to get the ball rolling on the acquisition of Grey's. Until then though, he had to clear his thoughts. And he didn't think he'd even be able to see straight if he didn't have Noelle as soon as possible.

"We need to get on with the wedding night," he whispered, his voice rough. "As soon as possible."

Her cheeks turned deep pink again and he felt an ache that started in his stomach and spread low to his groin. He wanted her so much it was beyond his experience. Again, she unmanned him. Made *him* feel like the virgin.

He didn't know how she managed to do that.

"I'm all for that," she whispered back.

"Not playing Mozart in your head, are you?"

"No. When I'm with you now it just kind of…flows. I hear music all the time."

He ignored the tightening in his chest and focused on that in his pants. It was safer. A bit more familiar.

"Come on."

He led her out of the chapel and back into the warm, dry evening. The limo was still there, idling in front of the chapel. He opened the door for her, she slid inside, and he joined her. As soon as the door was closed he pulled her into his arms, kissing her, tasting her, trying to sate the deep, gnawing hunger that seemed ever-present in him. A hunger that he didn't know if he could satisfy.

He could lose himself trying. And that didn't seem like such a bad prospect.

He couldn't remember the last time kissing had felt like the main event. Maybe the last time he'd kissed Noelle. Usually, at this point, he'd be undressing one of them, but at the moment, he simply wanted to taste her. Savor her.

To run his hands over her curves, delight in the fact that there was more to come. Sweeter. Sexier. Smoother. Drawing it out was heightening his pleasure in ways he'd never imagined it could.

He was so lost in the simple act of kissing her that he

didn't know the limo had pulled back up to the hotel until she pulled away from him.

"We're here."

"Yeah. Damn. I'm tempted to ask the driver to drive around the block a few times."

"A bed would be a decent idea," she said softly.

"One day though, we'll have to give the limo a go."

"Promise."

He opened the door and took her hand, drawing her out with him to the neon-lit entryway of the hotel. He watched as the colors alternated, white and red, casting different hues over her pale features.

"You really do belong in the spotlight," he said, his throat tight.

"I don't want the spotlight just now," she said, running her hands down his arms, the gesture innocuous but, in that moment, with her, enough to make his knees want to buckle.

"I don't either."

He took her hand in his again and walked quickly through the lobby, not caring if people stared, or if they knew just where they were going and what they were going to do.

Nothing mattered but Noelle. Having her. Being with her. Being in her.

During the elevator ride he was tempted to just hit the stop button and finish it there. But he wanted more than that. Longer than that. He wanted all night. To take her to bed and not get back up for at least twelve hours.

That sounded close to heaven.

When the elevator doors opened they moved across the hall to their suite door. His hands shook as he pushed the card into the lock.

He closed the door and she leaned against it, a slight smile on her lips.

"Noelle," he said. It was the only word he could think to say. It was the only word in his mind.

She kept her eyes locked with his, so sincere. So beautiful. She gripped the hem of her black tank top and pulled it over her head, revealing a simple black bra that shouldn't be anywhere near as sexy as it was. But it was hotter than any French lingerie he'd ever seen.

"I've never seen a more beautiful woman. And I mean that," he said.

"I've never seen a more beautiful man," she replied. "Return the favor already."

She didn't have to ask twice. He pulled his T-shirt over his head, gratified that she was affected by the sight of his body. Her breathing was more labored now, her cleavage rising and falling sharply.

"Your turn," he said.

She smiled and pushed that ridiculous leopard skirt down her hips, shimmying slightly as she worked the tight fabric over her curves. She was wearing a black…oh, he hoped it was a thong…that matched her bra.

"Your turn," she repeated.

He reached for the snap on his jeans, lowered the zip, his eyes on hers. They were round and riveted on his body. She didn't even try to hide her interest. Her reactions were honest, her desire for him easily seen.

It only made him hotter. Harder.

He shrugged his jeans down, along with his underwear, and kicked them to the side. The look on Noelle's face was enough to finish him then and there. She looked…fascinated, and hungry at the same time and it was doing things to him that he couldn't put a name to.

He closed the distance between them and locked his hands around her wrists, drawing her arms up over her head, against the door, as he pressed his chest against her breasts and kissed her. She arched against him, her hip brushing his erection.

He let out a rough groan and deepened the kiss, sliding his tongue against hers, reveling in the slick friction.

She wiggled against him. "Let me go."

"Why?" he kissed her shoulder.

"So I can undo my bra."

He licked the curve of her neck and blew against it, taking deep, masculine satisfaction in her shivered response. "I can do that." He used his free hand to snap the clasp open on her bra, letting it fall loose.

"It can't come off if you keep holding me prisoner."

"But I can work with this." He pushed the silky material up and revealed her breasts. He cupped her, sliding his thumb over her nipple. "Oh yeah, I can work with this."

She arched against him. "Ethan."

"What?"

"More. I can't wait."

"Patience is a virtue."

"I don't want to be patient."

"I've been patient," he said, lowering his head and flicking the tip of his tongue over her nipple. "I've been patient all day. It won't hurt you to wait."

She sucked in a sharp breath. "I think it will."

"I won't hurt you. I promise." He meant physically. He wished he could promise it in a deeper way. That he could swear he would slay her dragons and make everything better. But he was no white knight. Come to that, Noelle wasn't a princess locked in a tower. She was a woman. One who could take care of herself.

And that was something he found comfort in. Because God knew he wasn't up to the task.

He ignored the fierce tearing sensation in his chest and focused instead on her body. On touching her. Loving her. This was the way he knew how to do it. The best he could give. And he would give it all.

He abandoned her breasts and tugged her panties down her legs, sliding his fingers through the pale curls at the apex of her thighs, rubbing her moisture over her clitoris.

"Ethan…" His name was a plea on her lips and he couldn't get enough.

His whole body was hard, tense, needy. But he needed to give to her first. Needed her to take every last bit of pleasure that she could. He needed to give it to her.

Her lips parted, her head moving back and forth as he stroked her. She arched her body against his again, pressing herself more firmly against his hand. He penetrated her slowly with one finger and felt her tighten around him, a short sound of pleasure escaping her lips.

He let her ride out her orgasm and then slowly released his hold on her wrists. She slumped down the wall an inch, her breathing coming out in short, sharp gasps.

She moved and let her bra fall to the floor, then stepped out of her panties. She was naked now, so perfect. His wife.

His stomach tightened. It was so hard to breathe. Noelle was his wife. And it should make no difference to anything, because she wasn't his wife in any real sense. But it did. It suddenly made everything seem different.

So he kissed her again, because that felt good. It made sense.

And when he laid her down on the bed, he tried not to look into her eyes. Tried not to give in to the intense tugging sensation in his chest. But he couldn't manage either.

He looked at her, and he felt like he was drowning. It was like he was completely submerged in Noelle.

He took a condom from the bedside table drawer, an amenity always stocked at this hotel as well, and tore it open quickly, protecting them both. He put his hand on her hip and steadied her as he slid slowly into her.

He had to grit his teeth, hard, to keep from coming then and there, as she enveloped him. Body and soul.

She moved with him, against him, creating a rhythm he couldn't deny. He had no control here. He was lost, and all he could do was let go, let himself get sucked down into the undertow. He didn't have the strength to fight it. And he didn't want to.

He wanted Noelle. Only Noelle.

Always.

His orgasm roared through him, tore at him like a beast before it overwhelmed him completely. It went beyond pleasure, beyond anything he'd ever known. It consumed him. She consumed him.

They lay together, her head on his chest, smooth hands stroking him.

"Did you…sorry, I know you came against the door but did you…"

"Twice," she said.

"I'm usually a bit more considerate but this time…I couldn't think."

"That's okay."

It wasn't though. It was wrong. He needed to keep his head on straight. To have everything organized and together for his acquisition of Grey's. He didn't need to be obsessed with a woman.

More than that, he needed Grey's to matter. He would finally be able to see his father's face as he pulled the rug from under him, and it had to *matter*. Because it was all he had. It was everything he'd been working toward for years.

But right now, it felt like it didn't matter at all.

Noelle rolled over and blinked. It was early in the morning. And Ethan wasn't in bed. It didn't surprise her for some reason. Something had happened last night. And she wasn't sure if it was good or bad. Only that, for a brief moment, Ethan had looked...terrified.

It was all right. It only reflected what she felt.

Terror because Ethan had a part of herself she wasn't sure she could ever get back. Funny though, because he'd also helped her find pieces of herself she hadn't known existed. He had changed her. Or at least helped her figure out some ways to change herself.

It was scary to want someone so much. Scary but amazing. And it made her feel that she wasn't alone.

She got up and reached for the light switch. It illuminated the glossy, opaque glass wall opposite the bed, making it mostly transparent. She could see Ethan's silhouette. Naked. She was getting a view of his shower.

"Luxury hotel indeed," she said.

She watched as his hands slid over his body, her heart rate increasing. There was a certain illicit thrill in watching him like this. Was it what he'd felt watching her play the first time? When she hadn't known he'd watched her? Well, she hadn't been naked but she'd been bare in a way.

If only she could get more than just a sexual thrill from watching him. If only she knew what he was thinking. She felt her nipples tighten, her body aching to have him touch her, not simply to watch him as he touched himself.

She swallowed hard and walked across the room. She was naked, and she wasn't embarrassed. There was no way for her to be embarrassed. Not with Ethan. She was more herself with him than she'd ever been in her life.

She walked into the expansive bathroom and stood in front of the glass shower door. Ethan looked up, water running down his face, his perfect body, the droplets dipping and pooling into the well-defined grooves between his muscles.

"Hi. May I join you?"

He smiled, a purely wicked smile. "Always."

He kissed her, but differently than he had last night. More controlled. She tried to look at him, catch his eye, but she couldn't.

"Ethan?" He looked at her then. For just a moment. And what she saw in his dark eyes made her feel shaky. There was an emptiness there, a distance that didn't seem right.

But then he kissed her again. And his lips were so perfect. And the water was hot and soothing, and Ethan's touch was slick and arousing. So she focused on that.

And she tried to forget the horrible, haunted look in his dark eyes.

CHAPTER TWELVE

"WE'RE going to a small event in one of the high-roller areas tonight. Very exclusive."

Ethan rolled out of bed and Noelle watched each fluid movement with interest. The way his body worked, his muscle structure, his tan skin. It was all so deliciously different from hers. So very sexy. The kind of thing people wrote songs about.

She'd spent the majority of the day exploring it, but it hadn't gotten old. Not even close. The really scary thing was that he was only more enticing now that she knew him so well. Now that she knew just how good things were between them. Now, looking at him made her shiver with the anticipation of pleasure to come.

She was a lost cause.

"We are?"

"Yes. Our debut as a married couple."

For some reason that made her feel…she wasn't sure how it made her feel. Nervous and edgy somehow. She didn't feel ready to go and face people. Not knowing she loved him. Not after everything she'd given him. It felt so personal, and yet she felt as if she was wearing it, as bright and bold as any neon sign on the strip.

"Okay. I don't really have anything to wear."

"That's fine. I saw something I liked down in one of the hotel shops yesterday. I'm having it sent up."

She watched as Ethan dressed, as he covered the body she craved. He still looked good dressed. Though she'd rather picture him naked.

"I can pick my own dress…"

"And buy it too?"

His words cut much deeper than they should. "You know I can't."

"Then you'll wear what I pick out."

"Why are you acting like this?"

He breathed in deeply. "Like what?"

"A jerk."

"I'm just…this is a big thing tonight."

"You never let pressure get to you, Ethan."

"Then I'm allowed a day, aren't I?"

She tried to smile. "Of course. How long until this… thing?"

"Sorry I didn't tell you sooner. I got the call earlier when I went to order lunch for us. But it starts in a couple of hours."

"That's fine. I'm not that high-maintenance."

"No. I know."

The look on his face was strange, that cool distance still present in his eyes. She wanted to erase it. Wanted to bring back the warm man she knew and loved. But he seemed pretty determined to stay gone.

"I suppose I should take a shower. A non-peek-a-boo shower."

He gave her a wicked half smile and for a moment, she could see Ethan again. "I make no guarantees."

"I have to shave my legs."

"You fight dirty. And yet, I don't feel detoured."

"What am I going to do with you?"

His eyes darkened, his expression going flat. "I could ask you the same question."

The dress should have been illegal. He regretted choosing it. It was sexy in an overt way, and at the time, that had been the point. All of this had a point. He was feeling pretty regretful of the whole deal at the moment, at least the part he'd cast Noelle in, but it was too late to back out now.

This was why Noelle was in his life. This was what he'd married her for. He was letting it get muddled in finer feelings and things he had no business dwelling on. He needed to focus on the prize.

Tonight was the night to do just that. He would get what he needed, what he deserved. Tonight was the reason they were in Vegas. And he'd kept it from her. He was a bastard.

"This dress is a bit OTT, don't you think?" she whispered as he keyed in the passcode and pressed the elevator button that would get them to the exclusive high-roller's lounge.

"OTT?" he asked.

"Over the top," she tugged the tight black hem down, trying to get it to cover more of her legs.

"Not in the least. You look every bit the young, hot celebrity. And just like the sort of woman who could entice me into a quickie Vegas wedding."

"Is that the game, then?"

"You know it is." He put his finger on the button again. As if it might make things move faster. As if it might make the whole night move faster. So he could get on with it. So he could get Noelle out of his life and back to normal.

He ignored the sick, tight feeling in his chest.

"Yeah," she said softly. "I know."

And she didn't sound happy. Damn it that he cared. Damn her for making him care.

Why wasn't she what he'd just said? A pretty ornament. A decoration. Why was she so much more? All kinds of extra stuff he didn't need or want from her or anyone else. Why was he letting her split his focus? She was making him doubt what he was about to do, when it had been part of the plan from moment one.

The lift doors opened and he felt his scalp get tight, continuing down through his chest, his stomach. It was like he didn't fit inside himself anymore. He just wanted to climb out of his skin. He would have done, if he could. He didn't know why he didn't feel like himself anymore, why he felt so wrong. And so right. That was the really fearsome thing. He felt more right just standing with Noelle than he ever had before she'd come into his life.

He took her hand in his and led her from the elevator, trying to ignore the slow, spreading sensation of fire that began where their skin touched and made a direct trail to his chest. To his heart.

The hall leading to the high-roller room was long and narrow, the walls black, sleek and glossy, the carpet bright red. Something to make the people who used the casino feel like celebrities.

There were so many things about the place he didn't like. It was more his father's style. Maybe when the ownership of Grey's was transferred to him he would change it. Fix it. But then, this made money. It wasn't really about his taste.

The tacky would probably have to stay. The marks his father had put on the place would stay.

Something he'd have to get used to.

He looked at her again one last time before he opened the door to the private room. She was perfect, blond hair sleek, makeup expertly applied. Her wedding and engagement rings glittered on her well manicured hand.

She was the epitome of a trophy wife.

Thinking of her that way made him feel…it was wrong. They were partners. But tonight she would be playing trophy wife.

"Ready?"

She smiled. "Sure."

He opened the door and revealed an expansive room, all high-gloss and gold-plated. The true mark of nouveau riche. Overdone, overstated.

The room was crowded with couples, men who had women draped over them, fawning. One woman at the blackjack table had two men draped on her arm. A refreshing change, to Ethan's way of thinking. It was the only thing refreshing about the scene.

The rest of it was more of the same. People using other people for money. For sex. The kind of shallow existence his family seemed to aspire to.

That he aspired to. Except what he wanted was different. It *was*.

He scanned the crowd, past the gaming tables. His father was in the corner, a blond probably close to Noelle's age on his arm.

"This way," he said, tugging gently on Noelle's hand, leading her through the crowd.

Damien looked up from his companion, his expression not changing when he saw him. "Ethan. What brings you here?"

Noelle looked at Ethan, her expression filled with confusion. She hadn't known that his father would be here. That the show was for him. But every time Ethan had tried to explain, the words had stuck in his throat. She'd known he wanted revenge. He hadn't told her the part she'd play in it.

"Noelle and I decided to have an impromptu getaway. And wedding." He held her hand up, still clasped in his, and let his father see her rings. "I assume you know who she is. Noelle Birch."

His father's face drained of color, but his expression didn't alter.

He felt Noelle stiffen beside him, but she didn't speak. She didn't seem very present either. He looked at her, just a quick glance, but it was enough for him to see her blue eyes looking glassy, distant.

"Why did you come tonight, Ethan?" Damien asked, his tone implying that he knew perfectly well why. And that he didn't like it.

"To let you know that grandfather is signing Grey's over to me. All I needed was a wife, to prove how stable I was. How much more stable I was than you, and he was more than willing to pass it directly to me."

"You can't have…"

"I have," Ethan said, cutting him off. He turned and put his hand on Noelle's cheek. It was cold. "So now I have your company. I also managed to get one of the Birch women to marry me. Something you never managed to do. Funny how things turn out. Essentially, I have everything that you ever wanted."

As soon as he said the words, he wished he could cut out his own tongue. To treat Noelle like a possession…it wasn't something he'd truly thought through. Or maybe he had. Not simply to hurt his father, but to try and reduce her in some way. Because she was too much inside of him. What she made him feel was too big to handle.

He hadn't fixed anything though. No, far from it. He could feel the fracture between them, the crack in the bond they had built. And it provided him with no relief. Instead, it hurt like the severing of bone from tendon.

"What is it you hope to accomplish with this, Ethan?" Damien asked, pushing away from his date. "Proving the point that you're somehow a man of valor, even while you stand here with your trophy bimbo? You aren't any different. You aren't any better. You're just like me. You always have been, you always will be."

Just like me.

Ethan swallowed hard. "Regardless, I'm the one who walks out of here a winner." A lie. A bitter lie.

He tightened his grip on Noelle's hand and turned away from his father, heading back toward the door. Noelle released her hold on his hand and walked ahead of him, her skin icy pale. Her expression was set, strong, not betraying a hint of emotion. But he could feel it, radiating from her, echoing inside him.

She opened the door and walked out into the hallway. He followed her, his eyes on her, no one else, because she was all that mattered.

He closed the door behind them and followed her into the elevator. Neither of them spoke until the doors closed.

"Why did you do that to me?"

"I didn't do anything to you. It's an act, Noelle." The tension in him exploded, unraveling his control. "All of this is, it has been from day one, and you knew it then, and you know it now. What I said to my father, that was a part of it. I wanted him to face the fact that I did things right and I still came out ahead."

"But you didn't do it right! You lied. You cheated the game."

"Maybe I did, but I'm not the same as him. Someone had to show him. Make him pay."

"And you had to try and be the hero for your mother."

Pain sliced at him and he ignored it, pressed on. "Someone had to be."

"Maybe," she said. "But there was nothing—" She looked up at him, her blue eyes unveiled now, all of her emotion exposed. "—nothing more painful that you could have said. It wouldn't have been any worse if you'd called me your high-priced whore. Because that's what you said I was to you. You reduced me to nothing more than my name. One of your many acquisitions."

Anger boiled in him, at himself, at the damned heavy emotion that was crushing him beneath its weight. It drove him, compelled him to push back. And anger was much easier to embrace than the bigger, scarier feeling that was trying to claw its way into prominence.

"And I'm not the same to you, Noelle? Why did we get into this relationship in the first place? Because I had the power to give you back that wreck you call a home. Because you could use me to get your picture back in the paper, to climb back up onto your diamond pedestal. So don't play the wounded maiden. You got what you wanted."

"Fine. Maybe. But I didn't just parade you through a room and treat you like an object. I have never treated you like an object, or a means to an end. And until tonight, you hadn't treated me like one either."

"Tonight was what *this*, this thing between us, this whole arrangement, was all about. You know that."

"Yes," she said. "We made an agreement in the beginning, and I've held to it. And I knew that being on your arm was a part of that. But now you know me. And you know what my mother did to me, how she used me. I thought that might change something." She choked on the last words.

"It can't."

She looked down, and he looked past her, to where her expression was reflected in the high-gloss obsidian wall.

She looked tired. And sad. And he wanted to hold her. But he was the cause of her suffering, and wanting to be the one to ease it just seemed cruel.

"Well, fine then," she said. "You did it. That's all there is."

The elevator doors opened and neither of them moved for a moment. Noelle felt each beat lacerating her tender heart. She was being beaten, destroyed from the inside out by her own body. Her own emotion.

When they got to the hotel suite he closed the door behind them. The silence was like an entity between them. Real and powerful, hard to break.

"I suppose I'll see about getting my own room."

"You damn well won't," he growled.

He pulled her to him then, his kiss hard, fast, containing all of the rage and frustration and bitter anguish she felt inside herself. It tasted like her own sorrow. Like the ashes and ruin of heartbreak.

And she gave as good as she got. Everything. Because he wasn't allowed to just hurt her and walk away. He wasn't allowed to feel nothing, not when every breath seared her insides. She laced her fingers through his hair and held him to her, hoping to make him feel what she did. To feel all of the pain and desire and frustration.

He wrenched his mouth from hers and trailed hot kisses down her neck, leaving flames in his wake.

"Ethan. Please."

No matter what happened tomorrow. Or in the next hour. She needed him, with her, in her, now.

He pushed her dress up, that stupid dress he'd picked to make her look like a trophy.

"Say my name," she said, working his belt buckle and opening the closure on his slacks. "I need to know that it matters."

"Noelle," he rasped, his voice rough. He slipped his fingers beneath the edge of her panties and tugged them down as he leaned her back onto the bed, her legs still hanging off the edge. He got down on his knees in front of her and shrugged his pants and underwear down his hips, leaving them most of the way on. There wasn't time to take everything off. There wasn't enough time, period. There never would be.

She hooked her leg over his back and pulled him to her. He entered her in one smooth stroke and she locked her legs around his hips, holding him to her, reveling in this moment. In being joined to him. Because nothing made sense. Not how she felt about him, not how he seemed to feel about her. Or didn't feel about her. At least this was honest.

Here and now there was no acting.

She put her hand on Ethan's cheek, and he met her gaze, his dark eyes glittering in the dim light of the room. The tendons on his neck stood out, his breathing harsh, his heartbeat raging. She could feel his pulse echoing beneath her hand, pounding through her.

Every time he entered her, she wanted to take him deeper, to hold him to her longer. She slid her hands down to grip his shoulders, dug her fingernails into his back. He held her too, hands braced on her hips.

The pleasure was blinding, beyond anything she'd ever known. But it was secondary to the connection that was forged, stronger, more permanent, with each breath, with each movement.

He was a part of her. Drawing pieces of her away, bringing more substance back into her. Like sand in the waves.

She fought against her climax, because it meant the end. Because this was the end. She knew it. Knew it in every fiber of being. But it caught her, grabbed her. She reached the peak of pleasure as he found his and they rode the crest together, completely silent except for the harsh notes of their breath.

He withdrew from her body, but stayed on his knees, his arms resting on the bed. Noelle blinked and brushed her hair out of her face with shaking fingers. Every part of her was trembling, inside and out.

She rolled to the side, trying to put distance between them, trying to find a way to escape the pain that was clawing in her chest, pushing out the memory of the pleasure, the closeness they'd just shared.

She looked at Ethan. His face, his gorgeous, precious face. She had never loved anyone like she loved him. Had never needed anyone the way she needed him.

And she knew she couldn't do that to herself. She couldn't keep loving people who didn't love her back. She couldn't keep pouring herself into people who would leave her.

Because as hard as she had fallen when her mother had left, as devastating as it had been to lose her piano teacher, those two constants in her life, if she grew to trust that Ethan would stay…that he would love her when everyone else seemed unable to…she didn't know how she would survive it.

So she had to walk out now. While she had the strength.

She stood up from the bed and walked over to her suitcase. She found a pair of jeans that had remained unpacked and tugged them on beneath her dress.

"Noelle," Ethan said, his voice rough. "Stay with me."

She shook her head.

"Stay," he said again, more desperate this time.

"I can't."

"Why?"

She took a deep breath. "I have an audition next weekend. I haven't practiced at all while we've been here. I need to get back."

"So you can work on your music." It wasn't a question, neither was it an accusation. It was a statement, hollow, empty.

"Yes. You're right. That's why we had this whole relationship. That's the point of it all, you reminded me of that."

She looked at him. He was still on his knees at the foot of the bed and she wanted, more than anything, to drop to her knees in front of him and kiss him. But she didn't. She couldn't.

"I wish you would stay," he said again, his voice muted.

Her chest tightened and she feared her heart would burst from it. "I can't, Ethan. This…this is all fine for a few days," she said, indicating the gaudy room. "But it's not my life. My music is my life. It's what I need."

"Take my plane."

"No, I'll figure something out…"

"Take it. Dammit Noelle, take it." He stood and jerked his pants back up, reaching into his pocket and pulling out his phone. He opened it and punched in a number. "Have the plane fueled and ready to go. Mrs. Grey needs to get back to New York."

"That wasn't necessary," she said.

"It was. You're still my wife. And you will be until the ink is dry on the contract my grandfather sends over. Don't forget that."

No. Of course not. She couldn't forget why they were married. Certainly not for love. At least not on his part.

"I won't." She took her purse from the nightstand and ignored everything else. She didn't want it. She didn't need it. She just needed to get away from Ethan, needed to get out of her skin so she could escape the horrible, sick feeling of grief that was washing through her.

"He was wrong, you know," she said, her voice breaking. "You aren't like him. You're like your mother. You're like I was when we first met. You think...you think you're going to fix something in you by getting revenge, or by getting Grey's Resorts. Just like I thought having my career back would fix something in me. But it won't, Ethan. Not for either of us. It's not about things. It's about people. It's about love. And if you can't figure that out, if you can't find that, then you won't ever be happy. And nothing you have will ever be enough."

Ethan watched Noelle walk out of the room. She closed the door with a finality that rocked him. Still he watched. To see if she would come back.

He was a fool.

He had thought that somehow winning this game with his father, that somehow making Damien pay for what had happened would make him, Ethan...worth something. That he would suddenly be the man he needed to be to make things right. That holding the power, the Grey family legacy, would add some sort of value to him.

The boy who had been ignored by the two people in his life who should have loved him had been working toward this paper, pinning his hopes on it meaning something, for years. Hoping that revenge would prove him to be the better man, that having the family business pass to him would somehow prove him to be smarter, more worthy.

So now he had it. And it hadn't made a damn bit of difference. He wasn't better. He wasn't fixed. His entire life was shattered now, broken into a million unfixable pieces. He had lost Noelle.

He had everything that he'd wanted, that he'd dreamed of. He had billions of dollars and he had notoriety and fame, and yet she had walked away. He had banked on this moment. On somehow triumphing over his father and it mattering in some way, somehow removing the empty, unsatisfied ache inside of him.

Maybe because his own success had never impressed his father. Had never made his mother care.

Anyway, he had done it now, and in the process had increased his own power, his own bank balance. And it had only confirmed what he'd always suspected. Everything he'd feared.

That, as much as he'd wanted to place blame elsewhere, the problem was with him. Revenge had proven to be an empty thing. The acquisition of more hotels, even emptier. Noelle was right. No amount of material possessions could make a difference.

The problem truly was in him. He would never be enough. His love would never be enough.

And he loved Noelle. No matter how much he'd tried to deny it to himself today, no matter how much distance he'd tried to wedge between them with his actions in the high-roller room tonight, he loved her.

Even now that she'd rejected him, walked out the door when he'd all but begged her to stay, he loved her.

And he had let her go. Because when it came right down to it, he was afraid that if he had told her why he wanted her to stay, she still would have said no.

He hadn't been willing to take the chance.

CHAPTER THIRTEEN

It wasn't the number she dreamed of seeing on her phone, but it wasn't a bad number to have pop up either.

It was Jacques. Probably calling about last week's audition. She'd all but given up hope on that. But now he was calling, and she was really hoping it was good news. She glanced at the clock, and at the line of people that stretched out the door.

It wasn't a good time for her to take a break, and breaktaking was something she had to discuss with her supervisor. Because that was how her new job as barista at the Roasted Tea and Coffee Company worked.

She had a job. And she was learning it, a lot faster than she'd imagined she might. Steaming milk and pulling shots had come pretty naturally to her, and now she could make her own latte. Which was good, since Ethan wasn't around to buy her one. It was a small step on the road to self-sufficiency, but it was a step. One she'd been too scared to take before Ethan had come into her life.

That silly little job inputting data had done so much for her. And Ethan had acted as though she'd done it brilliantly. He'd always looked at her as if she was brilliant. And beautiful. But not the sort of beautiful other people talked about. He said it like he saw something deeper.

Hidden. Something she hadn't seen before he had shown it to her.

Noelle released the catch on the espresso grinder and let a fine dust of beans pour into the porta-filter. She twisted it back onto the machine and hit the button, watching the shot, making sure it took the right amount of time, that it was just the right color. There was a kind of art to this job too, and she found herself really enjoying it. She liked making people smile.

She'd give it all up to play on the stage again, but it was nice to have something else to do.

"Noelle."

Noelle looked at her co-worker, David, who was busy taking orders. "Skinny latte please, a sixteen-ounce, no foam."

"Got it." She put a pitcher of skim milk beneath the steam wand and nearly laughed out loud. Such a contrast from the over-the-top glitz of Las Vegas. Had it really only been two weeks? Two weeks since she'd seen Ethan? Two weeks since she'd touched him?

Then why did her skin still burn? Why did her heart still ache like this? More importantly, would she ever feel right again?

She clenched her teeth to keep from tearing up, something she'd done countless times in the past fourteen days. It was enough to drown in. She wasn't drowning though, she was *doing*. Living.

Because one major difference between having her mother walk out of her life and losing Ethan was that Ethan hadn't torn her down. He'd built her up. Told her she could do anything. He'd left her stronger. Even though he'd also left her broken-hearted.

You left him.

Only because she'd had to. Because someday, in the

not-too-distant future, when he got Grey's in his possession, he would have left. He'd shown her so much. Made her want more than surface fame and recognition. But he didn't seem to want anything more than what was on the surface.

She was starting to wonder if she should have taken the extra time, taken everything he could give. Some days it seemed like her pain couldn't get any worse anyway, so maybe it would have been better to take a bed that had Ethan in it, rather than her big, cold bed back at the manor.

Back at her decrepit old house. But at least it was hers. Ethan had sent those papers already, paid in full. And as far as the public was concerned, they were married. No one was paying close enough attention to realize they hadn't crossed paths in two weeks.

That was another thing she'd done. Gotten her house on the market. Soon she'd be able to move into the city, or just outside of it. Somewhere smaller. More practical.

Someplace where being alone didn't echo so much.

"Sir, I'm afraid you'll have to get in line."

David's distressed tone was answered by a harsh curse spoken in a very familiar Australian accent. She looked up and nearly melted onto the spongy rubber floor.

"Ethan?"

"You work here?" he asked.

He didn't look good. Well, that was a lie—he looked delicious. But he looked tired. Like he hadn't slept for two weeks. Like his whole body hurt him. He looked like she felt.

"Yes, I do. If I didn't they wouldn't let me behind the counter. Employees only."

"Right. Yeah.…right."

"Did you have something to say?"

"I've had a lot of things to say, for a long time. But you walked out on me. You left me on my knees."

People, David included, were staring now.

"May I take a break?" she asked, her eyes not leaving Ethan's.

"Please," David said.

She took her apron off and pulled the band from her hair, releasing it around her shoulders, before stepping out from behind the counter. "What?"

"Outside," Ethan said.

"All right. But I don't have long. Jacques just called and if I'm on a break anyway, I should return that."

"Oh. Jacques."

"About the audition."

"Of course." He opened the coffee shop door and held it for her. "How did that go?" he asked when they were out on the sidewalk.

"It was…he said I was a bit too dark. He wanted to hear something brighter from me. But I told him a different day."

"Why?"

"Because I didn't feel bright."

"Any idea why that was?" he asked, his voice rough.

"You know damn well why, Ethan Grey. What are you doing here? Do you need your trophy for something else? Is that it? Did you not twist the knife hard enough into your father?"

He shook his head. "No. I don't need a trophy. I don't want one either. I want you. You were never a thing to me and I…I behaved abominably. And you're right, it was the worst thing I could have done."

"Then why?"

"It was just what you said. You were right. I was look-ing for Grey's to give me some kind of validity. To bring me some sense of satisfaction and purpose that I didn't seem to have without it." He took a sharp breath. "I told my grandfather I don't want the resorts."

"But your father…"

"Can have them. Revenge is empty, Noelle. Vain. It was for myself. All that time I thought that it was for my mother, but it never was. It was for me. I was so desperate to keep blaming my father, to find a way to make it all about him so that I wouldn't acknowledge…I wasn't enough for her. Or for him."

"Ethan…"

"I wasn't as important as her job. I wasn't as important as her marriage. There were a few times when she told me…she wished she had never had a child. It was my fault my father didn't love her. And that day… If I hadn't blamed him…"

"You don't deserve any blame in that, Ethan. You were a child."

"A child whose parents barely looked at him. I… There's something broken in me, Noelle. I know that. But…I still want you. Even though I messed everything up, even though you should say no, and find a man who isn't damaged like this, I want you."

"Then why…" she choked up, her words stalling in her aching throat. "Why didn't you say this before I left?"

"Because I didn't think… I thought if you still didn't want me, even though I was getting more money, more power, then there was nothing I could ever say that would change it."

"You jackass. You thought I would want you if you had more money?" The stunned look on his face would almost have been funny if her chest didn't feel like a hole had been punched in it.

"It was never about you, Noelle. It was about me. Why

wasn't I enough? My mother was so miserable raising me she tried to kill herself. My father has never seen any value in me. Why should you be different? Not because you aren't amazing, but because I just can't seem to earn the love of people in my life. And I've always dealt with it. I've never begged for it. Until you. I'm begging you. And I'll get on my knees again if I have to. I want you to love me."

The image of him, so proud, so strong, ready to crumble at her feet, undid her completely. Two warm tears slid down her cheeks and splashed onto his arm.

"I do love you, Ethan. I have…loved you…for such a long time. But I didn't think you wanted love."

"I didn't. That's a huge part of why I acted the way I did that night in the casino. I was trying to force myself to get back to business. But I couldn't. And in the end I…I don't want to. Love hurts, and I've really gotten a dose of that in the past two weeks. But I've decided it's worth it. Because even though I've never been in so much pain before, I've also never felt so alive as I do because of you. Just because I love you."

"That can't be right." She shook her head.

"You don't think so?"

"No. Because that's how you make me feel. Like I can do anything. You've never tried to hold me back, or tell me I can't. You made me want to try at life again. And I was…scared, so I ran from you, from what you made me feel. But I don't want to run. I want to stay here with you."

"Here?" He looked around them, at the bustling sidewalk.

"Not right here, but you know what I mean."

He dipped his head and kissed her. Warmth flooded her and she felt her heart beat again.

"I want to ask you to marry me," he said.

"Then do it!"

"But I don't want to interfere with your career. With touring."

"Playing again…I want to play again. But it's not who I am. I get that now. I'm so much more than just the piano. Than what the public thinks about me. I'm me. And you helped me figure out what that means. I want to be with you, and if music fits into that, then I'd love to play. But it's not everything to me. It doesn't define me. And that… there's so much freedom in that."

"Then Noelle, will you marry me?"

"I'm married to you already," she said.

"I know, but we'll do it somewhere else, not in Vegas this time."

"I liked our wedding."

"In that case, will you stay married to me? Forever?"

"Yes."

"Thank you, Noelle, for loving me. Just me."

She leaned in and kissed him, her tongue teasing the edge of his lips. "It's not a hard thing to do, Ethan. You're exactly what I need. More than enough for anyone, and perfect for me. Even if I could have all the fame back, all of it and then some, the adoration of millions would never mean as much as having your love."

EPILOGUE

HE loved it when she wore red at the piano. He was certain she did it to tease him. And it always worked. Two years of marriage hadn't seen any of the spark dim in their marriage. If anything, it burned brighter now than ever before.

Ethan watched from the first row of the concert hall as Noelle started to play the grand piano, her fingers tripping lightly over the keys, her slender shoulders working with the rhythm.

The house was packed tonight, filled with people who had come to listen to her music.

Pride surged through him. She'd been playing in theaters along the east coast regularly for a while now, thanks to her resurgence of fame after playing in Jacques' orchestra. And now Noelle played her own music, on her own terms. Not in world-famous music halls as she'd done once, but she never seemed sorry about that. Not even for a moment.

Ethan picked up the program that she'd handed him before the start of the show and opened it. There was a handwritten note inside, done in Noelle's neat style.

Tonight, I'm playing a special song. The one I started in Australia all those years ago. I know how it ends now. Do you? Happily.

Ethan's throat tightened and he looked up at the stage, at the woman he loved. She looked back at him, her eyes shining in the spotlight as she played.

Later he would have to remind her of all the other things he'd taught her. After the show. And after he'd thanked her for all she had shown him.

And for bringing love into his life. Because there was no amount of fame or money that could rival the love they shared. Those things were easily lost, and they both knew it.

But their love was forever.

* * * * *

UNTOUCHED BY HIS DIAMONDS

BY
LUCY ELLIS

Lucy Ellis has four loves in life: books, expensive lingerie, vintage films and big, gorgeous men who have to duck going through doorways. Weaving aspects of them into her fiction is the best part of being a romance writer. Lucy lives in a small cottage in the foothills outside Melbourne.

CHAPTER ONE

CLÉMENTINE did a double-take in front of the ornate windows, almost pressing her nose up to the glass.

Lust—that was what she was feeling. Unadulterated desire.

In the window sat her Anna Karenina fantasy. Thigh-high, fur-lined, suede Russian boots.

She told herself she was only in St Petersburg for one more day after today. She deserved something to remember it by.

Five minutes later she was standing on the worn raspberry-coloured carpet inside, sliding one stockinged foot and then the other into her dream. She felt like Cinderella trying on her glass slippers. The real test was zipping them up above her knees. She was six feet tall and her legs held much of her height. She had shape to them. She had shape to all of her.

She almost gave a whoop of delight when the boots zipped up a treat.

The girl kneeling before her lifted the flaps. 'They can go higher. Shall we try?'

She spoke English, but in these luxury stores everybody did.

Without hesitation Clementine hitched up her burgundy leather skirt, feeling slightly naughty as she flashed her suspenders. She reached down and pulled the fur-lined suede up and up, to kiss the fleshy curve of her inner thigh.

Her legs looked impossibly long with the leather skirt clinging to her hips. Absorbed in her own reflection, she slung out a leg and stroked the fur meditatively. Out of the corner of her eye she caught a flash of movement behind her in the mirror, and looked up to collide with the gaze of a man standing by the door.

He wasn't idling in the doorway, lurking. He was purposefully filling the space. Announcing his presence up front. Owning it.

And he was looking right at her.

He had to have a head of height on her, and he was built to go with it, and Clementine would bet her last pair of designer knickers on that size being one hundred per cent lean muscle.

He was quite a sight. They didn't make men like that any more.

Maybe they had in earlier centuries, when Russian men went into battle with muskets, or even earlier when they needed to club things and skin animals to feed their families. Oh, yes, she could imagine him half naked and marked by claw-marks across his back and chest, bestriding the steppes. In fact—she nibbled her bottom lip—she could imagine that quite vividly.

But nowadays, in an age of technology and convenience and the liberation of women, you just didn't need men like this any more.

Except in bed. An unexpected flush of warmth moved through her body.

Imagine if he laid his hands on you.

Imagine if it was him adjusting the tops of your boots.

Her eyes flicked to the mirror and registered that the Cossack hadn't shifted an inch, but instinctively she just knew he'd moved some muscles because the look on his face mirrored her own: unadulterated fascination. With her. Male, down-and-dirty fascination. As if she was his own personal little sex show.

Clementine felt his eyes on her like a slow burn, sliding straight up the inside of her bare, exposed leg. It was that good, and almost as tantalising as being touched.

She should cover herself up, but after a year of keeping herself nice she was enjoying the attention. It was harmless. If this guy wanted to look, let him look. It wasn't as if he *could* put his hands on her. They were strangers. It was a public place. She was safe.

She was enjoying it.

She bent down, nice and slow, folding over one fur flap to reveal the length of her bare upper thigh and then the other. Then she ever so slowly tugged down the leather bunched at her hips and lengthened her skirt, inch by inch, as she had seen so many models do for the camera, until she was decently covered.

There. Show over.

Time to pay for the beauties, head back to the rats' nest where she was staying and catch up on some sleep. Except when she looked back at the mirror the Cossack was still there, holding up the world on those big shoulders. He'd folded his arms and Clementine registered powerful muscle under the strain of his jacket.

Her pulse leapt. He was every woman's fantasy, and also a little bit scary—not only because of his size. With his clear intent she got the absolute impression he was waiting for her.

A shivering awareness ran through her body like an electrical shock, but she got herself moving, fumbling with her handbag as she dug out the equivalent cost of her meals for the rest of the week to pay for the boots.

'You have an admirer,' said the girl, boxing up her old shoes with a discreet glance in the direction of the door.

'Probably a shoe fetishist,' murmured Clementine, but there was a smile on her lips as she said it.

Inhaling a deep breath, she swung round and headed for the exit—only to discover he wasn't there. She actually dropped a step, idling for a moment in the doorway, disappointed.

She emerged into the street and swung her designer bag as she headed south—and that was when she spotted him. Leaning against a limo, thumbs in designer pockets, running a gaze over her that sped up and slowed down depending on which part of her body he got hooked on. Clementine lost a breath and then her heartbeat raced.

Okay, Clementine, walk on, she lectured herself. *There's no way you're going over there and introducing yourself.* Guys dressed like that with limos on tap were not territory she wished to stray into. She'd already had her brush with his type. Never again. The industry she worked in was rife with women who cashed in on their desirability for a certain lifestyle. She wasn't one of them, and she wasn't starting now.

Serge fastened on the sway of her hips as she walked away, flashing those sensational thighs showcased by fur and sheer stockings. He knew what was holding those stockings up: delicate midnight-blue suspenders.

He had been leaving the jeweller Krassinsky's, where he'd left his father's wedding cufflinks to be repaired, and crossing the art nouveau atrium that linked several high-end stores in this building when he had spotted her through the shop's entrance.

A young woman bent at the waist, a leather skirt hiked up around her hips, as comfortable in the middle of the shop as if it had been her boudoir, her shapely bottom encased in burgundy leather, swaying provocatively. He'd seen two strips of pale flesh before the lacy tops of her stockings took over, attached to delicate suspenders.

It had ground him to a standstill.

When she'd started tugging up those boots lust had flashed through him like a lightning strike.

If she'd stopped there he might have dragged himself away, but all of a sudden she'd hooked out a leg and he'd got an eyeful of her inner thigh—that soft, fleshy curve at the very top of a woman's leg, pressed into prominence by the clasp of the stockings clinging to her legs. Serge had swallowed hard as she'd begun smoothing the fur right up to that spot.

That's the girl—a bit higher...very nice.

As if hearing his thoughts she'd lifted her head and met his gaze in the freestanding mirror. She'd frozen. Her face was heart-shaped, her mouth wide, her chin pointed. Despite the clothes, despite the pose, despite the lashings of make-up, she looked as if butter wouldn't melt in her mouth. He had waited for her reaction and been rewarded by a small private smile, and then she'd bent and slowly peeled the fur down to expose the tops of her thighs. To him.

Because it had all been for him. She'd known he was watching her.

Which had made it incredibly hot.

As her skirt had slithered down he'd known he'd be thinking not only about that spot at the top of her left thigh but also about her smile for the rest of his day.

He'd watched the girl switch her attention to the salesgirl—no longer his little show but simply a woman making a purchase—and it had chastened him. This wasn't Amsterdam. She wasn't on the market and she wasn't his type. The hooker look had never interested him, and whatever frisson she had got from the experience was over.

He'd left her to it, but as he'd handed his bag over to his driver he'd found himself lingering by the car, just waiting to see her emerge. Curious, interested.

She stepped out of the building in those ridiculous boots

and above the revving of his libido he got the full impact of a fifties pin-up come to life. Lustrous golden-brown hair, narrow shoulders, full breasts, curvaceous hips and a lick of a waist. Her legs were strong and shapely and went on and on. And on.

The realist inside him told him he should let her go. He had places to be, and it wasn't as if he couldn't find another woman to warm his bed.

Then she moved and he forgot about every plan he had for the rest of the day.

He knew the moment she noticed him. Her lashes dropped, screened her eyes, and she just took off, those sensational legs in those infamous boots eating up the pavement. Her leather skirt twitched provocatively over the bounce of her heart-shaped bottom. She'd be gone in a few minutes, lost in the late-afternoon crowd.

As if sensing his indecision, she chose that moment to turn her head over one pretty shoulder and give him a smile Mona Lisa would have envied. Subtle, but it was there. *Come and get me.*

Then she was off with a swish of her long hair.

Serge propelled himself away from the car, and with a brusque instruction to his driver to follow took off after her.

Clementine hadn't been able to help herself. She'd cast a last look over her shoulder, and when she'd seen his gaze was still glued to her she'd smiled. Apparently that was enough—because now he was coming after her.

Instinctively she sped up, her whole body tightening with anticipation.

When she checked again he was still there, impossible to miss, taller than anyone else, a big, insanely gorgeous man, with chestnut hair falling carelessly over his temples, curling at the base of his broad neck. In the bright sunshine she could see the faint shadow of where he'd shaved, and the square cut of his chin and the sheer bravado of his grin as he caught her looking.

She shouldn't be encouraging this. She should turn around on this crowded street and confront him. But she didn't. She slowed down. She put a little more sway in her hips and kept walking.

She checked again. He was clocking her, but not closing in. She felt relatively safe.

Serge pulled back his pace momentarily as Boots turned out of the Nevsky, watched her cross against the schizophrenic traffic, earning a few hoots and screeching tyres from drivers—probably more at the sight of those long legs than any traffic infringement.

She had a real energy in her body that translated into the sexiest walk he had ever seen on a woman. And what struck him was the fact that she seemed utterly oblivious to the chaos she caused around her.

He didn't want to lose her.

Clementine risked another glance over her shoulder but she couldn't see him. Disappointment slowed her walk, prosaic reality returning with every step. Game over. Damn.

Up ahead was the underpass. She hated those mucky tunnels, never felt completely safe, but it was the only route she knew. The boots were starting to rub, and without the distraction of her ridiculous sexual fantasy the worries of the day began to crowd into her mind.

Serge stood at the kerb and watched as she began to descend into the underpass on her own. He saw the danger closing in around her at the same moment, and without another thought launched into a run.

Bozhe, this woman took chances. She'd known he was on her tail, and now two men were honing in on her bag, flapping on that lavish hip, and she just kept walking, lost in her own little world.

She shouldn't be let out on her own. The thought briefly crossed his mind before the more savage *Take them down* intruded and he lunged into the underpass, aiming at the guy who was already reaching for the strap of her bag.

He grabbed her assailant by the scuff of his neck and dragged him off.

It was satisfying to use his body for something other than sitting in a plane and a car. He was fit—boxing and running took care of that—but to fight was in his blood and he hadn't had one in many years.

Not that it was proving much of a challenge. The first assailant launched a fist that he blocked.

Instead of acting smart and getting the hell out of the way, Boots was launching an attack of her own with her bag, smacking it with gusto into the back of the head of the guy nearest her.

She distracted him and the first guy got in a lucky punch, grazing his face. Fast was best, and Serge slugged him one, then zeroed in on the second thug who moved fast, snatching the bag she was flapping around as if it was a club.

At least she wasn't stupid. She let go, and the guy started running. The one on the ground crawled to his feet and took off, leaving Serge flexing his knuckles and alone with Boots.

'You let him go!' She was standing there in that short skirt, looking outraged.

At him.

Serge shrugged, rubbing his abused jaw. He didn't feel like explaining that beating both men to a pulp was the only way he could have kept them there, and that her safety had been foremost in his mind. Instead he opted for the more obvious standby. 'Are you all right?'

'They took my bag!' she wailed.

Foreign. British? Her voice was pitched low, slightly husky.

'You're lucky that's all they took,' he answered her in English. 'These underpasses aren't safe. If you'd read your guidebook, *moya krasavitsa*, you'd know that.'

She looked at him with clear grey eyes full of reproach.

'So it's my fault, is it?'

She had her hands on her hips now, stretching that white satin blouse across her breasts until the buttons strained. *Bozhe*, there was black lace under the white. This girl seemed incapable of keeping her clothes on. She was a walking incitement to the male libido. What did she expect was going to happen to her if she went around dressed like this?

Bizarrely, he wanted to tear off his jacket and wrap it around her—which would just ruin his view.

She wasn't quite what he'd expected up close. She was better, but in a less upfront, more feminine way, and the longer he looked at her the more other things began to leap out besides the obvious. Up close she was younger than he had imagined—closer to twenty than thirty. It was all that make-up. She didn't need it. Her skin was luscious, like a ripe peach.

She swore creatively, pushing the fringe off her forehead. 'What am I going to do?' she said fiercely.

He had the answer to that, but he would wait for her to suggest it.

Hands still firmly on her hips, she walked a few steps in the other direction, then turned and met his eyes properly for the first time. Some of the agitation had left her, and she turned up a face more interesting than conventionally attractive. She had thick brown eyelashes and clear grey eyes and a dappling of freckles across her nose.

She really was lovely.

'I'm sorry,' she said earnestly. 'I've been very rude to you. Thanks for scaring them off. You didn't have to, but it was a nice thing to do.'

He hadn't expected that—or her sincerity. He shrugged it off. He didn't need to get sentimental about picking up a girl in downtown St Petersburg. He only had to drop his gaze ever so slightly to remind himself she wasn't a shrinking violet.

'Don't men look after women where you come from, *kisa*?'

'I imagine they do.' She gave an awkward shrug, then another one of those little smiles of hers. 'Just not me. But thanks again.'

With that she took off, the slender heels on those boots clicking on the cobbles. She held out her arms stiffly from her body, as if balancing herself, a gesture that reminded him she had experienced a nasty shock.

He couldn't believe she was walking away.

Damn. 'Hold up.'

She looked over her shoulder.

'Can I give you a lift somewhere?'

She hesitated, looked at him with those doe eyes, and said, 'No, I don't think so. But thanks, Slugger,' and damn well kept walking.

Click, click, click.

CHAPTER TWO

GODDAMN. Unbelievable…

Clementine hobbled over a puddle, heading towards the light at the end of the underpass, cursing under her breath. She tried to focus on the practicalities. She would have to find the embassy. She would have to borrow money from her friend Luke. She would have to phone her bank in London. She would do it all once she'd had a little sit-down and a cry.

Her handbag was her lifeline.

It was her own fault. She was usually much more street smart than this. She'd been so wrapped up in her little fantasy with the Cossack she hadn't been paying attention. She'd ruined that too. She'd been too shaken, too tongue-tied to do anything more than try to block him out whilst she extricated herself from the situation even after he'd rushed in to save her.

Her chest gave a little flutter at that thought. He'd been magnificent. He'd just handled it. You didn't run into guys like that in London.

The light hit her face and, pulling awkwardly at her skirt, she ascended the steps. She was chilled despite the sun, and that was her own fault too. She should have changed out of this ridiculous outfit Verado liked her to wear, back into her street clothes. But there hadn't been time, and she'd left the bag of clothes at the store, and now she was wandering the streets of St Petersburg in great boots but frankly looking a little too uncovered for her own liking.

Emerging into the street, she hobbled over to a nearby kiosk and took a seat. She was really shivering now, and it didn't have much to do with her lack of layers. She supposed it was delayed shock, but she also felt naked without her bag—vulnerable. She was used to depending on herself and that bag had everything she needed to keep herself safe. She was beginning to wish she hadn't sent the Cossack away.

It was useless going back to her lodgings. She needed to head back into the city centre, find Luke.

That was when she saw the limo. It was idling across the road, one of its doors angled wide, and then she saw him, striding straight towards her. He'd removed his jacket and had his hands shoved into his pockets, so that the fabric of his superfine blue shirt pulled taut across a muscular chest and abdomen. Clementine's miserable thoughts dwindled to a virtual halt. He looked powerful and it wasn't just his size. It was the way he held himself, with tremendous confidence and that measured response to what was going on around him she had seen in action in the underpass.

But what he was giving her now was full sensual male interest. Clementine told herself she could handle men, but all her female instincts were telling her she couldn't handle *this* man at all.

He was so male as to be of another species.

Big shoulders, big arms, hard thighs—long and lean and coming straight at her.

He'd crunched bones for her, broken skin, shed blood.

'Come on, get in. I'll take you wherever you want to go.' He spoke abruptly, his voice deep and deliberate.

She just sat there, looking up, trying to clamber over the overwhelmed feeling to something more considered.

He lifted those big hands of his. 'I'm a good guy. I don't wish you any harm. You need some help, yes?'

'Yes,' Clementine said softly, distracted by the intensity of his green eyes.

'Are you staying far from here?'

Clementine knew she should tell him nothing and refuse the ride. But he had helped her. He had put himself at risk for a stranger. This *was* a good guy. This was a very, very sexy man. This would buy her a little more time with him. And she was so tired of looking after herself. It wouldn't hurt to accept a lift.

'Do you know where the Australian embassy is?'

'I'll find it.'

And she believed he would.

Serge gave directions to his driver, watched as those long legs folded themselves into his car, slid in alongside her, observed her scoot over to put a respectable distance between them. Then she shifted forward and leant down.

She was unzipping the boots.

The shell of each boot collapsed and she tugged one stockinged foot out, then the other, revealing her long legs in those sheer pale stockings that gleamed like silk. Her activity seemed unselfconscious, as if he couldn't possibly be interested, but of course she had to know what she was doing. She wriggled her toes and cocked a curious look at him up through her lashes.

'Sorry, honey,' she said. 'They're new, and they're rubbing.'

She pressed her knees primly together and folded her hands in her lap, utterly ladylike.

She was incredible.

'You're Australian? From Sydney?' His own voice sounded

hoarse, and he gave an inward laugh at his susceptibility to this woman.

'Melbourne.' She smiled, her eyes not quite meeting his. It was such a subtle smile. She kept her lips pursed, as if she was keeping a secret.

If only she'd stop rubbing her knees together. The *shub-shub* of the fabric was highly stimulating to his imagination.

'So far away. What are you doing in Petersburg? Business or pleasure?'

'Both. I'm here working.' She gave a little shrug as if it wasn't important. Those lips parted into a more open smile. 'But I've dreamed of seeing St Petersburg. It's so romantic, so full of history.'

'You like what you've seen so far?'

'Very much.' She gave him a sidelong look, making it clear she wasn't talking about the city—and didn't that just notch up the temperature in the car? She turned her head away, made a show of looking out of the window, exposing the length of her lovely pale throat, and he dwelt on the golden tendrils of silky hair tickling against her neck.

He decided to cut to the chase. 'When do you leave?'

She met his gaze, let him see those grey eyes, darker now than when he had first seen them. 'My contract winds up to-morrow.'

Two days. Perfect. 'Such a shame,' he mused.

'What do you do?' she ventured. 'I mean, you must do something—you're riding around in a limo.' She laughed nervously. 'You're either rich or something else.'

He laughed low, and watched the pulse in her throat give a little throb. 'Or something else,' he murmured, which clearly intrigued her.

'You're not one of those overnight millionaires you read about, are you, honey?'

'*Nyet*, sorry to disappoint you. I worked very hard for my first million.'

'Right.' Those slender hands fluttered in her lap. She was obviously attracted to him, but the money helped. His inner cynic gave a rueful shrug.

'This would be the moment to ask you, if you're not otherwise engaged, to join me for dinner tonight.'

He actually saw her swallow. She moistened her lower lip, dragging his attention to the contours of her mouth. She looked at him through her lashes. 'You work fast. I'll give you that.'

'You haven't given me much time.'

'Oh, I can't imagine that stopping you.'

'Nothing much does, *kisa*.'

She gave a negligent little shrug, a naughty sparkle in her grey eyes. 'Okay, Slugger, we'll see how you do.'

A challenge—and didn't he just relish that?

Lifting his head above the pleasure horizon, he made a quick judgement call. This girl clearly liked to play games, however guarded she was being now. It was reasonable to wonder how many other men she'd played them with.

He hesitated.

Did it matter?

This was his favourite type of female. A woman with a sparkle in her eyes and a willingness to just enjoy herself. No ties, no drama. No happy-ever-afters.

This girl was clearly that woman.

Libido humming nicely, he gave her body a comprehensive, less polite once-over. In response she surprised him. Her hands knotted up in her lap and her shoulders tensed. That little Mona Lisa smile flickered and vanished. She turned the lights down low on her eyes with those thick lashes.

Chastened, he put a clamp on his imagination.

It was a reminder that he needed to be kind and considerate and gentlemanly—as he would be with any other woman.

And look after her until she waved goodbye in a few days' time.

She was going on a date with the Cossack.

Clementine's imagination was beginning to gallop, but before it did perhaps she should take the opportunity to clear a few things up. But what was she going to say? *I don't make a practice of putting on sex shows for strange men? I've agreed to dinner but that's it. I'm a nice girl.*

But he *had* asked her to dinner, hadn't he?

And he'd rescued her.

That was huge. She was still feeling a little breathless over that.

And, honestly, how nice a girl *was* she?

He really should be rewarded.

A little smile formed on her lips.

She needed to think this through. She'd seen the way he'd looked her over, as if making a sexual inventory of the bits he'd like. She knew which way this road led and she didn't want to walk it again. Not even for a Cossack whose incredible green eyes made her tremble behind the knees and her nipples perk up.

He had one arm spread along the top of the seat, so that his hand hung just inches from her shoulder. He had positioned himself so he was angled towards her, long muscular legs stretched out. Without his jacket she could see the hard width of his shoulders and the taut flat belly delineated by the fitted dark blue shirt, crisp on his large frame. He really was mouthwateringly delicious.

For crying out loud—she had to stop this now! She didn't even know his name, or he hers. She could remedy that, at least.

'I'm Clementine Chevalier, by the way,' she said, sticking out her hand in a forthright fashion.

'Clementine.' His accent did wonderful things to her name. He took her hand and lifted it to his lips, and she felt the tingle all through her girly bits as he turned her endeavour to keep their interaction on a guy-to-guy basis into an old-fashioned gesture. The sort of gesture that got her just where her inner princess lived.

'I am Serge—Serge Marinov.' *Serj*, she pronounced silently, practised it a couple of times. It was far too sexy. She was such a goner.

Expectation shimmered in the air. The car had glided to a halt. Clementine registered belatedly that they were no longer moving and hit ground level as real life intruded again. She reached for her boots.

'Thanks for the lift.' She sounded breathless even to her own ears. 'Should I give you my address or shall I meet you somewhere…?' She trailed off.

'I will collect you,' he said, as if this was the only logical response, 'and I think you should let me handle the embassy.'

Okay. She wasn't going to argue over that. 'You really want this date,' she observed as he opened her door, helped her out.

He gave her an inscrutable smile. 'How am I doing?'

'How do you think?' She threw a feminine sway into her hips and preceded him into the building, enjoying herself far too much.

People were looking at them.

Probably wondering what a girl like her was doing with a guy like him.

She was wondering the same thing.

Clementine had pictured queues, waiting endlessly, forms to be filled in. Apparently Serge Marinov didn't live in that world. He lived in a parallel universe where you were taken

upstairs to a plush office and offered tea or coffee or something stronger, and where a senior official turned up in a neat
business suit and low heels, eyes lighting up as she focussed
on Serge. The woman was so poised and elegant, her flirta-
tiousness pitch perfectly low-key, giving Clementine a sick
feeling in the pit of her stomach. She knew women must fawn
over him all the time.

Yet he had saved her from who knew what in that underpass, and he'd asked her out to dinner, and now he was making a difficult situation evaporate. He was putting in all the
work. And within an astonishing half an hour Clementine
was sorted: passport, visa, bank account. All of it done and
dusted.

'Who on earth *are* you?' she blurted out as they descended
the marble stairs of the embassy building. It was shabby and
worn, but the interior had clearly once been a beautiful example of early nineteenth-century classicism. In any other
situation she would have lingered to take it all in, but right
now all she was interested in was the man beside her.

'I have a few contacts in the city,' he answered neutrally.
'Where can I take you now?'

Anywhere you want, a little voice sang. The boring, nice
middle-class girl part of her gave him her address, registered
his disapproval.

'Is it too far out of your way?'

'It's not a particularly savoury area.'

'I'm sure your car will be all right—I mean you can just
drop me and go.'

That stopped him in his tracks. 'I am concerned that a
woman is living alone in this building. Who arranged this
for you?'

'It's a work thing.' Clementine shrugged, feeling uncomfortable under his scrutiny. She put her game face back on.
'It's fine, really. I'm a big girl, Serge.'

It was the first time she had said his name and it ran through her like electricity. He seemed to like it too, because he was suddenly idling in front of her, blocking her view of the reception area and the street with his body. She liked it that she could barely see over his shoulder, even in her heels.

He seemed to read her thoughts, because he leaned in a little closer and said softly, 'You seem much too lovely to be staying there on your own.'

Clementine felt the backs of her knees give. She found her gaze buzzing on the line of his mouth. It was so unforgiving, yet there was a softness in his lower lip. She wanted to press her thumb there, see if she could coax a smile out of him. Just for her.

'You sure know how to sweet-talk a girl,' she said, as lightly as she could, but her voice came out a whole octave lower.

He leant in, his breath soft on her ear. 'Do you need sweet-talking?'

'A little,' she demurred, the sudden rush of response in her body embarrassing her.

He gave her a slow, knowing smile. 'I'll keep it in mind.'

This date wasn't just about dinner. She'd been a little slow on that score. Already she'd been planning her dress, and imagining candlelight and waiters bringing champagne and being romanced, when she should probably be thinking about lingerie and condoms.

It was stupid to feel disappointed. He was here now and all of this had started because of sex. And he expected it was going to end with sex. She was a big girl. She understood how it all worked. She'd learned the hard way that guys like this didn't date working girls like her with a view to a future. But she needed to make a decision about how she was going to handle that before she went any further.

Not that he'd pushed anything. Apart from that brief ges-

ture of his lips on her hand he had not laid a finger on her.
He was all well-mannered restraint. She felt completely safe
with him, and enormously grateful, and suddenly horribly
self-conscious—because all of a sudden she wondered if he
looked at her and saw what another man had seen in her unhappy past: a sure thing.

The Vassiliev Building. He wouldn't kennel a dog there. Yet
this warm, vibrant girl was sleeping there. Probably with a
lock on the door a five-year-old could snap.

If there were no funds she should be staying in one of those
concrete hotels that housed tourists. They weren't attractive
but at least they were safe. Well, this was the last time she'd
be sleeping here, so that problem was solved.

It still went against the grain to let her out here, and Serge
found himself accompanying her inside and up the stairwell.
She seemed embarrassed, as if the dire surroundings were
somehow her fault.

She'd been quiet on the drive across town from the embassy. He'd expected a little flirting, but she'd gone back to
pinning her knees together and she hadn't taken off her boots.
The mixed messages didn't bother him as much as watching
her let herself into that room and knowing he was going to
leave her there.

She was unbelievably trusting. She had climbed into his
car. She had given him her details. She'd probably open this
door to anyone.

'Keep this locked,' he said, thumping the doorjamb with
the side of his fist. 'Don't open the door to anyone you don't
know.'

She had sort of angled the door so he couldn't see inside.
Either that or she was worried he was going to lunge at her
now they were in stepping distance of a bed. Which didn't
make sense. She'd been more in danger of that in the back

of the limo. But he had no intention of rushing anything. A few hours wasn't going to make much difference, and he intended to work Clementine Chevalier over so thoroughly she wouldn't forget St Petersburg in a hurry.

It was going to be very mutually enjoyable.

If she stopped giving him these glimpses of vulnerability and expectation. As if simple consideration was something she hadn't much experience of.

He handed her his card. 'This is my number. Call me if you have any hassles. I'll be here at eight.'

She nodded, those grey eyes wary in her heart-shaped face. Then that sweet curve at the corner of her mouth made its appearance, and Serge fought free of an impulse to lean in and kiss her—because once he did that he'd be setting up a softer scenario than the one he had planned.

Straight up sex, not seduction. That was on the menu for tonight and tomorrow night.

He'd save the seducing for a woman who needed it.

CHAPTER THREE

CLEMENTINE lingered in her shabby rats' hole long enough to whip off her boots and slip on jeans and her trainers, then hightail it for the Grand Hotel Europe.

'You're doing *what*?' Luke slid his spectacles down to the end of his nose after listening to her story.

That those glasses were only for show made the gesture all the more endearing. They had known each other since Clementine's teenage years, when Luke had moved in next door. Meeting up with him again in a pub in London had been serendipitous. Without Luke, Clementine doubted she would have lasted more than a few months in London in that first year. He'd got her this job with the Ward Agency.

Clementine sat down on the end of his hotel bed. As head of public relations for the Verado shoot Luke got a whole room in the Grand Hotel Europe.

'It's just dinner, Luke.'

'No, he ogled you in a shoe store and followed you up the Nevsky—'

'And saved me.'

'Saved you—right.' Luke was all cynicism. 'Some guy stole your bag—'

'Two—two pretty nasty types. And then he just made the whole problem go away. Took me around in his limo.'

'Just you make sure that's all it is. Dinner.'

Clementine blew air up her fringe. 'Yes, Mum.'

Luke sat down beside her on the end of the bed. 'Sweetie, this guy isn't the one.'

'What one?'

'The one you're looking for.'

'I'm not—'

'Hey, Clem, remember who you're talking to. I was there last year, remember? To pick up the pieces. This guy is rich, right? Impressive? It sounds familiar to me. You're his type, darl, but he's not yours.'

No, she wasn't going to believe that. She wasn't going to let one bad experience alter the course of her life. But she had, hadn't she? And with Luke's reminder reality began to seep in fast. 'I don't know what's going to happen, but I really want to find out.' She could feel her face heating up.

Luke shook his head. 'I'm going to give you my mobile, okay? You ring me here at any hour. Wherever he takes you, you make sure you get the address, and if he wants to take you anywhere out of the city you say no—got it?'

'He's not a serial killer.'

'Probably not, but he knows you're a tourist. I can't believe you let some strange man ogle you in public.' But his blue eyes were twinkling. 'Those legs of yours should be insured.'

'They're not that good.' Clementine gave her thighs a pinch.

'They're sensational, princess. Now, listen to Uncle Luke—are you packing protection?'

Clementine blinked.

'Hell, Clem, I know you haven't been dating for a while, but nothing's changed, love.'

'Never rely on the guy,' intoned Clementine, wondering what Luke would say if he knew she'd never had casual sex in her life.

'Good girl.' Luke's expression softened. 'But you're not going to sleep with him, are you?'

Clementine went for an insouciant shrug, and Luke threw back his head and laughed. 'I'd love to be a fly on the wall when this bloke realises he's going home alone.'

'Maybe he just wants to get to know me better.'

Luke squeezed her knee. 'You go on thinking that, darl, and one day pigs will fly, my flirty little puritan.'

Puritan. Hardly.

She dated. Just not in the last twelve months. But mostly she worked. She'd been working from the age of seventeen, supporting herself in any number of menial jobs, studying at night school. It didn't leave a lot of time for relationships. Even friendships. She had loads of acquaintances—it went with her job—but only a couple of real friends. She knew the difference—just as she knew this date with Serge Marinov was a bit of fun to celebrate the end of her contract with Verado. She would flirt herself silly, and fantasise about what it would be like to be with a guy like this, and then—Cinderella-fashion—vanish at midnight.

Which reminded her... She retrieved Luke's condoms from her clutch bag and tossed them onto the nightstand.

She only did relationship sex, whatever Luke might think.

Given the circumstances of their meeting, she tossed aside her pile of short skirts and tight tops and took out the pale green satin dress she had packed for evenings out with her co-workers. On the hanger it looked plain, but once her curves had filled it, the wide belt cinching in her waist, it was something else.

Not that she was complaining about the curves. She couldn't help the way she was shaped, and despite all the good and bad attention it got her she wasn't going to waste her youth hiding behind acres of fabric. The pleated bodice covered up her chest modestly enough, and fastened in a halter around her neck, leaving what she considered her best feature—her shoulders—bare.

She wound her hair into a chignon and highlighted her mouth with deep pink lipstick, then slipped on her favourite strappy gold sandals.

From the window she saw a low-slung silver sports car enter the courtyard. It had to be him. She didn't want him coming up here again. It was too intimate, and it created a bit of a power imbalance she wasn't comfortable with.

There was an elevator in the building, but the concierge had advised her not to use it. She teetered a bit on her heels as she reached the bottom of the stairwell, and then she saw him striding towards her. She registered the moment he saw her—and that she had literally stopped him in his tracks.

'Hi,' she said, a tad breathlessly.

He wore tailored trousers, the shirt open at his throat was expensive, and the dark jacket screamed money. He was so physically imposing she ground to a halt. He didn't take his eyes off her, and there was nothing friendly in the look he gave her. For a moment all she saw was a flare of almost feral wildness in those beautiful Tartar features but then he was pulling it back, hooding his green eyes and covering the ground between them in a few steps.

Oh, Lord, she was toast.

Clementine drew her little clutch up to her waist, bent her elbows in a classic expectant pose, and waited for him.

'You look breathtaking.' His deep voice held the same appreciation she saw in his eyes, and for a giddy moment she thought he might bend to kiss her. But he merely reached for her elbow to guide her.

He looked so good—radiated such strength and confidence. What was it about this man that sent the blood thrumming through her body? It was all wrong, because this couldn't be anything more than dinner.

It was a lot more than dinner. If he could, he would have driven her straight to his place and set aside the 'getting to know you' niceties.

He couldn't help but admire her ability at sliding into a low-slung car. She had it down to an art form. Like much else. He watched her do it with only a slight hitching of her skirt and acknowledged she'd probably had lots of practice. Women like this required high performance cars—it came along with the body she had on offer, and Clementine was a piece of strategically engineered female design straight off the make-me-a-bombshell factory floor.

And he had her exactly where he wanted her.

He shut the door with an expensive-sounding *snuck*.

In under a minute he was beside her, his hand throwing the car into gear, taking in a discreet scan of that body.

'Ready?'

'As I'll ever be.'

Was she nervous? A little thrown by that thought, he let the motor throb and she actually jumped.

'Do it again,' she encouraged.

Smiling at her enjoyment, he reversed back towards the road with the expertise he'd built up with this car, aware he was showing off. He made a mental note. She liked the car. She liked surprises.

Then she opened her mouth and trotted out that cute little accent.

'So, where are we going, Slugger?'

'There's a place on the Neva I think you'll enjoy.'

He didn't want to take his eyes off her. How had he forgotten how much of a bombshell she was?

'This is an incredible car,' she commented.

'You like fast cars, *kisa*?'

She gave a little shrug. 'I guess. I like the rush.'

'I can open it up on the highway, but it's a no-go in the centre of the city.' He flicked a glance over her recumbent body. 'Why don't you sit back and relax and enjoy the ride?'

'I will.'

She had angled her body so that one leg was tucked behind the other, showcasing the long shapely line of her body from shoulder to breast and then to the luxurious curve of her hip and down her long, long legs to the clasp of her strappy shoes.

She was watching him; he could feel her curious gaze all over him. He almost growled as she said, 'I like the red leather. It looks expensive.'

They'd hit a snag in traffic, and instead of looking for a way out of it he leaned back and followed the length of her slender arm, the curve of her breast, lifted his eyes to the smile on her lips. Her eyes were gleaming mischief at him.

Everything about her told him she was practised at being provocative, but her smile and the look in her eyes spoke of the fun she was having with it.

'You like expensive things, *kisa*?'

'I really like it that you're rich,' she answered, batting those false eyelashes at him outrageously.

'And I really like a woman who appreciates leather. I liked your skirt this afternoon.'

'It's nice against my skin.' Her cheeks were starting to turn pink.

He had to ask. 'What else do you like against your skin?'

She laughed—that husky sound again. 'Warmth.' She suddenly sounded more down to earth. 'I get cold easily.'

'Good to know. I'll make it my responsibility tonight to keep you from getting cold.'

'You'll loan me your jacket?' Her eyes were sparkling. Her little smile had blossomed. 'Such a gentleman.'

He gave her a look, then a second look—as if to check and see that what he'd seen the first time hadn't altered—and then his eyes went all speculative. Male speculation.

Clementine drew herself together and settled back a little further in her seat. Maybe it was time to rein in the flirting.

She concentrated on the traffic outside, telling herself she could handle this guy. He asked her a few light questions about her time in St Petersburg and the atmosphere in the car settled down.

Feeling a little more confident, she covertly ran her gaze down the length of him. From his unruly close-cropped hair to the high planes of his face that revealed a southern Russian ancestry, the sensual jut of his mouth, the clean, solid lines of his jaw, down the strong column of his throat to his big husky body that made her cheeks burn. He was a sight to incite a female riot.

He looked at her again, and his eyes told her he knew exactly what she was doing.

Deciding to brazen it out, she said outright, 'I like your jacket.'

He smiled, forming appealing creases around his mouth that made him appear younger, more relaxed, as if he was enjoying her company. He got the joke. He'd play nice. She found she could relax.

The traffic eased as they went over the bridge. One of his hands rested lightly on the wheel, the other throwing gears as he negotiated the car in and out of snags and got them across town with a skill that mesmerised her.

Other images began to crowd her head and it was difficult to censor them. The way he had lunged at those men— all that aggression and cracking of bone—the way he had taken physical blows for her and scared those guys off. He'd done it because underneath all the *politesse* and courtesy he had shown her he was a big, strong, rough guy—and didn't it make all the girly parts of her tingle? She'd been on the money the first moment she saw him. They just didn't make men like this any more.

'You've gone quiet,' he said, in that deep, gravelly voice.

Pulling herself together, she slammed down the reply that was on her lips. *I was admiring the view.*

It really was time to pull the curtains on the flirting. She was having so much fun; it was like the old days, before she'd learned how her teasing could be misconstrued.

'I was thinking how light it is.'

'The White Nights are almost upon us. There's nothing quite like them.'

'It's a shame I won't be here to see them. But it's lovely right now. The light seems to mellow everything.'

He glanced at her. 'I find that too.'

She was something else, Serge reflected as he followed the twitch of her seductively rounded bottom into the restaurant. She was built the way women used to be, before diets and gyms and size zero. She was shaped this way because that was how nature had made her.

Mother Nature had done a superlative job.

He'd decided on an out-of-the-way place—small, cosy. There was a chance Clementine wouldn't like it. He'd brought a couple of women here before, watched them pick their way through the traditional Russian cuisine, listened to them dismiss their surroundings as *quaint*. But he was only in town for a couple of nights, and he loved the place. It was family run and noisy, and after eight there were gypsies.

Tonight wasn't about the location. It was merely a means to an end. But he wondered now why he had instantly thought of Kaminski's in relation to Clementine.

She was with him because she liked the money; she'd been pretty upfront about that with all her little flirty comments. Correspondingly, his feelings about this girl were down and dirty and basic. He had what she wanted, and she *definitely* had what he was after. Where he took her for dinner shouldn't figure into it.

Clementine tipped her head back as he escorted her inside, taking in the low-beamed ceiling. She scanned the room, already filled to capacity with diners. The décor was simple— round tables, wooden floors, murals of historical Russian scenes on the walls. He wondered what she thought of it.

She beamed at him. 'This is amazing. You are a dark horse. I expected a wine bar.'

The pleasure on her face took him off guard. Men's heads turned as they weaved between the tables and he felt an unfamiliar trickle of possessiveness.

Clementine seemed oblivious, giving him little backward glances over her shoulder as the restaurant's owner, Igor Kaminski, led them to their table. It brought back his uncharacteristic pursuit of her up the Nevsky, and fancifully he acknowledged that despite corralling her into a dinner date nothing had changed. She was still a step ahead, as elusive as ever, and he was enjoying it.

She gave an exclamation of delight as they reached their table, and he observed Igor grow about a foot as he gave her a potted history of the restaurant. Then she did that thing all women did as he seated her, smoothing her hands over her lavish hips and thighs to adjust her skirt. Somehow Clementine managed to turn it into a performance of female sensual pleasure. Igor stood there, a big smile on his broad, unhandsome face, watching her.

Am I supposed to hit him or order? Serge wondered, only half amused. He broke the spell by asking Clementine what she would like to drink.

She gave him one of those sweet little smiles. 'I'll leave it up to you.'

He ordered Georgian wine, and Igor returned with the menus himself, flanked by three men Serge knew were his sons. Clementine was enjoying herself, so he sat back and let the good-natured teasing unroll as *zakouski* was served and the men encouraged Clementine to taste—pickled mushrooms dipped in sour cream, different varieties of caviar, *ikra* fresh from the Caspian, salty *sevruga*. She washed it down with a mouthful of her wine, and Serge observed her trying to make sense of the heavily accented English, giving everyone equal attention.

Their table was busy in a noisy restaurant. This wasn't what he had pictured doing tonight. Food, alcohol, a little sweet-talking and Clementine gasping his name for a few enjoyable hours had been the plan.

Then Clementine leaned towards him and said, 'When does our date start, Slugger?'

Serge beckoned Igor over, whilst not taking his eyes off her, and murmured something to the owner. Their company evaporated, leaving them alone.

'Everyone's so friendly,' she confided over the rim of her glass. 'They certainly know you.'

'I think, *kisa*, the drawcard is you,' he observed wryly.

'Don't be silly.' As she slid her spoon through her soup her eyes teased him.

The little red candles in the glass bowls on the table between them cast a tantalising glow over her heart-shaped face. Her lightly tanned bare skin—what he could see of it—had the burnish of pale honey, extending from the curve of her shoulders, the slender length of her arms all the way down to those long-fingered hands and the gold bangles that clinked around her wrists.

A girl who looked like this, with the level of independence

Clementine exhibited, knew exactly what she was doing. She had to know what tonight was all about. She was going home on Saturday, which meant it had to be tonight or tomorrow.

The anticipation was beginning to burn.

'So, what is it that brings you here, Clementine?' He needed to do his bit—the what-do-you-do, tell-me-your-story routine—before the food and alcohol kicked in and he put thoughts of a soft mattress and his hard body into that pretty head of hers.

'Is it time to get to know one another?' she teased, wishing her tummy wasn't fluttering. She'd done this before—flirting in a public place. But it didn't feel public. It felt very, very intimate. Maybe too intimate for a first date.

He leaned towards her. 'Only if you want to, *kisa*.'

His eyes made her so aware of herself she was sure she was blushing. Trying to get back on track, she decided to fire some questions of her own at him.

'So you're a regular?'

'When I'm in town.'

'A different girl every time?'

'I've been known to drop in alone,' he replied, noticing the way her index finger had stopped drifting up and down the stem of her glass and she was gripping it now. What was the problem? Different girls? Did she need a little reassurance that he didn't make a habit of picking up women off the street?

Actually, this was a first—but he didn't want to draw attention to it, remind her they had only met this afternoon. For all her free and easy vibe, he was getting the distinct impression Clementine was more than capable of putting the brakes on this.

'So, tell me why you're in Petersburg?' He needed to distract her.

'I'm here for Verado—the Italian luxury goods company.'

'*Da*, I know them.'

'They're doing a promotion for their flagship store on the Nevsky. That's me—PR girl.'

Serge sat back, absorbing her pride in her job. PR. Of course. What else would a girl like this do but charm and influence people for a living?

'The grand opening is tomorrow night and then it's all over. Back to London.'

Serge had lost interest in her job. He was much more interested in the different lights he could see in her hair—golds and reds and browns. Was it natural? Probably not.

'I imagine you're very good at public relations?'

'I guess I am. I like people.' She noticed he was paying more attention to looking her over and it flustered her. 'I'm not that keen on Verado—all very old-world sexist misogynist management—but it's my job to make them look good, so I do what I can.'

Serge was tempted to comment that the fleapit she was currently inhabiting told him more about her job than words. Instead he said, 'What else do you do, Clementine, besides influence people?'

'Do you really want to know?'

There was something in the way she asked, angling up her chin but with a hint of vulnerability in her eyes. He hadn't expected that.

'Yeah, I do,' he said, surprising himself.

She gave him a curious look he couldn't read. 'Truthfully, not much lately. All I seem to do is work.'

'You're a beautiful woman. No serious boyfriend?'

She met his eyes candidly. 'I wouldn't be out with you if I had.'

Serge lounged back, rolling his shoulders, all big lazy Russian male.

Honestly, thought Clementine, what *was* it about men and competition?

He sipped his brandy, his eyes warm on her face, her bare shoulders.

'What about you?' She tossed back her hair, giving him her hundred-watt smile. 'Why isn't a rich, gorgeous guy like you taken?'

'Gorgeous?' He looked amused. 'Good to know I measure up, *kisa*.'

He hadn't answered the question. Clementine's smile faded. Okay, it didn't mean he was married or had a girl-friend or anything.

'So no one's waiting up for you at home?' The question sounded so gauche she could have kicked herself.

'No.' He settled his glass on the table. 'No one.'

It bothered her. He studied her suddenly tense face intently. 'What gave you the idea I was married?'

'A girl can't be too careful,' she said lightly.

Da, he could imagine an endless stream of guys hitting on her. Married men. Single. Hell, gay men. Any man with a pulse.

He had a personal distaste for adultery. He didn't fool around with married women, ever. So why in the hell did it annoy him so much that she had brought it up?

It was the idea of a married man making a play for her.

Any man.

Because he wanted her. For himself. Exclusively.

And why in the hell did he feel that at any moment she could get up, excuse herself from the table and never come back?

Clementine knew there was something about her that at-tracted guys like this. Good-looking, confident men, who thought they could bulldoze her into bed. And they always had money. Luke said it was her personality, but he meant her confidence. She was a girl who liked to dress up and flirt. She always had. She intimidated a lot of nice guys who were too scared to approach her, imagining every night of her week was booked, or who—like Serge—wanted to know why she wasn't in a relationship.

She had been. In two short-lived unsatisfactory relationships with nice guys who in the end had bored her silly. She recognised now that they had made her feel less like herself and more like the girl she imagined she should be. Clementine with the lights turned down.

Serge watched the emotions flickering across Clementine's expressive face. Her guarded eyes suddenly made him feel uncomfortable with his crass plan for a couple of nights' entertainment.

'You still haven't told me what you do,' she said, sitting back.

She genuinely wanted to get to know him, and something tightened up in his chest.

'I'm in sports management,' he replied, unease making him brief.

'Is it interesting?'

'Sometimes.'

Clementine's heart sank. He didn't want to share any information about himself with her. For a moment she was thrown back to that strange whirlwind of months, almost a year ago, when she had been pursued by another wealthy man who had dodged personal questions as he smothered her in unprecedented romantic attention.

After her last break-up she had gone back to dating casually—until Joe Carnegie. She had met him through one of her PR jobs and he'd been a client—which meant he was off-limits by her own personal code. But the minute the job was done he'd been on the phone, roses had been delivered to her door. He had encouraged her to play up to her 'gifts', as he'd called them, supplying her with spectacular dresses he could show her off in. They would arrive boxed before a date. He had groomed her for a role and she had let him.

She had been so naive.

He'd wined her and dined her and treated her like a princess. She had opened herself up to him so quickly, so easily. Until the evening he'd taken her to a swish restaurant, the night she had decided their relationship should move beyond the bedroom door, and presented her with a real estate portfolio. He had purchased her a flat—a place he could visit her whilst he was in town.

It had never been about her. It had been all about the way she looked on his arm and how well she would perform in his bed. And then it had got worse. A couple of days later she had read in the newspaper about his engagement to a French pop star, who was also the daughter of a leading industrialist. A woman from his own social strata. She had been something else all along. He had always intended her to be his mistress on the side.

The memory still burned. He'd done a job on her and she was still paying the price. She had told herself she wasn't going to let it ruin tonight, but already she was second-guessing Serge's motives. He had been nothing but a gentleman—but so too had Joe Carnegie. She'd already come to the conclusion long ago that she wasn't very good at working men out.

She looked around the restaurant, with its ambient lights and the laughter of other patrons and the wonderful smells of old-style Russian food, and realised she'd landed in yet another one of her stupid romantic fantasies.

'Excuse me,' she said abruptly, shifting to her feet. Serge rose. 'Powder room,' she murmured, unable to look at him.

The mirror in the ladies' reflected back her pale made-up face and she cursed her lavish use of the mascara wand, because those tears prickling in her eyes were going to leave tracks.

She wasn't sad. She was damn angry. With herself.

How in the hell did she get herself into these situations? Did she have 'sucker' tattooed on her forehead?

Two other women joined her at the taps, and Clementine made a show of washing her hands, checking her hair.

She looked up and recognised one of the girls as their waitress—one of the Kaminski daughters.

'Serge Marinov,' said the girl, making a sizzle gesture. 'Lucky you.'

Yes, lucky me. Clementine gave her dress a tug and shook her head at her reflection. She was being an idiot. She had an incredible man sitting out there in that restaurant, waiting for her, and she was hiding in the ladies' loo because one time some other guy had measured her value as low. It was time to suck it up and get on with her life. She was calling the shots, and if Serge Marinov had some stupid male agenda—well, she had one of her own.

As she approached the table he caught sight of her, and something akin to relief washed over his face.

Clementine almost ground to a halt. Well, fancy that. Guess who was on the hop. Confidence lifted her spine. He stood up as she approached, and she smiled to herself as he seated her.

'Miss me?' She couldn't resist the question.

'Every minute, *kisa*.'

'Are we still eating?'

'Coffee?'

'Tea.'

When the samovar came the gypsy entertainment had invaded the restaurant and it became impossible to be heard above the music.

Serge watched Clementine coming under the spell of the

performance, finding himself baffled by her. As the restaurant erupted into clapping she joined in, humming along unselfconsciously. When the performers came round to collect gold coins she fumbled in her clutch bag.

He reached across and laid a stilling hand on hers, tossed some money into the skirts of the girl.

Clementine shook a finger at him. 'I can pay my way, Mr Millionaire.'

'You're with me,' he replied, as if that said everything.

Clementine's inner princess sighed, but her capable independent outer working girl patted his arm. 'Come on, rich guy—let's get out of here and I'll buy you an ice cream.'

There was a flurry as they left. Clementine had made an impression on the Kaminskis, which was fine, but next time he came in here without her there were going to be questions. She was that sort of girl.

Hell, he had his own questions. Nothing had gone to plan. He should be rushing her across town right now to his place, after a meal spent trading sexual banter. Instead he'd spent the evening watching her enjoy herself—except for that bizarre moment he'd thought she'd got up and left the restaurant.

Walked out on him.

Even now he wanted to take her hand, weld her to his side, but she kept a neat distance between their bodies, held onto her purse with both hands, that classic little pose of hers complementing the sway in her walk.

Although it was after ten the evening was still light. They were so close to the White Nights of June. Serge shrugged off his jacket as they strolled down towards the embankment. The urge to slide an arm around her was very strong but he reined it in. Somehow this had turned into a real date. A first date.

Clementine looked up at him. 'Thank you for inviting me.

All I've been doing lately is working. It's nice to put on a frock and be taken out somewhere fun.'

Bozhe, she was so sincere. And he was buying it. It probably made him a sap, but there was something about her in this moment that made him want to believe her.

'You're a very easy woman to please, *kisa*,' he said at last, 'but the evening has hardly begun, no?'

Clementine hid a smile. 'Maybe for you, Slugger, but I'm beat and I've got an early start tomorrow.'

And didn't that just tie up all his expectations in knots and toss them in the river? Serge rolled his shoulders. 'Right,' he said—and everything fell into place.

She'd known all along tonight wasn't going to end in bed, which meant the little act in the car had been for her own amusement. He remembered the sparkle in her eyes, the invitation to laugh along with her.

He'd missed it because he'd been deep down in lust land.

Which meant tonight was a lost opportunity—for both of them. She was going home on Saturday, leaving him with a decision to make.

Was she worth the pursuit? Or—the better question—should he be messing with her? This nice girl? All sweet and sincere? And didn't that just get him in the traditional Russian male part of himself that he didn't make a habit of showing off? Where had he got the idea she wouldn't need seducing? Why *shouldn't* she make him work for it?

Instincts he didn't have a whole lot of familiarity with told him he needed to handle this delicately. Another, more familiar instinct was telling him to take her in his arms and drive every thought she could possibly have about other men out of her head—at least until tomorrow. It had to be tomorrow. Because she was going back to London on Saturday.

And if he didn't have her in his arms in one form or another tonight he was going to go crazy.

He reached and caught her hand—something he'd been wanting to do all night. She turned towards him, expression expectant, amused. He closed the space between them and lifted his other hand to hook one of her artfully liberated coils of hair away from her cheek. Her smile faded, her eyes grew a little rounder, her mouth softened.

'You're killing me, Clementine,' he said in Russian, and moved in to put himself out of his misery.

In that moment she made a soft little sound of dismay and to his surprise turned away, slipping her hand free of his with a nervous laugh.

'I still want to buy you that ice cream,' she said over her shoulder.

Ice cream. Not sex. Not even a kiss. Not tonight.

She began walking, swaying a little on those silly heels, and he stood there, stock still, gazing after her.

She threw him a backward glance.

'Coming, Slugger?'

She was going the wrong way. The ice cream vendors were in the other direction. But her question dissolved into a teasing smile, and without giving it a second thought he took off after her.

CHAPTER FOUR

SERGE had spent the morning listening to the argument that had broken out between the president of his company and the man he trusted above all others: trainer Mick Forster. Broadcast from the boardroom in the Marinov Building in New York City to the screen facing him, it had convinced him of one thing.

'I'll be at JFK tomorrow lunchtime,' he said briefly, and closed his laptop. He pushed away from the desk, striding over to the windows of his Fontanka Canal apartment.

He'd been out of the country less than a day and he already had problems with a young fighter, Kolcek, who was up on assault charges and getting a raft of publicity that was not the kind the organisation needed. More importantly they were behind on the stadium going up in New York—an ongoing issue—but his management team were scrambling in the onslaught of media attention, as evidenced by this morning.

He didn't like the look of it.

Yet all he could think about was that because of tardy contractors and a coked-up fighter who needed to be cut loose he was going to lose Clementine Chevalier.

Sexy, tempting, guarded Clementine. What *was* her game?

He'd taken her back to that dismal lodging last night, insisted on walking her up to her door. He'd been thinking more about the woeful security than infiltrating her defences when he'd lingered in her doorway. He'd seen once more the drab room, and then his eyes had lit on the condoms sitting on her bedside table right beside the door.

For a girl who didn't kiss on a first date she had come prepared.

Was she sleeping with someone else? Was that the problem?

She'd said she didn't have a boyfriend, but that didn't mean she wasn't sexually active. In fact it would be a crime against nature if she wasn't.

Except right now he only wanted her sexually active with *him*.

He acknowledged he'd been unusually disappointed by the discovery she wasn't quite what she seemed. For a few hours there he'd been enjoying the fantasy: man and woman out on a date, the simplicity and honesty of their interaction. Yet when it came down to it he would have left it there last night. Nice girls didn't feature in his personal life.

He wasn't in the market for a wife, or even a significant other, if that was the phrase, and the girl Clementine had seemed to be for a while there would have expected the whole romantic package.

He didn't do romance. He did sex.

And what a girl like Clementine was offering in all her luscious glory was clearly uncomplicated, sizzling sex. Oblivion between her lush thighs. The promise in those sparkling eyes at the beginning of the night. The complete lack of emotional ties a girl like that came with. The sort of girl who could be bought.

A former lover had once accused him of being cold-blooded, but he doubted that. It was why he picked his partners very carefully. Women to whom under no circumstances he would become attached. Women who liked what he could give them more than anything he might promise for the future.

He had seen what emotional attachments could do—the mess they created, the havoc they played with innocent lives. He had seen it played out in his parents' lives.

His father had loved his mother completely—taking over her life, turning all of their lives into a twopenny opera. When he'd died Serge had been ten years old and his mother had been devastated. Barely able to cope. He had seen both the intensity of love and the chaos it wrought when it went awry, or was simply taken away. His mother had remarried for financial reasons. Her second husband had beaten her for seven long years before she'd taken a familiar way out with an overdose of pills.

He had been away at boarding school, and later in the military. He had known nothing of her life until he'd stood by her grave with distant relatives who had spent no little time filling him in on the details of her disastrous second marriage—details no one had seen fit to give him during her sad life.

Emotional detachment came easily to him.

So last night, when Clementine had seen the direction of his gaze and blood-red colour had risen up to the roots of her hair, he had been curious to see how she would play it. She had kept her cool and stared him down. Before babbling. He had to go now. She had his number. He had hers. Maybe he could call next time he was in London.

At first he'd thought she was giving him the brush-off. He couldn't remember the last time that had happened to him. This gorgeous, sexy, clever girl who wanted him to believe she had the morals of a nun, or next to it, was handing him his walking papers.

Then it had all made sense. She had put the ball in his court—was waiting to be asked to see him again. His body was saying yes but his mind had gone stone-cold. Something about the entire scenario: foreign girl in a cheap hotel, holding back on any sexual contact, waiting for him to make this about more than a one-night encounter.

He hadn't been born yesterday. It wasn't going to happen.

He'd had no choice but to leave without making any definite plans with her, but as he had walked away down the dank, dimly lit corridor he'd glanced back and found she was peeking out into the hallway, drawing back as he caught her and closing the door.

And that was that.

Except he was still thinking about her after a conference call, an hour looking at complicated design plans and a lot of coffee. He hadn't slept well. Sexual frustration could do that. He'd had two cold showers—one on arriving home and another first thing this morning. There were other women he could call, but it was Clementine he was interested in.

He swigged another mouthful of coffee.

Where was she now? Working her little job? PR for Verado. He knew Giovanni Verado. High-end masculine luxury goods. She'd meet a lot of men in that job. Men with money—which was probably the point.

The nice girl had evaporated around about the time he'd spotted those prophylactics. If she wasn't sleeping with *him* on a first date, she was sleeping with someone—or planning to.

His mouth twisted cynically. She liked the money. She probably had several guys with the right cars, the right lifestyle on a string and she was working it. Girls who looked like Clementine, with that level of independence and confidence, were never single. There was always something going on.

Yet there was something else about her.

He could still hear her husky laughter, see her clapping her hands, singing along with the music last night although she didn't know the words and it was a foreign language to her. He remembered how she had been dismayed by his attempt to kiss her and then covered it up.

He wanted to phone her and hear her voice. He wanted to see her. More basically he wanted those long legs wrapped around him and her little sounds of pleasure urging him on.

But he was going to New York and time was what he didn't have. She'd said something about a launch tonight. He could turn up, try his luck.

A wry smile touched his mouth. Life wasn't about luck. It was about going after what you wanted with single-minded determination and not stopping until you had it. In business and personally.

No, better to ring and arrange to meet up with her. He didn't want to give her much choice, and in the flesh, in broad daylight, he'd be a little more persuasive than he'd been last night. He'd respected her boundaries but it hadn't got him far. He hadn't turned a single gym into a billion-dollar business without knowing when to push.

Clementine settled at a pavement table, thanking the waiter who brought her a coffee. Across the road was the Verado flagship store, where she'd spent the morning and most of this last week. She'd agreed to meet Serge at this café because of its proximity to work.

When she'd heard his voice a couple of hours ago her whole world had ground to a halt. She'd drifted away from the group she was talking to and said breathlessly, 'Serge,' and literally heard his intake of breath. His voice had been pitched lower then, darkly seductive in its accented rumble. She'd closed her eyes just listening to it, lost in the sensual spell.

She really hadn't thought he would call.

But he had, and now she was waiting for him because he

wanted to see her, speak to her, probably organise a second date. He'd have to be quick. Her plane flew out at four tomorrow morning. He was keen, though. Barely twelve hours had passed since they'd said goodnight.

He might ask her to stay a little longer, and a big part of her was considering saying yes—oh, hell, yes.

Imagining she had lost him last night had made her a little more reckless than usual this morning. She had lain awake going over every minute of their date, isolating everything that told her Serge was nothing like Joe Carnegie. All of her instincts told her he was a good guy. He hadn't pushed when it had been clear enough he had hoped for more. She wasn't going to read anything into that. All men wanted more. It was just some could be obnoxious about it.

What bothered her was that she had let Joe Carnegie come between them at a crucial moment. She had wanted to kiss Serge last night but fear had held her back. Fear of it only being some sort of sexual conquest on his part, of opening herself up to another man only to have her sensibilities ripped apart. It was only a kiss, she reminded herself, but she had never felt so strongly attracted to a man in her life, and she needed to be sure before she went any further.

Thinking about it now, she tried not to have any regrets. Serge hadn't walked away, and this morning he wanted to see her. He was keen. He liked her. He was making an effort.

Except he was late.

She glanced at her little watch, with its pretty diamond-studded face. She had bought it for herself soon after she'd landed the job with Verado. Most people had parents or significant others to help mark special occasions like that. A psychologist friend had told her it was important that when you didn't have those mainstays in your life to make an effort to look after yourself, and so she had. And every morning when she slipped it onto her wrist she felt she was taking care of herself.

I'll give him another five minutes, she told herself. He's only a quarter of an hour late. Maybe it was traffic. But definitely five minutes. Maybe at a stretch ten…

'Hello, beautiful girl.'

He was idling in front of her table, all height and muscles and testosterone. She took in the jeans, white T-shirt, brown leather jacket. He was freshly shaved, hair tousled, energy rolling off him in waves. Clementine didn't look at him so much as collide with his deep green Tartar eyes, and her heart began to do a thuddy thing that made it hard to hear over the pounding of blood in her ears.

'Oh, hi.' She endeavoured to sound casual.

He gestured abruptly to the waiter. 'What would you like to eat, *kisa*?'

'Oh, I can't stay,' said Clementine, getting herself together. 'I'm supposed to be at my job, and you're late, so I can only give you five minutes.'

He dragged a chair up close to her and straddled it. As he dropped in front of her she gave an involuntary jump. His sudden physical proximity made it very difficult to hold her ground and her first instinct was to retreat back in her chair. He smiled knowingly, as if her reticence was exactly what he was after.

'Give me five minutes, then.'

Unaccountably she flashed back to how last night had ended. Even now her cheeks grew warm as she remembered Luke's condoms, like neon signs pulsing on her bedside table. He probably hadn't thought anything of it, but she had blushed, and he'd certainly seen that, and she had spent last night tossing and turning—convinced he'd seen through her to the gauche girl she sometimes felt herself still to be. That was before Joe Carnegie had torn the scales from her eyes.

He was studying her face, her pink cheeks, lingering on her mouth. 'You are a gorgeous woman, Clementine.'

She'd been told that before, although it wasn't strictly true. She was far from being a beauty. Her nose was slightly too long, her chin a little pointed, and she had too many freckles…

'Am I?' She made herself hold his gaze. 'Is that what you came to tell me?'

'I haven't stopped thinking about you.'

Oh, she liked that. 'I'm flattered.'

His eyes were knowing, full of promise. They were playing some sort of game, she recognised, except she didn't know the rules.

'I've got a proposal for you, *kisa*.'

Clementine gave an internal sigh of relief. Mentally she began shifting her entire afternoon. Surely she could carve out a few hours before the launch, when all the work had been done, and she *had* planned to take a nap and get ready for the evening.

She really, *really* wanted to spend more time with him.

Serge studied her expectant expression and the rest of her, liking what he saw. She was all dressed up this morning, in a dark blue suit, but managed by dint of the pinched waist of her jacket and the cling of her pencil skirt to look outrageously sexy. In a classy sort of way. This look played havoc with his hormones in a way the tight leather skirt hadn't. He liked her all covered up. It made it more of a challenge to imagine what was underneath.

Well, here went nothing.

'I've got to fly to New York City tomorrow on business, I'd like you to come with me.'

Clementine felt as if she'd been slammed at speed into a wall.

'I'm staying in the penthouse suite at the Four Seasons for

a week. I think you'd enjoy yourself, Clementine—a little pampering, some nice restaurants, buying you some pretty dresses, see a show…me.'

Him. Clementine felt sick. She was thrust back in time to Joe's smooth delivery as she had bleated across the table at him, 'But I don't want you to buy me a place to live. Anyway, I have a place to live.' And he'd frowned and told her he wasn't spending his free time in London shagging her in a shared flat.

That brutal. And that fast she'd lost all her girlish illusions. The next morning the newspaper had shredded her self-respect.

'I understand it's presumptuous, but I need to be there, and I think we have something, Clementine. I'd like to explore that.'

She picked herself up and brushed herself off. 'Would you?' Her voice came out like a shard of ice.

It was happening all over again.

He was offering her stuff as if she were for sale. As if her body was for sale. Because *come with me to New York City, baby* wasn't an invitation to enjoy his hospitality without serving herself up to him on a plate.

More fool her.

All she'd wanted was a date. A chance to spend some more time with him, get to know him. All of it hopelessly naive.

Right in front of her was the reason she had tried to settle down with boys who didn't push, who weren't driven by their libidos—nice, gentle guys who in the end left her cold. Men like Serge were the other end of the spectrum—exciting, challenging, but fuelled by testosterone, confident in their ability to run the world on their own terms and by extension run her.

Well, she was running in the other direction. She'd learned her lesson. She wasn't some rich man's plaything.

She stood up so abruptly her chair almost toppled over onto the pavement. 'That's quite an offer, Serge, but I think you've got the wrong girl,' she said hotly.

He was on his feet, not looking so sure of himself now. She could actually see him thinking. Probably working out which girl was next on his list to invite for a little nookie in New York. God, men could make you feel like crap.

'Clem?'

She turned as Luke's hands closed around her upper arms.

'Are you okay, babe?' He was looking Serge up and down. 'Have you upset her, mate?'

Given any other situation, Luke's suddenly aggressive stance in support of her would have been amusing. It was kind of like a meerkat standing up to a Siberian tiger.

Serge's gaze had narrowed on Luke's hands, and she couldn't believe what she was witnessing. Did he actually think she now belonged to him? One date and her body was his to ship off to his penthouse for his use? Was he going to take on Luke? Because she didn't think her gentle friend was going to come off pretty face intact!

She shook her head at Luke. 'It's all fine, sweetie. Let's get back.' She cast Serge a frosty look. 'I'm finished here.'

Serge went cold. *What in the hell had just happened?*

Had he not been explicit enough in everything he'd offered her? It was a very lucrative deal over and above the sex. What was going on? Was she holding out for something else?

Okay, maybe he'd been a little cocky about it. But he'd been so convinced she'd say yes.

She'd said no. *Had* she said no?

And now she was with this metrosexual guy who was bristling like a guard dog at him.

As if he'd ever hurt a woman in his life. Suddenly what had seemed simple and straightforward felt like a huge mistake.

'I have your answer, Clementine,' he said formally.

'Forgive me if I've offended you. It wasn't meant that way.' He wasn't going to stand there and pressure her in this thug role he was beginning to feel he'd been cast in. 'Enjoy the rest of your stay.'

His good manners welded Clementine to the spot. All of a sudden the last few minutes seemed to have rolled up into a ball of confusion in her head. Maybe he hadn't propositioned her. Maybe it was up-front an offer to spend time with him— his best effort to fit her into his schedule. She knew all about seventy-hour weeks. He said he had business in New York City. It wasn't a pleasure trip for him. Maybe he just wanted to get to know her…

Had she read him wrongly? Was it just an innocent invitation from a very busy man?

Suddenly the entire world seemed to narrow down to that pinprick of vision she had fastened on the spread of Serge's muscular shoulders as he walked away.

Was she really never going to see him again?

You'll never meet anyone like him again, a little voice whispered in her head. You knew that yesterday—the moment you clapped eyes on him. You knew that he was special. You knew he had been made especially for you. He was your fantasy come to life.

And maybe you're his. Maybe he's feeling exactly the way you do and you've said those terrible things to him and you're never going to see him again.

What had she done?

What had she done?

Her feet were moving. She could see him a long way from her now. She wanted to run but it wouldn't be any use. She could see him getting into his car. She opened her mouth to call out to him but her throat had closed up, and then she just stopped, dead in the middle of the pavement, as his sports car swiftly rejoined the traffic.

She still had Luke's mobile. She had Serge's number. She began rummaging in her bag. What would she say to him? *I've changed my mind. I want to come. I want to see where this leads me...where you lead me...*

'Clem.' Luke had caught up with her. 'What is it, darl? What's going on?'

It was the reality of Luke's voice and the memories that came back with it that had her dropping the phone back into her bag, the frenzy of feeling subsiding. Luke had helped pick up the pieces when the Joe Carnegie incident had exploded in her face. She had slept in his and his partner Phineas's spare room for a week, and he had cared for her with all the kindness and tenderness she had never found in any of the guys she'd dated.

Serge Marinov was no different. She'd imagined him as her hero come to life, but her history told her the odds were against it ever working out.

Her best friend Luke was a reminder that she deserved more.

It wasn't in her nature to mope. There was work to do, and she was kept busy all afternoon sweet-talking the snooty representative of a high-profile fashion magazine who had been housed in the Grand Hotel Europe instead of the Astoria Hotel.

Try the Vassiliev Building, she thought, even as she twittered on about the incredible history of the Grand Hotel. The painful irony being she only had those stories because Serge had told them to her on their magical date. She must have been convincing because the woman, mollified, agreed to a larger suite in the hotel.

I can do this, she thought, walking through the lobby. She was spending the night with Luke, unable to face even one more night in the fleapit. Her dress was upstairs and she intended to take a long hot shower.

She had a party to go to. Parties she could do. It was men she had a problem with.

As she stepped into the elevator one of the species gave her a covert once-over and she narrowed her eyes, mean as a dunked cat.

She was still feeling prickly as she moved through the crowd at the launch. The fashion show didn't go smoothly, but it was the hiccups that made it fun. The models galloped down the runway—pretty boys carting luggage, wearing watches, flashing cocky grins at the cameras. Clementine did her usual meet-and-greet, brain switched off, dress switched on. She loved this black velvet evening gown. It was elegant and flattering, and Verado had loaned her a string of diamonds to wear around her neck. She was a walking advertisement tonight, and it suited her down to the ground. She was good at her job and it correspondingly made her feel good about herself.

If men thought she could be bought maybe it was time to start asserting her financial independence. She earned a reasonable living. She just had an expensive clothing habit. But she was twenty-five years old. It was time to stop living like a teenager and start looking towards her future. The fairytale husband and three children might never materialise—and given her romantic history and today's disaster it felt further away than ever. She needed to look after herself. Protect herself. And that meant settling into her career.

She was turning from one group of buyers to cross the floor to another when she saw him.

Six and a half feet of Russian male wasn't easy to miss. He was all dressed up in a tux, his unruly hair tamed. He looked devastating, a powerful man among many lesser men, and for a moment in time she merely stared. Until she recognised the older gentleman he was speaking to was Giovanni Verado himself.

Verado was a notorious womaniser. Probably swapping notes, she thought snappily. But in her heart she knew it wasn't true. Serge had been nothing but up-front with her, and she kept replaying his expression when she had thrown his invitation back in his face. He'd actually looked baffled.

But why was he here? He knew this was her job. She'd certainly blabbed all about it last night, revealing more than she was comfortable with now. She'd said some indiscreet things about Verado. Serge hadn't mentioned a connection to the owner. Serge hadn't said much of anything that was personal.

Her mouth suddenly felt very dry, her palms moist.

It didn't fit the character of the man she believed she knew to drop her in it. Why would he? Why would Verado care about her opinions as long as she did her job?

No, what was worrying her was that she suddenly realised she knew nothing about him other than the fact he made her senses whirl every time he looked at her, and she'd felt so safe and admired in his company.

Right now her heart was leaping into her mouth because he'd come, and it couldn't possibly be a coincidence.

He'd come for her.

A rush of nerves bubbled up in her tummy like champagne. All of the tales she had told herself this afternoon about Serge Marinov being just some guy disintegrated as she entertained the possibility that she was getting a second chance, and now she could give him one.

Clementine tugged at her dress, straightened her shoulders, and headed over. She wasn't going to make his finding her any more difficult than it needed to be.

There were a lot of people between them, and then there was a break in the crowd and she saw what she had missed before. There was a woman with him—a slender brunette in a sparkly blue dress. She was beautiful, perhaps around thirty, and she had her hand on his arm. It was that territorial display that stopped Clementine in her tracks.

Almost. She'd almost made a fool of herself.

Another woman. Well, that was quick. But what had she expected? Clearly it was exactly what he'd been thinking this morning in that fraught silence. Not, *I'm disappointed Clementine won't be coming with me.* Simply, *Where's the next in line?*

Her shoulders dropped. She felt as if she was getting a crash course in male mating patterns. Was it really that easy for him? She had opened herself up last night to a connection between them and she couldn't close it off so easily. Didn't it mean anything to him?

Clementine stuffed down the sudden sharp pain in her chest. She was such an idiot. Him and Joe Carnegie—both of them deserved flogging. Except, watching Serge now, she recognised he wasn't really anything like Joe. He hadn't hidden anything. He'd been up-front all the way. Probably in his world that was how these things were done. He was hardly going to be her *boyfriend* by any stretch of the imagination. She couldn't imagine him dropping by on a Friday night at her flat with a pizza and lying on the sofa rubbing her feet.

He turned his head suddenly and scanned the crowd, and Clementine froze. She knew when he found her because she felt it like a jolt down to her toes. She recognised the flare of those green eyes, how her own were probably huge in her frozen face. She waited for him to dismiss her, to turn away, but instead his features firmed. He looked resolved.

She spun around before she could see anything that would make mincemeat of her feelings and made her way blindly towards the bar. She needed a drink. She needed hard liquor and fast.

If I'd said yes I could be with him now, she thought helplessly. I could be in that woman's shoes. I could be going with him to New York.

She reached the bar and asked for a Bloody Mary. It wasn't something she normally drank, but she needed something sharp and unfamiliar to snap herself out of this mood. Before it arrived she felt him rather than saw him. The solidity of his body; the turning of other people's heads. There were people everywhere, brushing shoulders, bumping elbows, but she knew it was him.

She gravitated towards him like a planet to the sun and looked up into those eyes of his. She said softly, 'Yes,' then hopelessly, 'I wish I'd said yes. I should have said yes.'

He looked stunned, poleaxed. But at least he didn't look angry or, worse, amused.

I am crazy, thought Clementine. Why did I tell him that? He doesn't care.

Serge experienced the now familiar surge of frustration connected with this woman. What was she playing at?

As Clementine pushed her way through the crowd his first instinct was to pursue her. It was basically his foremost instinct where she was concerned, he acknowledged with more frustration. Yet all he could do was watch her vanish into the crowd, even as his thoughts curled possessively around her admission.

That's the girl. Run away. You won't be getting far.

He had to deal with Raisa before he tried anything bolder with Clementine, and that would take tact, but once he was free he would be going after her.

Clementine had better be able to run fast on those impossible heels of hers, because she'd just declared herself his and he was coming to collect.

CHAPTER FIVE

'DARL, can you cheer up? You're frightening the other passengers.'

'Sorry, I didn't get much shut-eye.' They were queuing to put their bags through at the airport, and at four in the morning she felt just about dead on her feet. But she manufactured a smile for Luke, remembering the old adage to fake it until you make it.

Which she would be applying to her life the minute she got back to London. The last couple of days had impressed on her as nothing else had the need to get back on track with her life. It was time to let the past go. She'd allowed her experience with Joe Carnegie to completely blow anything she might have with Serge Marinov right out of the water. He held a measure of blame, too. If he'd been less forceful she might have been able to navigate around his invitation. Instead they'd both hit a wall—his expectations versus hers— and he had moved on.

'Still thinking about the gorgeous brute?' commented Luke from behind her, resting his chin on her shoulder. 'I thought he was going to pop me one yesterday.'

'I'm sorry about that.' She squeezed his arm. 'I didn't mean for you to get involved.'

'He seems pretty keen on you, Clem.'

'What? No, that's all over.'

'Okey-doke. But I'm not sure he agrees.'

Clementine frowned and moved forward in the queue. Why was Luke speaking in the present tense? Why were people in the queue looking at her?

'Clementine.' His voice turned her around. Deep, dark Russian male.

Serge. So close to her she didn't know where to look. So she looked up and tumbled into his eyes again. It happened each and every time, and she couldn't work out why. Her breath hitched. She didn't know what to say.

His mouth eased into a knowing smile. 'Come with me now to New York, *kisa*.'

Go with him? She was boarding a plane... Of all the unreasonable...

'Are these your bags?'

To her astonishment a young man in a jacket and tie took hold of her suitcase and overnight bag.

'Just a minute—those are my things!'

Serge made a casual gesture with one hand and the guy froze mid-move.

'You have changed your mind?' That smile was still curling wickedly at the corner of his mouth, as if it couldn't possibly be true.

'No, I—' She looked around to find Luke madly nodding at her like a jack-in-the-box.

She rolled her eyes at him.

'Perhaps you would like to say goodbye to your friend and then join me.' Serge's eyes had narrowed on Luke. Clementine already recognised that slight hardening of his mouth.

He was jealous. Well, maybe a teensy weensy bit. Which reminded her...

'What about your girlfriend?'

'*Sto?*' He looked genuinely puzzled.

'Last night. Remember? She was your date. Or are there so many we start to blur?'

Luke snickered.

'Raisa is a friend, nothing more.' He actually sounded a bit affronted, as if he couldn't believe they were having this conversation.

The lady in front of her looked Serge up and down. 'I wouldn't trust him, love. Too good-looking.'

Too good-looking. It was an understatement. He was a big, tough gorgeous Cossack. Every other woman in the vicinity was glued to him.

Clementine bit her lip. It was funny, and she had to admit it was extremely exciting.

She deserved some fun—to be a light-hearted girl again instead of the cautious woman she had become, constantly second-guessing herself.

And he was here. He'd come for her. It was ridiculous to consider any of this romantic but she did. It was the most romantic thing that had ever happened to her.

'All right,' she heard herself saying, throwing herself off the emotional diving board. 'Why not?'

Satisfaction entered the look Serge was giving her, and she noticed a little breathlessly that his gaze took a round trip of her body but she decided to let it pass. Right now she just wanted to revel in her romantic moment.

Serge offered his hand and she took it. It was big and rough and enclosed hers completely. It felt unfailingly intimate. Even this man's hands were fantasy material.

'I'll call you when I arrive,' she said belatedly to Luke, who was grinning and gazing up at Serge like a fan girl.

'You do that, Clem. Have fun, darl.'

They had only gone a few hundred metres when she realised they were moving away from the public terminal.

'Where are we going?'

'My plane, *kisa.*'

'Your plane?'

'Private jet.' He glanced down at her and was met with a look of complete wonderment. Cynically, he wondered if that little bit of information was going to get him laid before the plane even took off.

She dug in her heels as they left the terminal and hit the tarmac. Ahead was indeed a private plane—a state-of-the-art jet. Nerves set in like never before. She yanked on his hand. 'Serge, I need to make a few things clear before we go any further.'

He looked at her impatiently. 'We'll discuss it on board.'

'No, we need to discuss it now. I have…' She didn't know how to phrase it, so she grabbed the nearest equivalent. 'I have some terms and I want to make sure you're okay with them. I don't want any misunderstandings.'

He gave her a look of sheer disbelief. 'You cannot be serious?'

Her heart stuttered at that. He wasn't going to be difficult about this, was he? It wasn't a deal-breaker?

'I am serious,' she said more crossly. 'And I want to be up-front about this.' She'd come to a complete halt, pulling free of his hand. 'I don't want to be treated like some girl you've just picked up.'

He made a sound of deep male frustration in the back of his throat. 'I have no intention of treating you as anything but a lady. Frankly, Clementine, in Russia we do not do things in this way. Would you not prefer some discretion?'

Baffled she gazed up at him. He would treat her *as* a lady? Why didn't that reassure her? Shouldn't he *consider* her a lady?

Suddenly it all felt too hard, and she decided then and there to let it go. She was reading too much into everything he said because she was having trouble trusting anyone. It wasn't fair to Serge, and it was going to ruin things before they started.

'We can discuss your terms when we're alone, *kisa*,' he said dryly. 'But I can assure you there won't be any "misunderstandings" as you describe it.'

She laid her hand gently on his chest. He felt so hard, and she could feel the shift of muscle as he took a deep breath. She affected him, and it thrilled her because it answered her own desire for him. But it wasn't anything she was going to act on unless it felt absolutely right.

She smiled up at him—her first for the day. 'I'm really glad you came for me, Serge.'

'You like the jet, *kisa*?'

'I guess.' She gave a gasp as he slid his arm around her waist and scooped her up into his arms.

'Serge!'

'*Da*—Serge.'

The sudden physical closeness wrapped around her and she melted. That fast she was a mess of hormones and longing.

He carried her as if she weighed nothing. Something long dormant inside her leapt in answer to his overt masculine display of physical strength and dominance. He was taking her over, and it was stunningly clear her body liked it.

Serge experienced a primitive satisfaction in having Clementine in his arms. He'd been anticipating this since last night. He'd been working towards it since he'd followed her down the Nevsky. Elusive Clementine, who withheld so much, only made him want more, to give her more.

Those terms of hers… Never had he been confronted with such a bald request from a woman. Did she imagine he wasn't going to cough up with the gifts? And how high exactly did she measure her favours? Not that it really mattered; at this point he was prepared to pay any price.

* * *

'How much does all this cost?'

Clementine ground to a halt in her silver slingbacks and did a three-sixty as she took in the hotel foyer. Understated elegance had never looked so expensive. Adding it to the limo from JFK, the posse of minders following them in another car, and not forgetting the plane—the private jet—the world was starting to resemble Oz, of the Wizard variety.

Serge waited, dark green eyes steady on her, his hand extended in a gesture to have her join him.

'Okay, Slugger—spill.' She sashayed up to him and slid her hand into his as if she accompanied wealthy, powerful men into hotels every day of the week.

'This sports management gig—who in heck do you manage?'

'Not who, *kisa*, what.' His expression was indulgent, as if she entertained him. 'I own a corporation that broadcasts and hosts boxing and mixed martial arts fights.'

Clementine batted her eyelashes at him. 'Wow,' she said. 'That's—wow.'

'I'm getting an impressed vibe from you, Clementine.'

The entire twelve hours of the flight—half of which she had slept—Serge had been an exemplary host, seeing to her needs before retreating behind his laptop and work. But she was definitely getting a more playful Serge now that they were on *terra firma*.

He ushered her into the elevator and the doors closed out the rest of the world. Serge's shoulders rose up in front of her and Clementine couldn't see anything else but him.

'Where I come from your line of business translates as very blokey. It explains a lot.'

And there it was—that little private smile he'd been waiting for.

He gently twined her hair over her shoulder and said quietly, close to her ear, 'And what does it explain, Clementine?'

She shivered in response. 'All the testosterone. That's why you were able to beat off those guys. You knew what you were doing.' Her own voice had grown hushed. She looked up at him.

'Since meeting you, *kisa*, it's been the only thing I've been sure of doing.' His admission, meant only to tease her, suddenly hit him as absolute fact.

She batted those lashes more slowly. 'You're not sure of me, Slugger?'

'Clementine, I have a feeling no man has ever been sure of you.'

His hand moved around her waist. He leaned in and gave her a moment to accept he was going to kiss her, and then his mouth was suddenly hot and moving fast against her own, opening her up with his tongue, tasting her, giving her no time to back away.

He hauled her up against him and Clementine turned to liquid heat. She moaned helplessly and slid her arms up around his neck, powerless against the feelings he was stoking in her. His body felt so hard against her own, and the slide of his tongue over her lower lip found an answering pulse deep down inside her. It was almost too much.

The doors slid open with a soft ping and Serge broke their kiss. It had only lasted a matter of moments, but it felt like for ever, and Clementine couldn't believe she'd got so carried away from one kiss. Mouth trembling, nipples pressing tight and hot against the lace of her bra, she pulled at her dress. The silk jersey had risen up over her thighs and her hair felt tangled and messy from his hands.

She watched him use a keycard on the door, trying to clear her head. She hadn't known a kiss could undo her, and suddenly all her certainty about what she was doing began to fall away.

Serge ushered her inside, his hand on the small of her back.

She needed to keep a clear head if she was going to navigate these waters. 'Wow,' she said inadequately as she stepped into sheer luxury. 'This is—incredible.'

The extravagance of the hotel suite was another reminder of exactly who Serge was. A rich man. Who could buy a great deal to keep himself happy. No doubt including women.

But not this woman. She needed to make that very clear to him. Somehow.

'I'm not that impressed, you know, Slugger. Money doesn't do it for me.'

'What *does* do it for you, Clementine?' He was smiling at her, that big, lazy Russian male smile, as if he knew something she didn't.

'Honesty,' she replied. 'Sincerity.'

The smile darkened to something else. She'd surprised him.

Her pulse was going thumpity-thumpity as she made her way slowly through the rooms—the living area, the dining room with seating for twenty-four, past the baby grand. She stopped to run her fingers down an octave.

'You play, *kisa*?'

'By ear.' She lifted her gaze to his heated expression and a rush of sweet arousal washed through her body. 'I'm a quick study.'

She backed away from the piano, realised Serge was measuring her with his gaze. She needed to keep her wits about her with this man. She needed to keep up the banter, hold him off a little longer until she got herself back under control. Beckoning to him with one manicured finger, she fashioned a smile. 'Come on, Slugger, we'll see what else we can find.'

Her heart was pounding as she strolled into the bedroom, knowing her big Siberian tiger was following.

Cheeks pink, breathing shallow, she put her head in at the *en suite* bathroom door.

'Now, that is one big tub.'

'Would you like to make use of it, Clementine?' he said from behind her.

'Not right now.' She was astonished at how steady her voice was.

She felt his body only centimetres from her own, and she tensed. She had to be smart about this.

She heard her zip start to slide down and suddenly knew she couldn't do it. It came over her in a panic, most unlike her, and she pulled away.

A few days ago she'd wondered if she could handle him. She was fast discovering her answer was no. A resounding no.

Jerking around, she put a hand up as if she were stopping traffic. 'Hang on a minute, Slugger, we've only just got here.' Her voice sounded ridiculously girlish. 'How about dinner and a movie first?'

She could feel the heat coming off his body, the slam of his breathing as his chest rose and fell just inches from hers. He slid one big hand around her waist, pulling her towards him, smiling that wicked smile of his, and she realised he wasn't taking her seriously at all.

'Hey.' She shoved at his chest with one hand and pulled on his arm with the other. 'I'm not playing, mister. Hands to yourself.'

She couldn't be serious? He frowned. By all that was holy, she *was* serious. Serge released her slowly, but Clementine backed up so fast she hit the doorframe of the *en suite* bathroom, banging her head.

Bringing up her hand to rub the offended spot, she blinked at him warily. 'I said dinner and a movie,' she repeated mulishly, not liking feeling this way—a little foolish and on the back foot.

She kept her eyes on his, daring him to argue her down.

She wasn't a newbie at this, but Serge Marinov was some-thing beyond her experience. She just didn't feel ready to be that out of control, and that kiss in the lift had rung some pretty significant bells. This man could very well annihi-late all her inhibitions, and she really, really didn't want to wake up tomorrow morning to a note on the pillow telling her thanks, he'd be in touch.

She wasn't naive. She got the impression Serge saw her as a lot more sophisticated than she actually was, and she prob-ably needed to talk to him about that. Which made dinner an excellent idea.

'Dinner and a movie?' he echoed. 'They're your terms, *kisa*?'

Clementine wanted to flap her lashes and tell him yes, but she'd been shaken up by what had just happened and it wasn't fair to Serge to keep up the flirting when she so clearly wasn't going to follow through.

'Not terms. I just thought it would be nice,' she offered. 'Normal.'

Nice. Normal. Serge was trying to get his head around what had just happened. One minute he was being lured by a siren into the bedroom, and the next he was shipwrecked on the rocks—an uncouth oaf who had come on too strong and not taken no for an answer.

He was thrown back to that café in Petersburg, feeling like a thug for upsetting Clementine. She was either playing a very clever game or he had got this all very wrong. If he had it wrong, and this less than sure of herself Clementine who kept appearing at inopportune times was the real deal, the traditional Russian male that lurked not far below his mod-ern sensibility was going to have a field-day. And he needed to keep that firmly in check.

He knew which way that led.

Either way, he wouldn't rush her. It would do both of them

a disservice. Especially if what was between them turned out to be as incendiary as he suspected it would.

Clementine decanted her clothes into one of the guest bedrooms, wondering what on earth she thought she was doing. Serge had got changed and told her he was going down to use the gym for a couple of hours. He would return to take her to dinner at seven.

She had hoped to spend a little time in his company beforehand, but given her actions this afternoon she hadn't felt in a position to try and dissuade him. He'd said something about having some excess energy to work off, which she might have interpreted as flattering. Instead it had just fallen flat.

Folding the last of her T-shirts away, she plopped down on the guest bed and smoothed one hand over the gold satin quilt. She was definitely in luxury land, with a man she didn't know nearly enough about, but there was a huge part of her that was singing out *squeee* as she threw herself down the rocky, rushing ravine she just knew this week with Serge would be. He'd almost pulled her over into the rapids with him this afternoon, but she'd balked at the last minute.

Cautious Clementine. She grimaced at Luke's nickname for her and checked her watch. Serge had been gone barely an hour. Smiling to herself, she began peeling off her clothes.

Serge repetitively drummed the gloves into the bag, feeling the shudder through his arms, relishing the impact. He couldn't believe the scene he'd had with Clementine. It took him back to being seventeen and not sure if it was all right to put his hand under a girl's top if she hadn't explicitly given permission.

Sweat blinded him and he pulled the punches, stepped away from the bag and reached for a towel, rubbing his face.

As he slung it over his shoulder he reached for his bottle of water.

'Is this what you're looking for?' Clementine stood in front of him, offering up the bottle with a little smile.

She was wearing a tiny pair of red shorts and a white tank top, and she'd tied all that hair back in a ponytail.

'Thanks,' he said, almost by rote, as every male cell in his body sat up and saluted.

'Can I have a go?' She indicated the punching bag.

'It might be a bit hard for you,' he responded, trying not to ogle her. Something Clementine was clearly aware of, judging by the little smile she was wearing.

His knowing, provocative little Clementine was back.

'Just give me some gloves, Slugger.'

He fetched a smaller pair for her hands and attached them himself, watching her expression as she tried not to stroke his body too obviously with her gaze. The urge to haul her against him and take what he wanted was very strong. 'Go in close,' he instructed. 'Little jabs. Keep your elbows up. That's it—don't pull back.'

Her concentration was absolute. She was really taking this seriously. His gaze dropped momentarily to the superlative curve of her bottom in those little shorts. Had she purposely come down here to shred the last fibres of his self-control?

She gave an *oomph* as the bag swung back and knocked her onto that bottom. She lay back laughing on the mat, looking up at him towering over her. As she watched he stripped off the sweat-soaked T-shirt he was wearing and stood there in only a pair of baggy long shorts that were barely holding onto his lean hips. There was something else stirring that made Clementine's laughter trickle into a deep sigh of feminine satisfaction. His shoulders and chest and back were powerful and heavily muscled, and there was a haze of dark hair arrowing down below his navel she longed to run her hands through. But after her little performance earlier in the day she didn't feel entitled.

He offered her a hand and she took it. One-armed, he literally pulled her off the ground and to her feet. As a display of strength it was breathtaking. But what really took her breath away was standing up so close to his barely clothed body, with her own hardly left to the imagination. He ran those green eyes over her face and then lower, to where her nipples were very clearly making themselves known.

'Are we really waiting until after dinner and the movie, *dushka*?'

His voice ran over her like rough velvet.

She licked her lips. No was on the tip of her tongue when other voices interrupted and Serge turned away, cursing under his breath.

'A public gym,' murmured Clementine. 'Whoops.'

Three men had come through the doors at the other end of the weights room.

'I'll hit the shower,' said Serge. 'You go on up. But keep the little outfit on.'

She narrowed her eyes and gave him a push to one rock-hard bicep. 'Dinner, Slugger. But I'll give you a raincheck for the movie.'

Clementine was surprised when Serge insisted on walking her out before returning to change and shower. He really was an old-fashioned guy in so many respects, and that was playing nicely with her inner princess. He wasn't just muscles and testosterone; he had some stellar qualities—manners being one of them.

She showered herself, and put on a red and gold kaftan dress that wrapped around and tied at the waist. It was simple, but she could dress it up with heeled sandals and she swept her hair up, attaching a red silk flower behind her ear. She layered on the kohl and the false eyelashes and painted her lips ruby-red.

She heard Serge's sports bag drop and scooted out to meet him. He took one look at her outfit and put up his hands. 'I surrender, Clementine. Dinner.'

She grinned.

CHAPTER SIX

THEY dined not in the hotel but at an exclusive restaurant on Manhattan's Upper East Side. The menu was contemporary French cuisine, but frankly, Clementine thought, she could have been eating sushi and she wouldn't have noticed.

The man opposite her in a suit and tie, all elegant Manhattan urbanity, fixated all of her attention. He hadn't rushed her off to bed, he hadn't pushed anything, and now he was dining with her in the most civilised surroundings imaginable. Their conversation ranged over her life in London, his here in New York, current events. But every time she allowed her gaze to settle on him—whether it be the breadth of his naked wrist beneath the fabric of his sleeve, the wide column of his strong neck so snugly contained in a collar and tie, the faint cleft in his chin that she imagined was tricky to shave—she kept picturing him standing over her, half-naked, dripping sweat and testosterone in that gym. Exactly as she had fantasised about him the first moment she'd clapped eyes on him.

Warmth pooled low in her pelvis and had been there for much of their meal. The wine and the soup and the main course and a blackberry dessert had all slid down, and her cheeks grew pink and her eyes sparkled as she listened to the deep, rhythmically accented voice stroking her senses, watching the changing colours in his sea-green eyes like the tides. She knew she had made the right decision in coming to New York with him.

No more cold showers, thought Serge as he helped Clementine out of the cab. His libido stretched and did a few push-ups in readiness.

They could have taken a town car, but she had wanted the 'fun' of riding in a New York City taxi cab—and who was he to spoil Clementine's fun?

Half of the sheer enjoyment he was having with her was watching her reactions to little things. She had the most expressive face he had ever seen, and it was because of that he knew her skittishness earlier had not been part of some ploy to stoke his desire for her or even some odd kink of her own. She genuinely hadn't been ready. But she was ready now—or his reading of female arousal was completely off-kilter.

Given the woman he was with, that was always possible.

So they were back to square one as the lift flew them skywards to the fifty-third floor, but he didn't attempt to touch her. He wanted to be very sure Clementine was on board with the programme. He also wanted to discuss a few terms of his own. He didn't want there to be any 'misunderstandings' when this was all over—and it would be over at some point. But thinking about the end before they even really began pulled him up short.

With another woman he would have discussed this long ago, but with Clementine he had delayed. Now there was a certain necessity in the moment to rush her into bed and to hell with everything else.

He hesitated to call it romanticism, but Clementine had early on introduced a certain element of that into their situation—he wouldn't call it a relationship—when she'd made herself so elusive in St Petersburg. He wanted to do this right. He wanted to do it the old-fashioned way and sweep her off her feet.

Which he did—after opening the door, gathering her into his arms and enjoying her gasp of surprise. Women loved to be carried, and Clementine was no exception to the rule. She wrapped her strong slender arms around his neck, her soft hair tickling his chin. What was different was how good it felt holding her this way. It probably had something to do with her elusiveness again. She couldn't run off, and all the muscles in her body seemed to dissolve as she submitted to his superior strength.

He'd never thought of himself as the sort of man who got off on proving himself to women, but her reaction to him lifting her off the floor this afternoon—a spontaneous gesture—and again being carried now was doing a power of good to his ego. Which boded well for tonight.

The lights in the suite were sensor-activated, and they showered across them as he carried her into the living area and she wriggled out of his arms. His intention was to take her off guard by kissing her and letting things run from there. And judging by his hardening body they'd be running pretty fast.

'Let's make some coffee and a little chat,' she suggested, tugging on his hand and taking a few backward steps, intending to pull him with her.

'Let's not.' He hauled her back in with one hand and she looked up at him, faint apprehension behind those steady grey eyes. Then her lashes dipped down and she seemed to make up her mind.

Slowly, cautiously, she reached up and wound her arms around his neck. But before she could press those soft lips to his he reached down and made short work of the bow at her waist, letting her go only to unravel the fabric that tied her kaftan together. He'd been studying that bow all night, in preparation for this moment, and the effect was well worth it as Clementine gave a shocked little yelp.

But she didn't try to cover herself, and when he began pulling the dress gently down off her shoulders she wriggled to give it a hand, pressing up against him in nothing but her sheer black bra and knickers. He fancied she was trying to shield herself. He felt rather than saw her step out of her heels.

She suddenly felt much smaller and somehow less assured in his arms. The dress slid down at his third tug and pooled on the floor. He ran his hand along her spine, coming to rest on the curve of her delectable bottom.

'I'm feeling a bit naked here, Slugger,' she said, but it was the nervous laugh that took him off guard. He hadn't expected her to be uncertain. 'Can't we do this in the bedroom, like normal people?'

'What is this "normal" you keep talking about?' he teased, his voice heavy with his arousal. 'This feels normal to me, *kisa.*'

'Not all of us normally swing from chandeliers,' she prevaricated, but he noticed she began pushing his jacket over his shoulders, and he helped her. Then she was pulling at his shirt-tails, but he wanted to see her face.

He tucked a finger under her chin, drew her eyes up to his. 'I promise no chandelier-swinging—even if you beg.'

Her grey eyes grew unbelievably soft, her whole expressive face somehow radiating a warmth and trust he knew he didn't deserve. For a moment he was distracted with the thought that the woman in his arms was taking all of this far too seriously for his comfort.

But his blood was pumping, and if he didn't learn every inch of her body tonight he was going to explode.

Clementine made his decision as she reached up and wound her arms around his neck. He gave way to the rush of desire he had to possess her, to know her.

Clementine heard him murmur something in Russian and his hands spread over her hips, moving down to cup her bottom as he drew her up to kiss her. His mouth was everything she remembered, hot, but tender this time, stealing her breath and any free will she had left. He seduced her with his mouth, kissing her mindless, until it was his body, hard and muscular, she began to explore helplessly.

She reached for the button and zip on his trousers, slipping her hand inside. She gave a little murmur of surprise. She gently learned his size and shape as he breathed heavily, his chest rising and falling with flattering intensity.

'Keep that up, *kisa,* and this may be over before we know it,' he murmured, his voice deep and dark in her ear.

'I don't believe that,' she whispered back, but he scooped her up and finally carried her through the other rooms and into the bedroom, lying her down on the slippery white satin quilting. Then methodically he began to unbutton his shirt.

Clementine lay back, biting her lip as she watched his big shoulders emerge and then his chest, broad and heavy with muscle, hazy with the dark hair she remembered, his powerful arms next, his waist, lean and defined.

Then he shucked off his trousers and boxers and long, muscular hair-roughened thighs and calves came into view, and what she'd had her hand on only minutes before. And then he came down onto the bed with her.

His hand cupped her face and he turned her mouth towards his before his lips brushed over hers, and then he was kissing her slowly, sensuously, dragging his fingers through her hair, loosing it so that it toppled down, a heavy mass that swam across his shoulder and bicep as he supported her.

His big rough hand curled into the underside of her left knee, stroked her there, moved up under the length of her thigh to squeeze the lush curve of her bottom.

Clementine trembled as his fingers pushed up the delicate silk of her knickers, anticipating every move he was making. But when his hand continued its exploration over her hip, dipping into her waist and smoothing up over her ribs, covering her breast encased in the same silk of her knickers, it wasn't familiar. He wasn't going for broke. He was taking his time.

His thumb made a slow perambulation of her nipple and his mouth caught hers again in a slow, sweet kiss as he gently handled her body.

'I knew you would have an amazing body,' he told her appreciatively, 'and it's more beautiful than I imagined.'

She reached behind and unhooked her bra for him, baring her breasts and trying not to show the faint ripple of anxiety she was feeling.

'It just gets better,' he murmured, that flaring gaze sweeping over her. He framed one breast with his hand, exploring the shape of her, bending his head to take her nipple into his mouth.

Clementine made a helpless noise and arched her back, the rhythms of her body taking over. She knew how to do this, or thought she did, but Serge seemed to know her body better than she did.

When she was almost crying with need and distraction he lifted his head, only to abrade her nipple lightly with the bristly skin along his jaw, watching her shudder. It had never been like this for her before—the want, the magic of having one hundred per cent of a man's attention on her pleasure. This man's attention—knowing, practised, skilled—was beyond her experience.

His hand slid down over her hip and he hooked a thumb under her knickers, and then he was sliding down the bed, settling between her thighs, and with a wink he applied his mouth to the heart of her.

Clementine threw back her head and whimpered as little starbursts of sensation blurred her vision. She felt swollen and ultra-sensitive, and when his tongue swiped over her clitoris she went with it, her cries filling the warmly lit room.

Serge shifted up over her, pausing only briefly to don a condom. Then suddenly he was inside her. He only gave her a moment to adjust before he was moving, and the sensations began to build again. She found her own body matching his rhythm. She clasped him around the neck and he forged his mouth to hers in deep open-mouthed kisses that mingled their breath and tongues with Russian words Clementine didn't understand but knew had to do with how good this was. His eyes were dark with pleasure and he kept making eye contact with her, as if testing the depth of her enjoyment but also letting her see his.

She could hear his deep rasping breathing, the heavy thump of his heartbeat, smell the warm musky scent of his male skin. A light sheen of sweat had broken on the broad expanse of his back and she luxuriated in that too, loving the intense maleness of him. Then it happened. An unexpected series of sweet, unending undulations crashed through her pelvis, spreading all the way out to her fingers and her toes, making the hair on her head stand up.

'Serge!'

'*Da*—Serge.' In response he thrust harder and faster.

Her orgasm met her and she rolled with it. She was contracting around him, and with a deep groan he released into her. It went on and on, spiralling through her body as she unravelled. As he subsided she sank back into the mattress, taking him heavily down on top of her, loving the sensation of being utterly consumed by him.

She closed her eyes and breathed him in. Her Cossack.

Clementine felt the absence of his weight even though he had only lain heavily atop her so briefly. He had his eyes closed and gave a couple of deep, gusty breaths, as if bringing himself back to reality. She knew how he felt. She hardly recognised herself in the woman who had clung to him and whimpered, encouraging him to do more, to make her feel more.

She turned her head on the pillow and looked at him. Beautiful. He'd called her beautiful.

She gathered the word up close and hugged it. She felt beautiful.

She reached out and touched his shoulder. His head tilted and his green gaze tangled with hers. Her heart gave a sudden lovely thump and her pulse kicked up.

Serge rolled towards her and brushed his thumb back and forth over her cheek, traced her mouth. 'I thought I'd dreamed you up in that store,' he said in a gravelly voice, 'but here you are. All mine.'

Clementine's eyes went soft as down even as Serge's own thoughts raced to a stunning halt. He didn't know what it was he wanted from her, but it wasn't this. Closeness…connection. What in the hell had prompted his soft words?

'Serge, make love to me,' she invited, lashes lowering, mouth soft, her body recumbent beneath him, parting her thighs in explicit invitation. She was a fantasy he had never known he had. Until now.

This at least he understood. This he could do. Again and again.

'My pleasure,' he said, and moved over her.

She drifted to consciousness to find herself alone. For a moment Clementine wondered if it had all been an erotic dream, before she rolled over into the space where he had slept and buried her face in his pillow, seeking out the remnants of his scent. No dream. All real. Luckiest girl in the world.

There was a tender ache between her thighs. In fact all of her was a bit achy. Memories assailed her—his hands on her, those skilful hands. A big smile spread over her face. Where had he learned to do those things? Had she really let him? When would they do it again? She sat up and winced. Maybe not this morning.

Should she get up and go and find him? What was she going to say? Maybe he wasn't a morning person. She definitely wasn't—with the exception of this morning. Sinking back onto his side of the bed, she luxuriated in her happy place. Nothing could ruin this feeling.

Stretching, she felt her hand land on something hard and cold beside the pillow. Curiously she rolled over, put her hand on a small red box.

Even as she opened it a chill was spreading through her chest.

Diamonds glittered from a black velvet bed. She couldn't even bring herself to touch them. There was a note attached.

Wear this tonight. I'll be back for you at seven. Dress up.

Clementine didn't know how long she sat there, cross-legged in the bed, the jewellery case abandoned beside her, the note shouting at her: *He's bought you; he thinks you're for sale.*

It took a while for the storm of feeling inside her to subside, but it did, and then she began to think more rationally.

Serge had no idea about her past. He couldn't know a piece of jewellery like this would push her buttons. Sensibly she told herself this was probably his *modus operandi*. Get the girl, drape her in something glittery—the same way other men bought flowers.

Oh, flowers would have been nice—to wake up to a little bunch of something beside her. Would have cost him a great deal less, too.

She wilted a little and gave a wry smile.

Serge Marinov might be a rich guy who flew in women to warm his bed, but that wasn't all he was. She'd seen enough to know this was a really good guy. She would never have slept with him last night if he wasn't.

He had been everything—tender and passionate and romantic.

He just didn't have a clue about the morning after.

She picked up the jewellery case and shoved it into the bedside table, then padded barefoot out of the bedroom. Out of sight, out of mind.

All morning long he'd been thinking about her. Through a tedious meeting with the stadium committee, a photo opportunity downtown at the Mayor's office, putting in a bid on some venues in California, his thoughts had continuously returned to the sleeping girl he had left at dawn.

Several times he'd almost rung her cell, self-preservation muscling in each time. The minute he phoned her he would be opening up a channel of communication between his working life and the woman in his bed. He'd never done it before. He wasn't starting now.

'Serge, you're not with us,' Mick's voice intervened, dragging him back into the present and his office in Upper Manhattan.

No, he wasn't with them. Serge corralled his stampeding thoughts about a six-foot girl naked in his bed and looked at the stats Alex had handed him. Mick's word was good enough, but Alex Khardovsky, president of the Marinov Corporation, always came up with cold hard numbers, and Serge knew at the end of the day you could trust figures. Unlike people, they never let you down.

'So you'll come down and have a look at the kid?' Mick was saying.

Dinner with Clementine. He was going to have to postpone it.

'I'll meet you there at seven.' He'd divert on his way across town and drop in at the hotel—enjoy a quickie with the beautiful girl he had left in his bed.

'I want to go over these figures with you, Serge. Can we grab a bite and meet Mick at the gym?'

'No, I need to drop in at the hotel. I'll take these with me.'

Alex grinned. 'A woman? I thought you seemed unusually upbeat.'

Usually Serge wouldn't have hesitated to affirm or deny a question from Alex. He was his oldest friend. They had been in boot camp together. Apart from Mick he was the only other person he trusted. Happily married for three years, Alex joked that the only excitement he got these days was observing Serge's revolving door policy on women.

But the memory of Clementine's soft grey eyes as he cuddled her close struck him as he opened his mouth, and he closed it. Shook his head briefly.

'We still need to talk about Kolcek,' said Mick flatly. 'You have to do more than a press conference, son. You need to put your face to the brand.'

Serge folded his arms. 'And I'm the poster boy for good clean living?'

Alex snorted, but Mick shook his head. 'Publicity's everything in this game, and you both know it. Your image is hardly what the moms at home are applauding, and that's what this political stunt over Kolcek is aimed at. The punters like to see you with a different airhead every day in the papers, but not the general public. You need to be seen with a decent woman at your side. Geez, I shouldn't have to tell you boys this.'

'I'm not playing the media game, Mick,' stated Serge with finality. 'The business is one thing, my private life another.'

'The problem being there's nothing private about it. What about that woman who spilled her guts about "my life with fight promoter Serge Marinov—the highs and lows of a jet-set playboy"'?' Mick threw the magazine he'd been carrying around onto the desk between them.

Serge ignored it. 'I barely knew the woman—slept with her twice. Once too many.'

Alex picked up the magazine. 'I'll show this to Abbey. She'll love it.'

Serge smiled, seeing the lighter side of it. Alex's wife took him to task about his lifestyle every time their paths crossed.

It wasn't until Mick and Alex were gone that he was given the opportunity to phone Clementine's cell. She gave him that breathless 'Serge' he was beginning to look forward to, and promised to be at the hotel in half an hour.

It was on the tip of his tongue to ask if she'd had a good day, but he knew the minute he did that he'd be feeding into a fantasy that she was in his life in any other way than his bed. His mind went back to the trashy magazine and the brunette he barely remembered. She'd sold her story for five figures, he'd heard. He couldn't quite picture Clementine selling anything.

He'd been right not to mention her name to Alex.

'See you then.' Her voice was in his ear, and was he just feeling extremely restless or did he hear a note of longing? Grinning, he rang off.

The penthouse was quiet as Clementine let herself in, but all the lights were on. She was sticky from her long day sightseeing, and wanted to bathe and get changed, but her heart had started paddling like a kayak up a canyon the closer she'd got to the hotel, knowing Serge would be inside waiting for her.

The intimacy they had built up, culminating in last night, felt a million miles away. Not being with him today, in the aftermath of their incredible night, had left her emotions close to the surface and she was feeling a little nervous—but also excited.

He was standing out on the balcony, those muscular arms of his spread on the railing, supporting him as he looked out over the city. From behind he was all masculine grace, with his lean height and the powerful spread of his shoulders. Clementine experienced an inner trembling as her body recognised what it liked. She'd never known anything like it when she was with him. It was as if the air between them lit up like sheet lightning.

She stopped on the threshold of the balcony. 'Hi,' she said, endeavouring to sound as casual as she could.

He turned around, and the intensity of his gaze was full of everything they had shared. The answering pulse in her body brought soft colour to her cheeks.

'Hi yourself,' he answered, as if he knew what was happening to her.

'Busy day?' She knew she sounded inane, but her heart was pounding.

'They're all busy, *kisa*.' He smiled slowly. 'You're late.' But it was said without animosity.

'Am I?' She knew she was. But he hadn't been beside her when she woke up. So let him deal with it, niggled the thought, and a little of her excitement fluttered away.

He strolled inside, shutting the glass doors on the city behind him, and casually reached for her. As his big hands slid over her hips, bringing her up against him, she experienced a flare of longing in her body that had nothing to do with the resistance in her head.

She waited for him to say something, allude in some way to this morning, but he merely bent his head and kissed her.

Clementine put her hands up to his chest and gently disengaged herself with a murmured, 'Not so fast.'

He released her, disconcerting her by patting her on the backside. 'Off you go, then.'

She looked at him uncertainly. 'I'll just go and change. I

won't be more than twenty minutes.' She hesitated, feeling a little shy all of a sudden. 'Are we going somewhere fancy?'

'There's been a change of plan.' He turned his back on her as he strolled over to the side table to collect his phone and keys. 'I've got to go downtown tonight. I can't take you out to dinner.'

'You're going out?'

'It's work, Clementine. Happens all the time.' His expression said *get used to it*.

'That's okay,' she replied, determinedly cheerful. 'I'll come with you.'

'You'll come—' He broke off, frowning at her. 'No, it's not a place for you.'

Her hand found her hip. 'What is it? A mosque?'

'A gym,' he said briefly. 'A lot of sweat and testosterone.'

'So a lot like last night?' she replied, scooting after him as he headed over to the wet bar.

He slowed to a halt, turned. Some of the tension eased around his mouth. He smiled. 'Maybe, but without the important addition of a soft landing.'

It was the smile that got to her. She narrowed her eyes. 'Did you just describe me as a soft landing?'

'You supplied the soft landing, Clementine. I would describe *you* as a miracle of natural engineering.'

Somehow it wasn't a compliment. It wasn't what you said to the woman you'd made love to for the first time and then abandoned the next morning. *Yes, Clementine*, a little voice niggled. Abandoned.

She didn't like the way he catalogued her body either—as if examining the parts he liked best. Guys did that to her a lot. It made her feel less than a person. She wanted him to see the whole woman—had imagined he had last night. But she guessed that wasn't the reality.

Unimpressed, she muttered, 'Careful with the sweet-talk, Slugger, you'll melt my knickers off.'

He grinned. He liked her like this—making him work for it. The other Clementine—softer, a little unsure of herself—put the wrong thoughts in his head. Thoughts of looking after her.

This Clementine could look after herself.

He relaxed.

'I'm going to freshen up,' she said stiltedly, a little afraid that when she came back he would be gone. 'It's been a long day.'

Serge didn't attempt to stop her. She had a right to be annoyed with him. He wasn't going to be able to do justice to her beautiful body this week with so much going on in the outside world. But he could make it up to her now—soothe that little temper of hers in a mutually satisfactory way.

Clementine satisfied herself by calling him every name in the book as she stripped off in the bathroom, stepping into the pressure-activated shower and letting the warm water do its soothing job. Where was the sweet, attentive man who'd listened to her over dinner and held her hand going in and out of the restaurant, who'd been so romantic with her last night?

Gone the way of the fairies, Clementine. Because he never existed. Now that he'd had her he'd cooled off. She'd heard about guys like him. Once the chase was over so was the romance. She snorted. She'd been such an idiot. The romance she'd been hoping for hadn't even got off the ground because there never *had* been any romance.

Serge knocked once, for appearances' sake, then opened the bathroom door. There she was—one of his afternoon's fantasies come to life. All six feet of naked Clementine, with water running over her pale honey skin, the graceful seashell-pink-tipped breasts, the narrow waist that only made the extravagant flare of her hips and bottom all the more dramatic, and those long, long legs.

She turned, sensing him, and those lovely eyes of hers narrowed.

'Don't even try it, Marinov.'

But he knew the battles he could win, and this was one of them.

Fully dressed, he stepped under the water stream, hands sliding around her. When she opened her mouth to swear a blue streak at him he took it as his invitation to lower his head and kiss her.

Clementine put up a good fight against her desire for him, holding off for at least five seconds before she spread her hands over his shoulders and pressed herself up against him. With his arms around her he felt solid and exciting, and everything fell away except for this. The way he made her feel. Beautiful, wanted, safe.

So many firsts, she thought later as she sat on the bed, wrapped in a big warm towel, knowing she needed to go and get dressed.

It was all playing through her head. Serge hadn't even removed his clothes—just unzipped and it had been happening, and her need had climbed with his at breakneck speed. What was wrong with her? She should have yelled at him—not had sex with him.

He was treating her like a convenience.

It was never more obvious than when he came out of the *en suite* bathroom, towelling dry his hair. He glanced at the digital clock and swore softly in Russian.

More disappointed with him by the minute, she said sharply, 'Going to be late, Serge? Never mind—just tell your friends you couldn't keep it zipped up. I'm sure it's not the first time.'

He dropped the towel to his side. He looked genuinely shocked.

Good. For five whole seconds she had a little payback.

But then he drawled, 'It's work, Clementine, and it's twenty-four-seven. Welcome to my world.' He threw the towel onto a chair and slid open a drawer. 'And, by the way, crudity doesn't suit you. I'd prefer you continued to behave like the lady you are.'

'Except when I've got my legs wrapped around your waist in the shower,' she shot back, hurt.

He flashed a charismatic smile over his shoulder. 'Exactly.'

Oh, boy. A streak of healthy cleansing anger ripped through her body. She was *so* out of here. His week of pleasure had just got foreshortened to one night. When he got back she'd be gone. Over the hills. Far, far away.

But even as she formed the thought of escape she dug her toes a little more firmly into the carpet. Oh, yes, Clementine, look at you running. Like *that's* going to happen. You've never been with a man like this and it's exciting, and despite everything you want to at least try and see if this can go somewhere better. Besides, he's got you wrapped around his little finger and he knows it. Why would he let you go yet? As long as he wants you you'll stay.

And with that all the anger fell away and all she felt was confusion.

What was going on? Was she sulking? Serge tugged on some briefs, pulled on his jeans. Glanced over at her again.

She was snapping at him as if he'd done something to disappoint her. Yet she'd climaxed around him in the shower. Hadn't she?

Was that the problem? Had she been faking it? The thought brought him up cold. He prided himself on giving a woman the pleasure she deserved in exchange for the gift of her body, and the notion that he hadn't lived up to Clementine's expectations wiped out any thought other than remedying that.

He strolled over and dropped to his knees at her feet. Clementine stared at him in astonishment as he tugged playfully on her towel, parting it to reveal her thighs.

'What are you doing?'

'Makings things better. Lie back, *kisa*, and think happy thoughts.'

He had to be joking. Clementine grabbed the towel and pulled it back down to her knees, tucking her legs up under her as fast as she could. 'Don't you dare.'

A challenge? A wicked smile lit up his face, but no answering invitation came from Clementine.

She glared at him. 'Your bedside manner needs a lot of work, mate.'

The smile was gone. In its place was disbelief. 'You love it, *kisa*.'

The sheer arrogance of the man! 'Love what? Being pawed at?' Her voice trembled a little with the anger and confusion she was feeling—waking up alone this morning, being abandoned again now. 'Sex isn't just physical, Serge. Haven't you worked that out by now?'

A muscle was ticking in his jaw and she glowered at him.

'And while we're at it, next time you decide to come into the bathroom ask before you take.'

Serge stood up slowly. 'Perhaps you should have kept the moaning down to a reasonable level, *kisa*, and then I would have heard the no.'

Visibly tensing, Clementine said hoarsely, 'I didn't say no. I just said you could have asked before invading my privacy.'

'Complaint noted,' he replied, jerking open a drawer. He wasn't indulging her temperament any further. He knew where this was going, and he didn't do female tantrums. She was being difficult for the sake of it because he was leaving her alone. Again.

Brought up short by that thought, he grabbed a T-shirt.

Yeah, okay, it wasn't the behaviour of a gentleman. But that was not what this was about. He tugged the T-shirt over his head.

What in the hell *was* this about?

He looked at Clementine as she sat on the end of the bed, tugging on the hem of that towel.

His conscience gave an unfamiliar jolt. He didn't want to leave her like this. Maybe he should cancel? Stay with her? *Bozhe*, this wasn't the way it was supposed to go. Where was the funny, happy girl he'd enjoyed yesterday?

There was something softer, more uncertain about her, and she looked genuinely upset.

'Are you okay?' he said roughly. 'I didn't hurt you? You're not sore?'

Her head snapped up and she made a little sound in the back of her throat that sounded suspiciously like a strangled scream. Clutching at the towel, she surged to her feet.

'You're a real prince—you know that?' she shouted at him, and with that enigmatic comment stalked out.

He'd never seen her lose her temper. It occurred to Serge he could have handled this better.

You're not sore?

Of all the humiliating things he could say to her—not to mention ridiculous. It told her volumes about how he saw her. Some silly girl who couldn't look after herself. Well, he had a surprise coming. She'd been looking after herself all her life, and she could deal with self-centred you're-with-me-babe men.

She yanked open drawers, slammed cupboards in the guest

room and rapidly dressed. She'd see about this *I've got to go downtown tonight.*

She had half expected him to be gone when she returned, and then she had no idea what she would have done. But he hadn't gone anywhere, and that tiny glimmer of hope she carried for this man flared a little brighter.

'If you want me to stay I'm coming with you,' she slung at him, burying her hands in her jeans' back pockets.

Serge stalled midway pulling on his leather jacket, his attention caught not by her statement but by what she was wearing. A fuzzy blue cashmere sweater which on another woman would have been casual, fade-into-the-background gear. Somehow Clementine's extravagant curves turned it into something else entirely. Something far too distracting for Forster's Gym.

It occurred to Serge in that moment that the only occasion when Clementine had actually been provocatively dressed was on that afternoon he'd followed her up the Nevsky Prospekt. Ever since she'd worn modest clothing, covering herself up from neck to knee. She didn't flaunt herself.

He hadn't considered it before, but she couldn't help being built like an old-time pin-up. A few lines of 'The Girl Can't Help It' flashed through his mind and he smiled to himself, shaking his head. He was losing his perspective if he'd started making up reasons for Clementine's sexual allure. She was a girl who could work the angles. Who knew her strengths and played to them—strengths he hadn't had enough of. Not yet.

'So don't even try arguing with me, Marinov. You really don't want to make me angry at this point,' she bulldozed on, then frowned suspiciously. 'Why are you smiling?'

Almost reflexively his eyes were drawn to her throat, where the diamond pendant was loudly not on display. Probably inappropriate, given what she was wearing, but he couldn't help but have his attention drawn to the little locket resting against the soft blue wool of the sweater.

It was a girlish locket, something clearly with sentimental value, and she seemed to be always wearing it. He had noticed that she tugged on it when she was agitated. She was tugging on it now. It bugged him.

'Apparently I've failed to make you happy, Clementine, and that's a problem.'

Damn right it was, she thought. And she wasn't going to say it was okay, because it wasn't. Shouldn't sex have brought them closer? She knew it was a naive view. Sex could mean nothing at all. But this wasn't normal. She was getting the distinct impression Serge was putting some emotional distance between them, and the message was *Burn up the sheets, but out of bed it's business as usual.*

It was probably time for some plain speaking. 'I'm not sure what's going on, Serge,' she said uncomfortably. 'You invited me to spend time with you, but I'm not spending time with you at all…' She trailed off.

His smile faded, and for the first time she saw the hard man she had glimpsed once or twice in Petersburg. 'You knew what you were getting into when you came with me, Clementine,' he said, almost formally. 'I'm making no apologies for that. I work hard. I play hard. What did you think you were signing up for?'

She shook her head in confusion. 'Signing up? I didn't know I was signing up for anything.' Then it hit her, his meaning, and two things happened. Her tummy dropped away and the chain around her neck snapped.

Clementine gave a reflexive gasp of dismay, looking down at the locket now pooled in her hand even as her head spun on the revelation this was some sort of sex date for him.

'I'll get it fixed,' Serge heard himself volunteer, unable to get over how upset she was getting, or how uncomfortable it was making him feel.

'I can take it to a jeweller myself.'

Her heart was pounding. She knew she was being too emotional, but sex had never been a casual thing for her. Deep down she'd known what he was about, but she'd jumped at the adventure of this and now she was having it. It was just she hadn't thought ahead to the consequences.

He didn't take her seriously. He might not even really like her. He just wanted to bed her.

Work hard. Play hard. Yes—what *did* you think you were signing up for, Clementine?

Silently she closed the door on the part of her that longed to be cared for and cherished, that believed she had a right to be loved—the hopeful, idealistic girl who had taken a chance in climbing aboard that jet with him. Instead she fired up the Clementine who'd been out in the world on her own for several years now—the Clementine who knew the score, who knew how to make a situation work for her.

There were two people in this arrangement. If she was having an adventure, she sure as heck was going to have some of this her way.

'I am coming,' she insisted, hands on her hips. 'I signed up to be with you, not sit around in a hotel room.' It felt good to throw his hateful words back at him. 'I'm surprised you get dates, Serge, if this is the way you treat women. Although I suppose the money helps.'

In an instant his Tartar heritage flared into life as his eyes narrowed and his expression hardened. '*Da, kisa*, the money helps.'

Somehow he had turned that insult around on her, and she stiffened, pressing her lips together. This was all going down the tube fast, and she didn't quite know how to save it.

'So what's it going to be?' she said fiercely. 'Can I come?' She couldn't quite bring herself to finish that with, *Or do I go?*

Serge pocketed his phone, his eyes travelling over her. She was a beautiful girl and she could stand up for herself. He liked it when she scratched. He wouldn't mind if she scratched harder. But it was the statement she was making with that tight, fluffy blue sweater that touched something softer inside him. For all her knowingness, Clementine really didn't have a clue.

He gave her a buried smile. 'As long as you wear a jacket, Boots.'

CHAPTER SEVEN

THE gym was a plain brick building. And Serge had been right about the sweat and testosterone. He introduced her to a man called Mick Forster, a fit guy in his fifties, who was polite but paid no more attention to her. All the other men in the room did three-sixtys as she moved through, and Clementine had never felt so conspicuous in her life. She was glad for once she had worn a neutral uniform of jeans, sweater and a vintage black velvet jacket.

She chose not to cling onto Serge's hand. She wasn't going to be the little woman on his arm. She folded her arms instead and wandered further into the gym, watching the athletes sparring, trying not to stare too long at any particular guy.

She was deep in man territory. It was nothing like her pretty pastel gym at home.

So this was how Serge had started out. Interesting.

She wandered back to find Serge deep in conversation with a group of men. She sat down on a bench. A short, strongly built young man slipped under the ropes and into the ring. A larger guy faced off with him, and Clementine watched with interest as they started feinting and jabbing, slicing the air with hands and feet. It was practice, it wasn't about breaking skin, and it was fascinating to watch how the men pulled their punches and kicks. It was a sort of masculine ballet.

She noticed no one sat down beside her. There was nothing friendly about any of these guys, but she suspected it wasn't personal. Her attention drifted back to Serge. He was talking in a low voice to Mick Forster, and they were both riveted to the sparring.

Then Mick said something, and it all happened at once. The blows made real contact. Clementine flinched as the men's bodies collided. She averted her eyes but the sounds kept coming—fist connecting with bone.

'Clementine, would you like to wait in the outer office?' Serge was bending over her, blocking her view of the ring.

She nodded, didn't argue. She felt embarrassed—and vaguely guilty.

'What in the hell did you bring *her* here for?' said Mick when Serge returned.

Serge felt an uncharacteristic surge of irritation with the older man. 'My private life isn't your business, Mick.'

'She's a distraction. You need to get your eyeline above her rack and back into the game, boy. A political move against this organisation and stadiums are going to close like mouse traps around the country.'

Serge's expression remained bland as he said quietly, but with lethal emphasis, 'If you refer to Clementine's rack again all conversations are over, Mick—you got it?'

Mick Forster rolled back on his heels. 'Well, well…' was all he said. Then, in a lower voice, 'Do you think she's up to holding your hand and being photographed at a few charity events?'

Five minutes later Serge emerged. Clementine stood up. 'Are you done?'

'We're moving, *kisa.*'

It wasn't the same as being done, but he swept her along

and seated in the car she said softly, 'I'm sorry. You were right. I shouldn't have come.'

Unexpectedly he pulled her in against him, pressing a kiss to her surprised lips—a gesture of comfort. 'No, you shouldn't have come—but that was my fault.'

'Who was he? The fighter?'

'Jared Scott. We're signing him.'

'Is that good?'

'I'm counting on it, *kisa*. We're throwing a lot of backing behind him.'

'How does it work? What generates the money besides ticket sales?'

'Gambling,' Serge said flatly. 'That's all it was initially. But the organisation reached sponsorship size about five years ago. When the boys go into the ring in two weeks' time here in New York they'll be covered in logos.'

'There's a match coming up?'

'We call them events. Don't even ask, *kisa*.'

Clementine looked away. After her performance in the gym she didn't feel she *could* ask.

He didn't know why, but he felt the urge to reassure her. He'd been struggling with it since she'd sat on that bed wrapped in a towel and looking lost. But his instinct for self-preservation made him hold off. He didn't want to set up that sort of dynamic in their relationship. But this he could do.

His hand squeezed her thigh and she looked up. 'It's pretty daunting for a woman to walk into that environment. You did fine.'

It was disconcerting to realise he had read her thoughts. Yet she was beginning to anticipate his. 'Am I going to see anything of you during the day?'

'You know why I needed to come back to New York, *kisa*. It's a busy time of year for me.' Serge endeavoured to keep his tone reasonable. He'd known this question was coming.

He got it from every woman he dated. They all wanted time he didn't have to give.

'It's just we've only got a week.'

Another predictable response from a woman who was proving anything but. It should have relaxed him. This should be familiar ground. This wasn't: 'How about you stay on after the end of the week?'

'Stay on?'

'After last night and today, Clementine, I'd be certifiably insane to let you go.'

'Oh.' He meant the sex. She was getting the picture.

He noticed she reflexively reached to tug on the locket that wasn't there.

'You're not interested?' He asked the perfunctory question, but of course she was.

'I have a job, Serge,' she said, her voice firmer than before. 'It was a bit of a cheek taking a week. I don't know if I could manage another.'

'Then quit.'

The nonchalance of a billionaire. Did he really think it was that easy for her? Or was it just a case of her job not meaning much to him?

'I can't just quit my job. It's a career, and it's important to me,' she spluttered. 'Besides which I've got a flat and a life to finance—not to mention it would look pretty dodgy on my CV.'

'Clementine, I don't think you understand what I'm offering you.'

She was plucking at her sweater now. Serge watched, fascinated, even as he endeavoured to work out what her problem was and exactly how much it was going to cost him.

'Two weeks in your bed in exchange for a career I've worked very hard for? I don't think so.'

'I was thinking of something more open-ended,' he said,

aware Clementine was about to turn him down flat. And how in the hell he'd opened himself up to be shot down he had no idea. It was Petersburg all over again—standing in that street, feeling like a thug for upsetting Clementine, when all he'd wanted was to see her again. To go on seeing her.

Yet he wasn't quite able to get the words *I'll make it worth your while* out of his mouth. He told himself it was because he'd never actually had to say them to a woman. The women he chose to be with understood the unspoken contract: mutually enjoyable sex, a certain lifestyle made available to them, and at the end—and there was always an end, sooner rather than later—a reward in the form of jewellery or something else that softened the edges of what was essentially a sexual contract.

Or an interview in a trashy magazine. But the women who had done that were always the ones with whom he'd had only glancing contact.

Clementine looked at him with those soft grey eyes he remembered from last night.

'I don't know, Serge,' she said with quiet dignity. 'You haven't made much of an effort so far.'

Sto? A dark flush of colour moved over his high cheekbones. His male pride sat up and took notice. Not made much of an effort? What exactly did *that* mean?

'It's not as if I saw anything of you today, and after last night that felt...weird.'

'Weird?' He repeated the word as if she was speaking in another language. Something about her simple, straightforward manner was riffling through his hard-won masculine detachment.

'I felt a bit...used,' she confessed.

He shifted beside her, his eyes narowing. Clementine viewed the change in him warily.

'What is it you require, Clementine?'

He spoke so formally, his accent thickening attractively on her name.

'Time. With you.'

She asked for the moon, he thought, challenged all the same.

Diamonds were so much easier.

Yet a wild sort of certainty about how this would play out focussed him on the one thing she seemed to be asking for that he could give her.

Time in his bed. Time with him. Time for both of them.

Clementine wondered what his silence meant. She could read him a little now, but she wasn't that good.

'Serge?'

A slow, elemental smile lit up that mouth she had longed to soften with hers the very first time she'd met him.

Never had she felt like this with a man before. From the very start he had lit something inside her. She felt like a woman when she was with him, and not a gauche girl stumbling through life. She didn't want it to end. She didn't want to give him up. But she didn't want to lose her self-respect if he only thought of her as a convenience.

'I will make time.' His green eyes had darkened. He reached for her, and suddenly she was wrapped in those muscular arms and being kissed in the way she had dreamt of being woken this morning.

Clementine was up early every morning thereafter for the rest of the week. She made sure of it. It meant she was sleeping lightly and waking often, but come six a.m., when Serge stirred, her eyes were open and she was waiting for him.

She would steal her arms around his neck and hold onto him, talk drowsily about what she had planned for the day: a gallery, a ride downtown, a walk through Central Park. Serge would listen, and gradually she'd eke out a little of what he would be doing. She gathered he wasn't used to explaining himself, but he was making a manful effort on her behalf. It was a start.

On the Friday, lack of sleep caught up with her. It was light on her face that woke her, and she surfaced to an empty bed. Her heart sank. Because it told her what she'd been steadily avoiding since that first morning after: this wasn't the beginning of a relationship, it was a sexual fling.

People had them. She had girlfriends who slept with men for no other purpose than sexual enjoyment. It was a natural part of life. Apparently.

But she didn't. She had relationship sex—the sort that had a framework of mutual caring and a view to a future together. That both of her relationships had been ended by her, neither truly touching her heart, did not make it any less true. She had gone into them with an innocence, a belief in love, until Joe Carnegie showed her exactly how base the relations between men and women could be.

And that experience haunted her. She hadn't realised how much until she'd met Serge. It hung over her like Damocles' sword. She was frightened of giving too much of herself to him, of opening herself up and having Serge reduce it to something sordid.

She thought she knew him—he was sweet and generous and attentive—but waking up alone now, as she had on that first morning, brought it back to her. How they had met, where they were now—in a swish hotel, with him continuing on with his working life, her life on hiatus.

Sitting up, she looked dismally around the room.

She never got over the luxury. But it felt empty without him, and worse, it made her feel uneasy. After all, it wasn't as if they actually had a proper relationship.

The half-open door came wide and Serge wandered in with

two coffee mugs, his eyes settling on her. 'You're awake, *dushka.*'

'Serge.' She couldn't hide her pleasure at seeing him.

'Cover yourself up, or I won't be responsible for my actions. And we have to move. I'm taking you to the Hamptons for the weekend.'

'Now?'

His gaze settled on her naked body. 'You're purposefully making this difficult. *Da*—now.'

Clementine leapt out of bed and ran for the door.

Serge watched her bottom wobble tantalisingly out of view. He liked waking up in the morning with Clementine warm and sweet, draped across him, and he wasn't about to pretend even to himself that he didn't; he even got a kick out of phoning her during the day and hearing that breathless 'Serge', as if she couldn't believe he had called her and would drop everything to fly to his side. Which she never did. Not Miss Independent. For all her demonstrative shows of affection he had a sense of her hovering like a butterfly, not quite sure of her perch. The analogy was apt—delicate, whimsical, difficult to hold. Her elusiveness remained, despite the week they had spent together.

It probably explained her hold over him.

It was clearer to him than ever that being a girl on call to a rich man was not a scenario Clementine truly understood. He was beginning to suspect he was her first foray into this world. If her wide-eyed reaction to the penthouse suite hadn't told him that, her refusal to wear the diamond necklace confirmed it.

He was beginning to suspect she had no idea what any of this was about—and that made two of them.

The helicopter ride out was thrilling. The view of the city below was like a movie. As they came in over the Atlantic

coast Clementine leaned down to take in the curling break-
ers on the beach below.

'You have no fear, *kisa*,' Serge shouted above the roar of
the rotorblade.

'I have a few, Slugger—just not of heights,' she sang back.
'Tell me that is *not* where we're staying?'

A beautiful large white house, set down beside dunes falling away to the beach.

On the helipad he took her hand in a casual gesture and
led her towards the house. 'Welcome home, Clementine.'

'You live here?'

'I'm thinking about buying it. I'm leasing at the moment.'

'What about St Petersburg?'

'Winter. When I can.'

For the first time she realised it made sense for him to have
a base in the US. It hadn't occurred to her before. His business interests in the main were here. He wouldn't be living
out of hotels.

He was just living in a hotel with her.

Unease slid through her but she pushed it aside. She was
here now. He'd brought her here now.

'Can you take me on a tour of the house?'

He gave her that flashing grin that told her he enjoyed surprising her.

'It will be my pleasure,' he said, with a note of formality
that shouldn't have surprised her. He'd pulled out this traditional Russian male several times since she'd been with him
and it always got to her.

It made her trust him a little more—made her want things
from him she couldn't have.

Which was dangerous thinking. Just looking around this
huge, airy house she couldn't help but be conscious of the
gulf between them. He took this level of luxury for granted.
She wondered what he would say if he saw her shared flat,

with its two bedrooms and a showerhead over the bathtub? Picturing Serge in her tiny bolthole brought a wry smile to her lips. Picturing him in her bath made her laugh out loud, and he angled her a curious but amused look.

'What is funny, *kisa*?'

'I was thinking—what's a middle-class girl from Melbourne doing in a Russian billionaire's summer house in East Hampton?' she replied cheekily.

'Enjoying the amenities,' he shot back. 'It's all at your disposal, Clementine. The tennis court, pool, games room, theatre, and of course the Atlantic Ocean.'

They had reached the other end of the house and stepped out onto the deck, extending like the prow of a ship out towards the grassy dunes and the Atlantic beyond. The sea breeze lifted Clementine's hair and wrapped it around her neck.

'It's huge. You *cannot* live here all by yourself.'

'I'll use it for entertaining this summer.' He shrugged. 'And I'm not living here alone at the moment. I've got you.'

Clementine tried not to enjoy that comment too much, but she had to drop her chin to hide her smile at his words. He really was being very sweet. Ever since that conversation in the car, coming back from Mick Forster's gym, he'd been everything she needed him to be—attentive, considerate, looking after her needs. It was very easy to forget she was only here on a break.

Although he'd said he wanted more. And after a week so did she. She looked up at him, wondering how to broach the subject. It was hard for her. She'd been let down so often in the past. People wanted you around as long as you were entertaining or useful or fulfilled a function. Her own parents had taught her well. She came second, never first. Serge was making an effort right now, but she knew it couldn't last. She was already foreseeing the end of all of this, when one day she woke up and discovered she'd overstayed her welcome.

She was still thinking about it when Serge left her to go and make some calls. Even on a weekend break his work didn't stop. As she wandered around the state-of-the-art kitchen, opening cupboards, checking the cooking utensils, imagining the meals she could prepare in here, she mused ruefully that it wasn't other women she needed to worry about with Serge. It was the business that was her rival. If she was going to stay with him she needed to get a job, and it occurred to her that with the Marinov Corporation facing a huge public relations exercise in the media at the moment her skills might be put to some use.

She was tired of spruiking fashion. She wanted something to get her teeth into.

But mostly it would be nice to show Serge the smart girl wrapped in the sexy girl package.

Serge reappeared in quarter of an hour, stripped down to a pair of boardshorts and nothing else. Clementine went a bit weak at the knees, but told herself there was no way she was going to strip him naked and do anything remotely sexy with him in the kitchen, because it was broad daylight and anyone could walk in.

'How about we go for a swim, *kisa*?'

Her lustful thoughts dissolved as her face fell. 'I don't have a bathing suit.'

He winked at her. 'All taken care of.'

'I'm not wearing something that belonged to some random woman you brought here.'

For a moment Clementine fancied he was going to say something about those random women. Then he shrugged. 'I had a buyer bring in a summer wardrobe for you, Clementine. I checked your size from your existing clothes.'

'You bought me clothes?' She struggled to keep control of her voice.

'*Da*—I'm a prince.'

She searched his eyes for a hint of ownership, but he looked relaxed.

Okay, he was turning it all into a bit of a joke. She could relax into that. This wasn't about her in a designer dress on his arm. This was casual. This was just between them. This was his summer home.

He'd brought her to his home.

She needed to relax.

Then she flushed, a little disconcerted by the notion of Serge knowing her measurements.

'I'm waiting to be chastised for buying you clothes, *kisa*,' he drawled.

'You'll be waiting a long time,' she replied loftily, tossing her hair. 'But those bathers better be more than postage stamps.'

It was bliss to frolic in the cold Atlantic surf. Clementine had grown up beside the beach, and it was what she missed most living in England. There were beaches, but nothing like what she was used to at home.

Serge swam with her. He was a different man here. She'd noticed it even as the spit of land had come into view from the helicopter. He laughed with her and teased her, and seemed to have left the city and all his tensions behind.

As they strode out of the surf she felt confident enough to bring up the subject she'd been rehearsing in her mind all day.

'Serge,' she ventured, 'I've been thinking about what you said—about my staying on here.'

He tugged her closer, his gaze appreciative of the virtually transparent red bikini clinging to her wet skin.

'That sounds promising.'

'I was thinking maybe I could work for you. You must have a huge PR department?'

The sexual heat was doused with a bucket of reality. '*Nyet*—no, definitely not. It's not a place for you, *kisa*.'

'What do you mean? I'm fabulous at my job.'

'I have no doubt. But you won't be working in the fight game, Clementine. Not while you're with me.'

She looked at him sadly. Why did he have to bring that up? The sense there was a time limit on everything? She wanted to forget that, to be in the moment with him if the moment was all he could give her.

'Listen.' He took her chin between his thumb and index finger. 'I can send you in the direction of any number of high-profile fashion firms in this city. Getting you a job, beautiful girl, is not a problem.'

She hadn't thought of that. His contacts. The water foamed around their feet. 'I'd prefer to get my own job, Serge.'

'Does that mean you'll stay, *kisa*?' He slid his hands behind her shoulders.

She tossed her ponytail. 'I could be persuaded.'

He had her. Serge tried to ignore the rush of hot excitement that thought brought with it. Any other woman arranging her life to suit his would have rung serious warning bells, but he wanted this. He didn't want Clementine going back to London. He needed her a little longer—just until this craving for her was worked out of his system in increasingly inventive sex.

Except it hadn't been particularly inventive. His imagination came up with the scenarios, but the reality was that when she was in his arms he found it became much more about losing themselves in one another, in the kissing, the touching, but especially her soft touch. She didn't display any skills, or even really initiate anything between them. Not that he gave her much time to. He couldn't get enough of her, and the only thing that slowed him down was the impression Clementine was still adapting to him and the realities of their sexual relationship. Sometimes she would have a vulnerable look on her face, and instead of stripping her naked he would just cuddle with her—which, he told himself, proved nothing except that he was sensitive to her needs, and that made her more susceptible to future approaches.

That night the sex was fast and furious and then finished. Clementine fell into a deep sleep almost immediately it was over.

He'd worn her out. The thought stroked a male ego he hadn't known needed stroking. Yet he lay awake long afterwards, with the moonlight spilling over the bed and Clementine's face illuminated in the pale light on the pillow beside him. She was the most beautiful woman he had ever seen. But her features were slightly irregular, there were freckles all over her body, and she had the most endearing snore. Why all of this should enhance her beauty he didn't know. Only it did.

He must have dozed, because he awoke to hear her voice soft in his ear. She was telling him things, and at first all he did was listen. How overwhelming it had been for her, arriving in London three years ago, not knowing anyone, all the trouble she'd got into, the jobs she'd endured. But always she'd kept thinking: *I can't go back. I can't put my tail between my legs and go home. There's a bigger life out in the world for me.*

He figured he was only hearing all of this because his eyes were closed. His mysterious little Clem was opening up, and he wasn't about to let the cat out of the bag by shifting an inch. He could feel her hair sliding over his arm and chest, the warm press of her breast and belly and leg. He was thinking how sweet she was, confiding in him like this.

She had run into her old schoolmate and neighbour Luke in a pub— 'You remember Luke? He was going to punch you on the nose.' And suddenly her life had started to open up. On Luke's advice she'd switched to her first good job with the Ward Agency, spruiking for up-and-coming fashion designers. Her name had got passed on until she'd landed the job with Verado.

She told him how Luke had always told her it was who you knew before it was what was you did, and how she tried to make every contact count. She had learned to work a room, learned to make the most of what she had and flirt up a storm, and as a result she'd got jobs.

Da, he got that. He'd worked out for himself the sexy-girl persona was just that—something designed to get attention. He just hadn't connected that to her working life. But it made complete sense. It was why he never got that sexy girl in his bed. He got someone better, a lot less knowing, a lot more real, sensual, genuine.

As he lay there, debating whether to roll over and get up, pull the cord on this little confessional skydive, she nuzzled his neck and he opened his eyes to look down at her.

'When I first left the army I floundered around trying out a mess of jobs.'

She gave a little gasp. 'You're awake?' She sounded dismayed.

He took in her wide, worried eyes, the heat mounting her cheeks. What had amused him, and then felt a little too much like real intimacy, now changed colour again. The urge not to embarrass her made him keep talking. About selling mechanical parts on the black market, about a failed attempt to set up a trading company, about the gym training prize fighters he'd owned, which he'd almost lost when the trading company went bust but had ended up becoming his way out and up.

'Why did you get interested in the fight game?' she asked.

'Started in the army—fighting for money. I graduated to organising matches. It's not a lenient sport, *kisa*. It's better to be behind the scenes.'

Instinctively Clementine reached up and gently touched the bridge of his nose. 'Is that how you broke it?'

'Twice. It happened a long time ago. I don't even remember the pain.'

She stroked his chest. 'I don't like the idea of you being hit.'

'I'm a tough guy, *kisa*.'

'What about your family? What did they think about you being involved in the sport? What about your mother?'

'My mother died when I was nineteen.' He spoke quietly, calmly, as if reciting facts. 'She took pills.'

Clementine lifted her head, her forehead pleated with concern.

'We'll never know if it was suicide. Possibly. Probably. Don't look so dire, Clementine, it was a long time ago.'

'Your mother?' she said softly, stroking him.

'Let me tell you something about mothers, *kisa*. Mine married young. My father was an engineer—idealistic, probably bi-polar.' He slanted her a curious look, unable to believe he was telling her all this. She had stopped stroking him and her eyes were pinned to his. 'My parents loved one another with an intensity that didn't allow any air into the relationship or any light into our family life. It was two performances of *Turandot* daily.'

Clementine stayed silent, trying to form a picture of what his childhood must have been like. He stretched, as if the telling of the tale was cramping his muscles.

'Papa stepped in front of a car one afternoon when I was ten, and everything changed. Mama remarried a couple of years later. My stepfather and I didn't see eye-to-eye and I was shipped off to military school. Before you feel sorry for me, *kisa*, it was the best place for me. I rarely saw my mother and sister after that. My stepfather made a fortune out of the fall of communism and promptly lost it—put a bullet in his head. Mama wasn't far behind him. So you see—an opera in four acts.'

Clementine was silent for a moment, and then laid her head on his shoulder.

'Yes, you are,' she said softly.

'I'm what?' he enquired in a rough voice.

'A tough guy.' They were quiet together for a long time, and then she confessed, 'I don't want to go back to the city.'

It was the closest she had come to voicing how uncomfortable she was feeling, living in a hotel suite with him.

'Room Service beginning to pall, Clementine?'

He was teasing her, but there was something else in his voice. A sadness. Perhaps a leftover from his revelations, or maybe he was just over the whole impress-the-girl routine.

'It's a bit impersonal, isn't it? I hadn't realised until we came here. Being in this house is more like real life.'

Serge suddenly felt uncomfortable, and it wasn't a familiar sensation for him. Impersonal wasn't working here for him either, in this house with the ocean pounding at their doorstep. He'd brought her here to talk terms, make definite the parameters of their future relationship, but the girl lying in his arms didn't fit those terms. He'd just shared more with her than he'd shared with all the other women he'd ever known combined.

He heard himself saying, 'How about we take on some more real life?'

She looked up. The light in her eyes smote him.

'I'm taking you back to my townhouse, Clementine. I think the whole hotel scenario has worn thin, no?'

He had a home in the city. Yet they had been staying in a hotel for a week.

For a moment Clementine's whole world tipped, and everything that had come before took on a new, harsher light. Her stomach just dropped away. 'I see,' she said softly.

'Don't see too much, Clementine,' he said quietly, and she nodded—which was about all she could do.

It wasn't personal that he had chosen a hotel to get to know her, to make love to her, she thought with a savage desperation to make this all right again, to make it nothing like Joe Carnegie, to make it all romantic and hopeful again.

But nor was it personal that he had now decided to let her into his life, she acknowledged painfully. It was just a choice he was making—probably for his own comfort. She moved fast after that, making an excuse that she needed the bathroom and locking herself inside, running the bath water strong and hard to block out the sound of her tears.

CHAPTER EIGHT

THE drive back into the city gave Clementine a chance to process events as she watched the scenery zip by and surreptitiously observed Serge, who was very quiet. He liked to drive. She had seen that in St Petersburg. They had no room for their luggage, of course. That was coming separately. Clementine had only her handbag, which she jumbled through now, trying to find some of the barley sugar she always carried around with her.

Serge glanced at the objects beginning to clutter her lap.

'What have you got in there? Buried treasure?'

'Very funny.' Giving up on her surreptitious hunt, she just shook her bag's contents out over her lap. Ticket stubs, a pen, bits of paper, a tissue—all dropped out, fluttered down. She found the barley sugar. And Luke's two condoms.

'Going prepared, Clementine?'

She flushed and began stuffing everything back into her carry-all. Then was annoyed with herself for being embarrassed.

'Luke gave them to me back in Petersburg—for my date with you, if you must know. As if you were going to get lucky on our first date.' She couldn't resist adding, 'You had to fly me to a fancy hotel across the world for that.'

Serge was glad he was doing a low speed and that the car

was a fluid machine to guide, because her words had him veering towards the centre of the road.

He glanced at Clementine. 'Put your hand in my pocket.'

'Serge!'

'Go on. I won't bite.'

Rolling her eyes, but curious, she reached into his jacket pocket and retrieved a small box. She opened it.

'My locket!'

'I had it repaired.'

She hadn't looked at it since she'd slipped it into a drawer beside the bed. Serge clearly had.

Dipping her head to clasp it around her throat, she experienced a wave of affection that she felt awkward about expressing. Not now that she had a much clearer-eyed view on their relationship.

'Don't tell me it's a memento from an old boyfriend,' he said in a gravelly voice.

'I bought it for myself when I turned eighteen.' She held up her wrist. 'I got this watch for myself when I signed up with Verado.'

Serge frowned. 'You purchased these yourself?'

'Why not?' she said defensively. 'Someone once told me if you don't have people in your life to mark important occasions you need to do it for yourself.' She manufactured a grin. 'Which for me is just an excuse to shop.'

No one to mark important occasions. It shouldn't bother him but it did.

'Clementine, a beautiful woman should not be buying herself jewellery.'

She gave him a bright, dismissive smile. 'Men are always buying me gifts, Serge, I just choose not to accept them.'

His knuckles rose to prominence on the wheel. He didn't want to hear about other men. But he got the message. Loud and clear. She was thinking about the diamond necklace. He wished he'd never given her the damn thing. Given? He'd left it for her to find with a note. Thanks for your services. He didn't allow himself to look back, but this was one incident he wished he could go back and change.

Yet she hadn't confronted him over it in so many words. He knew exactly where it was. In the bedside table, on his side of the bed, untouched. As far as a statement went it was pretty loud.

'You haven't talked about your family,' he said, clearing his throat. 'I assume you have them? Parents?'

Clementine looked at him sharply. He gave her a reassuring smile and her defensiveness wobbled. She nodded slowly.

'Happy childhood?' he pressed, not sure where he was going with this but feeling a bit like a drowning man grasping at sticks.

'Not really.' She suddenly became fascinated with her hands, examining her nails as she talked. 'They divorced when I was five.'

'Brought up by your mother?'

'I was handballed between them—Mum in Melbourne, Dad in Geneva. He's a journo—war correspondent. Always chasing something, whether it's a conflict, a story, a woman.' She shrugged her shoulders, dealing privately with the mixture of anger and grief she always felt when speaking about her parents. 'Mum remarried. I've got three stepsisters but I don't really know them. I left home at seventeen and I haven't been back.'

Serge frowned. 'Seventeen is young for a girl to be out on her own.'

'It is, but I managed.'

It explained a lot. Her independence, her ability to take him on, but also that vulnerability that had been worrying him.

'So you don't miss your family?' He didn't know why he

was pursuing this, only he found he needed to know more about this side of her life, and until now she had never spoken about it.

'Not much to miss,' she replied briefly, looking down. 'I was still at school when I left home. I ended up working a slew of menial jobs during the day, did school at night. I wasn't getting anywhere so I made the decision to do what so many other people my age were doing and try London. I don't regret making the move. I always felt like there were opportunities out there in the world for me, and I want to take them whilst I'm young enough to enjoy them.'

Clementine suddenly wished this conversation had never started up. Talking about her parents always stirred up painful memories. A childhood where nothing was certain, all power in the hands of two adults who seemed to be nothing more than overgrown toddlers careening out of control on dodgem cars, herself alone and unprotected between them, had given her a strong need to protect herself.

At twenty-five she knew her past was beginning to take a toll. Professionally she was fine, but her personal life had never really got off the ground and now it was dead in the water.

Until this man.

Don't see too much, Clementine.

No, she wouldn't. But he wanted to be reassured she wasn't jumping the gun. That she could be the girl he wanted. The no-strings girl. But *could* she be that girl or was the price too high?

It was time to protect herself again.

She gripped her knees, and the gesture wasn't lost on him. 'Serge, can I be frank?'

He actually looked taken aback and she almost smiled. Were there worse words you could say to a man? It always prefaced something they would rather not know.

She smiled thinly. *Lucky you, Serge, you're going to get exactly what you want to hear.*

'I'm not naive,' she continued. 'I know you live for your work. Relationships are way down on your agenda. I also know that you want to keep me out of that part of your life—you want to keep your distance. I get that you chose to take me to a hotel rather than your townhouse.'

He looked as if he wanted to say something, but she got in there fast.

'You're telling me not to get serious about any of this. I get it. I understand all you're offering is an opportunity, not a long-term relationship.' She affected a casual shrug. 'It's okay. I'm cool with that. That's what I want too.' *Liar, liar, pants on fire.*

Serge stilled.

This should be his moment of relief. Instead it hit him like a sucker punch.

'An opportunity?' he said slowly, turning the phrase over like a rock and observing all the nasty things crawling out.

For the first time in over a week he was reminded of the girl he'd first met in St Petersburg. The girl he'd imagined had several guys on the go, working her advantages. From their first night together the notion had been rendered laughable. For all her innate sensuality Clementine was not a practised lover. In fact she had given the impression of being swept away by her feelings. It was a big part of why being with her felt so different.

Up until a moment ago he would have discounted her claim. Yet now knowing a little about her past put a slant on his perspective. She was clearly tougher than she looked. This was a woman who had survived on her own since she was a teenager. She didn't need his protection. She didn't need coddling. She was telling him exactly what he should be celebrating hearing.

'So my finding a job makes sense, don't you think?'

He looked over at her. She flashed a bright, brittle smile.

Nyet, nothing made sense.

The next day Clementine spent her time alone, making the rounds of several fashion labels before one bit. Her CV now had Verado's name as a calling card. All her hard work in St Petersburg had paid off. The fashion label Annelli were launching a campaign over Christmas, to brand their jeans with an up-and-coming young Hollywood actress. If she was interested in joining their team they had a job for her.

The work was in New York City. There wouldn't be a problem with her visa. It was all lining up. Yet she hesitated to take the job.

In a cab uptown she thought about what all this meant.

She wanted a lot more from Serge than she suspected he ever intended to give her. You didn't take a girl to a hotel when you had a perfectly good home across town. He had never meant this to be anything more than a no-strings fling and in the Hamptons, desperate to hold onto her dignity, she'd dismissed the depth of her feelings and given him his 'Get out of Jail Free' card.

Because she did have feelings for him—and she wasn't going to deny them to herself even as she hid them from him. And the longer they were together the deeper those feelings were growing. She so desperately didn't want to be his good-time girl. She knew the impression she had given him in St Petersburg. She had hoped he knew her better now. But a week of heady lovemaking and not much else had left her teetering on the suspicion that this was always going to be a sexual affair for Serge and little else, and his luxury lifestyle only confirmed it. Why would he want more when his looks and money could bring in beautiful women from all over the world?

He had invited her into his home now, prodded her inner voice. It was something.

But it wasn't an invitation into his life, which was clearly taken up with his business.

Which was why she hesitated to take the Annelli job. Whatever he said about her not working for him, it grew more and more appealing the longer she thought about it. Being with Serge was going to mean lots of late-night drop-ins on gyms and plenty of travel, given the far-flung nature of the sport in Europe and the States. To be in his life she needed to be in his business. She could prove to him she was much more than a warm body in his bed and that she could play with the big boys too. Maybe that was a way forward for them?

But the overarching issue was the need to keep her independence, and that meant finding an apartment of her own. Being safe meant being independent. She'd learned that lesson the hard way with her parents, and had it reinforced by her experience with Joe Carnegie. Never again would a man consider he owned her simply because of the financial disparity between them.

She hopped out of the taxi on East 64th and jogged across the road towards the line of 1920s townhouses.

Serge's house had come as a lovely surprise. It was a proper home—eleven rooms over five levels. Ridiculously large for a single man, but what interested Clementine was how unpretentious it was. Completely restored, it had an old-fashioned simplicity that told her a great deal about the man she was living with, and it was oddly comforting.

She fired up the laptop in Serge's study and called up his website, navigating her way through to the schedule of matches. She knew he would be at the match on Friday night for a couple of hours, which gave her a window of opportunity to see him in action.

He didn't need to know, and it would help her build up a sense of how to approach him about a job. She booked a ticket on-line and shut the laptop with an uneasy feeling that she had just crossed a line with Serge. If he found out he wouldn't be happy.

Serge checked his watch and then looked at the screens in the control room. The stadium was filled to capacity, the main event would soon be underway, and he could leave and drive back into town and have a late dinner with Clementine.

He was enjoying their little arrangement. He had never cohabitated with a woman before, would have run a mile if anyone had suggested it to him. Although Clementine was quick to remind him she was effectively on holiday and that once her working visa came through things would naturally change. They weren't actually living together.

She'd said that to him. *We're not living together, Serge.*

As if he needed to know where he stood. As if she was warning him off. It was starting to get on his nerves.

And she kept talking about this apartment idea. He told her there was no hurry, but it didn't stop her talking about it…

Almost as if thinking about her had conjured her up the small screen in front of him suddenly filled with her face. The wide cheekbones, pointed chin, grey eyes fluttering as she looked around, oblivious to being broadcast on a large screen.

'Hold that camera,' he said to the tech in front of him, and leaned in.

The cameras always panned in for a pretty girl, and Clementine with her lovely face, her wealth of hair down over her shoulders, in tight designer jeans and nipped-in jacket was just that. Possession gripped him behind the neck like a vice.

She was out there. Alone.

Serge registered all of this as Alex said something about going down and showing himself in the owners' box if only to make the media happy.

'That girl,' said Serge to his minder. 'Find out what seat she's in.'

'Do you want me to fetch her, boss?'

'You do not touch her,' Serge snarled. 'I'm going down. Phone me through the info.'

Alex caught up with him as he jogged down the maze of corridors.

'I thought you were seeing some Australian woman.'

'I am.'

Seat 816 FF. She was up in the gods. He had a detail of security with him as he closed in on her. She had that tight expression on her face he recognised. She wasn't comfortable with all the noise or the people around her. Good. It might teach her a lesson.

He didn't expect the look of relief on her face when she saw him—nor did he expect his instant reaction, which was an answering satisfaction. She knew who she belonged to. Then her gaze slid by him to his security, and she frowned and looked back at him uneasily.

He didn't say a word, merely extracted her from her seat. She looked up into his eyes. 'Serge, you didn't need to do this.'

'You made it necessary with your actions, Clementine.' His voice was clipped. 'I'm sure you've got an explanation as to what you think you're doing, but I haven't got time to hear it.'

He put his arm around her. From a distance it might seem a tender gesture but Clementine knew when she was being frogmarched.

Trying to defuse the situation, she laughed uneasily. 'Geez, Slugger, what are you going to do? Arrest me or something?'

'I'm going to put you somewhere safe and you're going to stay there. I don't have time to babysit you, Clementine. This isn't a local gym and a controlled environment.'

Clementine felt a pang as she remembered her embarrassing reaction when he had taken her, on her insistence, to watch the sparring. She had interrupted his working life. His important working life. And she was doing it again—only on a grander scale.

She hadn't meant to. It wasn't supposed to be like this. If he hadn't come and plucked her out of the crowd she'd still be sitting up there, him none the wiser, nothing disrupted.

It was his problem with her, and she wasn't going to take the blame.

As they approached the glassed-in owners' box she hissed, 'Maybe if you'd just issued an invite instead of shutting me out I wouldn't have had to buy a ticket.'

'*Kisa*, if you ever pull a stunt like this again there won't be any invites. Anywhere. Period.'

And with that he pushed her in front of a group of strangers and said to the nearest woman, 'Kim, this is Clementine—Clementine Chevalier, Kim Hart.' And around they went—introductions, handshakes. Hard men and heeled-up women with big hair. Clementine felt quite demure by comparison. She wondered if anyone else could hear the edge in Serge's voice or if it was just her own private horror show. Then he plopped her down in a central seat and had someone put a glass of white wine in her hand. And was gone.

Clementine watched him leave, trying not to look too panicked. He would come back for her? What had he meant, no more invites? Had she crossed some sort of relationship line she didn't know about?

A blonde whose name Clementine had forgotten leaned

forward and tapped her on the shoulder. 'So what's it like being flavour of the month?'

'Ignore her,' said another voice to her left, and the woman Serge had introduced as Kim slid into the seat beside her. 'First event?'

'Yes, I'm looking forward to it,' she responded, a little blindsided by Serge's words and then by the 'flavour of the month' comment. Doing her best to shrug it off, she switched on her job brain and queried, 'So what's the deal here? How is everyone connected with the Marinov Corporation?'

Kim was the chatty type, and she seemed to have a comprehensive knowledge of the business. She rolled off the fighters' agents, the sponsors present, pointed out different key staff, then settled into the nitty-gritty of the fighters, their stats. None of which interested Clementine in the slightest, but as Kim chatted she was able to look around, soak in some of the atmosphere.

About thirty-plus people circulated in the luxurious environment of the glassed-in box, milling with drinks and nibbles. There were little screens everywhere, with different matches being broadcast from outside the arena. Outside the glass windows rock music was pumping, but it was only a rhythmic thump that came to her faintly.

She was suddenly glad to be in here.

'When it gets going we wander down and take ringside seats,' explained Kim. 'Jack, my partner, number-crunches at the top of the tree for the corporation. Completely unglamorous. This is the only exciting part of his job—getting ringside seats.'

'Where's Jack?'

'Over there.' Kim pointed him out, a rangy-looking guy in his mid thirties wearing jeans and a jacket and somehow contriving to make them look like a suit. Clementine knew the type. She looked at Kim. 'Do you think I could have a chat to him? I'm interested in how everything works.'

Serge returned to fetch Clementine for the fight. He found her with a male audience—what was new? Two accountants and Liam O'Loughlin, his deputy head of promotion. She'd pushed back her jacket and had her hands on her hips, and whatever she was saying the guys were riveted to her.

'Why can't you huddle with the girls and behave yourself?' he asked as he walked her away.

'I don't know, Serge. Maybe I get a little bored talking about nail colour.'

'That's not what I mean, *kisa*, and you know it. A third of my management team are women.'

'I know.'

He looked as if he was about to say something, but the wall of noise hit them as they stepped out of the box and there was no chance for further conversation. Serge wrapped his arm around her, instantly separating her from the world in his embrace. As she looked up she had her fifteen seconds of fame as she saw them reflected on the huge screen above the ring, and then flashing logos for sponsors, car companies, sports drinks. She tried to catch them all, but Serge was walking her fast.

The combination of lights, music and an excited crowd had Clementine's blood pumping, and she could see Serge wasn't unaffected. He might be focussed on the bottom line, but he did enjoy the hoopla on some level. She hadn't noticed it before but there was a real feel for showmanship in putting on a spectacle like this, combined with meticulous planning. Serge was a planner—she got that—but this was another side to him.

It appealed to her.

Ringside seats meant they were right on the action. This time Serge introduced her in a general way to the people sitting with them, including two famous male faces that had Clementine tugging on Serge's sleeve as they sat down.

'*Da, kisa*, it is,' he responded, sitting back and stretching out his long legs. He looked like a king on his throne, thought Clementine, highly amused.

'I'm not impressed,' she said. She was—but not for any of the more obvious reasons. Having these faces ringside was publicity. It was effectively labelling the brand. The fight game was an old one, but a rap artist and a young Hollywood actor brought a different vibe to the arena. 'Serge, how much is this costing you? Setting aside the sponsors?'

He gave her a flashing smile. 'Don't worry, Clementine. I can still afford to keep you in the style you're accustomed to.'

For a moment the volume was turned down, and all she could hear was the thump, thump as her mashed-up heart made itself known. Serge hadn't noticed a thing—his full attention was on something someone was saying to do with the match. Clementine slid her hand away from his and folded her arms. Serge didn't even notice. He just rested his forearms on his knees and sat forward.

The match was starting, but it didn't much matter any more. Serge had just made it very clear how he saw her. His feelings for her were about as meaningful as the spectacle they were enjoying tonight.

She was arm candy. She was, to quote, 'the flavour of the month'. He didn't take her seriously at all. Showing him her professional skills wasn't going to change a damn thing.

The fight started and Clementine braced herself. It was the reaction of the crowd more than the thudding contact of bodies in the ring that reverberated through her. She felt each and every time bone hit bone. She could feel Serge's attention being dragged away from the fight to her, and she kept her chin up, trying not to flinch.

Serge's arm was around her and his mouth at her ear. 'What in the hell did you come for, Clementine?'

A job description, murmured a snarky little voice, but she didn't voice it.

'I'm okay, Serge. Don't make a big deal of it.' She lifted her head, made herself look at the ring.

Serge made a sound low in his chest and stood up, startling the people around him. He had hold of her hand.

She wanted to resist, but it was embarrassing enough. He escorted her towards the exit, ignoring everyone else to get her through, his minders running ahead, clearing a path. Most people were focussed on the fight, but Clementine felt humiliated as Serge dragged her grimly away from the lights and pulsing rock music that had made him his fortune.

Serge was silent as they drove at speed out of the venue and along the highway. He barely said a word to her other than, 'Get in.' That suited her. She couldn't believe how high-handedly he was behaving.

He remained silent as they entered the house. Clementine took off her jacket and went straight upstairs. She didn't want to go to bed. She didn't want to pretend this was normal. But it was late, and there was nothing else to do, so she went into the bathroom to take off her make-up and undress. She put on her pyjama bottoms and a T-shirt—the least alluring bedwear she had.

Then she climbed into bed and sat there and waited. And waited.

He wasn't coming to bed.

Well, good. She didn't want him there. All the descriptors went flying around her head: arm candy, flavour of the month, good-time girl. Who in the heck did he think he was, implying she was with him for what he could give her financially? She was independent. She worked. She'd never relied on another person for anything.

Yet the way she had felt tonight hadn't been all bad. A part of her had liked his high-handedness, had enjoyed being the girl welded to his side. The sheer physical impact of him, his charisma, the way people leapt out of his way—she had seen it through others' eyes and she'd liked it.

He owned that world in a way she hadn't quite comprehended before. He was a man who reigned over an empire which celebrated machismo, and apart from the massive profit turnover it came with a huge element of sex appeal.

If you were that kind of woman.

Clementine lifted her hands to her hot cheeks and shook her head in amused despair. He had been drenched in sex appeal tonight, and just thinking about it was making her fidget. Who was she kidding? Everything about Serge got her going, and he knew it.

She'd been doing her best all week to keep him at arm's length, to protect herself by being the independent woman who had her own life and wasn't looking to him to offer her anything more than what he had given any other woman. She had her pride, and she'd been stuffing her own needs behind it and leading with her chin.

But now she didn't bother to hide her relief when he finally came up. Stripped down to jeans and a T-shirt, he looked like the big tough guy he was and she was honest enough with herself to admit she liked that. She liked it enough to want to shove aside her anger and hurt and climb him like a tree. Her pride kept her sitting cross-legged in the middle of the bed, but she was going to be honest with him for a change. He was a tough guy—he could take it. And so could she.

'We need to talk,' he said bluntly.

'Yes, we do,' she fired back. 'And I'm going first. Now, you listen up, Slugger. I'm much more than your current squeeze. I'm very good at my job, and your little fighting empire would be lucky to have me, and if you think my living here equals being kept by you, you've got another think coming. Okay?'

He was silent, just watching her. He didn't even blink. The atmosphere began to crackle with something and Clementine shifted uneasily on the bed.

'Are you listening to me?' Her voice quavered a little.

In reply Serge stripped off his T-shirt. As muscle and taut male skin came into view Clementine lost a little bit of concentration.

The T-shirt dropped to the floor.

'Serge?'

'You went behind my back,' was all he said, eyes hooded, gaze resting on her mouth.

She moistened her lips, shifting a little on the mattress.

'Do you have any idea how I felt, seeing your face on that screen and knowing you were out there in that crowd?'

His voice was low, intent, and he wasn't really asking a question. He was telling her.

Clementine's heart-rate kicked up and began to gallop.

Yet for some reason she thought this was the best time to throw herself off the emotional pier and blurt out, 'No, I *don't* know how you felt, because you never talk about your feelings.'

A tight smile sat at the corner of his mouth, as if he knew something she didn't. 'Well, guess what, *kisa*? I'm going to now.'

'That's good,' she prevaricated, giving a little 'oh' as he yanked down his jeans. He was naked and he was aroused and he was palming a condom from the drawer beside the bed, and Clementine wondered just when the talking part was going to take place.

He flipped her onto her back and came down over her, pinning her with his larger body. He did it so fluidly that one minute Clementine was sitting upright, fretting, and the next she was flat on her back staring into the eyes of the man who had rescued her from those thugs in the underpass.

'Now,' he said with slow deliberateness, 'let's talk about how I feel, Clementine. How about how I felt when I saw you alone in that crowd?'

He swept her T-shirt up over her head and bent to nudge a pointed rosy nipple with the stubble of his chin.

'How about how I felt when I saw you flirting with men who work for me?'

He took that nipple deep into his mouth.

'I don't know how you felt,' she gasped, but she was getting the picture.

Her body began to sing as his hand went south under the elastic of her pyjamas, testing her readiness. She'd been ready from about the time he'd said, 'We need to talk.'

'I felt like *this*.' He stripped her of the pyjama pants and cupped her bottom. Her thighs fell open of their own accord and she welcomed him as he thrust into her, a single stunning stroke. 'I felt like this, Clementine.' And he moved inside her harder, with a single-mindedness that wound her up with him, until she felt all the anger and tension in him turning into something that overwhelmed them both.

It seemed to Clementine they lay there for a very long time afterwards, just catching their breath. Her own was coming in rapid pants as she felt the throbbing in her body subside.

What had that been about?

Serge climbed off the bed and disposed of the condom in the *en suite* bathroom. Clementine watched him as he padded slowly back to the bed. He lay down beside her and pulled her body into the shelter of his. He laid a kiss on her shoulder, saying nothing. It was then Clementine realised he hadn't kissed her mouth—not once.

Yet this had felt more intimate than anything that had come

before. Wasn't he supposed to be angry? Wasn't she supposed to be too? Instead she felt closer to him than ever.

Serge pulled her in tighter. What in the hell was he doing? When he'd seen her on that monitor his only thought had been to reach her. Everything else had been blotted out but the need to keep her safe. And he hadn't. He'd shoved her up ringside and everything had come undone. It was still coming undone. She made him act rashly. He'd taken her home and acted rashly again. And he suddenly had no doubt given any provocation this rashness was going to continue. Unless he made a conscious effort to stop it.

'Is that how you felt?' she whispered, turning her head to look at him, her eyes half closed, her expression so sultry he knew they were about to repeat it all over again.

'I don't know how I felt,' he admitted in a deep voice, his accent pronounced, and something in his tone snagged all Clementine's attention away from her body, still sensitised from his touch. 'But I do know now you're safe.' His arms tightened around her.

'Yes, I'm safe, Slugger,' she and answered, and reached up and patted the big arm slung around her, sounding more confident than she felt. Inside everything was knocked off kilter. As if she didn't quite belong to herself any more.

But what did that mean? That she belonged to Serge?

CHAPTER NINE

SERGE took a coffee and his cellphone out onto the deck and stood in the cool morning light as it dappled down through the leaves above. This was his sanctuary in the city—a green garden, an oasis kept in exquisite shape by people he paid.

Having the people in his life on a payroll made everything so much easier, cleaner. Nobody's emotions got involved.

Last night his behaviour in bed with Clementine had been the opposite. Hard, messy, and very emotional. The sex as a result had been incredible. The only thing that could have improved on it was not using a condom, and the fact that he'd actually considered that thought put the brakes on any future plans he had with this girl.

He'd never once not used a condom. Ever. He didn't have the sort of relationships where that was possible.

Yet he hadn't been thinking last night—not with his head and not with his body. It was how she made him feel that had been driving him, and it had translated into the best sex of his life. He'd shown little finesse, just a need to dominate her, leave his mark. He'd taken her again, with no more consideration than the first time, and she had met him with her own scaling need, and then again, with a slower, more soothing cadence, whispering things to her in Russian he could never get away with in English before sleep claimed them.

But that first time had rocked them both, and everything

that had followed held its echoes. And he would have been blind not to see how dreamy she was this morning. He'd heard her singing to herself in the shower. Hell, he'd been humming to himself until he'd realised what he was doing.

This was all without precedent.

Something about seeing her at the show last night—her fragility coupled with her independence, the sheer chutzpah she paraded around, going after what she wanted, and his inability to stop her doing exactly as she pleased—had loosed something primitive in him.

He'd known it was there. His grandmother had told him stories about his father's legendary passion for his mother, his jealous rages, the theatrics of their marriage. He didn't remember all of it—only a father whose moods had moved from highs to lows at frightening speed. He remembered that—and a mother who had been frail and ethereal, appearing to be caught up in a drama in which she didn't quite know her lines. She had only been eighteen when she gave birth to him, and not much older than he was now when she died.

He didn't want that kind of passion in his life. He didn't want to be out of control. He needed to take a big step back. Put some air between them.

Clementine came down the stairs in her runners and cargo pants. She hadn't even fiddled with her hair this morning, just left it to its natural wave. Lipstick and mascara were her only concessions to making an effort. For the first time since she was fifteen she didn't feel she had to. She felt beautiful. Serge had made her feel beautiful. She could still feel his body stunning hers, the impact of their coming together, the tension winding tighter and tighter in him until it had given way and he had been heavy and peaceful in her arms. She'd felt so powerful—like a sex goddess. A thought which put a little smile on her lips.

She'd decided before falling asleep last night to drop the

whole 'this is your life and this is mine' front and give them both a chance. Serge had demonstrated how much she meant to him. Nobody behaved that way without being borne along on strong emotions.

The fact he hadn't been in bed when she'd re-emerged from the bathroom this morning had been the only blip on her radar. She'd wanted to leap back on him and make him prove to her all over again that she hadn't dreamt last night.

She planned on taking him market shopping with her this morning, and couldn't believe how much she was looking forward to it. Back home it was her favourite Saturday morning activity. Stock up the cupboards, have lunch out with friends, maybe see a film in the afternoon. It was the sort of stuff you did with a boyfriend.

She found him on the phone, pacing the long hall between the staircase and the kitchen. His attention was immediately with her, but he averted his eyes as he continued the conversation. She went on into the kitchen to collect the eco-bags.

As she turned around she realised Serge had blocked the kitchen doorway. His hair was all ruffled and he needed a shave. The phone was dangling from one hand.

Her hormones were jumping and she couldn't wipe the happy grin off her face.

He didn't even crack a smile. 'I'm going down to Mick's gym. I'll be back around midday.'

He looked and sounded so distant—nothing like the man whose arms she had fallen asleep in last night.

The sun slipped in Clementine's sky.

'Then I've got a team of people coming over to debrief at one.'

The sun fell out of her world, and it was in that moment as she stood there clutching the bags to her waist that she realised just how deep in she was with this man.

This man who put his job before everything—or rather had chosen to today. After last night.

'You might want to organise the day for yourself, Clementine.'

So now she knew where she stood.

It hurt. It hurt so much she couldn't bear to look at him. Part of her wanted to yell at him. *Is this too hard for you, Serge, a bit too real?* But looking at him standing there, emanating power and self-control and a level of success she couldn't even fathom, she suddenly felt horribly ordinary, with her save-the-planet hemp bags and stupid, simple morning at the market, and was glad now she hadn't had a chance to open her mouth.

He'd want her out of the way. So he didn't have to be reminded of how he had lost himself inside her body last night, had revealed a part of himself he didn't want to show. It was the only explanation she could come up with, and it made her feel about an inch high.

He didn't trust her enough to understand she would protect him. She wouldn't be reckless with his feelings.

But he was with hers. Look at him—master of the universe, and me making nice with the shopping. She looked down at the bags in her arms.

'I'm going marketing,' she said, making a hopeless gesture with the bags. 'I thought you might like to come.'

But now I know you don't.

'You know I have a shopper for that stuff,' was all he said.

It was on the tip of her tongue to say, *And I know there are women who will sleep with you for money*, but her pride was too strong. He might see her as another one of his many conveniences, but she was here because she loved him.

She loved him.

In the middle of his big state-of-the-art kitchen, with flagstones underfoot and every possible mod-con a man could want in his life, making her feel never more redundant to his needs, she realised the one thing guaranteed to break her heart.

It was just sex for him, and she began to shatter into tiny pieces.

He pulled out his wallet and in front of her started peeling off notes.

For one horrified moment she couldn't move, and then the words came out as if torn from her gut. 'I can pay for a bag of apples, Serge.' And she turned around as she said it so she didn't have to face him.

She jumped as he took hold of her hips. For a strange disconnected moment it felt as if he was going to embrace her, and instinctively her body drifted up against him as he dragged her close, all the angry heat inside of her pooling in her pelvis even as her mind shouted *no*. But he was shoving the money into her back pocket instead.

'Get yourself something nice.'

He actually patted her on the backside.

He had to know what he was doing. He had to know how he was hurting her. It gave her the backbone to walk away, clutching those bags tightly to her chest. If she had the guts she'd walk away from him for ever, but she didn't have that amount of courage. Not yet. Not after last night.

The soft reminder of who she had been earlier that morning—the happy girl who had been floating on cloud nine—manifested itself in the thought: where was the closeness and belonging and sharing? Where had it gone?

Serge wasn't sharing anything this morning except his open wallet.

It burned.

It was still burning a few hours later, as she schlepped with her bags up the steps. The boxes of groceries were on delivery, but she had carried little delicacies herself: cheeses and a French wine, and some lovely Chinese tea, and those god-awful pickled herrings Serge liked.

She'd done it all despite being arm candy.

Flavour of the month. That was her.

Carrying the groceries.

As she approached the kitchen she could hear male voices. She left the bags on the bench and wandered curiously but warily into the drawing room. Serge was on his feet. About a dozen other men were sitting and standing around the room. Expensive weekend casual was the dress code, but the guys didn't look like your typical buttoned-down execs. The atmosphere vibrated with tension, and Serge didn't look happy. Her self-pity evaporated.

Only a couple of people noticed her at first, and then like an avalanche the focus of the room turned on her, the same male interest she'd been getting since she was fifteen.

Serge glanced up. The look on his face said it all and her heart sank. She took a backward step, then stood her ground. Thirteen pairs of male eyes—all directed at her.

Serge moved to her side, introducing her to the men in rapidfire succession and then gently but inexorably leading her to the door. 'We've got a lot to discuss, Clementine. It could take a while.' His tone clearly said *make yourself scarce*.

'Fair enough.' Feeling excluded, but knowing it wasn't personal, she retraced her steps and set about piling up a few plates with bruschetta, olives, cheeses, opening up a bottle of wine.

She had an idea this was about the fallout from the Kolcek disaster, and from the conversation drifting in it sounded as if she was on the money.

A heavy-set man with tattoo sleeves on both arms peeking out of his T-shirt came into the kitchen.

Behind him was Liam O'Loughlin, the promotions guy she had spoken to yesterday. She already knew she didn't like him. He compounded it by copping a look down the front of her shirt as she picked up an empty hemp bag and began folding it.

Then another man and another strolled into the kitchen, and suddenly she was standing by the island bench surrounded by five big men, all of them clearly starved of female company if their slightly inane expressions were anything to go by.

'Is this a convention or something?' she enquired smartly, to hide her subtle unease.

'Alex Khardovsky—president of the Marinov Corporation. Serge and I are old friends.' The heavy-set guy reached over the bench and shook her hand. 'Heard a lot about you, Clementine.'

Clementine's smile didn't falter, but she couldn't help the cold trickle at the idea Serge had talked about her, wondering what he had said.

'You've domesticated Serge Marinov,' said Liam O'Loughlin smarmily. 'Many women have tried and failed.'

Clementine didn't respond. She hated this sort of drivel and she really didn't like guys who couldn't keep their eyes to themselves.

'What I heard was that you worked in PR for Verado, Clementine,' interrupted Alex.

'That's right. Lots of free golf clubs and cigar clippers.'

The men laughed. Clementine pushed a glass of wine towards Alex and began pouring a couple more glasses. She didn't bother with Liam O'Loughlin.

'So you guys are all here about that fighter who's up on assault charges, right?'

'It doesn't go away,' answered a fair-haired guy with the buzz-cut.

Here goes nothing, thought Clementine, and addressed Alex.

'Your problem is managing the fallout from that big famous trial, right? You had trouble a few years ago with the media about some of your fighters' extra-curricular activities and now it's all coming back to bite you.' She pushed the platters of food towards the other men. 'Seems to me what you need is a blanket print, cable publicity blitz, pushing what's great about the sport and taking the emphasis off this over-the-top macho rubbish. Highlight the athleticism. Maybe get some of those fighters to turn up at high-profile charity events— and not on their own. You want wives and kids in tow.'

She looked up and saw Serge leaning against the door-frame. She hadn't known she was so nervous until she re-alised she wasn't alone. Confidence had her straightening her spine.

'Keep going,' said Alex, grinning. 'I'm taking notes.'

Clementine blew air up her fringe. This still wasn't easy.

'Yes, well…you need to get more women into your front row. Lots of famous guys there last night, but stag. Plays up to the problem you've got with Kolcek—young guys, too much testosterone, too much money, running around disrespecting women.'

'So what you're saying is the fight game isn't appealing to soccer moms?' said Liam dismissively.

'What I'm saying is you've got a problem with a thug image, and if you're serious about changing that you need to leave the theatricality in the ring and think about projecting the reality of the business, which is professional athletes en-gaged in highly staged combat.'

'You wouldn't consider coming and working for us, Clementine?'

'Why, Alex…' she looked at Serge over the rim of her glass '…I thought you'd never ask.'

Serge had watched the guys, one after another, follow Clementine into the kitchen and the hairs had gone up on the back of his neck.

It was macho posturing. Clementine could take care of herself. But he'd told himself he would just check up on her—he'd do the same for any other woman he was with. There were a lot of men in the house, and for all Clementine's confidence it wouldn't be easy for a woman to handle.

Yet here she was, one hand on an outswung hip, telling Alex exactly how he needed to run his publicity machine.

A dark voice prodded him. What had he expected? Her to suddenly go all shy and play the role of his girlfriend? He reminded himself he didn't want that. He wanted the sexy girl with no ties. Well, look—he was getting it. In spades.

Provocative. Used to male attention.

It was how she got through life. She'd told him as much but he'd never actually seen it in action.

This was a woman who had survived on her own since she was a teenager. She was tougher than she looked, than she seemed when he had her wild and pinned under him.

She looked up at that moment and caught sight of him, and he actually saw some of the tension he hadn't noticed in her body leave her. Every male protective instinct in his body stood on end. She finished her little spiel and sipped her wine and met his eyes.

And because of it he moved in to stake his claim.

'Poaching my secret weapon, Aleksandr?' Serge didn't take his eyes off her as he spoke.

Alex grinned, and all the guys stirred like cattle sensing a stampede. Liam O'Loughlin was already edging his way out through the other door.

Yeah, back off. Serge couldn't believe how proprietorial he was feeling.

'She should have been sitting in there, cutting our job in half,' said Alex, looking genuinely impressed.

'Just offering a few suggestions,' Clementine said sweetly.

Alex picked up his drink. 'There's a job offer on the table. Think about it, Clementine.' He gave Serge a conspiratorial nod. 'Serge got my number.'

Clementine eyed him cautiously when they were alone, as well she might, but he merely said, 'Keeping me on my toes, *kisa*?'

'I don't know what you mean.'

'Yeah, you do.'

She tensed. 'What's the problem, Serge? Surprised I've got a brain?'

'I'm well aware of your intelligence, *kisa*. It's how you work the room, your entirely female skills I'm referring to.'

For a moment she looked blank, and then his meaning dropped into place. 'You haven't complained before,' she said stiffly.

'It was directed at me.' A dark demon was driving him. 'I get that you're a friendly girl, *kisa*, but I don't appreciate you showering it around.'

Suddenly the hard shell was gone, and all he could see was the utter shock on her face and the flutter of confusion in her eyes before she shut down.

'Okay—fine. Whatever.' She pushed the plates towards him, her hands visibly beginning to shake. 'Here—I've made this for your guests. There should be a delivery of groceries around four.' She knocked over a glass bottle as she bumped against the bench in her haste to get away from him. Righting it, she mumbled, 'I got those awful herrings for you—more fool me.'

For a few moments Serge didn't move. He didn't know what was going on between them. He didn't understand why seeing her surrounded by other admiring men had made him so damn jealous that he couldn't see straight. He didn't even understand why he'd left her this morning.

The herrings brought him up short for a second too. She was shopping for him?

Then he noticed for the first time the tremble in her body, her refusal to look at him. He took hold of her arm. 'Clementine.'

She swung around, and for a moment he thought she was going to hit him, but she merely yanked her arm away and he let her.

'Don't worry, Serge,' she said sharply. 'I won't be turning up at your gigs any more. I know my place. I've got it pretty clear now exactly where you see me in your life. If I didn't get it before you've spelt it out now.'

She dashed out of the kitchen before he could stop her. Not fast enough he hadn't seen the flash of tears in her eyes.

Yeah, he was a real prince. He'd finally made Clementine cry.

CHAPTER TEN

IT TOOK him ten minutes to clear the house. Alex lingered the longest, took him aside on the front steps.

'What are you doing with that girl, Serge?'

'Come again?'

'The look on your face when you came into the kitchen was priceless.'

'If you could translate, Aleksandr, it might make more sense,' said Serge dryly.

'That's right—play dumb. I saw you last night. You care about her. She's not one of those bimbo airheads on your revolving door policy, she's a savvy woman. I really might employ her, *Seriosha*, then what are you going to do?'

'Fire you.'

'Touché. You know, Mick's right. You turn up with her at a few charity events and we're cooking with gas again. How about a magazine spread? "At home with Serge Marinov and the lovely Clementine".'

'You've either lost your ever loving mind or you're looking to see stars,' commented Serge, folding his arms.

'I'm not the one shacked up with Jessica Rabbit crossed with Martha Stewart.' Alex laughed and bounded down the remainder of the steps, heading for his car. 'She had groceries, man,' he shouted. *'Groceries!'*

Serge went back inside and took the stairs by threes. The

bedroom door was half ajar and he knocked a couple of times. 'Clementine?'

He'd expected to find her spread across the bed crying into a pillow, or whatever it was women did when they were put out, but the room was empty. The bed was made—nary a crease thanks to Housekeeping.

Where in the hell was she?

In the end he found her on the roof garden. She was kneeling on the ground, pulling weeds out of pots. She barely acknowledged his presence.

'First you go grocery shopping, now you're gardening,' he commented. 'This domesticity has got to stop, *kisa*.'

'Yes, well, I don't have anything else to do. You're gone most of the time and I don't have a job. So I do domestic, okay?'

He hunkered down beside her. 'Last night, Clementine—'

'Yes, I get it, Slugger,' she interrupted. 'I overstepped the mark or the boundary or whatever it is. It won't happen again.'

Serge was silent for a moment.

'I didn't want you at the event last night because it's violent,' he said with deliberation, 'and you don't react well to violence, Clementine.'

She wanted to snap, *I wasn't talking about the match. I was talking about afterwards.* 'You put me in a ringside seat,' she protested instead, turning her head so she could look him in the eyes.

'Because you were there, and I didn't want you out of my sight. I made a bad judgement call.'

'You didn't want me out of your sight?' she repeated, trying to make sense of it.

'It's my responsibility to look after you.'

The hairs prickled on her body. She was nobody's responsibility. She looked after herself. The minute she started believing Serge was going to do that was the moment this all came crashing in—as it had this morning.

He wasn't going to protect her. He wasn't going to love her. He was just her lover. Her current lover. She was a big girl. This was the way the world worked. Serge's world worked.

'You're not my dad, Serge. You're my—' She broke off, at a loss for a descriptor. Embarrassment prickled along her neck, worse than before.

'Your father lives in Geneva,' interposed Serge smoothly, letting her know she was right to hesitate. 'Do you ever see him?'

She avoided talking about her parents whenever she could, but suddenly her father seemed like a much safer topic than whether or not Serge was her boyfriend.

'No, not for many years. We had a falling-out when I was fifteen and I've never been back. I was a bit of a handful in those days.'

'Unlike now, when you're a pussycat.'

Clementine smiled a little. 'Why do you call me kitten all the time?'

'Because you're cute and playful and then you scratch me.'

She waved the gardening fork. 'Better be careful, then. I'm armed and dangerous.'

'What about your mother?'

'She presents a breakfast TV show in Melbourne. She was never home and when she was we fought. Mum and Dad were both barely out of their teens when they had me—it's why they married—and neither of them had much interest in a baby. So I grew up with a lot of childminders and nannies and fights until I was ten, when they finally split for good. Only then the fun started. The commute. Twice a year to Geneva.'

'Not fun?'

'You're kidding? A twenty-four-hour flight by myself, and then I'd be there a week and one of dad's girlfriends would arc up and I'd be hurtling back to Melbourne again. Both of them are self-obsessed—or should I say obsessed with their careers? I decided a long time ago when I have my babies I'll be staying home with them.'

'You want children?'

'One day. Don't you?' She asked the question out of interest, without thinking of the overtones.

'No.' He plucked the gardening fork out of her hand and stabbed it into one of the pots. 'But you're right, Clementine. Kids need a stable home and two loving parents.' Then he surprised her by stroking his hand gently over her head down her back to the ends of her hair. 'I'm sorry you didn't have that.'

Nobody had actually said that to her before, and the simple acknowledgement touched something raw inside her. She bent her head, enjoying the feeling of him being there with her, stroking her, offering comfort.

'Now I get it.'

'What do you get?' she asked suspiciously.

'This fierce independence of yours.'

Clementine closed her eyes, feeling herself losing her grip on the hard realities she needed to keep at the forefront of her mind. This thing with Serge could very well be temporary. She couldn't go swooping down the romantic slippery dip as she had their first night in New York and last night, because she'd only end up by herself in a heap at the bottom.

'Come on.' He stood up, offering her a hand and she took it uncertainly. 'There's somewhere I want to take you,' he said.

'Can I go like this?' She indicated her crumpled pants and dirt-stained T-shirt.

'You're fine. I like you a bit rumpled.' He put an arm around her. 'There was one thing I wanted to say about last night. Not the fight—afterwards.'

Clementine swallowed and tried to look casual. 'Oh?'

'You asked me how I felt. It feels good, Clementine. Being with you feels good.'

He took her downtown to his charity. A brown mission building in Brooklyn, housing a recreation centre for disadvantaged children.

'We have them in every city where we have venues,' he explained as they walked together through the gym. 'Here and in Europe.'

'This would be great publicity, Serge. The best antidote to Kolcek is to show what you're doing here.'

'Yeah, Mick says the same thing.'

'Mick Forster? The guy I met at the gym?'

'*Da*, he was the first trainer who would work with me when I got to the States. I wouldn't be where I am without him. He's the best in the business.'

Serge was speaking so freely she decided to take advantage of the moment. 'So what's Mick's great idea?'

'Well, for one I stop getting papped with women falling out of their dresses outside private parties.'

Clementine elbowed him hard in the ribs. 'That's not true! *Is* it true?' Some of her sweet enthusiasm evaporated, and he noticed she put a little space between their bodies. Then, more uncertainly, 'I hesitate to ask, but what are "private parties"?'

Bozhe, this woman could bring him to his knees.

He'd better get this over with quickly. 'The business I'm in, *kisa*. There's a lot of money, illegal gambling, drugs, you name it. Although we've done our best to clean it up. And there's always women. I'm healthy, clean as a whistle. Always used condoms. But I'm not one of the white bread guys you're used to. I've seen a lot and I've done a lot.'

He was nothing like the guys she was used to. Clementine knew it was silly to be shocked. She'd seen what he did for a living. She'd seen the women at those events. She'd seen the way they looked at him. He probably had phone numbers coming out of his pockets. Even that night she was with him.

The little show she'd given him in that shoe shop, which had seemed so daring to her—women probably did things like that for him all the time. Probably much more daring things.

Serge watched the emotions flickering across Clementine's expressive face. He shouldn't have told her. He'd upset her.

She gave him that negligent little shrug she'd perfected, but he knew now it covered up a lot of insecurity. 'Still doesn't tell me what private parties are.'

'It doesn't matter.' He closed the gap between them and pushed her fringe up out of her eyes. 'That's all over.'

A wave of warmth swept through him as he looked into her anxious eyes and experienced an overwhelming urge to protect her from his past. She had a lot of swagger, but she could be incredibly sweet at times. This was one of those times. It was sitting on his 'traditional Russian male' button and not getting off.

'So what are Mick's other ideas?' she surprised him by asking. Clearly the subject of other women was not a topic she wished to dwell on. Which suited him fine. He hadn't even thought about another woman in the time they had been together.

Which brought him up short.

'You'd be Mick's dream come true, Clementine. What you said to Alex about putting a wife-and-kids gloss on things is right up his alley.'

'Is Mick married?'

'Hell, no. He wouldn't be half so good at his job if he was.'

Clementine worried at her bottom lip. 'So I guess he doesn't approve of your wild lifestyle because it reflects back on the corporation? Or at least it does now, since Kolcek.'

'Wild lifestyle? Are we not in bed every evening before ten?'

Clementine blushed and shook her head. 'Maybe,' she said slowly, 'you need a woman who's not falling out of her dress?'

Serge's arms came around her. 'How about out of her cargos and T-shirt? And might I say this is a very good look on you, Clementine?'

She rolled her eyes, and Serge experienced an upswing in mood. Things felt better between them again. Whatever had been knocked awry had been restored by bringing her here, and for some reason he wasn't going to examine too closely that tight knot in his chest was gone.

He could do this. He could do light and easy and friendly. He could do sexy sweet girl who drove him a little crazy. He could do all the things that stopped short of out-of-control passion.

'So, do you want to use *me*?' she ventured, turning up her eyes to his.

'It would be ungentlemanly to ask, Clementine.'

He was gently teasing her, but Clementine was suddenly very clear on what she wanted. This was a way to test the waters—to move the relationship in the right direction. Last night had revealed he had strong feelings, but he was clearly fighting it. Maybe this was a way to give him a gentle nudge that didn't feel too real-life. A practice run.

'I think it's a dangerous idea to couple your personal life to the public face of what is essentially a business,' she said slowly, 'but I do think Mick has a point. If you have a media profile—Serge, *do* you have a media profile?'

His mouth twitched. 'A very slight one.'

'But enough to be photographed leaving parties with inappropriate women?' She tried to sound cavalier but it came out a little stiltedly.

He actually looked slightly embarrassed. Well, good—so he should. Private parties? She could just imagine…

'Maybe it would be good for you to be seen doing a few conventional guy things. With a woman.'

'But where would we find such a woman? This paragon of virtue, good manners and incredible hotness?'

He was teasing her. That was good. That meant he wasn't backing away from her. 'I don't know, Slugger. Maybe just whistle one up?'

'You're determined to get involved, aren't you?' But there was something in his expression—something that was inviting her in.

'I want to help you,' she said, suddenly feeling a little shy—which was a new feeling for her.

She hoped he was reading her right, getting the hint. Surely he could see how much he meant to her? *Tell him*, a little voice prodded. *Tell him how you feel.*

Instead she put on her professional smile, stroked his arm flirtatiously. 'I do this for a living, Slugger, just leave everything to me.'

He put an arm around her, but she noted the caution was back in his eyes. 'We'll see.'

'Public face of the Marinov Corporation,' said Clementine, feeling rather as she had when she'd first walked into that ritzy hotel with Serge a few weeks ago: kicking like mad to stay afloat. 'It'll take some getting used to,' she confessed, glancing across the table at Alex. 'I've done stuff like this before—I've just never actually been the product.'

Alex smiled at her, all charm. 'You'll do fine. Relax.'

Mick Forster strolled into the kitchen ahead of Serge, who clearly wasn't relaxed. He vibrated with tension. Clementine wondered how she could take that down a few notches.

Mick whipped off his perennial cap as he spotted

Clementine sitting at the big oak table. Serge introduced them and Mick sat down gingerly at one end, a good metre from where Clementine was curled up with a coffee.

'I hear you made a good impression on Alex,' said Mick bluntly, narrowing his into-the-wind blue eyes on her. 'Do you think you can do it in front of eight politicians and a camera crew?'

'Well, Mick, I don't know,' replied Clementine, looking at Serge. 'As long as I remember to take the gum out of my mouth I'm sure we'll be fine.'

He didn't crack even a millimetre of a smile. He hadn't been smiling since she'd agreed to do this. Was he having second thoughts? She knew *she* was.

'This is just a front up,' said Serge, folding his arms. He looked so intimidating for a moment even Clementine drew back a little in her chair. Mick and Alex both looked warily at one another.

'She has her picture snapped, I do the press conference, and then we leave. No chit-chat. She doesn't speak to the press.'

No mention of doing it this way to make any of it easier for *her*, Clementine thought a little hopelessly, then nipped her self-pity in the bud. She wasn't going down that path. She had come into this eyes wide open. It was what it was: an opportunity to help him out, an opportunity to make something of what they had between them. She wasn't giving up on them without a fight; it was just right now she felt like the only person in the ring.

'I want to be sure Clementine knows what she's up for,' said Alex slowly, as if testing the waters. 'You'll be answering questions, Serge, but she'll be facing the scrum outside.'

'*Nyet*—no paps. We go in the back way. Only legit media.' Serge spoke quietly but it had its effect. The other two men stayed quiet.

'Listen, boys, I'm aware I'm going to be a handbag tomorrow,' Clementine interrupted, straining for her voice to be unnaturally high and cheerful in the tense atmosphere. 'I look good. I don't say much. I'm flashbacking to my last job.'

Nobody laughed. Nobody even twitched.

'Nah, we *want* you to speak,' said Mick finally. 'If you don't you may as well be one of those other airhead bimbos...' His voice fell away into a taut, uncomfortable silence.

Other airhead bimbos. Clementine didn't know where to look.

Ever since she'd put the proposal to Serge, Clementine had been wondering if she was out of her ever loving mind. Now Mick had pointed out what she'd been too blind or dazzled by the notion of putting a public stamp on their relationship to face. She'd be hanging her dirty laundry out for everyone to see. Anyone who was interested in the Marinov Corporation would have some idea about Serge's sexual past. She couldn't call it romantic, and there was a huge chance she was about to be showcased as a bimbo who'd made it past round one and that was about all.

Clementine suddenly felt hideously exposed and her hands found their way into her lap, winding around one another so she had something to hold onto.

She took a deep breath. She wasn't a bimbo. She wasn't going to be considered one. And this little exercise would ensure she could keep her head held high. She could handle tomorrow.

Be careful what you wish for, Clem, she told herself under the shower as she freshened up before dinner that evening. She was going to show her skills, but not in quite the way she'd wanted. In her haste to offer herself up she'd overlooked one fundamental flaw in her thinking: this wasn't about how he felt about her; it was about what she could do for him.

She'd done what she'd sworn she would never do again. In her desperation for his love, to come first with Serge, she'd forgotten her own life lesson from her parents. People wanted you around as long as you were entertaining, useful or fulfilled a function. And right now she was doing all three. She'd rushed headlong into it in her desperation to keep what she'd had a glimpse of the other night in his arms.

God help her, she wanted this to be different from what both of them had known in the past. He with his endless string of women and she with her two unsatisfactory, half-hearted relationships.

Well, she'd ensured she was in it for the long haul now—or at least until the Kolcek furore settled down and the spotlight turned to the next media frenzy. But none of this was really what she wanted. 'Come live with me and be my significant other in order to counteract media speculation over my until now playboy lifestyle' left something of a sour taste in her mouth.

She wanted a real commitment from Serge. It was time to acknowledge that, if only to herself. Pretending to be his significant other wasn't going to achieve that.

For the first time since she'd arrived on US soil with him she was beginning to wonder if any of this was worth it. It was starting to feel as if she was running after him, and it wasn't a good feeling.

She was just getting out of the shower when she heard her phone buzzing. Heavy-hearted, wrapping herself in a towelling robe, she answered it and gave a heartfelt sigh. 'Luke!'

Serge heard her voice and continued dressing in the other room, one ear on her improved tone. She hadn't sounded so upbeat all day and it bothered him. Events had coalesced all at once: the press conference, Mick's advice—which he usually heeded to his benefit—and Clementine offering herself up, the answer to Mick's prayers. She was so damn *willing* to help out.

Using Clementine in this way—and as every hour passed

that was how it was shaping up—was going to make it more brutal than it needed to be when they severed ties.

It was time to let her know this domestic idyll was over. He'd known it yesterday morning. He couldn't have a repeat of the night before. Last night he'd found concentrating on her physical needs helped keep whatever this was between them within bounds—shifting the sex up a notch to a game of skill where the name of the game was her pleasure, not how he felt when she was soft and sweet in his arms. But he would have had to be blind, deaf and dumb not to hear the emotion in her voice as she cried out his name, or see the question in her eyes before she drifted, exhausted, off to sleep. She knew the difference now. She knew he was holding back.

But he didn't have a choice. It had never been that way with anyone before, and it could never be that way between them again.

'No, I don't know,' she said, her voice suddenly pitched lower. 'No, I haven't rented anything. I might be back. I don't know.'

His heartbeat slowed.

'It's not quite what I expected.'

She was thinking about going back to London?

Every muscle in his body went on high alert. His fingers slid away from the buttons of his shirt.

Clementine gone.

This house empty.

He stood there, his head bent, breathing steadily, deeply. He told himself it was for the best.

Usually a chat with Luke lifted her spirits, but tonight Clementine felt worse than ever. It was his questions: about Serge, about her plans. They'd made her realise she couldn't make plans because none of them involved the man she loved.

She was allowed in, but only so far with Serge. Even now

their intimacy felt forced, and all about the business. Instead of making her feel more secure, as she had hoped, putting herself forward as public girlfriend only made her feel lost. Because it wasn't true—and having your picture in the paper didn't make it so.

Worse, their emotional intimacy the night of the fight hadn't been repeated. Serge was as attentive as ever, driving her pleasure, but she felt his restraint like a slap in the face. It clearly wasn't what he wanted. It was as if now she had seen how good it could be every time he touched her was a reminder of what they no longer had.

She inhaled deeply as she advanced on the kitchen. Cooking smells. Serge had only a skeleton staff, and they were never here on weekend evenings, so she knew *he* had to be cooking.

Unable to believe it, she lingered in the doorway, just watching. He looked sensational. A male animal out of the wild and giving a good impression of being domesticated.

'You're cooking.'

'I can also make beds, sweep floors and clean toilets with a small wire brush. Army training.'

'I'm impressed—although a little put off by the toilets.'

'I thought we could eat and watch an old movie and have an early night.'

Clementine told her heart not to leap but it did.

'Before D-Day?'

'You don't have to do this, Clementine.' He was suddenly deadly serious and her heart thumped in response.

'No, I want to, Serge. I want to do this for us.' She could have cursed at the slip of her tongue. She'd meant to say *you*, hadn't she?

Serge's benign expression didn't slip. He merely handed her a glass of red wine. 'To us,' he said, clinking her glass with his, but his eyes remained cool and almost watchful.

* * *

Although she'd had a dress picked out for the occasion, at the last moment it looked all wrong.

She should be good at this. She employed this skill all the time in her job. Making people see what she wanted them to see, shifting points of view, spruiking the product. Except today the product was herself, and the girl trawling through her ad hoc wardrobe wasn't finding anything. Serge put his head in the door.

'You've got fifteen, Clementine.'

'Yes, fine,' she said distractedly, not wanting to ruin a moment of today by making them late. Serge must have some nerves. He was facing a hostile media.

He hesitated, and suddenly his arm shot out and he whipped her green dress out with its hanger.

'Wear this.'

She'd worn it on their first date and she wondered if he remembered. Probably not. Why would he? And it would definitely not do.

'Thanks. I'll be with you in ten.' She purposely turned her back on him and reinstated the green satin to its place, reached for another dress with a great deal more material.

Serge consulted his watch. He could hear Clementine rushing about, the sounds of drawers closing, doors creaking, little swear words. Something about the noise she was making, the trouble she was going to, touched a part of him he was not familiar with. *I'm going to miss this.* The thought moved through him, leaving only a troubled sense of having lost something in its wake.

But she was coming slowly down the stairs, as if the last frantic quarter of an hour hadn't happened, dressed in a yellow linen high-necked dress that skimmed her breasts and hips and fell to her knees. Without a cinched-in waist her extravagant curves looked much more understated. She was playing her role. He was suddenly glad she hadn't worn the green, it brought back memories of the sweet, elusive girl he'd followed down the embankment and he didn't want those today. If he was half the man he'd built himself to be he wouldn't entertain them ever again.

Clementine did a little twirl at the bottom of the stairs. Her fragrance wrapped around him—something with damask roses, as familiar now to him as the woman who wore it. It was in the bathroom, it was in the odd piece of her clothing he'd find lying around, and it was on his pillow every morning.

She looked up and used both hands to tug at an imaginary misalignment of his suit jacket, then smiled at him, 'I think we're ready, Slugger.'

She was so lovely she took his breath away.

But there were other beautiful women in the world—as many as he wanted. Other women with toffee-coloured hair and legs that went on for ever and grey eyes. But not soft ones. He wouldn't be caught by soft eyes again. They could get under your skin. Like now.

'Anything I need to know, Serge, before we hit the road? Any last words of advice?'

'Only that you look beautiful.' He had said it a hundred times to her since they'd met, but it was only now he noticed the way the muscles beside her mouth flicked down, as if she were momentarily cringeing before the compliment sank in completely.

Because she'd heard it from a lot of men and it didn't mean much to her any more? What meant more to Clementine was to be praised for her abilities. He knew that about her now, and he fully intended to do that when all this was over. She needed to know he appreciated everything about their time together, and he could tell her now he knew she was going home.

'Do I?' she said, looking up at him, her face open and unguarded—the way she was, he realised, when they were in bed. But there was something else in her eyes. Something almost uncertain. 'Do I look beautiful? Because I'm not really. I think it's just more make-up and confidence.'

He curved his hand around the back of her head and kissed her. Her mouth fluttered under his, surprised, cautious, before her lashes swept down and she gave way. He actually felt it, the moment of her submission, and it pounded through him like big surf.

She made him feel as if he was the only man ever to do this to her. It was a fantasy, but he was going to allow himself just a little more of it before they let one another go for ever.

And it was a reminder of why he *had* to let her go—because whatever was between them was too much, too powerful. It threatened to sweep too much of what he'd worked so hard for away.

'No other woman comes close,' he said softly against her mouth. The truth, but he forced himself to release her, put air between them. 'Clementine, do you have your passport?'

'Pardon?'

'We're not going uptown, *kisa*, I'm taking you to Paris.'

CHAPTER ELEVEN

'WE CAN'T do this. What about the press conference?' blithered Clementine as he handed her into the car. He'd barely given her the time to run upstairs and grab her passport.

'Alex can handle it.'

Clementine couldn't take her eyes off him. Why was he doing this? It was irrational. It didn't make a lick of sense.

She knew Serge. He wouldn't be running away from a confrontation. He took life on, fists swinging. It was one of the things she loved about him—his willingness to front up, take it on the chin. It was something they shared.

'Serge, I have no luggage. I have nothing.' Practical considerations began to line up as she realised this was actually real. She was going to Paris.

'You've got me, *kisa.*' And he gave her that lazy Russian male smile that told her she didn't need clothes, didn't need underwear. She wasn't going to be seeing much of Paris.

Distracted for a moment by some pretty powerful imagery, she shook her head. She wasn't going to let him get away with palming her off. 'Serge Marinov, talk to me.'

He made a dismissive gesture, as if it wasn't worth talking about. 'It's not such a big deal, Clementine. All you need to know is I have no intention of using you—now or ever. It was a ridiculous idea and it was never going to fly. Happy?'

'No—yes.' She made a frustrated noise. 'Confused is what I am. How long have you been planning this?'

'Since last night. I heard you on the phone to your friend, and I got the impression you were a little homesick, *kisa*. I thought you might miss Europe.'

'No, I—' She broke off, unable even to start that sentence, which ended in *because I love you*. She put her hand on his arm. 'Serge, what are we doing? What's going on?'

She was asking him about what this did to the boundaries of this temporary sexual relationship of theirs, and she knew he knew it.

His green eyes caught hers. 'I'm taking you to Paris, Clementine, because in two days' time it's your birthday. I thought you might like to mark it with a trip somewhere special—for both of us. Something we can remember.'

Everything had been so awful, she realised for the first time, and now suddenly it wasn't. It was better than wonderful.

Happiness bubbled up from some spring inside her she hadn't known existed until that moment. It spurted like a geyser, and she did the only thing a girl could do in that moment. She flung herself across the seat at him, wrapped herself around him and sang, 'Thank you, thank you, thank you.'

And it had absolutely nothing to do with Paris and everything to do with this dear, generous man.

Serge felt slightly stiff beneath her onslaught, but his arms enfolded her. She buried her head in his shoulder and sniffled.

'You cannot cry, Clementine, this is good news. This is fun for us.'

She drew back to frame his beautiful male face with her hands. 'Yes, lots of fun,' she agreed, eyes wet, biting her lip.

Did he have even the faintest idea how much this meant to her? Probably not. But that didn't take an ounce of specialness out of his gesture.

'You're such an emotional girl, Clementine,' he teased. 'Where's my happy, funny girl?'

'She's here.' She flung herself back into his arms. She would make an effort to be more of what he wanted. She wouldn't drip all over him. She would be absolutely herself, with her big, sincere Slugger to back her up.

This was the second hotel she'd walked into with Serge, and it was a lifestyle she could get very used to. Lavish surroundings, invisible staff making their lives feel effortless...

There were surprises everywhere for her: the view of the Plâce de la Concorde, the drawers full of slinky underwear, the *armoire* layered with evening gowns and dresses for the day. Enough for her to change twice a day for a week.

How had he come up with all this?

'Personal shopper.' He shrugged it off, watching her fingering the *eau-de-nil* silk of a sheer evening gown. With his shirt open at the collar, sleeves pushed up, hair rumpled, lounging back on the vast bed, he looked like a rather louche king, surveying all he owned.

'Put it on, Clementine, so I can take it off.'

She smiled over her shoulder at him. Slowly she began to unzip, shimmy and strip. She unsnapped her bra and worked down her knickers. She didn't turn around. Then she stepped into the silk gown. It felt cool, like water on her skin, and she shivered although the room temperature was pleasant. Slowly she turned around, having no idea how it looked on her until she met Serge's eyes. Her throat ran dry. Her pulse sped up.

He was off that bed and had her flush against him so fast all she could do was squeak, 'Don't you dare hurt my dress!' and then sigh.

They had dinner in a restaurant overlooking the Seine, with a view of the lights of Nôtre Dame. Clementine wore her dress, unscathed.

The next day they wandered through the city, visiting a few tourist sites but mostly meandering. Until they washed up on the doorstep of an exclusive jeweller, when Serge took her hand and said, almost formally, 'Allow me to do this for your birthday, Clementine.'

What could she say? It was an entirely novel feeling, being escorted into a jeweller's, being sat down and having endless pieces brought out for her selection. Everything was expensive. Walking through the door, Clementine had fancied the rarefied air they were breathing must cost at least an arm and a leg. Yet she didn't feel awkward at all. It felt amazingly special. *He* made her feel special.

In the end she chose a pair of pink diamond earrings.

Her taste was praised by the staff. Serge said merely, 'Happy?'

'Happy.' It was an inadequate word for how she was feeling, but Serge seemed content with it.

Her birthday dawned cold and a little misty—very unusual for June—but the day turned into a picture-perfect summer's day. Serge had organised a balloon flight over the Loire, and lunch and an overnight stay at a private *château* he explained was owned by friends who were happy for them to put it to some use. Clementine had ceased to pinch herself, but leaning against the stone terrace rail of a sixteenth-century *château* drinking champagne, rubbing elbows with her gorgeous Russian lover, was not something she was going to forget in a hurry. And she said so.

'I've made myself memorable, then, Clementine.' His voice was warm, as if the day had pleased and mellowed him as well as her.

'I can't imagine anything more perfect. I can't imagine I'll ever forget this for as long as I live.' She made a sound and screwed up her eyes. 'Oh, Lord, I can't believe I said that. I sound so gauche.'

The champagne had loosened her tongue. She was at the end of her second glass, Serge noted, amused.

'You sound very sweet,' he replied.

'Worse!' She laughed. 'Believe me, Slugger, no woman wants to be described as sweet.'

'Incredibly sexy, then.' He plucked the goblet from her hand and slid his hands down over her hips. 'Time for bed, Clementine.'

'It's still very early, Serge,' she teased.

'Yes, but we'll be having a long night,' he replied.

He was incredibly skilled, Clementine thought the next morning, as she ate her egg and drank her orange juice on the bedroom balcony and gazed out over the dark forest that shielded the *château* from the main highway. Once the kings of France had ridden here to hounds, when much of this pastureland had been forest. Serge had told her yesterday afternoon as they explored the grounds. They shared a love of history, along with so much else. He was the best company she'd ever had.

It all went far beyond the sex, which was skilled, but not what she wanted. Not any more. He had been almost driven last night to choreograph everything that occurred between them. *Careful* was another word that came to mind. He was also romantic in a formal sense, as if searching for ways to please her out of a catalogue of 'What Women Like'. But she knew how different it could be between them when he allowed himself to let go, to feel something other than sexual gratification. It would have been her best birthday present— she would have forgone everything else: *château*, earrings, the perfection of the day—for just a few moments when she felt once more like a part of him. But it wasn't to be, and she had no idea how to change that.

'Serge…' she said out loud.

He wandered out to join her, fully dressed in slightly formal attire, as if their returning to Paris merited a modicum of style. Clementine felt a little underdressed beside him in her robe, hair unbrushed, but she had a pretty chiffon layered frock to wear today, and she was wearing her birthday earrings.

Was it her imagination or was he a trifle distant this morning? He'd been up before she had even woken, and the echo of that morning in New York had passed through her before she'd remembered how perfect the last few days had been and how unnecessary it was to worry.

'What is it, *kisa*?'

'Can we talk about last night?' She moistened her lips. 'It was amazing, but—is there something I should be doing? Something you want from me?'

Serge had gone very still. In the process of pulling up a chair to sit opposite her, he instead pushed the chair in and stood behind it, looking down at her. It rather put her at a disadvantage.

'What do you think you should be doing, Clementine?'

'I—I don't know. You can just seem a little—distant sometimes—when we're together—and I want to—talk about it.'

He picked up a piece of toast. 'Yes, well, *dushka*, some things can be talked to death. If I wanted a professional in my bed I'd pay one.'

She took a breath. Okay, he was sensitive about this. 'I wasn't talking about technique,' she told the salt shaker. 'I was talking about emotions. We don't seem to connect in that way any more.'

He made a gesture of impatience and walked back into the room. 'You're talking in riddles, Clementine. What's the problem? Endless climaxes not enough?'

'It's not about that.' Why was he getting angry?

She understood men could be touchy about these things, so she stood up and went to him, slid her arms around his waist from behind, laid her cheek against his back. He didn't reciprocate, but he didn't shrug her off either.

'Sex isn't just about an orgasm, Serge. You know that as well as I do.'

His whole body seemed to grow, harden, pull away from her, but she held on.

'*Da, kisa*—it is. Between us it is.'

And just like that the bottom fell out of her world.

'What?' She gave a nervous little laugh and her arms slid from his waist as he literally stepped away from her.

'Clementine,' he said gently, but he didn't reach for her, 'this is all very romantic—Paris, dropping out of the world for a while—but we have always had just a sexual relationship. You are an incredible girl, and I'm a very lucky man, but it doesn't go any further than this.'

'Are you breaking up with me?' The words came out in a low, hard voice she didn't recognise as her own. 'Did you bring me to Paris to break up with me?'

'Hell, no.' He suddenly looked uneasy, and the knowledge shafted through her like the blade of a sword. He *had* been going to break up with her. It was just for some reason he'd changed his mind.

But he wasn't going to love her. Ever.

'You do know this will end. Everything ends.' He closed the distance between them and took her hands in his. 'I'm not going to lie and say you don't mean a great deal to me—you do.'

She wanted to curl up in the corner of the room and die.

But her pride wouldn't let her.

'Good to know, Slugger,' she said softly. She pulled her hands free and walked back out onto the balcony. He let her go, didn't follow her. He would know she wanted to cry. He was probably used to crying women. No doubt he'd passed through a lot of them.

'Clementine, it's not over.' His voice was husky, and some part of her snatched hold of that as proof he wasn't as unaffected as he pretended to be.

'No,' she said, forcing the cheer into her voice. But it fell flat. 'I just don't like talking about it. Can we change the subject?'

'We're driving back to Paris in an hour or so. There's no rush,' he said slowly. 'I thought you'd like to go out to Versailles. I think Marie Antoinette probably appeals to you, Clementine.'

She closed her eyes. He knew her so well. Yet not well enough to know she was in love with him. If he knew that, surely he wouldn't be so cruel. Surely he would lie to her. For a little longer.

Well, she was going to lie to herself. She was going to pretend she could be with a man who wasn't ever going to love her, if all he could give her was 'a great deal'.

To mean 'a great deal' to someone was something. Wasn't it?

She knew then what she had to do. Book a flight home. It was over.

Serge was angry. He didn't think he'd ever been so angry in his life. It was that cold, settled anger that could sit in your gut for days, weeks, months. It kept him silent on the drive back up to Paris. He had a pretty good idea what was keeping Clementine silent. What had he expected? She was going to chatter and sing silly songs and trade barley sugar kisses with him as she had on the way down? He'd lost that girl for good. In an act of necessary sabotage.

Yes, his anger was of the settled kind, and it wasn't going to shift, but he could feel it growing exponentially as he navigated the pretty Paris streets in the sports car and Clementine started talking about how clean Paris was compared to

London. When she had exhausted that topic she moved on to that international conundrum the weather.

'I'd like to have some time on my own,' she told him in a *faux*-sweet tone as the valet took care of the car. 'Do you mind if I go up to the suite alone?'

It was about then the anger burst. *'Da,'* he said, 'I do mind.'

She gave him a look that could incinerate and stalked ahead of him through the hotel. He didn't hurry. The anger felt good, it felt justified, and it had nothing to do with Clementine.

She had closed the door on the bedroom and thrown herself on the bed. He kicked the door open.

'Get out,' she said shifting her legs off the bed.

'I sleep here too, *kisa.*'

'I told you to get out.' When he didn't shift she said, 'Do you know what's wrong with you, Serge?'

'Go ahead—inform me.'

'You're a male chauvinist pig. You live in another century, and it's not the last one.'

He slanted her a dark look. *'Da, kisa.* You know, I had a sixteenth-century ancestor who kept fifteen wives—a couple for each day of the week. He had no trouble keeping them in line, but I guess he just hadn't met you.'

Somewhere in there was a compliment, she thought uneasily, but it got lost in the concept of fifteen wives and the way he was looking at her. All of a sudden she didn't want to be on the bed. She felt entirely too vulnerable to him.

She knew he could overwhelm her in moments—not with his expertise, although that was considerable, but with his sheer maleness, and feeling as vulnerable as she was she didn't know how she was going to cope.

She knew she could say no and Serge would stop. But no wasn't coming, and all of a sudden the only thing that was going to work was skin on skin.

All Serge knew as he came over her on the bed was that

desire crashed through him, stronger than he had ever felt it. He was driven to possess her and he would.

His father had been this way with his mother. Scenes on scenes. Crashing doors, shouting, dramatic gestures. As a child it had been terrifying. As an adult man he had been fleeing his father's legacy—a great passion destroyed in the blink of an eye.

And right now he just didn't know what it all meant any more.

He needed the sweet hot centre of her body, how it felt driving inside her, the oblivion of reaching release, of knowing nothing but pleasure with this woman who was driving him to such extremes.

Yet as he settled on top of her and began to kiss her the kissing grew slower, deeper, prolonging this time they had together. It wasn't out of control, it wasn't frenzied, and he knew then what he had been fighting.

Not Clementine. Not his past.

Himself.

What he was capable of and the fear he wouldn't be capable of it at all.

True love—deep and abiding. As if a grand passion in all its wrenching glory was all he could have and he might mistake that for the other kind. The real stuff. But the other side of that coin held by a fearful boy was a yearning for both— to love exaltedly and to love simply and truly.

Clementine's lashes fluttered down, all the resistance going out of her. The pink colour spread across her chest, up into her face, mounting her cheeks. He tugged her hair gently free of its tie and then he had his fingers spread in the silky weight, and her hands were softly caressing his neck, down over his shoulders, his back, as tantalising as a feather. She kissed him as if it nourished her. She clung and she said his name.

He slid down her body and pleasured her with his mouth until she was trembling, and he kept going until she peaked. Then he positioned himself and stretched her, filled her, rocking into her with gentle, slow strokes until she was murmuring incoherently and locking her thighs around him. The feel of her breasts rising and falling between them, the sweet tickle of her breath on his neck, was almost too good.

'So beautiful, Clementine,' he whispered, unable not to gaze his fill of her. 'The most beautiful girl I've ever seen.'

Her eyes spilled over with tears. He gently pressed his mouth to each eyelid, catching them with his tongue.

'Sweet Clementine,' his mouth murmured against her skin, his movements increasing in tempo.

She lifted her hips, took him deeply into her, threw her head back and made a sobbing sound as her internal muscles tightened around him. He gave way with a deeply satisfied groan, the pleasure hurtling through his body at force. But it wasn't enough. He wanted more from her. Twice more he took her as the evening wore on, absorbing the heat of her body, the scent of her skin, the clash of his body giving way to the sweet clutch of hers. Until he had her limp and quiet, breathing softly beside him.

Clementine released a ragged breath and wondered why, after the most intense sexual experience of her life, she couldn't get enough breath in her lungs. She sucked in as much air as she could and turned her head, ate up the sight of him, eyes shut, chest labouring as he caught his breath, the sheen of sweat lightly glossing his skin. He had been so generous, so passionate, so much everything she wanted. Except he didn't love her, and he wasn't going to love her.

She had been wrong all along. He had never seen her as anything different from the women who had preceded her and would probably come after her. She wasn't going to mistake his tenderness, his gentleness in the act of sex, for feelings he didn't have for her.

He rolled over, and suddenly those dragon-green eyes were enmeshed with hers. Despair gripped her. In a moment she would lose herself again in wanting this to be real. But it wasn't. Tears she couldn't repress filled her eyes, spilled over, made a mess of her face.

Serge cursed and drew her in against him. His arms were tight around her, but instead of comfort it only reminded her of what she had lost.

'Don't cry, sweet Clementine, don't cry,' he murmured.

Except those words didn't mean anything, did they? Nothing was going to change, and one day—sooner rather than later—it would all be over and her heart would be smashed to smithereens.

'Tell me what's wrong?'

'I don't want it to end,' she wept, unable to hide her true feelings any more.

His Tartar blood turned his expression wild and fierce as he caught her face between his hands. 'It's not ending. Listen to me, Clementine, nothing is over.'

For an endless moment Clementine held herself in the bright circle of his assurance, the words *But you don't love me* dying on her lips, because her next words, *And I love you— so very much*, would tear this moment apart.

She couldn't do it. She couldn't tell him how much she felt when there was nothing in him to answer it. Instead she let him draw her close into his arms and listened as he began to croon to her in Russian, his hand moving in circles on her bare back. Gradually her crying fit subsided and she lay still and broken.

She lay there for a long time, until by his deep even breathing she was sure he was asleep. It wasn't even nine o'clock, but it felt much later to Clementine. It felt like an endless day that was never going to be over.

She had faced up to this when she was a seventeen-year-old girl, knowing the only way free of the emotions tearing her apart was to go out into the world on her own and make a new life.

She was a twenty-six-year-old woman now, and it should be easier. Except it wasn't. The pain was tearing her up like the claws of a wild animal and she couldn't stop it. And the longer she lay here in this bed the harder it was going to be to get up and force herself to go.

Extricating herself as carefully as possible, she silently dressed, packed her suitcase with her old clothes, and sat down to write Serge a note on hotel stationery.

She didn't know what to say and in the end she simply wrote her name—*Clementine*. One name to add to his many. She put the note on the bedside table, pinned it down with the red jewellery case, and took a last look at his sleeping form. His beautiful male face looked so peaceful—as if he'd let go of something that had been hurting him and now all she saw was a kind of relief.

One day I will feel that way too, she told herself.

'I *will* get over you Serge Marinov,' she whispered.

But the force of her emotions threatened to overwhelm her again, because something told her she never would. Not completely.

She had to protect herself. It was time to go.

CHAPTER TWELVE

THE bright lights in the main terminal at Charles de Gaulle airport seared Clementine's sensitive vision, and she made a stop at a chemist and bought a pair of cheap sunglasses, an eye-pack for the flight and some aspirin.

As she crossed the concourse she found herself looking around for him. As she queued, as she waited, even as she went through Security she kept half expecting to hear that dark Russian voice, to turn around and tangle in his eyes again. But what good would it do anyway? He didn't love her. He wasn't going to love her. The past weeks had been a fantasy. She had been right in that little shop when she had first seen him—a Cossack out of a historical epic. Ridiculous, hopelessly romantic, it didn't stand up to the light of day. He wasn't going to chase her. Not any more.

It was truly over. It was time to get on with her life.

As she bumped along the aisle to her seat in cattle class her thoughts flashed back to the private jet, and it brought home to her just how unreal her time with Serge had been.

In less than two hours she would be on her adopted home soil and life would begin again—more or less as it had been when she'd left months before. She remembered how she had felt back in St Petersburg when she'd thought she had lost him, the little lecture she had given herself about putting her experience with Joe Carnegie behind her once and for all, getting on with her life in a proactive fashion.

But now she was finding it hard to picture her flat, had forgotten Joe Carnegie, and couldn't fathom how she was going to drag herself through the next few days, let alone get a grasp on her dreams and ambitions once more. Because she had allowed herself to dream with Serge and those plans now lay in ruins.

One step at a time, her weary mind acknowledged.

As her head touched the back of her seat she closed her eyes. The noise in the plane ceased to touch her as the emotional strain took its toll and she slept.

It was five o'clock in the morning when Clementine emerged from the airport with her luggage. She wondered how she was going to get a taxi—briefly considered phoning Luke until she realised the hour. People jostled her as she ground to a halt on the concourse, but she had a suitcase, a piece of hand luggage and a shoulder bag to deal with and only two arms. She fumbled in her handbag for her purse and the money for a coffee. She needed to take a breath before she gathered herself together and thought about getting home.

Out of the corner of her eye she saw her suitcase lifted and swung out of her line of vision. She gave a cry of, 'Hey!' before her gaze ran up six and a half feet of muscle-honed male in jeans and a jacket and a blue T-shirt she remembered that brought out the intense green of his eyes. Her shock turned to heart-stuttering confusion. Then he hauled her hand luggage under his arm and took off.

'Serge!'

For a moment shock held her immobile as he strode off. With her belongings.

'Serge!' She took off after him. 'Wait! What are you doing?'

She dodged and weaved through the wave of people coming in the other direction, but she was hardly going to lose him. He stood head and shoulders above the crowd, and he wasn't in a hurry. It was just the length of those long, purposeful strides.

'Stop! *Stop!*' she shrieked, no longer caring what anybody thought of her. He'd come for her. She threw herself at his back the precise moment he ground to a halt and landed smack against those big shoulders, her hands going up to steady herself.

He dumped all her luggage and turned around, his expression so fierce she took a backward step.

'*Da,*' he said fiercely. 'It's good you have to chase *me* for a bit. How does it feel, Clementine, being the one on the hop? Isn't that one of your Australian expressions?'

'I don't know,' she said unthinkingly, still coming to terms with his presence. 'How did you get here?' It was the least important question that came to mind, but her brain seemed to have short-circuited.

He made a 'no importance' gesture—so like the Serge she loved, king of his own fiefdom. As if the practical considerations of life that so bedevilled the general population had nothing to do with him.

'You like to run, don't you, *kisa*? Ever since I first laid eyes on you I have been chasing you. Why would it be any different now?' His tone was almost meditative, but his eyes were charged and as wild as she had ever seen them.

'I'm not running. I've come home. The holiday is over, Serge. You made that clear. You took me to Paris to break up with me.' Her voice shattered over those words. 'The most romantic time in my life and you took it and you smashed it.'

The colour left his face as her words sank in, and for a moment she experienced a modicum of satisfaction that he understood how truly awful that experience had been for her.

Then a deep sadness began to invade her, its tendrils reaching into every corner of her body.

'That wasn't my intention,' he said, in a deep, fractured voice. 'Clementine, please believe me—it was never my intention to hurt you.'

But you did.

Her whole body was howling and he was just standing there, looking fierce and troubled and desperate.

'Go and find yourself another girl, Serge,' she said heavily. 'I'm sure there are thousands of women in New York City alone who would be happy to take my place.'

He reached for her, leaning in, and suddenly all she could see was the turbulence inside of him and something else. Something tender—something awakened by her words.

'Where do you get this from? When have I looked at another woman since I met you?'

For a long moment her heart felt too big for her chest. If only he meant a word of that. But she knew it couldn't be true. She shook his hand from her arm. 'You have a history, Serge. Do you think I was living in a bubble back in New York? Everywhere I went I heard about your airhead bimbos. This is what you're like with women.'

'Not with you, Clementine.'

'We were having sex, Serge,' she hissed. 'Sex—that's all it was. You told me that's all it was. You spelt it out. How am I supposed to feel? How am I supposed to deal with that? I don't have casual flings. I'm not built that way.'

'I know you're not.'

She shook her head, shaking out the soft, persuasive sound of his words. Meaningless, empty words.

'I'm not coming back with you, Serge. It's over.'

He caught her hand. 'No.' It wasn't a plea. It wasn't a request. It was a statement of fact. *No.*

It gave her the much needed anger to power herself up.

'Get over yourself, rich boy.' She shook his hand off. 'You're not that irresistible.'

He didn't shift and suddenly she wanted him to know how badly he'd hurt her. But she also wanted him to know he was nothing special.

'I met another guy like you, Serge, a year ago. A rich guy who thought he just had to throw his money around and everything would belong to him. He dated me for six weeks. He dressed me, he asked me to wear jewellery he'd loaned me, and then he offered me an apartment because he didn't want to slum it in my flat. The problem was he was engaged the whole time and had no intention of me being anything other than his mistress. Just another guy looking for no-strings sex with an easy girl.'

Serge was looking at her as if she'd punched him.

She took a deep breath, lowering her voice. 'Except I didn't sleep with him. Because it means something to me, Serge, when I share my body. And the only reason I'm telling you any of this is so you understand what I risked when I came with you to New York City.'

'Clementine—'

She heard him say her name but she barrelled on, full of emotion, hardly knowing what she was saying or revealing any more, and not caring.

'I didn't date for a year afterwards—until I met you and took a chance. You fit the profile, Serge. Money, charisma, the sort of guy who owns the world.' She shook her head in disgust. 'But I thought, He's a good guy. I should look beyond the outer trappings to the man underneath. But in the end, Serge, you're worse than he is because you made me believe you cared about me. All that other guy did was make a fool of me.'

Serge was silent, then he said roughly, 'You should have told me.'

'I'm telling you now. I just wanted to go on a date,' she said stonily. 'I wanted to be a normal girl for a change, who gets dated instead of propositioned.'

'I never propositioned you.'

'Sure you did. You asked me to come with you to New York and my first thought was, Great, another jerk. And guess what? I was right.'

'We ran out of time,' he said softly.

'I know. That's why I said yes. Because I thought just maybe I'd give you the benefit of the doubt. I thought you saw *me*, Serge, the real me. More fool me.'

'I do see you.' Serge touched her cheek, and when she flinched turned her face to make her look at him. 'I *do* see you,' he repeated, his finger curling possessively under her chin.

'No, you don't see me at all. All you see is what everyone else sees—sexy Clementine working her stuff,' she said bitterly. 'You made that very clear yesterday. It's about sex, you said. Just sex.'

'That is not true, Clementine. I lied to you.'

She went very still.

Serge's whole body had drawn taut. 'I didn't want to feel this way about you. My parents had passion in their marriage, Clementine, and it wiped out everything else. My father thought loving meant annihilating the other person. I vowed I would never do that, and whenever I found myself getting close to a woman I would pull back. Until you.'

His eyes softened on her. 'Everything about you has been different. From the moment I saw you in that little shop, saw that smile of yours, you invited me in. It was like being a kid again, following you down that road, and when you wouldn't let me look after you I was stumped. I couldn't leave you there.'

His green eyes, so fierce as she'd flung her accusations at him, grew tender and their gazes locked.

'I've been chasing you ever since.'

She blinked.

'I'm in love with you, Clementine.'

She felt her legs give. She sat down heavily on her suitcase and Serge dropped to his knees beside her. In the middle of an airport terminal, under harsh, unforgiving lights. But all Clementine saw was the man she loved in front of her, on his knees, declaring himself.

'Then why did you push me away?' she whispered hoarsely, not really believing what he was saying.

'Fear.'

Her chin came up. It was a huge admission for a man like Serge to make, and she met the sincerity in his eyes and believed him.

'I didn't want to be like my father,' he admitted tautly. 'I didn't want to destroy the woman I loved. But, God help me, Clementine, when I woke up and found you gone I knew I'd destroyed what we had anyway. I was exactly like my father.'

He took her hands and held them between both of his—a strangely formal gesture that shook her to the ground.

'You tell me I don't see you, Clementine, but I do. Because we're alike, you and I. I see a girl who has been on her own far too long. I see a girl who takes chances and not all of them work out.' He swayed in against her until they were eye to eye. 'I see a girl who when she gets scared runs away. I'm not going to let you run away from me, Clementine. I will chase you to the ends of the earth if I have to. I love you. I will always love you.'

He took a deep, sustaining breath, as if making a declaration of intent. 'I'm a Marinov, and that is how we love our women.'

Clementine's heart stuttered, and then began to thrum to

a deeper beat. Hope was blooming inside her and it hurt too much—because she'd been disappointed so many times in the past. People promised to love you, but love wasn't always enough. Careers and personal desires got in the way. She'd learned that with her parents.

Serge seemed to sense her reticence. He let go of her hands and reached around her waist instead, suddenly so close he was her whole world.

'I've been in hell, Clementine, because I knew I'd driven you away. At the *château* I wanted to take my words back. In the car I wanted to take them back. I tried to show you in the hotel but it wasn't enough. When I woke up and found you gone I knew it wasn't enough. I didn't give you the words you needed because I found them so difficult to say—because I knew once I said them there was no going back for you and me. It's for ever. You *do* understand it's for ever, Clementine?'

A lava-flow of emotion pushed past the hard pylons she'd erected to protect herself and she laid her hand against his chest.

Serge gazed down at her hand, acknowledging the familiar gesture.

'Please don't be just saying that,' she said.

His eyes met hers, and she was stunned by the look of blatant hope in his. He wasn't holding anything back from her any more.

'Be with me, Clementine. Love me. Be mine.'

All the breath seemed to have left her body. It would be so easy to just give in. But she wasn't a little girl any more, hoping others would give her what she needed. She knew now she had to ask for it.

'I want to know first what it would be like, being yours?' she said softly, her voice growing more sure. 'Because I value my independence, Serge.'

She gave him a little smile, and his eyes lit with such a fierce light it felt slightly overwhelming.

'I will tell you what I want,' he said, his accent thickening the words. 'I want to live with you and work beside you and fill our house with friends and family and have babies with you. I want it all. But I don't know how much you want, Clementine.'

She swallowed. 'You told me once you didn't want children.'

'Clementine, I've said a lot of things I wish you'd never heard. When my father died he left behind chaos in his wake. I vowed I'd never do that. But I'd been living a half-life until I met you. I want to live fully, in the moment, and I want children with you and I want to grow old with you.'

'I took a chance, hopping in that limo with you all those weeks ago,' she said shyly. 'I can't see why I shouldn't take another chance now.'

'Forget the limo. You came across the world with a man you hardly knew.' Serge's fingers tightened around hers as he meshed their hands together. 'But, *kisa*, you must never, never do that again. Have you any idea how dangerous it is?'

She looked at their joined hands, wondering how that had happened.

'You've never felt dangerous to me. I always feel safe with you, Serge.'

'I want you to feel safe. I want to look after you, Clementine. I don't want you out in the world on your own. It takes years off me just thinking about it.'

'Then don't think about it, Slugger.'

She drifted up against him with a little smile he recognised. He kissed her softly, tenderly, with growing depth.

She wound her arms around his neck, forged that deep physical connection she had had with him from the beginning simply through the press of her body to his. But now she knew what had been there all along—the emotional link that had been forged between them, highlighted yesterday when he had moved over her on the bed and showed her he loved her because he hadn't had the words for how deeply he felt.

Now she understood. Serge didn't always have the words, but he had been showing her all along.

He looked into her eyes.

'Will you be my wife, Clementine Chevalier?'

A whole host of feelings cascaded through her, but the predominant one was certainty.

'Yes, of course I will. Was there ever any doubt?'

Serge began to chuckle, his chest vibrating with sound.

'What's so funny?'

'Oh, my elusive Clementine—was there ever any doubt? But I have you at last.'

'You always had me, Serge. You just had to ask.'

'I'm asking, *moya lyubov.*'

My love.

Clementine's heart caught on that sentiment. Happy tears sprinkled her eyes and Serge took her in his arms and kissed her.

'Come on, Boots,' he said with deep satisfaction, 'let's find a hotel. I want to be alone with you.'

* * * * *

A QUESTION OF
MARRIAGE

BY
LINDSAY ARMSTRONG

Lindsay Armstrong was born in South Africa but now lives in Australia with her New Zealand-born husband and their five children. They have lived in nearly every state of Australia and have tried their hand at some unusual, for them, occupations, such as farming and horse training—all grist to the mill for a writer! Lindsay started writing romances when their youngest child began school and she was left feeling at a loose end. She is still doing it and loving it.

CHAPTER ONE

'FOR crying out loud, Luke,' Jack Barnard said *sotto-voce* as he eyed the retreating, ramrod-straight back of one of the most militant women he'd ever met, 'why the hell do you put up with that…that gorgon? Getting anywhere near you is like trying to break into Fort Knox!'

Luke Kirwan grinned and picked up the list of messages his secretary had just presented him with before departing indoors. 'Miss Hillier?' he drawled. 'Believe me, Jack, she's invaluable for keeping…' he paused '…students of the female persuasion at bay.'

Jack Barnard stopped looking irritable behind his spectacles and laughed aloud. 'Don't tell me they still make a nuisance of themselves? It's not a problem I would have a problem with, by the way. Herds of sweet young things panting to be in one's bed. Mind you—' he looked reflective '—with the delectable Leonie Murdoch in one's life, perhaps not. Is that what this is all about?' He gestured comprehensively to include the house behind them and the garden around them.

Luke Kirwan rubbed his blue-shadowed jaw and squinted up at the home he had only recently moved into. It was a two-storeyed, attractive, hacienda-style home perched on Manly Hill, a bay-side suburb of Brisbane. From the terrace, where he sat enjoying a beer with his long-time friend Jack Barnard, who was also his solicitor, they had sweeping views out over Moreton Bay towards North Stradbroke Island. 'Maybe,' he said pensively and shrugged. 'Maybe not. I was looking for an investment when it came on the market, then I thought it might be nice to live here.'

Jack Barnard regarded his friend quizzically. It was hard

5

to imagine a more unlikely professor of physics—and one of the youngest to gain his chair at the university he taught at. Because Luke Kirwan was about as far removed in looks from the proverbial absent-minded professor as one could get. Tall, lean and dark with a hint of rapier-like strength, he also possessed a pair of brooding dark eyes that made him look arrogant even when he wasn't—although there was no doubt he could be arrogant.

Add to this a boundless energy, a fine intellect and the capacity to look through people who bored him with complete indifference—and you had the kind of man women found electrifying, Jack Barnard mused ruefully. He himself, he went on to think also ruefully, was much more the archetypal professor. He was short-sighted and supremely absent-minded.

But it was on his mind as he surveyed Luke Kirwan that a worm of discontent might be niggling away at his friend. One would have thought that, by now, Luke and Leonie Murdoch might have tied the knot—they were a spectacular couple and had been together for a few years. In fact he, Jack, had been quite sure it was about to happen when he'd first heard about the new house. Now, though, he wasn't at all sure of it.

'May I point out that you spend very little time at home, Luke, so this could all be quite wasted on you?' he said, and added delicately, 'Have you and Leonie fallen out in any way?'

Luke Kirwan gazed expressionlessly out over island-studded Moreton Bay as it danced and glittered beneath a clear blue sky. Then he transferred that enigmatic dark gaze to his friend and said with a quizzical little smile playing on his lips, 'Jack, what will be, will be.'

'In other words, mind my own business?' Jack hazarded wryly.

'In *one* word, exactly.'

*   *   *

A week later, Aurora Templeton set her teeth and commanded herself to stop shaking.

True, she was breaking into someone's house at the dead of night, but only to remove something that rightfully belonged to her. So it wasn't stealing. It wasn't really breaking and entering because she had no intention of breaking anything, as for entering—yes, well, that could be a moot point, she conceded as she shaded the torch with her gloved fingers. But if you couldn't retrieve your property by any other means, what else were you supposed to do?

She'd also thought this out thoroughly over the past week, she reminded herself, and now was no time to get the wobblies.

But the fact was, it was more nerve-racking than she'd anticipated. Despite having lived, not that long ago and for a long time, in this solid, two-storeyed, hacienda-style house set in its lovely garden—which was how she came to have a key and the knowledge that an easement ran behind the house leading to another street—it was impossible not to feel intimidated by the consequences of being caught in the act of what some might consider robbery.

It was also a heavily overcast night, humid and very still but poised eerily, one couldn't help feeling, for a good storm.

All the more reason to get it over and done with, she told herself briskly, and inserted the key into the deadlock of the laundry door. It opened smoothly and noiselessly. Not that there was anyone home, she'd made sure of that.

The new owner was interstate and she knew that no new burglar alarms, locks or vicious dogs had been installed. Indeed, without a key to the deadlocks, the house was virtually impregnable—all the windows had decorative but effective wrought-iron Spanish grills to protect them, all the doors were thick, solid, hardwood timber.

She slipped silently through the laundry and kitchen into the hall without the aid of her torch after allowing her eyes to adjust to the darkness, and had to smile faintly at how her teenage years came back to her. The laundry door had been her favourite means of entry when arriving home after her curfew had expired.

But she put the torch on, although veiled again by her fingers, for one swift glance around the hall in case the new owner had laid his furniture out differently, to see that there was still the same clear path to the bottom of the stairs. Then she froze and flicked it off at a slight sound. Just a tiny knock really, but it was difficult to establish its source.

And she waited motionless for a few minutes, in her black jeans and polo-neck sweater, with her heart beating uncomfortably.

How she didn't scream as something furry wrapped itself around her legs, she never knew, but the large cat then sat down beside her, purring quietly.

She swallowed and bent down to stroke it, feeling much less as if she should take flight—the cat had obviously made the noise because there was no one else at home, simple, she told herself. And she flicked the torch on briefly again, before she stealthily made her way to the staircase and began to climb it one carpeted step at a time, counting beneath her breath and avoiding, from sheer habit, the fifteenth step that creaked.

Perhaps it was this that rendered her less cautious, she was to wonder later. Because to be silently enfolded into a pair of strong arms as she reached the top step took her supremely by surprise and paralyzed her for several heart-stopping moments. Then terror got the upper hand and she screamed and pummelled so vigorously, the two of them started to topple over in slow motion.

'Oh, no, you don't, lady!' she heard a masculine voice breathe huskily, but as she twisted like an eel she must have taken him by surprise, because the rest of what he'd been going to say was smothered by an exclamation of pain and she felt him go slack just long enough for her to evade his grasp, jump onto the banister and slide down it. Then she raced across the hall and kitchen, out through the laundry, locking the door with the key that was still in it, and sprinted across the back garden, jumped the fence and raced down the easement as if all the demons from hell were on her heels.

She'd had the foresight to park her car two blocks away. Although the easement led onto a different street from the front entrance to the house, she'd thought it wise in case anything went wrong and it could be identified. But, out of the heavily overcast sky, a clap of thunder at last rent the pregnant night and heavy rain began to fall.

'Thank you, thank you up there!' she whispered devoutly, although she was almost instantly soaked to the skin. 'A good storm has got to muddle my tracks, surely!'

'And just repeating the local headlines: the storm that ravaged the southern and bay-side suburbs of Brisbane last night is estimated to have caused close to a million dollars' damage to homes in its path… This is Aurora Templeton for Bay News.'

Aurora pulled off her headphones and steered her chair on its trolley tracks to the other end of the console. Her programme director gave her a thumbs-up sign and she got up stiffly and walked out of the studio. Her morning radio news shift was over and she couldn't be more grateful, not only because she felt as if she'd been through a wringer, but the consequences of her actions only hours ago had kicked in to plague her conscience with a vengeance.

She couldn't avoid looking around constantly or expecting a heavy hand to fall on her shoulder. And it had been the stuff nightmares were made of to wonder whether she would have to broadcast a police report of her own misdemeanour—thankfully not, but there was no guaranteeing it wouldn't be on tomorrow's news!

Why you never stop and think, Aurora Templeton, is a

mystery to me, she castigated herself bitterly and repeatedly on the way home.

Her new town house, in the Brisbane suburb of Manly, was pleasant and comfortable—or would be when she sorted the clutter.

Manly was an eastern suburb of Brisbane, south of the mouth of the Brisbane River on the shores of Moreton Bay. Because of its bay-side position, lovely breezes and views as well as its geographical make-up—a steep cliff running adjacent to the shore atop of which were some wonderful old houses—it had become fashionable again but it was also home to a large boat harbour.

Many of the boaties who enjoyed the waters of Moreton Bay, with its twin guardians of Moreton and North Stradbroke Islands, moored their boats in the Manly harbour so the suburb had a distinctly nautical flavour.

Aurora didn't have a view of the bay from her new town house although she did have a small garden and a courtyard. But she'd had no idea, when she'd come home a couple of weeks ago from six months overseas, that she'd find the family home sold, that her retired sea-captain father would have taken it into his head to buy a yacht and decide to sail around the world solo.

She'd lost her mother when she was six and been brought up by her father, when he'd been home, at boarding-school otherwise, and by a devoted housekeeper, Mrs Bunnings—known affectionately as 'Bunny'—in between times. But she'd also spent a lot of time travelling the world with her father and, at twenty-five, she had a Bachelor of Arts degree, she was fluent in several languages, cosmopolitan, well able to take care of herself and had embarked on a career in radio broadcasting.

None of that worldly education had managed to eradicate a daredevil streak in her character, however, which had often seen Bunny despair of her. And it was this that Aurora blamed as she brewed herself a cup of coffee in her new town house, the morning after she'd broken into Professor Luke Kirwan's home.

Well, not only that, she amended the thought as she inhaled the coffee aroma luxuriously. All sorts of things had gone towards creating the debacle, not the least her father's sudden decision to sell their home without even consulting her, then go sailing off into the wide blue yonder a bare few days after she'd got home and *before* she'd remembered her diaries.

She took her coffee to the lounge and curled up in a winged armchair, and thought back down the years.

She'd always been a compulsive scribbler, an inveterate diarist. Not that you would know it from the face she presented to the world but, deprived of her mother at an early age and separated from her father for long periods, an only child with no other close relatives—all of it had created the need in her for some kind of a lifeline, which was what her diaries had become: her companions that never deserted her.

The discovery, when she was about twelve, of a loose brick in the never-used fireplace of her bedroom that revealed a cavity in the wall behind it, had been a wonderful cache for them. She'd used it right up until she'd gone overseas, convinced her dreams, fantasies and innermost thoughts were quite safe from prying eyes.

But it wasn't until she'd rung Bunny to tell her that she was home and to discuss the turmoil of Ambrose Templeton's unexpected actions that she'd remembered them.

Bunny had been delighted to hear from her and able to tell her that she had been kept on, three mornings a week, as a cleaner for the new owner of Aurora's old home. That was when a vision of the fireplace in her old bedroom had floated through Aurora's mind and her mouth had dropped open...

It hadn't taken long to occur to her, however, that the

normal course of action, simply ringing the new owner and explaining about secret caches and diaries, was, at the same time, inviting extreme curiosity in any normal person who most probably would not be able to resist having a look first for themselves… Just thinking about it made her break out in a cold sweat.

So she'd rung up and tried to make an appointment with Professor Luke Kirwan, Professor of Physics, she now knew, without giving a reason other than saying it was important and personal, and with the thinking that, once she was in the house, she could explain then and retrieve her diaries herself so that no one could get to them first.

Only to discover that the professor himself didn't take calls at home at all. He had an extremely officious secretary to do it for him during working hours, long working hours at that, and an answering machine he never responded to at other times.

Nor was this secretary—and Bunny had told her what a dragon the woman was, always sneaking up behind her to check what she was doing—at all interested in making an appointment for Aurora with the professor without good reason, saying he was far too busy at the moment unless she could state her case.

Aurora had thought swiftly, then explained that she was the previous owner's daughter, she'd been away at the time of the sale and she'd just like to check that nothing of hers had been left behind.

'Definitely not,' Miss Dragon Hillier had said coldly down the line. 'I checked the house myself and you can rest assured there was nothing that shouldn't be here! Good day.' And she'd put the phone down heavily.

Aurora had taken the receiver from her ear and breathed fierily. But she'd forced herself to calm down and devise Plan B. Of course! She would simply roll up, after office hours, and corner the professor in his den without his dragon lady protector. But this professor of physics had proved to be extremely elusive. She'd rolled up to her old address five times in as many days to find no one home. The fifth time had been when the germ of an idea had started to niggle at the back of her mind.

'What's he like?' she'd asked Bunny, over the phone. It had occurred to her to ask Bunny to get her diaries for her, but she'd discarded the idea immediately on the grounds that she could lose Bunny her job—especially since Miss Hillier was a such a sticky beak. But would a few simple questions do any harm? she'd pondered.

'Don't know, I've never met him, only the dragon, she hired me on your father's recommendation,' Bunny had replied. 'And he's always gone by the time I get to work and doesn't seem to come home during the day. Mind you, it's only been a few weeks, but I'll tell you what, love, I think he's a regular old fuddy-duddy. She's certainly as fussy as can be and I guess it comes from him!'

'Has he made any changes, Bunny?' Aurora had asked a little hesitantly. 'And has he got a wife or—'

'Nope, he's a bachelor. Can't for the life of me understand why he wants to rattle about in a house that size—he doesn't even have a dog, although there is a cat. As for changes, none so far although I heard her talking to a builder on the phone to get a quote to brick up the fireplaces in the bedrooms, the ones your dad always used to say were such a waste in a climate like Brisbane.'

Aurora had almost dropped the phone. 'I see,' she'd said rather hollowly.

'You OK, pet?' Bunny had enquired, then continued without waiting for an answer, 'Must say the place is beautifully furnished, lots of antiques that take a powerful lot of dusting, mind. You would think he'd have a dog to guard it all, especially as he's away an awful lot, apparently. I also heard her book him an air ticket to Perth for next weekend, flying out Friday, coming back Monday, but they didn't even change the locks as new owners often like to do. I guess the old place is pretty hard to get into when you stop to think about it, though.'

'Yes.' Aurora had swallowed. 'Yes.' And she'd let Bunny ramble on for a few minutes more before ending the conversation. Then she'd up-ended the contents of the suitcases Bunny had packed with her clothes and personal possessions that had come from the house, and fallen on an old wallet to find her laundry door key still sitting snugly in a zip-up compartment...

She came back to the present with a sigh. She still might not have done it if she hadn't rung once more and tried again to get past Miss Hillier, this time to be told flatly that the professor was busier than ever and would she please stop bothering them! There'd also been a curious innuendo in the other woman's scathing tones that she'd been unable to pin down but it was almost as if she, Aurora, should be ashamed of herself for some reason—it was this strange insinuation that had added fuel to the flames and made her decide to take things into her own hands.

So what to do now? she wondered. Would the professor and his dragon lady secretary associate her calls with this home invasion? Should she step forward and confess?

The phone rang as she was thinking these thoughts and it was Bunny, deliciously full of news. Believe it or not, the professor had been robbed! Well, Bunny had gone on to explain, he'd come home early from Perth on account of some virulent bug that had laid him low and put himself straight to bed, only to wake around midnight ravaged by a headache and thirst. He'd stepped out of his bedroom, stood for a few minutes wondering where the light switch was as often happened to people in new homes, then, despite feeling extremely groggy and unwell, had noticed a strange light at the bottom of the stairs.

And, when someone had begun to ascend the stairs, between wondering whether he was hallucinating and definitely not feeling well enough to grapple with a burglar, he'd stayed quite silent until the intruder had literally walked into his waiting arms—only to knock himself out briefly in the ensuing mêlée.

'You don't…say!' Aurora commented feebly at this first break in Bunny's narrative. 'Is…is he all right? Was anything stolen?' she forced herself to add.

No, nothing was missing, Bunny reported, but that could have been because the intruder had been disturbed; no, he was back in bed but mainly because of a virus he'd picked up and—here Bunny chuckled—would you believe it? He'd actually left the front door ajar when he'd come home which was, according to the police, tantamount to issuing any stray burglar who happened to be 'out and about casing joints' an open invitation!

'How…bizarre!'

Bunny agreed, still chuckling. 'Talk about the absent-minded professor! Although, he was pretty crook.'

'So…so what are the police going to do?' Aurora asked.

'Well, love, there've been a few burglaries in the area, apparently, and they suspect there's a bit of a gang at work, must have been them, they reckon, but they didn't sound too hopeful of pinning them down on this one. In all the chaos of the storm—we got three broken windows and the garden is kind of flattened—they can't find any evidence of anyone being on the property.'

Aurora swallowed, mainly with relief, as Bunny chatted on about how she'd been given the day off. And when Aurora finally put the phone down, she thought she might have had a very lucky escape; she told herself she would *never* do anything as foolish again, but there still remained the problem of her diaries…

It took her a week to acknowledge that she would either have to come clean with the professor and resign herself to either he or Miss Hillier reading them before she got to them, or resign herself to having them bricked up for ever, assuming the builder doing the bricking up didn't find them.

Then, out of the blue, came a ray of light. Her programme director, Neil Baker, asked her if she'd like to accompany him to a house-warming party. They'd actually met overseas and laughed at one of life's little coincidences that they should be working together back in 'Oz', but there'd never been any romantic spark between them.

'You wouldn't be between girlfriends, Neil?' she teased.

He grimaced and confessed that he was, but he'd been invited to bring a partner to this party, to which his ex-girlfriend had *also* been invited, and... He paused and looked awkward.

'OK, I get the picture.' Aurora grinned. 'Where and when?'

'Luke Kirwan has got himself a new pad, somewhere up on the hill. Know him?'

Aurora coughed to cover her start of surprise. 'Er...no. You do, I gather?'

'Yep. I was at uni with him. Like to come? It's this Friday night, semi-formal and I'll take the present.'

'I...yes.'

The thing was to look as little as possible like a cat burglar, Aurora told herself as she studied her wardrobe early on Friday evening.

Of course, it would be even better if she could persuade herself to come down with a sudden bout of flu and give up the whole idea of going to this party at all, but...

She flicked back her long streaky fair hair and planted her hands on her hips. Who did this professor and his watchdog secretary think they were? Common courtesy alone was entirely absent from their behaviour and if they thought they could brush her aside like a troublesome, somehow rather shameful fly, they could think again. She would go and, if the opportunity presented itself, she would retrieve her diaries.

She chose a flamenco outfit she'd picked up in Spain, a long flounced skirt with pink flowers on a dark background and a white blouse. She pinned a fake pink gardenia into her hair and studied her reflection.

It was almost a boyish little face beneath the glorious hair but redeemed by a pair of thickly lashed, sparkling green eyes that were little short of sensational. At barely five feet two, her figure was neat, compact and very slim.

She started to smile at herself in the long mirror as she kicked the skirt aside and raised her hands above her head—it was a beautiful outfit and she always felt wonderful in it. As if she could dance the flamenco all night but, not only that, even without her mantilla, she always felt as if the clothes and the dance were a sensuous celebration of her femininity.

She lowered her arms abruptly—perhaps those were not the right vibes to be giving off at Professor Luke Kirwan's house-warming? Perhaps she should dress to be as inconspicuous as possible rather than trying to look the opposite to a cat burglar? She frowned, then shrugged as the doorbell rang—it was too late to change now.

'Wow!' Neil Baker looked suitably impressed. 'You look absolutely stunning, Aurora.'

'Thanks.' She got into his car and stowed her fringed shoulder bag at her feet. It was a little bulkier than normal because it contained a green rubbish bag and a length of strong fishing line as well as her lipstick, comb and a hanky. She smiled at Neil as he started the engine for the short drive to her old home. 'Tell me a bit about this friend of yours?'

'He's really brilliant, but he's a good bloke for all that. There was a rumour that he and a girl called Leonie Murdoch were about to get hitched—maybe this is a surprise engagement party too,' Neil theorized, 'because I can't see why he needs a house otherwise. There's a hell of a lot of old money in the family, family homes and a sheep station out west—here we are!'

Aurora opened her mouth as she stared at her *old* family home lit up most attractively tonight, and it was on the tip of her tongue to tell Neil that she was no stranger to this house and why, just in case she met someone she knew, but the moment seemed to pass without her being able to get it out. Then she saw how many people were streaming into this house-warming party, and it didn't seem to matter—she would only be one insignificant guest in a big crowd.

But once she was inside, she did take the precaution of asking Neil to point Luke Kirwan out to her because she had every intention of avoiding their host as much as was possible. Only Miss Hillier, fortyish, upright, groomed within an inch of life and looking every bit the martinet she sounded, had been at the door to greet guests.

'Uh…' Neil looked around the throng as glasses of champagne were pressed upon them—a catering firm had obviously been hired '…oh, there he is! Over by the piano. I think I'll wait until things settle down rather than fight through the crowd to introduce you, if that's OK with you?' he added, but rather distractedly as he scanned the throng intently.

'Fine!' Aurora said, more enthusiastically than was called for, as she gazed through the crowd at the man beside the piano. Actually there were two, but one of them wore thick glasses, had thinning fair hair, was short and wore an Argyle tie with a mustard corduroy shirt beneath a baggy tweed jacket. He also had a pipe in his hand.

No one could possibly look more 'donnish', she decided and smiled inwardly. So that was Professor Luke Kirwan. No wonder he had to employ a dragon lady to run things for him because he literally exuded the kind of fuddy-duddy ineffectualness one associated with an absent-minded professor.

Which was not how you could describe the man standing next to him, she mused as she felt herself relaxing beneath the vastly less than threatening presence of the man she'd grappled with at the top of the stairs on that never-to-be-forgotten night.

No, another kettle of fish altogether, the second man beside the piano. In fact, downright arresting might be a good way to put it, she decided.

Tall with brushed-back dark hair, he had a wide brow, smooth skin, high cheekbones and slight hollows beneath those good bones as his face tapered to a hard mouth and a jaw-line that indicated this was not a man to trifle with. He also had dark, brooding eyes and he was leaning negligently against the baby grand looking cool, slightly bored and capable of a rather damning kind of arrogance if he chose.

From what she could see, he wore indigo designer jeans, a midnight-blue shirt beneath a faultlessly tailored navy jacket and a shot-silk amethyst tie. He also had a glass of something in his hands which he twirled now and then before putting it to his lips, draining it and setting it down decisively. As he straightened and his dark gaze roamed around the crowded room briefly, she saw that he was even taller than she'd suspected with wide shoulders.

Well, well, Aurora found herself thinking as that indifferent gaze failed to be impressed by anything it saw and he turned away—what have we here? A hawk amongst the sparrows? A real man amongst us? I wonder what he does for a living? Could he be a corsair in disguise, a better-looking, more dangerous James Bond than any of them, a modern-day Mr Darcy?

This time an outward smile twisted her lips because it was just that typical flight of fantasy that made it so difficult for her to allow anyone to read her diaries…

Over the next two hours, the party got noisier and merrier. She also got separated from Neil, who still hadn't got around to introducing her to Luke Kirwan for the simple reason that as soon as he and his ex-girlfriend laid eyes on each other, they were drawn together like a pin to a magnet and determined, it appeared, to have things out with each other despite being in the middle of a party.

'Look,' Neil said awkwardly to Aurora as his ex-girlfriend glowered at her over her shoulder, 'I'm sorry about this but—'

'Forget about me, Neil.' Aurora chuckled. 'If looks could kill I should be six feet under by now, which tells me she's still very interested in you, so go for it! I can take care of myself.'

Neil looked both grateful and exasperated at the same time, but, five minutes later, neither of them were to be sighted.

Aurora shrugged, still amused but also aware that she was a free agent now, which simplified things considerably. She could put her plan—of wandering upstairs in search of a powder room but nipping into her old bedroom to get her diaries—into action, and she could leave the party whenever it suited her without anyone being the wiser.

Before she got to implement any of it, though, she'd wandered outside onto the terrace to drink in the view she knew so well and loved—the Manly Boat Harbour by night with its millions of dollars' worth of yachts and all kinds of small crafts tied up to the jetties—when a disco struck up on the terrace and couples drifted out to dance.

And she was actually thinking that this was a livelier kind of party than one would expect of an absent-minded professor when a deep voice behind her drawled, 'May I have this dance, señorita?'

For some reason the hairs on the nape of her neck stood up as she turned slowly, then she knew why—it was the man who'd been standing beside the professor at the piano.

She took an unexpected breath to be on the receiving end of that dark, worldly gaze, but said lightly, 'Oh, it's you.'

He raised an eyebrow. 'You were expecting me?'

'Not at all, señor.' She smiled faintly. 'I got the rather strong impression not much about this party was of any interest to you.'

A glint of something like mockery entered his dark eyes. 'When did you get that impression?'

She shook out her hair and opted for honesty against confusion at being caught in having 'sized him up', so to speak. 'When you were leaning against the piano looking bored,' she said with a glimmer of mischief curving her lips.

'That must have been before I caught sight of you,' he countered, then frowned slightly. 'Are you—unaccompanied?'

'I am now, although I didn't start out that way.' She looked wry. 'My escort met his ex-girlfriend and they've disappeared. I'm not sure if they're making up or tearing each other to bits, but something intensely dramatic was going on between them so I decided to withdraw rather than get my eyes scratched out.'

'Then he wasn't the love of your life?'

'No way. I was only filling in *because* they'd split up!'

'I think he needs his head read,' the man remarked thoughtfully. 'Do you dance, señorita? It would be a pity not to do that gorgeous outfit justice.' His gaze roamed up and down her figure.

'That's what I always think when I'm wearing it,' Aurora replied simply, although conscious of a tremor running through her, sparked by that heavy-lidded dark gaze on her body. And she knew instinctively that her sensuous pleasure in herself, brought on by this outfit, had communicated itself to this stranger—in other words it had been a mistake to wear it. But how was she to have known she would bump into the one man who would sense that, where others mightn't?

She also caught herself thinking that this stranger was

dynamite, and she should possibly exercise due caution or she might find herself willingly led down the garden path…

That was nonsense, she immediately corrected the thought, another flight of sheer fantasy! All the same, it wouldn't go astray to take care.

She said, whimsically, 'I won't treat you to a full flamenco, though.'

'Could you?'

'I took lessons in Spain a few months ago. They called me the pocket señorita.'

He studied her upturned face until she moved restlessly beneath the way his gaze took in her eyes, then rested squarely on her mouth before he said pensively, 'Why do I get the feeling you could be a pocket dynamo all round, Miss…?'

But Aurora, who found her heart beating abnormally and her senses all at sixes and sevens beneath not only the way this man was looking at her but everything about him, clutched a straw of sanity. 'I'd rather remain anonymous at the moment,' she said with a delicious look of fun in her eyes. 'If you don't tread on my toes or have sweaty palms I might reconsider, but I'm not promising anything.'

He didn't reply, only inclined his head, took her in his arms and swung her into the beat of the music. Then he stopped and frowned down at her again, but only for a moment before he rather absently steered her through the dancers.

As for Aurora, she also found herself dancing mechanically for several reasons. A determination not to be overly impressed by this man on such short notice, but also because of a prickling sense of *déjà vu*. Why, though? she wondered. She was quite sure she'd never met him before—he was not the kind of man you forgot—so it had to be because she was back on the terrace of her old home, only—that didn't seem to fit.

'Have I offended some other, unnamed principle of yours,

Miss Anonymous? Body odour or bad breath?' he drawled, breaking her out of her frowning reverie.

Her eyes widened. 'Uh…no, sorry, nothing like that at all! You smell quite nice in a manly way.' She inhaled delicately. 'I'm not partial to overpowering aftershave or cologne on men.'

'Neither am I,' he said abruptly. 'You, on the other hand, use a particularly delicate, floral perfume.'

'Thank you! It is rather nice, isn't it? I have it specially made up for me by a friend who is into that kind of thing.'

'So it's—uniquely yours?' There was a rather intent little gleam in his eyes as he asked the question.

'Yes. Do you have a problem with that?' she asked curiously.

'No. Why should I?'

'I don't know. You just looked a bit—' she shrugged '—censorious about my perfume.'

He smiled faintly. 'I think it all goes towards making you rather special.' He held her away and looked down at her consideringly before raising his eyes to hers. 'Do you have anyone in your life—when you're not helping hapless men friends out?'

Aurora, once more clasped in his arms, began to dance again. 'I don't think we know each other well enough to go into that. Unless you'd like to set the ball rolling by telling me about your love life?' She raised an eyebrow delicately at him.

'In point of fact I happen to be—unattached at the moment,' he responded gravely.

'And on the prowl,' Aurora suggested with an undercurrent of irony.

'What makes you think that?'

'Could be that my antennae are picking up those vibes about you,' she replied ingenuously. 'In fact, I warned myself to be on guard against being led down the garden path not long after we started to dance.'

He laughed, and there was something curiously breathtaking about it despite Aurora's wish to be unimpressed by him. Because it revealed a vitality that made you want to laugh too, and made you want to get to know this man, who could be so damningly bored at times then respond so fascinatingly to something you'd said—so that you felt absolutely fascinated yourself.

'I have yet to resort to leading a girl down the garden path,' he denied, 'although the opposite may not be true.'

Aurora blinked and wrinkled her brow. 'You have a problem with girls leading *you* down the garden path?'

'Occasionally.'

They danced in silence for a while as Aurora digested this. She wasn't sure if he was serious, although it was not hard to imagine him cutting a swathe through the female population. She said, eventually, 'How old are you?'

He looked briefly taken aback. 'Thirty-seven, why?'

She smiled wisely. 'Then it's about time you got yourself a wife, I would think, not only to keep *you* on the straight and narrow but to discourage women from making fools of themselves over you.'

'Are you suggesting yourself for the position?' he came back smoothly and with a mocking little smile playing on his lips.

'Not at all,' Aurora replied airily. 'I plan to have a lot more fun and adventure before I embark on marriage, domesticity and maternity.'

'And do you think these things work to plan?' he queried, rather dryly, she thought.

'For me they do—so far, anyway!'

'How nice,' he commented, and said no more for a time.

But it was not long before Aurora realised, as they danced, that it was far easier said than done to remain impervious to this man. He danced well, holding her lightly and certainly not imposing any unwelcome familiarities on her. In fact he was being a very correct partner—but that could be a mockery, she found herself thinking darkly.

There was certainly a quizzical gleam in his eyes from time to time as he so carefully observed the proprieties. Almost as if he knew exactly, damn him, how wonderful he was to dance with even so correctly. How easily his well-knit body moved to the rhythm—how impossible it was not to feel rather stunningly aware of him even held so lightly in his arms.

'You were thinking?' he murmured, his dark eyes resting wickedly on her flushed face, after he'd twirled her expertly so that her skirt belled out beautifully, and brought her back safely into his arms.

'That's for me to know and you to ponder upon,' she replied, and was annoyed to hear herself sounding defensive.

'Then I'll tell you what *I* was thinking, Miss Anonymous. That we dance so well together, there are certain other—activities,' he said, barely audibly, 'we should be able to lend ourselves to excellently.'

Aurora took a breath and felt her cheeks redden, but she was unable to prevent herself from replying in kind as anger also coursed through her veins. 'Really?' she said gently. 'I should warn you that I don't take my clothes off on first encounters.'

He took the opportunity to look right through her clothes, then raised a lazy eyebrow at her. 'A pity, but it might create a riot here and now, wouldn't you agree?'

'Perhaps I should rephrase,' Aurora started to say.

He laughed softly. 'Perhaps. That is cutting to the chase rather rapidly.'

'You started this,' she reminded him, trying valiantly to sound cool and unflustered, although she was kicking herself mentally.

'I may have,' he agreed, 'but I was thinking along the lines of extending the pleasure we take in dancing with each other...' he paused and looked down at her significantly until she had to look away with a mixture of embarrassment and self-directed ire '...to another, quite lovely level that wouldn't, however, require us to undress.'

Aurora missed her step and marvelled bitterly at the ease with which he redirected her to the rhythm. And it was impossible not to silently contemplate another 'lovely level' with this man, right there as she was, in his arms, with their bodies touching when the music brought them together.

It should be impossible, she mused. She was not an impressionable girl, she was not particularly naïve, but she had the distinct feeling that this man had somehow got past her defences with his mixture of intriguing looks, his arrogantly bored air and his exquisitely polite handling of her that, at the same time, had activated all sorts of reactions in her. Nor did his approach—guaranteed, one would have thought, to prove she was being 'toyed' with—stop her from wondering what it would be like to be somewhere private with him.

What would happen? she even found herself wondering. Would she allow herself to be kissed—the next level he appeared to have in mind? Would she be able to resist if he was as good at it as he was to dance with?

She stopped dancing abruptly and looked at him lethally. 'All right, you've had your bit of fun. I think we should part company now.'

'Why? Didn't you tell me you were into "fun" for a good while yet?' His gaze rested pointedly on the curve of her breasts beneath her blouse, then flicked up to her eyes with a mixture of derision and irony.

Aurora compressed her lips and took hold. Enough of this, she told herself. She'd come here for one reason tonight and it certainly wasn't to get waylaid by a man, however gorgeous. Make that downright *dangerous*, she reflected with an inward little shiver. And as the music changed it presented her with the perfect escape.

'Fun—oh, yes! Let's see if you can really dance,' she teased, and whirled herself out of his arms as the rhythm changed and she started to do the twist expertly along with the rest of the dancers.

When it came to an end, everyone was hot and laughing and fanning themselves, but her partner took her hand and said, 'Well? Do I qualify to get your name now?'

'Tell you what,' she suggested, 'I really need to powder my nose. If you could find me a long, cool drink in the meantime, who knows?' And she regained her hand and melted away into the crowd. A quick peep over her shoulder once she was inside told her that another woman had claimed him.

All the better, she thought as she found her bag, unobtrusively scanned the staircase and, seeing it deserted, slipped upstairs. No one knew better than she that there was a downstairs powder room for just these occasions, but surely a guest in a supposedly strange house could be forgiven for going upstairs?

And, in the proverbial twinkling of an eye, she'd let herself into her old bedroom. The room was in darkness but she waited for a few minutes, then moved forward cautiously, feeling for the bed and finding a bedside table. She had her hand on what felt like a lamp when the door opened and the overhead light went on. She froze, then swung round to see the man she'd danced with anonymously standing in the doorway.

'So,' he said with soft but unmistakable menace, closing the door behind him without turning, 'I was right.'

'I...I...' Aurora stammered '...I...was looking for a bathroom. I couldn't seem to find the light, that's all.'

He smiled grimly. 'Again? I'm only surprised you didn't bring your torch with you, Little Miss Spain, who didn't want to tell me her name.'

Aurora blinked and licked her lips. 'I don't know what you mean.' She backed away as he moved towards her, and sat down unexpectedly on the bed. 'I don't know what you're doing here either. Please leave, and I'll find the bathroom on my own.'

'Give me one good reason for *not* telling me your name,' he countered.

She swallowed and thought frantically, then decided that the closer she could stick to the truth, the better. She tossed her hair with more spirit than she actually felt. 'I don't believe in being bowled over by men on first encounters.'

'As in allowing yourself to be attracted to them even when it's already happened?' he suggested, with a wealth of satire in his dark gaze. 'Or wearing provocative outfits,' he added meaningfully.

Damn, Aurora thought, that hadn't been such a good idea after all; and could think of nothing to say, so she merely shrugged.

'But tonight was our second encounter, wasn't it?' he drawled then. 'Aren't you forgetting the way we…bumped into each other at the top of the stairs the last time you invaded my home?'

Aurora's mouth fell open and her eyes were suddenly huge. '*Your* home! Who…who are you?' she said in a strangled kind of croak.

'Luke Kirwan,' he replied, looking altogether taller, tougher and much more dangerous than she'd imagined earlier. 'And you're not getting out of here until you tell me what you're so determined to steal from me, señorita.'

CHAPTER TWO

'YOU can't be!' Aurora gasped, absolutely thunderstruck.

He studied her narrowly. 'Believe me, I am. And this is *my* house, in case you've devised a ploy to confuse things somehow or other.'

'But…but…who's the other one, then?' she stammered.

'Other what?'

'The man you were standing with next to the piano—the man who looks just like a prof—' She broke off and bit her lip.

Luke Kirwan frowned and she saw him concentrate for a moment, then look fleetingly amused. 'Jack Barnard?' he suggested. 'He's my solicitor, but what has that got to do with any of this, señorita?' he enquired coldly.

Aurora swallowed painfully and closed her eyes as she grappled not only with the folly of judging people on their appearances, but also having that prickling sense of *déjà vu* explained to her in this manner. She had been in Luke Kirwan's arms before—not for long before she'd started to pummel and struggle with him, but long enough, obviously, for it to have imprinted itself on her subconscious.

But, it suddenly occurred to her and she clasped her hands together tightly, if that was all *he* had to go on, a similar sense of *déjà vu*, then he didn't have a leg to stand on…

'I think I know what's going through your head, my pretty,' he drawled as her lashes flew up. 'How do I know it was you at the top of the stairs the last time you tried to rob me? I'll tell you. Same height, same petite figure, same…' he paused and looked wry '…athleticism but, above all, same unique—as you told me yourself—perfume.' His dark eyes glinted sardonically.

29

Aurora's lips parted and her eyes widened. Then she closed them again and barely stopped herself from saying caustically that, for a man groggy with some kind of virus, he'd taken in an awful lot about her and no one would buy it anyway!

But he spoke again, and this time there was a grim warning underlying his words that caused her to tremble inwardly. 'Of course, finding you creeping around my bedroom, when there's a clear sign downstairs directing people to a *downstairs* bathroom, adds a lot more weight to my evidence, don't you agree?'

Aurora looked around properly for the first time. It had never occurred to her that the new owner would not use the master bedroom, but that was exactly what Luke Kirwan appeared to have done. Her old bedroom was now definitely, although luxuriously, furnished for a man.

'I preferred the view from this room,' he said, as if reading her thoughts.

Damn, she thought again, and forcibly prevented herself from wiping her face.

'Well, Mr Kirwan,' she said after a moment's thought, 'I am sorry for inadvertently invading your bedroom but you're mistaken. I didn't see the sign downstairs so it couldn't have been so very clear. As for all the rest of it, whatever it is, I...' she tilted her chin and gazed at him imperiously '...I'm happy to forget about it if you would be so kind as to direct me to a bathroom. I'll even leave your party then, since you cherish these amazing suspicions about me. In fact, nothing would induce me to stay,' she finished proudly.

He laughed softly as he took in the hauteur of her expression, the set of her small chin, her very straight back and the outraged bearing of her slender figure—even seated on a bed. 'You're a rather brilliant actress, aren't you?' he commented. 'But the only thing that's going to get you out of here is telling me who you are and *why* you're here—'

'I've told you that!' she interrupted.

'So you have. It doesn't wash, though.' He studied her comprehensively, right through her clothes again, in fact, so that she started to boil beneath that dark, insolently intimate gaze. 'What is beginning to wash is something a little different,' he continued leisurely. 'Could you even be a groupie, señorita, who devised a rather novel way of getting through my secretary's net?'

Aurora's mouth fell open. 'I have no idea what you're talking about!'

'No?' The scepticism in his expression was chilling. 'Never heard of student groupies? Girls? Believe me, it's an occupation for some of them; it would appear to be the only reason they're at university in the first place,' he said with damning scorn.

Several things suddenly came clear to Aurora, including his secretary's manner and why he never answered the phone himself, but the shock of it all rendered her speechless.

Giving him the opportunity to continue with lethal satire, 'Why, yes. Heaven alone knows what bizarre scheme you'd concocted the other night—looking for something to steal from me to blackmail me into bed with you, perhaps?' He raised an eyebrow at her. 'But your actions tonight have been loud and clear—coyly refusing to tell me your name, being a seductively mysterious guest—and so on,' he finished flatly.

To be thought of as a coy, student groupie throwing herself at his feet in a rather 'novel' manner caused Aurora to lose her temper completely. 'Look here—' she bounced off the bed '—I've had enough of this. Will you get out of my way before I scream the place down?'

'Scream away,' he invited. 'The only thing that will achieve is to have me call the police.'

'What?'

'Oh, yes,' he said. 'In fact, you have a choice. I'll leave

you here for a period of sober reflection. When I come back, either you tell me the truth or I do get the police.'

'If you think I have any intention of staying here,' she spat at him, 'you're mistaken!'

'No, I'm not. I propose to lock you in, you see.'

Aurora flew at him, prepared to scratch his eyes out, only to find herself caught in a grip of steel. 'Let me go!' she gasped through pale lips.

'I'd rather let an enraged tigress go.' He pinioned her hands behind her back. 'I've also got something of a score to settle with you, Miss Spain. Let's see if you kiss as well as you do—other things.'

'I never kiss under these circumstances. I'm perfectly capable of biting, however,' she warned through her teeth.

He smiled crookedly. 'What circumstances do you kiss under?'

'I need to be in love or on the way to it, like any normal girl,' she replied scathingly. 'The last thing I can imagine with you, Professor. For one thing, you're too old for me, for another the mere thought of doing it under duress turns me right off!' Her green eyes were proud and defiant.

'OK.' He released her pinioned hands but transferred his hands to her waist. 'In exchange for no duress, could I get a promise that you'll keep your fists to yourself?'

'I'm not promising anything!'

'Then how about…' there was the glint of wicked amusement in his dark eyes although he spoke gravely '…proving to me that I am too old for you?'

'You must think I'm still in my cradle,' Aurora retorted, 'to fall for that old line!'

'On the contrary, before I discovered you sneaking around my bedroom, I thought you were gorgeous, certainly of the age of consent—' his gaze roamed up and down her figure '—and quite stunning.'

Aurora's lips parted and, before she could think of a suitable rejoinder, he drew her into his arms. She breathed once, jerkily, but, to her horror, the spell of Luke Kirwan once again began to weave itself around her. And no twelve-year age difference was going to save her, she realised—not that she'd said it as anything but a crushing, heat-of-the-moment snub.

To make things worse, she also realized from the smile twisting his lips that her thought processes were about as easy for him to read as an open book. 'Look,' she began uneasily, 'this is insane! You can't just do it...'

'I can and I'm going to, so save your breath,' he recommended. 'Don't tell me there isn't the slightest curiosity on your side?'

He moved his hands on her hips and she went to say something, stopped with her lips parted as all sorts of sensations started to run through her—and not only physical. Knowing that part of the dangerous attraction of this man for her was that she was playing with fire, for example. *See if you can be unaffected by this, Little Miss Spain,* she mimicked in her mind, because she had no doubt that was the gauntlet Luke Kirwan was throwing down. But it would be madness to take it up...

He did it for her. He took advantage of her confusion to withdraw his hands from her hips and cup her face lightly at the same time as he captured her green gaze so that she was unable to look away. 'Small, neat and stylish—whatever else it is you are, my would-be robber, and, I suspect, delicious. Let's see.' He lowered his head.

Aurora trembled as his lips touched hers, but he said against the corner of her mouth, 'I was right: sweet as a peach, señorita.' And started to kiss her properly.

The crazy part about it was that he made her feel as sweet as a peach while he kissed her lingeringly, but not only that. He himself felt so amazingly good it was almost impossible to remain unaffected. How did he do it? she marvelled as he ran his hands down her back and laid a trail of feather-light kisses down her neck. With great restraint, she answered herself. This was no stolen, victory kiss—he was far too clever for that, damn him, she thought.

This was a skilled assault that made her skin feel like silk as those cool, dry lips wandered across it, and the way his hands found the curves of her body made her heartbeat triple. This was a man who made not one blunder while her senses rioted and she began to drink in the feel of him through her pores.

His height, those broad shoulders, the interesting hollows of his face, which she found herself wanting to touch, the crisp cotton of his shirt, the hard, taut length of him that she was now resting against as he stopped kissing her, with not an ounce of defiance left in her but one embarrassingly girlish word on her lips—Wow!

To her everlasting gratitude, she managed to stop herself from actually saying it as he put her away from him and steadied her before releasing her.

'Well?' There was sheer devilry in those dark eyes as he posed the question.

Aurora breathed deeply and had to suffer the indignity of him restoring some tendrils of hair behind her ears and straightening the collar of her blouse before she could think of a response. Then she could only fall back on the truth. 'I'm speechless,' she said huskily and licked her lips.

He raised an eyebrow at her with a mixture of amusement and mockery. 'I'll take it as read, then. And I'll leave you to—compose yourself.'

'I didn't necessarily mean I was bowled over or anything...' she began to protest not quite truthfully, but stopped with her eyes darkening. 'You're not still going to lock me in!'

'Oh, yes, I am, sweetheart,' he said coolly, then looked amused. 'By the way, there's an *en*-suite bathroom through there.' He pointed. 'Never let it be said I inconvenienced a guest even if they are burglars or groupies—and I'm now quite sure it was you that dark and stormy night.' He turned on his heel and walked out and Aurora heard the key turn in the lock before she was able to think of a thing to do.

'I don't *believe* this!' she said through gritted teeth, then sank back onto the bed to drop her face into her hands as she marvelled bitterly on her sheer bad luck and wondered what to do next. Of course, it was obvious, she thought. She had no choice but to come clean, yet it went supremely against the grain to be outwitted by this man and there was no guarantee he wouldn't insist on reading at least some bits of her diaries...

Several minutes later she got up and went into the bathroom, where she washed her face and had a drink of water. Then she returned to the bedroom and went straight to the fireplace. The brick came out easily; her diaries were still in the cache. She removed them, put them into the plastic bag from her shoulder bag and tied the fishing line to the bag. She turned off the light and went to the window that was so impossible to climb out of because of the wrought-iron bars—apart from being one floor above the ground.

Five minutes of silent, intense scrutiny of the shrubbery and surrounds below yielded nothing, no movement at all. Her old bedroom was not directly above any window on the ground floor, so she felt quite safe as she manoeuvred the rubbish bag awkwardly through the bars, lowered it to the ground to be swallowed up amongst some flourishing hydrangea bushes, and threw the line down after it.

Then she switched on the light again and looked around. Despite the luxuriousness of the bedroom, a thick-pile silvery blue carpet, matching curtains and bed cover, there was only one chair, a wooden antique that matched the marvellous bureau but looked highly uncomfortable.

She shrugged, slipped her shoes off and retired to Luke Kirwan's bed, where she propped the pillows up behind her and picked up the book on his bedside table—a murder mystery, as it happened. And she'd finished the first chapter when she heard the key in the lock. She made no move to get up and that was his first sight of her as he came into the room—propped against his pillows, looking gravely at him over the top of his book.

Inwardly, Luke Kirwan was amused. This girl had enormous nerve if nothing else. Not that she lacked other qualities, he conceded. A delicate figure, unusual beauty—her hair and eyes alone were stunning—a flair for clothes and the kind of *joie de vivre* that was infectious. The fact remained, he reminded himself, that discreet enquiries downstairs had shed no light on who she was, and the story of coming with someone who'd deserted her for an ex-girlfriend was most likely another invention.

'I do hope you're comfortable—or, after what passed in here before I locked you in, is that an invitation to join you?' he said with an undercurrent of sarcasm.

'Not at all.' Aurora closed the book, got up and slipped on her shoes. She added, as she shook out her beautiful skirt and ran her hands through her hair, 'It was your idea to lock me in, not mine, so I couldn't see why I shouldn't make myself comfortable. How do you do, by the way? I'm Aurora Templeton.' She held out her hand.

He crossed the room to take it, and felt it tremble briefly in his. It was the only sign of inner nerves he could detect, however. Her back was as straight as ever, her chin elevated and those stunning green eyes proud.

'Why do I get the feeling this is not to be a—*penitent* confession—brought on by sober reflection?' he murmured a little wryly.

Aurora took her hand back. 'Because you really have only yourself to blame, Mr Kirwan. You and your secretary, that is. This preoccupation with guarding you from "groupies" is what brought this all about. I find it a little hard to believe that any kind of a real man needs to go to those lengths anyway, but, be that as it may—if I could have got in touch with you by any other means, I would not have had to resort to this.'

'Hang on—resort to robbing me, do you mean?' he queried quizzically.

'No. Reclaiming my property,' she stated.

'Really, you're going to have explain better than that, Aurora Templeton.' He paused and narrowed his eyes. 'Why does that name ring a bell?'

'From the number of messages I left on your answering machine that you ignored?' she suggested with irony. 'But you also bought this house from my father,' she explained. 'This was my bedroom.'

Luke Kirwan blinked.

'And this,' Aurora continued, turning towards the fireplace, 'was my secret cache from the time I discovered it when I was about twelve.'

He followed her across the room and ducked his head to look into the fireplace. He observed the brick and the empty cavity in the wall, put his hand into it and whistled softly. 'I see,' he said as he straightened.

'Good!' Aurora said briskly. 'Now, you may or may not have been aware that I was overseas at the time the house was sold—'

'I had no idea Ambrose Templeton had a daughter,' he said, and pulled a handkerchief from his pocket to wipe his hands.

'Well, he does,' she said flatly, 'and I can prove it. But I didn't even know the house had been sold until I got home, just a few days before he took off on his round-the-world voyage. And it was only after he'd left that I remembered the cache and something that was very precious to me in it.'

'Why the hell didn't you just say so?' Luke Kirwan demanded.

'I would have, if I could have got here *first*—to make sure no one got to it before I did.'

'What was this precious something?' he asked with a frown. 'A heroin haul or the crown jewels?'

'Very funny, Mr Kirwan.' She eyed him sardonically.

'No, but precious enough to me. And when I couldn't get past your secretary, not to mention being treated as if I were a piece of rubbish even after telling her who I was; and when I could never find you home, I remembered I still had a laundry key, and I decided to take matters into my own hands. Don't you think you might have done the same?' she asked gently.

He blinked. 'So—you didn't use the front door?'

'I didn't have a front door key,' she said simply. 'I'd left all my other keys with my father. As a teenager, the laundry door was my—' she grimaced '—preferred way of coming home when I was late.'

He was silent for a long moment, watching her narrowly. Then he said abruptly, 'Did you know I was supposed to be away that night?'

Aurora took her time. This was the tricky bit because if she didn't tread carefully, she could involve Bunny. She frowned at him. 'Were you? What a pity you weren't. I *was* kicking myself for not taking into consideration that you had to be an extraordinarily light sleeper. I swear I didn't make a sound and, believe me, I've had a bit of practice at it, but...' She shrugged.

'You didn't make a sound,' he said slowly. 'And I came home early because I was ill. I got up to go downstairs to find an aspirin or something when I saw this strange light at the bottom of the stairs.'

Aurora smiled suddenly. 'I haven't had much luck, have I?'

He considered, then gestured with his forefinger. 'There's still something that doesn't quite gel, Aurora Templeton. What was it you thought you left behind in that cache that was so precious you couldn't tell anyone about it? I really think I need to see it,' he said pensively, 'before I can believe this story.'

'You can't because it—they—weren't there after all. My diaries,' she said simply.

'Your…*diaries*?'

She nodded. 'My innermost thoughts and secrets that I would hate any strange, prying eyes to see.'

He took a long moment to think around this, then said with a frown, 'If they're not there now, what's happened to them?'

'I think my father must have removed them,' she replied. 'Like any conscientious parent, he probably went through a stage of wondering whether I was on drugs or whatever. I did go through a slightly wild stage,' she confided, 'although certainly not that wild. But I'm now faced with the lowering thought that he probably knew about the cache all along. And my guess is that he packed the diaries up and forgot to tell me.' She sighed ruefully. 'We had so little time together and he was so excited before he left. He's sailing round the world single-handed. I don't know if you knew?'

'I didn't deal with him personally. Can you check it out with him?'

'Yes. He's got a satellite telephone on the boat.'

'So that explains that,' he said slowly. 'You must have confided some pretty intimate thoughts to your diaries to be so paranoid about getting them back unseen by other eyes?'

The slightest tinge of pink entered Aurora's smooth cheeks. 'Would you like any old stranger reading your diaries?' she countered, however.

'I don't keep one, so I don't know,' he replied with the glimmer of a smile. 'What do you do for a living, Miss Templeton?'

She told him, adding, 'I also have an afternoon music programme that I compere three times a week. In between times I volunteer my time as a radio operator for the local Coastguard Association. I'm really quite respectable.'

'So you say,' he commented. 'But, seeing I don't know you from a bar of soap and neither does anyone else, apparently, just how did you get into this party?' he enquired.

'I came with Neil Baker—he's my programme director

and a friend of yours, apparently. It, at the time,' she confessed with a glint of mischief in her eyes, 'seemed like divine intervention, when he invited me because he'd broken up with his girlfriend—and I told you the rest of it.'

'Ah, Neil,' he murmured, 'yes, he is a friend.' But he continued to study her thoughtfully and in a slightly nerve-racking way.

'Does that set your mind to rest about me, Mr Kirwan?' she asked. 'Look, I apologize. The whole thing was rash and misguided—I'm a little prone to that kind of thing but, I can assure you, your secretary did brush me off like a troublesome if not to say somehow shameful fly; I did leave messages for you that you never responded to and I did call to see you at least five times but you were never home.'

'I've been out west a lot lately. So—' he shrugged '—what would you like to do now, Miss Templeton? Go back to the party?'

He took Aurora by surprise. 'Is that all you've got to say?' she asked incredulously.

He eyed her. 'What more is there to say?'

'You could at least apologize for putting me in this awkward position in the first place!'

'Putting you in an awkward position,' he marvelled, his dark eyes suddenly full of wicked amusement. 'You may not recall this, but I did get bitten, scratched and finally knocked out in our first encounter, not to mention made to look a fool.'

'I did not bite you!' Aurora denied hotly. 'Nor did I scratch you—I had gloves on and you must have knocked *yourself* out.'

He raised a quizzical eyebrow. 'Nevertheless, it was like having an angry kitten, spitting and clawing in my arms. Well,' he amended, 'after the first impact of a slim, rather gorgeous little body and, of course—that *unique*, haunting perfume.'

This time his dark gaze was pointedly intimate again as

it stripped away her outfit and dwelt on the curves of her figure beneath it—any doubts she might have had that he was mentally undressing her were embarrassingly laid to rest by the way her body responded to his scrutiny. She could feel herself growing hot and bothered and more than aware of her fluttering pulses.

'I think I'll go home now,' she said unevenly. 'You didn't happen to notice whether Neil had surfaced, by any chance? Not that I need him—' She stopped frustratedly.

'I saw no sign of Neil.'

She shrugged. 'Doesn't matter, I can get a cab.' She picked up her bag.

'Why don't you stay?' he suggested. 'It's only eleven o'clock. I'm sure the party has a bit of life left in it yet.'

She returned his dark gaze with as much composure as she could muster. 'No. No, thank you—'

'We danced well together,' he said meditatively, then grinned. 'I gather it was a case of mistaken identity, your dancing with me at all?'

'Yes, it was!' She eyed him with a mixture of frustration and annoyance. 'Neil pointed out this man who looked exactly like a bumbling, absent-minded professor to me. It never occurred to me it was *you* he was pointing to.'

'My apologies,' he said gravely. '*I* hesitate to point this out to you, but it's never wise to make snap judgements about people on appearance, although Jack has enough of a sense of humour to see the funny side of it,' he assured her.

'Blow Jack,' she retorted bitterly. 'And I have no intention of dancing with you again, Mr Kirwan, because I'm now in a position to make an *informed* judgement on that subject. This meek air you're assuming is entirely false, you're laughing at me behind it and it doesn't blind me to the fact that you're a wolf in sheep's clothing. You even kissed me without one jot of concern for what my preferences in the matter were!'

He smiled satanically. 'Bravo, Aurora—I like that name,

by the way. Your preferences, incidentally, didn't seem to be so contrary to mine,' he pointed out.

'Oh!' She ground her teeth. 'I'm off!' She picked up her bag and slung it over her shoulder.

'Allow me to call a cab for you.' He reached for the bedside phone and did just that. Then he said, although still looking amused, 'Please don't hold this against me but, just to be on the safe side, I'll come down with you and see you into it.'

'Be my guest,' she spat at him, 'but I'm not a burglar or a groupie!'

'Yes, well—' he sobered, and that tough, dangerous side of him was in evidence for a moment '—be that as it may, as you remarked to me, Miss Templeton, and while you may be neither, you do have slightly strange notions about breaking into people's houses and apportioning the blame.' He strolled to the door and opened it. 'After you.'

And to Aurora's extreme indignation, he escorted her downstairs and out onto the porch, and he handed her into the waiting taxi—he even paid for it. But his parting shot was the most humiliating.

'I would have a little more faith in human nature, if I were you, Aurora. You may find life a little less dangerous— unless that's how you get your kicks?'

She argued the matter out with herself during the short drive home in the cab. She paced up and down her living room for ten intense minutes and even consulted her goldfish on the matter, but nothing could alter the fact that there was no better time to retrieve her diaries than right now, while a noisy, crowded party was still in progress. And nothing could alter her determination not to be bested by Luke Kirwan. With the net result that half an hour later, dressed all in black, she was cautiously making her way down the easement once again.

The party was audible as she approached the house from

the rear. As Luke Kirwan had predicted, it still had plenty of life left in it. But as she flitted through the garden like a soundless shadow, no one accosted her, no one was about. The only problem was, there was absolutely no sign of a green rubbish bag stuffed full of her diaries in the hydrangeas below her old bedroom window.

CHAPTER THREE

'MISS HILLIER, my name is Aurora Templeton,' she said down the phone the next morning, a Saturday. 'I would like to speak to Professor Kirwan and, unless *you'd* like me to come and lie down on the front doorstep and go on a hunger strike, don't you *dare* fob me off!'

'That won't be necessary, Miss Templeton,' Miss Hillier replied smoothly. 'Professor Kirwan thought you might like to lunch with him today. Would twelve-thirty be suitable?'

Aurora ground her teeth as she felt, this time, rather like the fly who'd walked into the spider web. Consequently, she said coolly, 'One o'clock would suit me better.'

'That's fine,' Miss Hillier murmured. 'We'll see you then.'

'OK,' she said as she marched out onto the terrace of her old home at five past one, 'hand them over, Mr Kirwan. My diaries.'

Luke Kirwan didn't rise from the cane chair he was lounging in. There was a table for two set for lunch on the terrace and the pool, just beyond, sparkled invitingly beneath a clear blue sky. There was absolutely no sign of a party having been held the night before.

And he summed Aurora up comprehensively, from her tied-back hair, her yellow blouse and white shorts down to her yellow canvas shoes before he said lazily, 'Good afternoon, Aurora. Isn't it a beautiful day? By the way, I was wondering about your legs, but they too are quite stunning.' His gaze returned to them thoughtfully.

Aurora clenched her fists, then swallowed several times

to calm herself and negate the effect of his gaze on her legs. 'I didn't come here to make chit-chat,' she stated.

He lifted his eyes to hers and they were amused, but with a glint of irony as a tinge of pink coloured her cheeks at the same time. 'Why don't you sit down and have a glass of wine instead?' he suggested. 'It might be just what you need after a sleepless night.' He raised his glass to her.

'How did you know—?' She bit her lip.

'You look a little peaked,' he drawled, and got to his feet at last to pull out a chair for her. In blue jeans and a grey T-shirt, he looked casual but big and very fit.

Aurora hesitated, then sank down into it. She also took the glass of wine he poured for her, although absently. 'How did you know,' she began again, 'that I'd dropped them out of the window? I assume that is what happened?'

'You assume correctly.' He sat down. 'I just thought,' he mused, 'that I should take some precautions. It was, after all, only your word I had to go on last night. So I stopped and asked myself what I would have done with anything I had come by—shall we say illegally?'

'There was nothing illegal about it at all! At least by now you must know that.'

'I certainly do.' His gaze was so amused as it rested on her, she flinched visibly. 'But at the time, with Neil having done a bunk—'

'I told you why!' she interrupted fiercely.

'Yes,' he murmured gently. 'Once again I must point out I had no way of knowing if you were telling me the truth.'

Aurora suddenly took a large swallow of wine as some intuition told her that she was in for a battle of wits on a scale she'd never encountered before. 'Now we've sorted it out, though—OK, I concede it was *all* my fault and offer my sincere apologies—could I have my diaries back, please?'

He studied his wine, then raised his dark eyes to her. 'Did

you come straight back to crawl amongst the hydrangeas last night?'

'Uh…no. I spent at least half an hour trying to persuade myself I was…mad.'

'Just as well, we could have bumped into each other—and look what happened the last time we—er—bumped into each other,' he said humorously. 'How often do you have these kind of losing battles with yourself, Aurora?'

She looked at him steadily and refused to reply.

'OK—another tack,' he said wryly. 'What made you unable to persuade yourself you *were* mad?'

She tightened her fingers around the base of her glass as she also attempted to stem the flow of the truth from her lips, but found herself unequal to the task. 'A thorough desire not to be outwitted by a man such as yourself, Mr Kirwan,' she said coldly. 'I don't happen to approve of you in the slightest!'

He laughed softly. 'Because you decided I was on the prowl?'

'Yes,' she said.

'That is unequivocal!' He narrowed his eyes and studied the set of her chin and the warring light in her green eyes until a slight smile twisted his lips. 'There wouldn't also be a slight sense of pique at allowing yourself to—contemplate the pleasures of being led down the garden path by someone as unacceptable as myself?' he queried.

'When did I do that?' Aurora responded, then clicked her tongue. 'OK, but you were to blame for that. I didn't ask you to dance with me and I certainly didn't ask to be kissed!'

'No,' he mused, 'nor could you be held to blame for deliberately deceiving me—about your plans to invade my home again, I mean—since it wasn't me you thought you were dancing with.'

A slight chill ran down Aurora's spine, but Miss Hillier intervened at this point. She wheeled a trolley onto the terrace and invited them to help themselves to lunch.

A few minutes later Aurora was staring at a plate of cold meat and salad in front of her. She picked up her knife and fork, then put them down. 'Have you read them?' she said, her green eyes direct and cold.

'Your diaries? I've glanced through them. For substantiation of your story purposes—who would not have?'

She flinched inwardly but said witheringly, 'So much for trusting human nature! What...' she paused '...do I have to do to get them back? I should warn you to think carefully, Mr Kirwan, before you reply. You've mentioned the police to me. I'm perfectly capable of going to them and reporting blackmail.'

He grinned. 'I see we understand each other, Aurora. However, the police still have an open file on you.'

She gasped. 'You are going to blackmail me!'

He shrugged. 'I just thought it might be a little awkward for someone with as public a profile as you have even to be mentioned in terms of home invasions. I listened to one of your news broadcasts this morning, incidentally. You have a lovely voice on the radio.'

'Before—' Aurora controlled her voice rigidly as she ignored the compliment '—you tell me what it is you require in exchange for my diaries, Mr Kirwan, may I tell you you're wasting your time? Nothing would induce me to sleep with you, my diaries included. If you're that desperate why don't you call on your army of groupies?' she concluded with genuine scorn.

'You've jumped the gun once again, Aurora. I certainly don't expect you to sleep with me immediately.' He helped himself to a crusty brown roll and a pat of yellow butter. 'Although, you must admit you weren't that averse to kissing me.'

'Forget about that,' she ordered, causing him to look wry. 'What did you have in mind?'

'Getting to know you better,' he said lazily.

'Oh, come on! You must think I came down with the last

shower! To all intents and purposes, you're literally rolling
in women—' She stopped as he laughed, and she blushed.

But she soldiered on almost immediately. 'Don't forget
you yourself told me about the groupies! And I've since
remembered Neil mentioning a girl called Leonie something
or other—he even thought last night's party might be a surprise engagement party. What are you, Mr Kirwan? A sex
maniac?'

But if anything, Luke Kirwan, as he placidly ate his lunch,
was even more amused. 'No,' he said at last. 'Although I
don't usually kiss girls without some kind of an interest in
sleeping with them.'

Aurora's mouth fell open and she stared at him incredulously.

'Why don't you eat your lunch?' he advised, and continued, with lazy irony, 'I would have thought that was human
nature. But if I were a sex maniac, do you think I'd go to
the lengths I do to protect myself from an army of groupies—as you put it?' He took a leisurely sip of wine. 'After
all, you yourself fell foul of those measures.'

Aurora started to eat after another long moment of incredulity, but only because she couldn't think of a thing to
come up with to contradict this. Then she had a thought.
'What about Leonie whatever-her-name-is?'

'She need not concern you,' he said serenely.

'You're wrong. None of this concerns me, so let's have
no more—nonsense!' Aurora said briskly.

'Very well. What would you like to talk about?'

'Nothing. I just want my diaries back!'

'Then I'm sorry but there's nothing left for me to do until
you finish your lunch but—enjoy the view.' He put his knife
and fork together; his plate was as clean as a whistle whereas
she had hardly made any inroads into her meal.

She ate silently for a while, then said intensely, 'If my
father were here, you'd never get away with this!'

'No,' he agreed.

'How can you sit there and admit you're a bastard?'

'I wouldn't go that far.' He raised his eyebrows ruefully. 'Nor have you heard my proposal. It's actually quite honourable.'

Aurora pushed her plate away, her meal unfinished, and looked heavenwards. 'OK, hit me with it. Then I'll tell you exactly what I think of it.'

'In exchange for allowing us to get to know each other better, I'll return one diary per date you have with me. Incidentally, I only intend to keep the last five, that's the last five years so our...agreement would extend for five dates. After that, who knows? The rest you can have back now.'

'And if I don't agree to this?'

He shrugged. 'I guess I'll get to know you through your diaries.'

Aurora's mind worked furiously.

'Don't,' he said softly.

'What?'

'Concoct any more schemes to burgle me.'

She chewed her lip as she gazed at him, trying desperately to come to grips with not only the situation but the man himself.

At last she said abruptly, 'There's got to be more to this. I mean, if you really expect me to believe that your proposal is honourable in any way at all. It's still blackmail, and as for the ''getting to know me'' line—' she shot him a sparkling green look tinged with satire '—there's another line that I'm all too familiar with—men will be men.'

'Go on.' He looked at her attentively.

'How about this—for every girl with a curve, there are several men with an angle. Your angle has got to be quite original, Professor Kirwan, but it doesn't blind me one bit!'

He grinned. 'Anyone would think you'd swallowed a phrase book, Aurora. Got any more?'

'No.' She paused and frowned heavily, then said slowly,

'I still don't see. I mean, I may have attempted to burgle you and outwit you, I certainly don't *like* you, however you may have induced me to kiss you and dance with you—believe me,' she said candidly, 'all the rest of it has well and truly wiped that out! So, unless you have a monumental ego, there's got to be something else behind it.'

She paused again, then looked at him sharply. 'Tell me more about this Leonie person?'

'This Leonie person,' he repeated and grinned. 'I'm only glad she's not here to hear herself referred to thus. Her name is Murdoch, by the way. Uh…we had a relationship, we no longer have a relationship, that's all.'

'How long?'

He shrugged. 'Three years.'

'Oh, yes? And you broke up recently?' Aurora enquired.

'Fairly recently.'

'As in a week or two ago?'

He didn't respond but he didn't look the slightest bit discomfited either.

'So either you're on the rebound or looking to show Ms Murdoch a thing or two,' she mused aloud. 'We already know you're on the prowl so…I guess that makes more sense as to why.'

He said nothing.

'I still think it's despicable. Surely you should be old enough to be above playing games with women?' She gazed at him severely.

A smile tugged at his lips, but he replied gravely, 'Perhaps you got it right first time—men will be men. You're very attractive, you know,' he added.

Aurora thought back over the last five years of her life. And for a second it trembled on her lips to tell him he was welcome to keep her diaries and read every word. But a sinking feeling in the pit of her stomach told her she just couldn't do it. It would be like handing her heart and soul to him, although who was to say she could trust him not to read them anyway?

'By the way,' he murmured, 'I packed and sealed the five relevant diaries separately and they're in my safe where no one can get to them, not even Miss Hillier.'

'If that's supposed to reassure, it doesn't, not on any front,' Aurora said cynically.

'You'll just have to trust me.'

She muttered something derogatory and gazed at him broodingly.

'Miss Hillier has made a Mississippi mud cake to die for,' he continued. 'Should we proceed to the coffee and dessert stage since you don't appear to be interested in finishing that?' He gestured towards her plate.

'For a secretary, she's a most amazing all-rounder,' Aurora commented dryly.

'She is. I don't know what I'd do without her.' He rose, collected their plates and took them indoors. Five minutes later, he returned with a tray of coffee and cake. The Mississippi mud cake looked superb in its coating of glistening, smooth dark chocolate with some crystallized violets grouped in the centre, and there was a bowl of whipped cream to go with it. The coffee, in a plunger pot, also smelt divine.

Luke Kirwan cut the cake, placed a large portion in front of Aurora and courteously passed the cream. Then he poured the coffee.

Aurora picked up a cake fork and, with it poised, said, 'What did you have in mind for our first date? Not that I'm agreeing to anything yet and I wouldn't call it a date either— my role of being a stopgap until I bore you rigid, too, because you're jaded, disillusioned or whatever. I think that's a more accurate summing-up of the situation, don't you?'

He merely said, 'Dinner this Wednesday.'

She ate a bite of cake—it *was* superb—and licked some chocolate from her fingertip, then demolished her slice of chocolate heaven and looked longingly at the mud cake. Luke responded with a grin and cut her another slice. 'Just— dinner?' she asked cautiously.

'Aurora,' he murmured, 'despite your protestations to the contrary, I think we may have already crossed a certain divide between a man and a woman. Perhaps it's different for women, but men don't generally fantasize about gorgeous, shapely little bodies without their clothes if they're feeling platonic.' And he allowed that dark gaze to drift over her in a way she remembered all too well.

Causing her to miss her mouth with the cake fork and end up with a blob of chocolate on her upper lip. She muttered a curse and snatched the napkin he offered her. Then she pushed her plate away determinedly, reached for her coffee-cup and tried desperately to banish the memories of being kissed by Luke Kirwan and how her body had felt in his arms.

'But on Wednesday—dinner will do,' he drawled.

She stared at her cup, then looked at him seriously and silently.

'If you didn't enjoy dancing with me, you certainly gave a good imitation of a girl who was revelling in subjecting me to all her feminine powers and wiles,' he said softly.

She swallowed and knew she couldn't deny it. Even the memory was making her feel restless in that special way only a special man could make you feel.

'And you didn't take the opportunity to bite me when I kissed you.'

His words fell into the continuing pool of silence but, although Aurora couldn't tear her gaze away from him, although she could feel herself blushing, a desperate sense of needing to retaliate against this man before she was swamped by those memories started to grow. He might have made her feel uniquely feminine, he might have kissed her more pleasurably than any man ever had, but he was still blackmailing her. And if she wanted her diaries back she was going to have to fight for them, obviously, but also fight not to fall under his spell…

She looked away at last. 'Where?'

'RQ,' he said. 'They have a nice dining room.'

RQ, as she well knew, was affectionate shorthand for the Royal Queensland Yacht Squadron based at Manly, and they did have a nice dining room. 'Are you a member?'

He shook his head. 'But my brother is. He and his wife are up from the country for a couple of weeks of cruising on the bay—they will also be there on Wednesday night.'

Aurora put her head to one side and thought for a bit. To discover there was something else running through her mind, something to do with evening the score between them or—perhaps even a desire to prove to this enigmatic, at times infuriating man that, on a level playing field, she was well able to hold her own.

As in being quite capable of dealing with the dangerously attractive side of him, as in having her feet quite firmly planted on the ground and not being susceptible to being toyed with? she wondered. Was that what she was contemplating? Surely not, yet…

She shrugged. 'I suppose I can't get into too much trouble on the venerable RQ premises or in front of the family, although that's a bit of a surprise—OK.'

'I don't know why I'm not damned with faint praise into thanking you humbly for such magnanimity,' he said wryly.

Aurora smiled coolly for what seemed like the first time for a long time. 'I'll tell you why—humble and Professor Luke Kirwan is a contradiction in terms, that's why.'

'Do you really think so?'

'I know so,' Aurora said. She stood up. 'Thank you for lunch. And I would advise you that, although I've decided to have dinner with you on Wednesday, don't…' She paused and sought the right words.

'Don't get any ideas?' he suggested.

'Exactly.'

He stood up himself and strolled towards her. She didn't move but her eyes widened, then narrowed.

'Relax,' he murmured. 'I'm not going to lay a finger on you. But I think it would be a good idea to allow our dates to follow our—natural inclinations, Aurora.' His gaze slipped up and down her body.

She swallowed uncertainly and trembled visibly, causing an absent smile to cross his lips.

'You might,' she said huskily at last, 'but I have no doubt I'm dealing with someone who could not be termed a gentleman.'

The smile grew. 'Just think how much more exciting it could be, though, especially for someone into fun and adventure as you are, Aurora.'

She licked her lips as her pulses leapt because she had no doubt that being with Luke Kirwan could be all those things—then reminded herself that it would also be a bit like sleeping with the devil. She was going to need a long spoon as it was, she thought chaotically. And did the only thing she was capable of—turned on her heel and walked away.

'Just a moment, Aurora,' he said. 'Don't forget these.' From behind a large pottery urn that held a ficus tree, he produced a green rubbish bag. 'I'm sure you'd like to count them, if nothing else.'

She set her teeth, then walked regally back to him where she accepted the bag from him. 'Do I actually have to count them?'

'No. You can trust me on that too.'

'Personally, I don't think I can trust you any further than I can throw you!'

'But you'll have dinner with me on Wednesday night?' he queried gravely.

'Not from choice, Prof,' she said. 'Not from choice. Would you like to name a time?'

He did so and added that he would pick her up, so she gave him her address and, this time, succeeded in leaving in as dignified a manner as it was possible to at the same time as toting a bulky green rubbish bag—and quite sure her tormentor was laughing at her silently.

'Enjoy the party on Friday? I'm really sorry I abandoned you,' Neil Baker said to Aurora on Monday morning, when their shift ended.

They were drinking tea. It was a cool, wet morning and Aurora wrapped her hands around her mug. 'It certainly was a lively party,' she commented neutrally, then grinned a little wickedly. 'Did you and your girlfriend make up or did things get worse?'

Neil sighed. 'We are back together but I don't know for how long. Mandy is…it's a case of can't live together, can't live apart.' He gazed at his mug. 'Oh, well, we'll see. What did you think of Luke?'

Aurora shrugged. 'Quite impressive and not what you'd expect. He doesn't look particularly scholarly.' She heard the dry note in her voice.

But Neil appeared to miss it as he replied enthusiastically, 'That's the beauty of Luke. You'd expect him to be dry and desiccated, but he surely isn't.'

'So I gather. Tell me about this Leonie Murdoch? You mentioned you thought Friday night's bash might have been an engagement party?'

'Ah.' Neil looked rueful. 'I was a bit out of date there, apparently. Mandy knows Leonie and it would appear that they've broken up just when everyone thought they were getting engaged—two days before the party, in fact; the party was more Leonie's idea than his, apparently, then it was too late to cancel. He needs his head read. Mandy sides with Leonie, of course—girls sticking together, kind of thing—and puts all the blame on Luke, but in this case I have to agree. Leonie Murdoch is a ten! If not to say an eleven or twelve!'

Aurora blinked. 'That gorgeous, et cetera, et cetera?'

'In a word, yes. She's also very bright and brainy, she's a stockbroker.'

'So,' Aurora said slowly, 'she's upset about the break-up?'

'Well, she's putting on a brave face, but Mandy reckons she's devastated underneath. Luke…' Neil paused '…has always had women running after him. So the concept of monogamy could be a little foreign to him.'

'You don't say!' Aurora's expression was full of disdain.

'Why—' Neil focused intently on her suddenly '—do I get the feeling you didn't like him?'

'I…it's a long story, but men who are God's gift to women bore me silly.'

'I don't think he gets around like that!' Neil protested.

'You're not a woman,' Aurora pointed out. 'And you're the one who mentioned monogamy.'

'Yes, but…' he paused and frowned '…what exactly happened between you two?'

'Nothing much,' Aurora replied airily, then subsided. 'But I'm having dinner with him on Wednesday and I'm not sure—I'm even less sure now that it's a good idea.'

Neil stared at her, then blinked twice, but appeared to be bereft of speech.

'You're comparing me with Leonie Murdoch and finding me wanting?' Aurora suggested.

'I…well, no…I mean—'

'Don't lie, Neil,' Aurora said with a gurgle of laughter. 'I could see the circles of your mind spinning in your eyes. She *must* be quite something because, although I'm not a stockbroker or a "ten", I don't have two heads or anything like that, do I?'

'No, no. Of course not. No,' he insisted. 'In fact, you're something else yourself, Aurora. Enough to make Mandy absolutely furious with jealousy, as it happened, but—'

'Not quite in their league? The Luke Kirwans and Leonie

Murdochs of this world?' Aurora suggested, still smiling as she posed the question. 'Well, we'll see.'

'Aurora,' Neil said a shade apprehensively, 'don't let anything I said…I mean, I shouldn't have…I was only theorizing…' He stopped helplessly.

'Don't worry, Neil, I won't,' she promised, with her eyes very green and very bright—something that would have put the fear of God into Bunny and her father, and didn't, as it happened, reassure Neil Baker much either.

Luke Kirwan was early when he came to pick her up on Wednesday, but she wasn't even changed when he knocked on the door of her town house.

'I'm sorry,' she said as she opened the door, 'but there's been a bit of a kerfuffle at the Coastguard. A yacht stranded on a sand bank on the South Passage Bar. So my shift went overtime because the person due to take over from me went out on the rescue boat.'

'Oh.' He looked her up and down in her white boiler suit with the Coastguard logo and studied her thick plait. 'Are they all right?'

'Yep. They got them towed off safely, but there was a woman aboard having hysterics, which didn't help.'

He smiled. 'You don't approve, I gather?'

She shrugged. 'It was pretty scary stuff. But I just don't think you should be out on boats if you don't think you can cope with emergencies.'

'Do you do any of the actual rescue work yourself?' he asked.

'No. I'm just a radio operator. Look, come in and help yourself to a drink.' She led the way into the lounge and pointed to an open cocktail cabinet. 'I promise you I'll be fifteen minutes at the most!'

'You don't have to rush. If I can use the phone, I can ring the club and leave a message to say we'll be a bit late.'

'I like rushing,' Aurora said. 'With plenty of time to get

dressed I can change my mind about what to wear at least half a dozen times and still end up unhappy with my choice.'

'Oh.' His lips twisted. 'Then please do rush, Aurora. I wouldn't like to see you unhappy.'

It took her five minutes to shower, five minutes to dress and the last five to apply a minimum of make-up and brush out her hair. Despite all this activity, she reminded herself of how she'd decided to play this evening. Quite normal, friendly even, but definitely not susceptible to any satanic overtures from Luke Kirwan. She grabbed her bag, shoes and a scarf in passing.

'There,' she said to him as she arrived back in the lounge. 'Is that a demonstration of power dressing, sheer masterful organization—or what?' She slipped on her shoes and raised her hands to gather her hair and comb it with her fingers, preparatory to tying it back with the scarf.

He was sitting in the winged armchair but he stood up and put his hands into the pockets of his fawn trousers, worn with a beautiful blue linen shirt. And he took in her emerald chiffon blouse with its stiff collar and cuffs, her sleek long black skirt with a slit up the thigh to reveal sheer black stockings, and high black heels. Her scarf matched the blouse and her bag was embroidered with black, gold and emerald beads.

'Not only that, but I think the result is masterful too, although beautiful would be a better way to describe it,' he said finally.

Aurora lowered her arms, conscious suddenly of the way her breasts were outlined beneath the chiffon, and shrugged. 'So long as I don't disgrace you in front of your brother and his wife, not to mention RQ! Shall we go? Oh, didn't you want a drink?'

He paused and held her gaze in a way that made her aware that her slight confusion to do with the outline of her body being on parade beneath his dark eyes was all too apparent to him. And it wasn't until she'd turned faintly pink that he said politely, 'Thank you, but no. I thought I'd wait.' He looked around. 'I've been talking to your fish.'

Aurora grinned. She had a small, colourfully embellished tank but only two goldfish so far in it. 'One of the good things about Annie and Ralph is that they don't talk back to you. I could swear from their expressions that they do listen, though.'

'Their expressions actually change?' he asked quizzically.

'Once you get to know them, yes, certainly. I thought of getting a bird, but I really feel sorry for birds in cages, so fish seemed to be a good alternative.' A glint of mischief lit her green eyes. 'Better than talking to yourself, surely?'

'What about your diaries?'

'Well, now.' She shrugged and wondered if this was his unsubtle way of reminding her about the hold he had over her. 'I've been a little circumspect there lately. Thanks to you. But I'm sure I'll get back into it.'

'I hope you do. I'd hate to be responsible for curtailing your creative genius.' His lips twisted at her dark expression and he said then, obviously changing the subject, 'Do you feel claustrophobic at all, living here after the house?'

Aurora, still smarting from the fact that he'd had the nerve to mention her diaries but determined not to show it, launched into a random speech. 'I haven't really had the time for any claustrophobia to kick in. But as town houses go, it's nice, isn't it? I know it's a bit cluttered at the moment—I've got all the treasures from the house that Dad couldn't bear to part with. Of course, he had to part with a lot, which actually annoyed me somewhat but—' She stopped and grimaced. 'Don't let me ramble on! Oh, by the way, since you brought the subject up, perhaps I should give you this.'

This was a key that she picked up from the bureau. He took it and studied it as it lay in the palm of his hand. Then he raised his dark eyes to hers. 'The spare laundry key, I take it?'

'Yes.'

'I'd forgotten about it,' he said with a faint smile and a teasing little look.

She raised her eyebrows ironically. 'I hadn't.'

'Thank you.' He slipped it into his pocket. 'So you have no further plans to burgle me, Aurora?'

'Obviously not. And I certainly don't plan to be a suspect because I have a key to the house in my possession should you ever really be burgled.'

'I see,' he said thoughtfully. 'I gather I'm not forgiven, then?'

She bit her lip. It hadn't been part of her plan to let him know she wasn't going to be a willing victim to his black-mail scheme, but she could see this might be easier said than done. If only he hadn't mentioned her damn diaries on top of making her feel edgy in a very physical way! So how to regroup?

She didn't; she made things worse if anything, but couldn't help herself. 'If you didn't…somehow keep making me feel as if you'd like to…' She stopped frustratedly.

'I'd like to go to bed with you?' he suggested mildly.

'Yes!' Her green eyes were fierce and her fists clenched. 'Believe me, I have no intention of allowing that to happen.'

'Then should we go to dinner instead?' He consulted his watch. 'It is getting late now.'

'Is that all you've got to say?' she demanded.

'You've used that line before,' he reminded her.

Aurora turned away, ground her teeth, then picked up her bag and marched to the door. He followed her, shrugging into his tweed jacket, and waited while she locked the door behind them. She dropped the keys into her bag but when she glanced at him through her lashes it was to disturb such a look of humorous appreciation in his eyes, she was flooded with all sorts of sensations. But the chief ones were to feel disconcerted instead of annoyed—and rather young.

CHAPTER FOUR

'I MIGHT have known,' Aurora said as she slid into the front seat of his yellow, convertible Saab.

Luke Kirwan glinted an unspoken question at her.

'That your car would be in keeping with everything else that is so misleading about you,' she elucidated. 'Mind you, it's very nice, trendy and yuppie, et cetera.'

He said ruefully as he drove off, 'Is that how you see me—trendy and yuppie?'

Aurora shrugged. 'Scholarly was the last thing that entered my mind when I saw you, as we both know.'

'What about nice?'

'No, nice didn't occur to me at the time either,' she conceded, 'and, to be honest, neither did yuppie.'

'So what did occur to you, Aurora?' he queried as he turned into the RQ car park.

She considered briefly. 'I'd rather not say at the moment.'

'Is this going to be a test like sweaty palms and treading on your toes?'

She tilted her chin and favoured him with an enigmatic green gaze. 'Perhaps.'

He laughed softly, then said, 'As a matter of fact, this car appeals to the engineer in me, that's why I drive it.'

'I might have believed that if you'd gone for a black one,' she said gravely. 'But yellow? Surely that has to be a statement of some kind?'

'What colour car do you drive?' he countered.

'A sort of pearly watermelon pink,' she said demurely. 'But then I'm not a professor of anything.' She shrugged. 'I'm also a girl and expected to be colourful.'

He pulled the yellow Saab up in a parking slot and

switched off the engine. 'So you are—colourful,' he re-marked. 'OK, I fully intended to get a neutral colour only to find I couldn't resist this one. I don't know what hidden facets of my character this indicates, but it gives me a deep sense of satisfaction to be seen driving this car and this colour.'

'See?' Aurora smiled sunnily at him. 'It's quite easy to be honest when one really sets one's mind to it. And I don't hold the colour of your car against you at all, so long as you're honest about it.'

'I'll store that piece of information away for future reference,' he said a little dryly. 'Nor is it the time and place to go into the fact that I haven't been intentionally dishonest with you—'

'It isn't,' Aurora broke in to agree. 'We're definitely late now, Mr Kirwan. Not only that, I'm starving!'

But although he opened his door and the overhead light came on, it was a long moment before he got out. And it was a curiously heavy-lidded gaze he subjected her to that set her skin tingling just when she'd been congratulating herself that she'd got the reins back in her hands, so to speak. The reins of not falling for the dangerously attractive side of Luke Kirwan as well as playing her own game.

He said nothing, however, then he did get out, leaving her feeling shaken and not at all sure—of anything.

Barry Kirwan and his wife, Julia, were already seated and waiting for them.

Barry was in his early thirties, as tall as his brother but sandy-haired and playful. And Julia Kirwan was one of those down-to-earth, straight-talking girls, although attractive with big blue eyes and a very short cap of fine, fair hair.

But it was obvious they both felt slightly awkward at first, as if trying to assess how serious Leonie Murdoch's replacement might be in Luke Kirwan's scheme of things. When one of Aurora's coastguard colleagues came over to the table and congratulated her on the way she'd handled the afternoon's drama, the ice was broken immediately, though.

'Was that you on the radio this afternoon?' Barry said incredulously. 'We were out on the bay at the time and we listened to it all—you were fantastic!' he said enthusiastically. 'Especially the way you calmed that poor woman down.'

'Thank you,' Aurora responded, and the evening perked up considerably as they talked boats and boating, and sheep stations—Barry managed two of the family properties—and Aurora's career as a radio broadcaster.

Then Julia suggested they visit the powder room and Aurora had been enjoying herself so much, she didn't stop to think about what she might be letting herself in for...

They were touching up their make-up side by side when Julia looked at her in the mirror and said straightly, 'Do you know about Leonie, Aurora?'

Aurora capped her lipstick and ran a finger around the outline of her mouth. 'Yes, as a matter of fact, although I've never met her.'

'We all thought Luke bought his new house because they were getting married.'

'So I believe,' Aurora murmured, not looking back at Julia in the mirror.

'I just thought I ought to warn you,' Julia went on, 'that he could be in a...dangerous frame of mind.'

Aurora's lashes lifted and their gazes locked in the mirror. 'In what way?'

Julia shrugged. 'In the way that if he still wants Leonie, but on his terms, say, then he might, well...use someone to make her jealous.'

'What different kind of terms could he have in mind other than marrying her?' Aurora asked.

'Perhaps he wanted her to give up her career to fit in with his own. Look—' Julia hesitated, then went on frustratedly '—it's just that they were such a great couple, no one can believe this has happened. So I…perhaps I shouldn't have but, anyway, I felt conscience-bound to say something.'

'Thank you, Julia,' Aurora said, although she was actually thinking that in different circumstances she might have found the other girl's candour more like a natural talent for meddling. 'But I'm not serious about Luke so you don't need to worry.'

Julia turned from the mirror for the first time and regarded Aurora directly. 'It wouldn't be hard to join a long line of women who thought the same,' she observed.

You, too, before you married his brother? it crossed Aurora's mind to think from nowhere—but she was just on the verge of dismissing the thought as being uncharitable, if nothing else, when Julia turned away as a faint pink began to creep up her neck.

Aurora blinked, then popped her lipstick into her bag at the same time as she thought, Glory be! Luke Kirwan had a lot to answer for. But all the better, really. All the more ammunition to add to her arsenal…

The evening broke up not long after that.

It was eleven-thirty and Aurora said ruefully, 'Oh! I've got to get up at five tomorrow, I really should be getting home to bed!'

Luke stood up. Of the four of them, he'd probably said the least, Aurora suddenly realized, yet he hadn't looked bored or as if he hadn't been enjoying himself.

But when they'd parted from Barry and Julia, after Barry, at least, had enthusiastically expressed the hope that they'd meet again, and were walking to the car, Luke said, 'That wasn't so bad, was it?'

Aurora grimaced. 'No. In fact I think I did an awful lot of the talking.'

He looked down at her, amusedly.

Aurora stopped walking. 'You were not nearly so loquacious,' she remarked. 'Were you being inwardly superior?'

'Did I look as if I was?'

She considered. 'No. But, now I come to think of it, it was a bit like a test of some kind.'

'Well, you came through with flying colours, but it wasn't.'

'I...so why were you so quiet?' she asked slowly.

It was another overcast night, windy and with ragged clouds pursuing a bright new moon. When the moon evaded the clouds, trees surrounding the car park cast stunted shadows and the wind bore not only a salty smell on the air but the unmistakable jangle of a marina close by as it sped through the shrouds of many a yacht. It also lifted Aurora's hair and fluttered her emerald scarf as she waited for Luke Kirwan to answer.

'I was slightly—preoccupied, I guess you could say,' he replied at last.

'Work?' she hazarded, then looked rueful. 'Groupies? Or—are you sure you weren't measuring my social skills up against Leonie Murdoch's?'

'Perfectly sure. I was wondering what it would be like to kiss you again,' he said, quite casually.

Aurora's immediate reaction was to back away hastily, which brought her up against the yellow Saab, causing Luke Kirwan to smile faintly, and add, 'I don't intend to find out here and now.' He produced the keys and opened the door for her.

It wasn't until they were driving along that she could think of anything to say, and then the words burst out against her better judgement. 'All evening?' she said incredulously.

'On and off.' He shrugged. 'Don't you see yourself as kissable? I would have thought I demonstrated otherwise on Friday night.'

Conscious of the possibility of walking into a trap, she said stiffly after a slight pause, 'That's got nothing to do with it. I—'

'But don't you?' he persisted.

'Of course I do—that's to say, *when* I think about it, which is not—it's not one of my preoccupations…I knew you were going to tie me up in knots!' She looked at him bitterly. 'And thank heaven I didn't know about it at the time!'

He laughed. 'How do you think you might have reacted?'

'I'd have probably been all hot and bothered,' she replied tartly.

'As in filled with revulsion or—wondering how a certain set of circumstances between us has failed to be amenable to your planning?'

'I…I'm not sure…how do you mean?' she asked disjointedly.

He pulled the car up outside her town house, switched off and turned to her. 'Your decision to hold me at arm's length, Aurora, if not to teach me a thing or two at the same time.'

Her eyes widened and her lips parted.

He waited, with grave attention. But when she could only look crestfallen, a wicked little smile twisted his lips. 'I'll see you in.'

'It's OK, I…I'll be fine.'

'I was only intending to walk you to your front door.'

'Gallantry I could live without,' Aurora muttered, then looked embarrassed.

His smile deepened as he got out and came round to open her door.

'Thank you,' she said, attempting to step out regally but catching her heel in the hem of her skirt so that she actually toppled out into his arms.

They closed about her and he picked her up and sat her on the bonnet while he disentangled her heel. He studied her shoe for a moment, then slipped it carefully on her foot at the same time as he murmured, 'What a pity I'm not Prince Charming. This is also coming adrift,' he added, and put his arms around her neck to retie the scarf around her hair. Then he rested one hand on her shoulder and traced the line of her eyebrows delicately with a fingertip. 'There, all present and correct,' he said wryly.

Aurora could still feel his fingers on her foot, the nape of her neck and her eyebrows. For some reason, the way he'd handled her in those places, although with the lightest touch, had left a tingling sensation behind, but not only that. She was uniquely conscious of everything about this tall man who had spent the evening contemplating kissing her.

She breathed in the clean linen fragrance of his shirt tinged with pure man, and thought she'd like to see him without a shirt because she had the strong feeling he was fashioned rather beautifully beneath his clothes. Then there were those eyes, that hawk-like look sometimes and the fascinating hollows beneath his cheekbones; and the way he'd picked her up as if she were as light as thistledown.

But it was also the little things he did and the way she responded to them, she thought, as if being intensely familiar with this man whom she barely knew, who tidied her hair, smoothed her eyebrows and restored her shoe to her foot, was almost second nature to her. How strange, she marvelled. It's as if he knows me better than I know myself, otherwise I'd be resisting and resenting him rather than thinking how nice it is…no, really, Aurora, you need to take a stand!

'I swear,' she responded at last, 'that I am jinxed at times and never more so than in relation to you, Luke Kirwan!'

'I don't know about jinxed,' he replied with a lurking smile. 'It could be that someone up there likes me—since I swore I wouldn't be so obvious as to attempt to kiss you goodnight.'

'Are you going to?' she asked.

'Put it this way, would you like me to, now we're…in such close contact?'

'That's—well, at least that's an improvement,' Aurora commented, more for something to say as she sat on the bonnet, desperately trying to withstand the sheer niceness of being so close to him. 'You didn't give me any choice the last time.'

'Actually, sitting there, especially if I step off the pavement—' he did so '—makes you just the right height for me to kiss comfortably now—another consideration,' he said.

'I'm sorry if I'm not tall enough for you,' she said tartly.

'Strange you should mention that,' he commented gravely. 'I did believe I had a preference for taller girls, but it seems to have flown out of the window lately. You don't contravene my preferences in any other respect, I should add.'

'Oh! That's—'

'Great legs, but I've told you about those; lovely skin; fantastic eyes and a figure to—'

'I think you should stop right there, Professor,' she said ominously. 'I hate the idea of being totted up against a set of preferences!'

'You're welcome to return the compliment,' he replied mildly. 'What do you usually go for in a man? By the way, you were going to tell me what you thought of me on first impressions earlier—not trendy and yuppie, apparently.'

'But not scholarly either, remember?' she said with some irony. 'Uh—a latter-day Mr Darcy—was one of them anyway.'

He laughed softly. 'Proud?'

'Proud, bored, dangerous—I was right.'

'Bored? Perhaps,' he conceded. 'But proud? I don't see where you got that from.'

'You wouldn't.' She studied him darkly. 'It's the last one I'm concerned about at the moment, though. You do happen to have me trapped on the bonnet of your car. Not to mention the rather public aspect of it.'

'Aurora, you're absolutely right. I did think I mightn't be able to help myself—from kissing you. You feel so nice.' He moved his hands down her arms to clasp her waist. 'You smell so nice. And it was a rather memorable experience the last time we did it.' He stopped and looked into her eyes with a little glint of mockery in his own.

Aurora trembled suddenly and was conscious of a crazy desire to say—Just go ahead and do it, Luke, because now I can't get it off *my* mind! But she bit her lip instead.

He smiled crookedly and lifted her down. 'I shall bow to your good sense, however, as well as proving I'm not dangerous at all!' He released her and strolled around to the driver's side. 'Goodnight, Miss Templeton. Sleep well! I'll be in touch some time.' And he slid into the Saab and drove off with a casual wave.

Leaving Aurora on the pavement prey to a veritable Pandora's box of emotions and sensations, one of them being that he was laughing at her... But it was only when she gained the sanctuary of her town house that she gave rein to emotions.

'Who the hell does he think he is?' she asked her goldfish as she stood in the middle of her lounge with her hands on her hips, having flung her bag down on a chair ungently.

But the even more annoying thought, she discovered as she started to pace the room, was her own reaction to him. Talk about behaving like a dewy-eyed schoolgirl, she marvelled, and groaned aloud as she thought of herself stranded on the pavement by a deep sense of disappointment while he drove off waving...

So, how to set the record straight? she pondered. By having nothing further to do with Luke Kirwan, she answered herself severely. Simple as that and for once in your life, Aurora Templeton, *don't* be tempted to redress things or...give back as good as you got!

What about her diaries, though? was her next thought.

The next morning, when she got home from her early news shift, she received an unexpected visitor—Miss Hillier.

'Oh! This is a surprise,' she said when she opened the

door, then her gaze fell on the parcel in Miss Hillier's hands. 'Is that—'

'I don't know exactly what it is,' Miss Hillier said. 'Professor Kirwan asked me to deliver it to you. May I come in for a moment, Aurora?'

'Well, yes.' Aurora led her into the lounge. 'Would you like a cup of tea?'

Miss Hillier sat down. 'No, thank you.'

Aurora hesitated, then sat down opposite, to find herself on the receiving end of an unnerving stare.

She cleared her throat.

Miss Hillier put the parcel down on the table. 'Aurora, although I don't know what this is, and although I do now know you're not what I first thought you to be, I think I should still warn you that you could be playing with fire.'

Aurora chewed her lip, then said tersely, 'What is he really? The devil in disguise?'

Miss Hillier blinked. 'How do you mean?'

'I happen to *know* that he's not exactly a gentleman, but this is the second warning I've had on the subject.'

'He can be a *perfect* gentleman,' Miss Hillier said stiffly, then stopped and sighed. 'But there's obviously some game going on between you two and I can't help knowing…well, that since he broke up with Miss Murdoch he's been… different.'

'I should hope so,' Aurora said, tartly this time. 'Because if the way he's dealing with me is his usual *modus operandi* then he's nothing but a cad, albeit a very attractive one.' She looked ceiling-ward.

'Men,' Miss Hillier said slowly, 'are…can be…difficult.'

Aurora laughed unamusedly.

'But I did believe he was very much in love with Miss Murdoch and to see him, so very soon, attaching the interest of another woman just…it doesn't make sense!' she finished frustratedly.

'It's beginning to make very good sense to me, Miss

Hillier,' Aurora said grimly. 'He's trying to make her jealous.'

Miss Hillier blinked again. 'If you know that, why are you going along with it?'

'I'll tell you.' Aurora reached for the packet, stripped the wrapping and revealed one her diaries. 'You remember that attempted burglary? It was me, trying to get my diaries back.' And she explained it all.

Miss Hillier sat transfixed for a long moment at the end of it, then she said helplessly, 'If only you'd told me...'

'If only I had,' Aurora agreed in a heartfelt way. 'But there's something that makes it impossible for me to...' She stopped and got up to pace around with her arms folded. 'Not only that, but he's holding the police file over my head.'

'Oh, he wouldn't...would he?'

Aurora stopped in front of Miss Hillier. 'You tell me, you know him much better than I do.'

Miss Hillier hesitated. 'He...doesn't like to be crossed,' she said at last.

'I gathered that.' Aurora took a breath. 'You could end this farce, Miss Hillier. You could surely point out to him how...low he's being.'

Luke's secretary stood up. 'I don't—' she started to say, but Aurora interrupted.

'I mean to say, not only you—but his own sister-in-law has warned me about getting my fingers burnt. Personally, I suspect Leonie Murdoch is the one you're more worried about, but on one thing I do agree. I have four more "dates" to endure with Luke Kirwan and I am literally under siege.'

'To...to sleep with him?' Miss Hillier asked dazedly.

Aurora shrugged. 'When he sets his mind to it, he can be dynamite.'

'So you're not entirely unaffected by him?'

Aurora paused. 'Sadly, I didn't know who he was at first and I found him, let's just say, intriguing.'

'I'll do what I can,' Miss Hillier said abruptly. 'But I'm now very worried about him. All this is extremely out of character. He's obviously much more affected by the break-up with Miss Murdoch than I realized.' And she took her leave.

Why do I get the feeling I'm the last person anyone need concern themselves within all this? Aurora asked herself with considerable irony.

She got a response that same evening, just after she'd finished reading her five-year-old diary—a mistake, she had to concede. It was the year she'd fallen passionately in love with a married man, not that he'd ever known about it, but all the impossible and exotic scenarios she'd dreamt up to bring them together were there on the pages in black and white.

'Nice try, Aurora,' Luke said casually down the line when she picked up the phone, 'but Miss Hillier is not subornable.'

'Then she's a disgrace to her sex,' Aurora shot back.

'Oh, I've been given a piece of her mind, all right. But short of burgling my safe herself, there's not much else she can do. Incidentally,' he drawled, 'I gather Julia had a go at you as well?'

'She did. *Incidentally*,' she parodied, 'we're all of the same mind. That you're using me to make your ex, or whatever she is, jealous.'

'You're wrong, you know,' he said lightly. 'The more I see of you, the more I want to get to know you. But there is the other way to do that.'

Aurora looked down at the diary in her lap, and flinched. 'Doesn't it mean anything to you that I have to *despise* you for this?'

'Well, you still haven't slapped me, bitten me or told me to go to hell—in certain circumstances—so I'm not too sure about that. And it's only four to go now—are you seriously afraid that you can't resist me for four more dates?'

Aurora couldn't speak.

He waited a moment, then said merely, 'I'll be in touch.' And put the phone down.

It was three weeks before she heard from him again.

Three uncomfortable weeks during which she felt as if she were on an emotional roller coaster. Mainly because there was one small area of her that could not entirely hate Luke Kirwan, impossible as it seemed.

She composed and rehearsed fiery, cutting speeches. She visualised getting him so besotted with her that he would be devastated when she walked away from him. She also visualised Leonie Murdoch walking away from Luke Kirwan, but as the days passed she lost a lot of her bite. In fact, she even started to feel outraged in the opposite direction...

How could he spend a whole evening wondering about kissing her, then leave her dangling for weeks?

To make matters worse, she was all too aware that the ambivalent state of her mind was responsible for these unreasonable cross currents in her thinking on the subject of a blackmailer.

Then there were Neil's questions to field. He'd been intensely interested in how the dinner had gone, and, perhaps fuelled by Aurora's disinclination to expand upon it, asked her several times if she'd heard any more from Luke.

Or, she paused to think one day, had Neil been recruited by Mandy, on Leonie Murdoch's behalf, to report on the state of play between herself and the professor? His keenness for the subject seemed a bit excessive otherwise.

In a bid to disengage her mind from the topic, Aurora threw herself into properly organizing her new home, and took up gardening. She also spoke to her father a few times. He was having a whale of a time exploring Pacific islands, which she was happy to hear but it was impossible for her to relax. Then it crept into her mind that, despite a busy, fulfilling life, she was lonely and even the company of a blackmailer would be better than none...

She was actually gardening when this thought struck, and she reared back from it physically, as if the rose bush she was planting had plunged its thorns into her flesh. And that was how Luke Kirwan found her when he came to call—kneeling upright on the lawn and staring into space as if she'd been mummified.

In fact he said her name twice before she responded, and the way she responded was to be like a thorn of embarrassment to her for quite some time. She turned, nearly toppled over in surprise and said, spontaneously speaking her mind, 'Oh—go away, please! You've complicated my life enough as it is!'

'I beg your pardon, Aurora?' he drawled.

Of course she blushed scarlet, and when she wiped her face she left a streak of dirt on it. Then she tripped on her trowel as she staggered to her feet and had to suffer the indignity of his helping hand to restore her balance, but not only that—the quizzical set of his eyebrows and the fact that he was trying not to laugh.

Then he said, 'I've come to take you out to lunch, but perhaps you'd like to clean up first?'

In spite of her several causes for deep embarrassment, Aurora was instantly moved to express her own satirical reaction. 'You didn't think you ought to call first? In case I wasn't here or I had something else on, or—I simply might not have wanted to go to lunch with you?'

'Well?' he said mildly. 'Are you any of those things—apart from obviously being here?'

'I...' She gritted her teeth. 'I...need to think about it.' And shrivelled inwardly at such a feeble response.

He didn't laugh. He did say, 'May I come in and have a cup of coffee with you while you do?' Which was as good as laughing at her, she felt, and he added, 'Then we could make a decision about lunch.'

'Would that constitute one date or two?' she asked acidly.

'I might be able to see my way to making it two,' he replied.

She eyed him, then shrugged and turned away. He followed her inside via the front patio and through the lounge to the kitchen where she put the kettle on.

'May I?' he queried.

'May you what?'

'Make the coffee while you have a shower? I'm sure you'll feel better for it.'

Aurora looked down at herself. She wore an old pair of khaki shorts with a once-white T-shirt now yellow with age, her knees were dirty and her feet were bare. 'Can you? Without Miss Hillier to hold your hand?'

'Yep.' He grinned. 'If you have a plunger pot and real coffee.'

Aurora looked heavenwards and produced not only a plunger pot but coffee beans and a grinder. 'There. The only thing you don't have to do is go to Arusha to get it.'

'It so happens I've been to Arusha,' he commented.

'So have I.' Her expression indicated this was no big deal.

'Well, we could swap experiences,' he suggested comfortably.

Aurora studied him—he was in the same jeans and grey T-shirt as on that never-to-be-forgotten lunch occasion at her old home. Not quite the corsair, the better-than-any-of-them James Bond or the Mr Darcy she'd first imagined him as, but not because he was any less physically impressive, just better known to her now. Only, she thought gloomily, that made him all the better—or was it worse?

She shook her head, left the kitchen and went upstairs with no further ado.

This time she took her time. It was half an hour later when she came back down wearing a straight skirt to just above her ankles, taupe cotton with tiny white dots, and a short white sleeveless top. Flat, strappy sandals completed her out-fit and her hair was damp and up in a knot.

Luke Kirwan rose on her arrival, boiled the kettle, poured the water into the plunger pot and brought a tray on which he had assembled cups, milk and sugar and some biscuits into the lounge. What he had occupied himself with while he'd waited was a sports programme on television, she saw.

She sat down opposite the tray, which he'd placed on her unusual coffee table—an elephant bearing a round brass ta-ble-top.

'Feeling better?' he asked.

'Yes, much better, thank you.' She plunged the coffee and poured two cups. He took one and sat down in the winged chair.

'You've—' he looked around '—sorted the chaos. It looks very nice. I take it you and your father did a lot of travelling together?'

'We did. I just wish I was island-hopping with him in the South Pacific at the moment,' Aurora replied, unwisely as it happened.

'That bad?'

She stilled in the act of stirring her coffee and slowly placed the spoon in the saucer, very conscious of the nar-rowed way he was watching her. 'What do you mean?'

'Have I complicated your life to that extent, Aurora?'

'No! Of course not,' she denied. 'I…it's just that…I feel a little flat at the moment. Probably the natural consequence of coming back from a six-month overseas trip myself, that kind of thing.' She flipped a hand casually.

'So what did you mean earlier?' he asked.

She thought for a moment. 'It must be obvious. Until I get all my diaries back, you have complicated my life. Unnecessarily, what's more.' She studied him with her chin lifted, her eyes challenging.

'I…' He paused and raised an eyebrow. 'Unless you sus-pect I'm about to take advantage of you here and now—'

he looked around '—or during what I had in mind for lunch, I don't see what's so…difficult about it all.'

'You wouldn't,' she retorted unwisely.

'Then why don't you explain, Aurora?' he invited.

She took a deep breath, and all the nervous tension she'd endured for the last weeks rose to the top, killing stone-dead any ploys she might have devised for beating Luke Kirwan at his own game. 'Don't think I don't know,' she said intensely, 'what you're up to. You're not going to be satisfied until you have me so besotted I'll willingly go to bed with you!'

An alert gleam entered his dark eyes but he said nothing.

'And I know why,' she continued, past all good sense now. 'Yes, your break-up with Leonie may have a lot to do with it, but the other reason is—you hate the thought of not being able to click your fingers at a girl whenever the whim takes you!'

'It is rather a novelty,' he agreed mildly.

She stared at him.

'You didn't expect me to admit it?'

'I'm just trying to work out if it makes you better or worse—' She stopped abruptly and bit her lip—it was the second time she'd entertained that sentiment in the space of half an hour.

'But the other reason I have, Aurora, is that you never bore me,' he said.

'What…what about Leonie?'

He sat back and stared absently into space. Then his lips twisted into a dry smile. 'I'm amazed at everyone's concern on that score—Leonie and I agreed to come to a parting of the ways.'

'End of story?' Aurora suggested with irony.

'Yep. By the way, my sister-in-law, my secretary and anyone else you may have been taking advice from on the subject—'

'Mandy Pearson, for instance,' Aurora put in.

'Ah, Mandy.' He looked sardonic.

'I haven't *spoken* to her,' Aurora said hastily. 'I wouldn't even have known of the connection if it wasn't for Neil—he was the one who, well, in response to a little fishing I did he...' She shrugged.

'Spilt the beans? Anyway,' Luke said, 'none of them are entitled, or indeed competent, to comment.'

Aurora considered this. 'If all that's true, why do you need to blackmail me?'

'Are you suggesting you'd allow me to continue to get to know you without holding onto your diaries?' He raised a dark eyebrow at her.

Aurora hesitated. 'I see your point,' she said at length and shivered suddenly.

'What?' he queried.

'I don't know if I like you or hate you—I don't know if I could trust you.'

'There's only one way to solve that,' he observed.

'Perhaps—all right,' she said with sudden decision. 'If you consider this two dates, I'll have two more with you. Then, when I get my diaries back, I...might reconsider.'

'You mean reassess your judgement of me?'

'And exactly what your intentions are, Prof,' she said with some acerbity.

'I shall look forward to it—so, you will come to lunch?'

'Yes. Where?'

'Well, since it's such a beautiful day, I thought we might take the fast ferry to Dunwich, then a taxi over to Point Lookout, have a swim, then a long, leisurely lunch before we get the ferry back.'

Aurora simply couldn't control the dawning of sheer delight in her eyes. 'I love Point Lookout,' she said helplessly.

He took her hand. 'Then why don't you get your costume, a hat and some sunscreen?'

'What about you?'

'My gear is in the car.'

'All right. But I'll need my hand back,' she responded with a mischievous glint in her eyes.

He looked down at her hand and thought how small it looked in his, then his dark gaze drifted all over her. And it occurred to him that it was true—he wasn't normally attracted to small girls, but this one could be an entirely different matter.

'Thank you for a wonderful day,' Aurora said as the Saab pulled up outside her town house much later that day. 'Would…would you like to come in?'

Luke shook his head, but slid his arm along the back of her seat. 'Thank *you* for a wonderful day, but I've got some work to do. And just to reassure you that I do keep my word…' He used his other hand to open the glove box and he pulled out two packets, which he put in her lap. 'Only two to go,' he murmured.

Aurora looked down at her diaries in her lap, and came tumbling down from the clouds. 'OK,' she heard herself say, 'I guess I'll hear from you when…whenever.'

'Aurora—'

'No. A deal is a deal, Luke. Goodnight.' She had her bag at her feet, which expedited a swift departure, but, for that matter, after one restless movement he didn't try to stop her, although he didn't drive off until she'd opened her door and switched on a light.

Then she did hear the Saab roar away and she walked dazedly into her lounge to curl up in her wing chair and rub her face miserably.

It had been a wonderful day. They'd done everything he'd suggested, but it hadn't only been the beauty of North Stradbroke Island and Point Lookout or the surf they'd swum in, the long lunch or the ferry rides across a placid and lovely Moreton Bay that had made it so magical. It had been Luke Kirwan.

The gorgeous but dangerous man on the prowl she'd seen the night of his house-warming had not been much in evidence, although she had found herself suddenly the object of palpable envy from her own sex throughout the day. But he'd also made her feel intensely alive and as if she was operating on all cylinders because he was mentally challenging to be with. They'd talked a lot during the day about all sorts of subjects.

Other things had appeared to be, mysteriously, more stimulating too. The wonderful seafood they'd eaten for lunch had acquired an almost sensuous quality to be eating it with him while they'd also enjoyed a bottle of wine. The thick grass beneath her bare feet as they'd strolled through the old Dunwich cemetery while they'd been waiting for the ferry home, the lovely old trees, the timelessness of the One Mile anchorage where the ferry came in—it had all sung to her very soul because he'd been there with her.

But, despite being surprisingly easy to handle, he was also physically challenging, she had to acknowledge. She'd discovered during the day that Luke Kirwan was breathtakingly beautifully put together. In fact, that was just what it had done—taken her breath away when they'd stripped to their costumes on the beach and the lean, clean, strong lines of his body had been revealed to her.

And when they'd come out of the water to stand side by side on the sand, sleek and dripping, she'd found she'd been able to feel and taste as if they were doing it, the final act of intimacy between a man and a woman. But beyond a lurking glint in his dark eyes as they'd skimmed her slim figure in a rose-pink bikini that had told her she was equally desirable, no more had come of it.

And now this, she thought bleakly, coming back to the present. She looked across the room to where she'd put her diaries down. A calculated reminder that this was a game to him? It had to be. What was more she, incredibly foolishly, had done all the things, bar one, she'd accused him of trying

to achieve with this game. Even to feeling disappointed that
he hadn't come in for a nightcap and kissed her goodnight.

Two more dates, Aurora, she thought unhappily, and you
won't know if you're on your head or your heels and all
over a blackmailer. There has to be a way out of this...

Perhaps he had never had any intention of reading her
diaries, she wondered suddenly with a faint spark of hope.
But it subsided almost immediately. Even if that were true,
she was still under siege for whatever reason, but it didn't
seem likely to be a long-term commitment.

If nothing else he was on the rebound—how many times
had she had that pointed out to her, after all? And there was
something about his own reticence on the subject that was...
She considered for a moment. A little scary?

There was only one way to find out, she told herself. Was
she game to throw down the gauntlet? No more dates until
she got her remaining diaries back?

CHAPTER FIVE

THE next morning, out of the blue, Neil approached her with an exciting proposition—a talk-back show of her own.

'You mean I host it?' She stared at him wide-eyed.

'Yes—don't look so surprised.' He grinned. 'Once a week is what we have in mind with a guest in the studio who you will chat to first, then we'll open up the lines. We'll provide you with a research-assistant-cum-secretary. And the choice of guests will be something you and I will hammer out together; but we feel you're well-enough informed, you're well-enough travelled, certainly articulate enough, et cetera, to handle it and you're obviously of good character. But it will be a lot more work. How say you, Miss Templeton?'

'I say yes!' Aurora beamed back at him. 'This is *wonderful*—thank you, Neil!'

'My pleasure! Er—how's it going with Luke?'

Aurora stilled and felt a lot of her euphoria evaporate. 'Why?' she asked cautiously.

'I believe Leonie is mounting a reconciliation movement.'

'Oh.'

Neil raised an eyebrow. 'Are you still seeing him?'

Aurora rose. 'Not anymore, Neil. At least—not after tonight.'

'Aurora—'

'Neil—' she smiled down at him '—don't worry. Without so many people to keep me informed, I'd be working in the dark!' And she went to walk out jauntily but stopped in her tracks. 'What has good character got to do with it?' she asked with a frown.

'Well, the public wouldn't take kindly to a bank robber on their air space, and, once you open the lines to them, if you do have a skeleton in your closet someone could well embarrass you on air with it.' He eyed her humorously. 'So now's the time to come clean if there is anything deep and dark in your past, Aurora!'

'No, there's nothing…'

Nothing but an open police file on me and two of my diaries still in Luke Kirwan's possession, she thought for the tenth time in the space of an hour as she paced her lounge when she got home from work. So what to do?

Just go and explain things to him? If nothing else, it would prove to her once and for all what kind of a man he really was. But, say he was the devil in disguise, she mused, wouldn't she be handing him a real hold over her that could affect her career for ever?

She sat down and rubbed her temples distractedly. Most of her instincts told her that Luke Kirwan would drop this game if she put her case fairly and squarely. But, as was faithfully recorded in one of the diaries he still had, her one previous relationship with a man had proven beyond doubt that her instincts, on the subject of men, were not that reliable. At twenty-three she'd thought she'd fallen deeply in love but it had turned sour on her.

The love of her life had turned into a frighteningly possessive, jealous man and she'd had to fall back on her father to help to extricate her from the relationship…

Her father! She sat up suddenly. Even if she could just talk to him on his satellite phone! But she slumped back almost immediately—what would that achieve, other than worrying the life out of him wherever he was—which was somewhere in the middle of the Pacific Ocean?

Then her phone rang and it was Luke with a proposition. Barry and Julia were having a house party on the family sheep station, Beltrees, the coming weekend, and Julia had rung to ask if he would like to take Aurora.

'You're kidding!' Aurora said flatly.

'No,' he replied. 'And we'd fly so you'd still be able to work on Friday and Monday. I think you'd like Beltrees. And most people fall for my father although, I should warn you, he's a bit of a character.'

'He…would be there?' Aurora asked cautiously.

'Certainly.' He paused and when he went on she could hear the amusement in his voice. 'I think this would definitely qualify as a two-diary date, Aurora, and, well, it's entirely up to you what happens from then on.'

'I…see,' she said slowly.

There was a short silence, then, 'Are you all right, Aurora?'

She made a concentrated effort to perk up. 'I'm fine! OK. It sounds…fun.'

'Good. I'll get in touch later in the week. Bye.'

'Bye!' She put the phone down and stared at it with a most curious thought in her mind in the circumstances— what about Leonie's reconciliation attempt?

They flew to Beltrees in a light plane that belonged to the property.

During the preceding days, she'd worked hard on the approach she should take over this weekend and had decided that since she'd got three of her diaries back by being, mostly, herself, that was how she should continue. If she could, she'd thought several times, because things were much more serious now. It therefore came as a pleasant surprise to find that Beltrees itself was a help…

Situated between Charleville and Quilpie in south western Queensland, the station was in the heart of sheep country and, while it could be prone to drought, or flood, while it was often flat and not very interesting country, Aurora was in for a pleasant surprise. A good preceding season had turned it into a carpet of wild flowers.

'I can't believe it,' she said wonderingly of the splashes of lovely colour on the red soil as they floated down to land.

'You're lucky,' Luke said. 'It doesn't happen often like this.'

'Only every seven years or so,' the pilot contributed. 'OK, here we go.' He touched the plane down gently and they rolled to a stop at the end of a dirt strip. 'You're the last of the party to arrive,' he added.

'Who exactly is in the party?' Aurora enquired as they drove in an open four-wheel drive past a picturesque old wooden shearing shed and yards.

'Not sure.' Luke shrugged. 'All Julia said was that they were having a house party and would I like to bring you? But she comes from a big family.' In jeans, a khaki bush shirt and short boots with a broad-brimmed Akubra on the seat beside him, he fitted into the landscape well.

'Did you grow up here, Luke?' she asked.

'I did. And broke my father's heart when all I wanted to do was escape.' He looked around, then down at Aurora with a smile lurking at the back of his eyes. 'Sheep bore me to tears. On the other hand, it was a marvellous spot to observe the heavens.'

'So that's how it all started? With a passion for astronomy?'

'Mmm... But also phenomena such as artesian basins, water tables and rivers that run inland like Cooper Creek. So my time wasn't exactly wasted. Here we are.'

He pulled the vehicle up and Aurora blinked because Beltrees homestead was about as far from a typical Queensland homestead as one could get. Built of sandstone, it was long and low, had a steep red roof with a central gable, also sandstone, all the window frames were wood and it looked like trout lodge from the Scottish Highlands rather than a farmhouse in outback Queensland.

This impression was reinforced by the fact that the house, framed to the rear by trees, looked out over a lake, complete with swans, beyond a smooth green lawn.

'Luke!' she said in awed tones. 'Are you sure you're not

mad? This is incredible. Is there anything else you haven't told me?'

'Such as?'

'Well, it's not only incredible, it simply shouts—now I come to think of it,' she said on a descending scale, 'Neil did mention something about old money and family homes. I see what he means!' She turned to him urgently. 'I only brought one dress, all the rest are jeans and shorts.'

He laughed. 'You don't have to worry about clothes. When my mother was alive, she liked things to be, well, formal, but Julia is much more easygoing. By the way, my father is a little absent-minded—he often speaks his thoughts aloud, so don't be surprised. But he doesn't stand on ceremony and he hates people calling him Sir David.'

Aurora's mouth fell open. 'Sir David Kirwan? Knighted for his contribution to the wool industry? How come I never connected you to him?'

Before Luke had the chance to answer, Julia and Barry, with several dogs at their heels, came to meet them. And it was not until much later that night that Aurora was alone with Luke again, although she did find herself alone with Julia for a few minutes when Julia showed her to her room. Nor did Julia desert her outspokenness.

She said, 'You might be a little surprised about this, Aurora?'

'I am, Julia. Especially since I've been told Leonie wants him back.'

Julia sat down on the bed and grimaced. 'Don't hate me for this, but it wasn't my idea. Barry insisted I ask you. But then, for some strange reason, Barry was never a great fan of Leonie's and he has also insisted that I stay out of it. So, welcome to Beltrees, Aurora, and please don't feel you need to be wary of me.' She smiled what appeared to be a very genuine smile.

Aurora smiled back after overcoming a moment of complete surprise. She also thought—Good on you, Barry! At least one of you is prepared to judge me on my merits. It was only some time later that it occurred to her this was an inappropriate sentiment...

It wasn't a big house party by Beltrees standards, Aurora discovered.

Two other couples, one of which comprised Julia's sister and brother-in-law. The second couple were friends from the district and Aurora was the only stranger in their midst. But everyone welcomed her enthusiastically, almost overpoweringly so, in fact. Because she was not Leonie Murdoch, she surmised with an inward little grimace, but they were all trying to put it out of their minds?

She didn't get to meet Sir David until they were gathered in the lounge for pre-dinner drinks, and he was a different matter.

Fortunately, the one dress Aurora had brought was a little black number, sleeveless and round-necked, then A-line to just above her knees. It was quite plain but classy, and she tied her hair back with a tissuey gold scarf. The only problem was shoes, of which she had a nice black pair, patent with a narrow gold rim around the sole, but they were almost flat. Oh, well, she thought, there was nothing to be done about it, but she would have loved a bit of height.

And despite Luke's claims of Julia being much more easygoing than his mother, it was an elegant company that assembled in the lounge before dinner. In fact, it was an elegant house filled with marvellous antique furniture and paintings, and sherry was served from a crystal decanter.

Then a tall old man with a shock of white hair and shaggy eyebrows strode into the room, saying, 'OK, where is she? If she's ousted Leonie, she must be something else!'

'Dad,' Barry protested, 'I thought we agreed that subject was taboo—oh, hell!' he added helplessly.

'As a matter of fact, she is something else,' Luke said smoothly, into the awkward little pause that had developed.

'May I present Aurora Templeton?' He took Aurora's hand and drew her forward.

Aurora swallowed for some reason and looked up into a pair of dark eyes not unlike Luke's. 'How do you do?' she said politely. 'I've been told not to call you Sir David, but I don't know what else to call you.'

'Good Lord!' David Kirwan studied Aurora intently, from her tied-back streaky fair hair to her black patent shoes, then turned to Luke. 'Is this cradle-snatching or what?'

'She's twenty-five,' Luke murmured. 'As I recall, you were fifteen years older than Mum.'

'But…' Luke's father turned back to Aurora '…well, she couldn't be more different from Leonie if she tried!'

'So I've been told,' Aurora remarked, 'although, never having met the lady, I'm unable to form my own opinion. But she obviously has a formidable reputation—I wouldn't let my lack of inches fool you, however,' she added with a sparkle in her green eyes. 'I actually broke into your son's house once, knocked him out, and I haven't been able to get rid of him ever since.'

'Aurora,' Luke said gravely, 'that is playing with the truth a little.'

She turned her gaze to him. 'It's what you yourself accused me of, Luke,' she responded equally gravely.

'By gosh, a right sassy little one!' David Kirwan gazed down at Aurora. 'Do you know, I think I might see what he sees in you. And, come to think of it, Leonie's last tip on the stock market was a lousy one.'

Everyone started to laugh and David Kirwan took Aurora's hand and led her into dinner.

'You bowled my father right over,' Luke said when they were strolling, at his suggestion, beside the lake before going to bed.

'Oh, I think it would be fairer to say he's reserving judgement,' Aurora replied, and stopped to gaze at the reflection of the house lights on the smooth, dark surface of the water. And when she shivered because the night was cool, he took his jacket off and put it around her.

'Maybe, but he's enjoying himself along the way.'

'He's rather a sweetie.' They came to a bench and she sank down on it. 'What a marvellous night. It's a little hard to associate this—' she waved a hand '—with the dust and rigours of an outback sheep station.'

'Plenty of blood, sweat and tears went into the creation of Beltrees. But my father had the foresight to diversify into other things rather than ride completely on a sheep's back.'

'Did you break his heart, Luke?' She looked up at him as he stood before her on the lake's edge.

'Not really. Barry is more than happy to take my place and I still keep an eye on the business side of things.'

'I would have thought you were a son to be proud of.'

He shrugged. 'I suspect he has grandchildren on his mind these days. Barry and Julia don't seem to be in any hurry to provide them and I'm definitely…dragging my heels.'

She thought for a moment, about how Luke had been during the evening, and wondered about the disenchantment she'd sensed in him. Not that it was anything to concern her, she told herself. She had one clear goal to concentrate on, and why, for example, he might have decided to present her to his father should not be allowed to deflect her from that goal. All the same…

She patted the bench beside her. 'Sit down for a moment,' she invited, 'and tell me which star is what.'

He grinned and sat down. 'There's the Southern Cross—'

'I know *that*—are you feeling dangerous again, Luke?'

He was silent for a long moment, then, 'How did you know?'

'I could tell you were dangerous from the first moment I met you—remember? Although that was in a different context, of course, but some of the signs are the same—a bored sort of arrogant aura. Is it…was it because your father brought up Leonie?'

He slid his arm along the back of the bench, around her shoulders. 'We do antagonize each other sometimes, Dad and I. He's not quite as absent-minded as he would like everyone to think—the Leonie reference was no doubt a well-thought-out ploy to point out the error of my ways to me.'

'Why did you bring me along, then?' Aurora queried. 'You must have had some idea that it would happen.'

'Because it seemed like a good idea to get it over and done with.'

Aurora grimaced and unthinkingly laid her cheek on his shoulder. Then she realised what she was doing and went to sit up, but he stilled her.

'Relax,' he said. 'No one can see us.'

'It wasn't that…' She paused. 'Perhaps I *feel* like the error of your ways now.'

He laughed softly. 'On the other hand, you couldn't be more aptly named for an astrophysicist, which is my speciality. I guess you know what Aurora means?' He looked down at her.

'The dawn—I was born just as the sun rose!'

'A little bundle of joy. But in meteorological terms an aurora is a luminous, sometimes richly coloured display of arcs, bands and streamers in the sky and there are two famous ones: aurora borealis and aurora australis. That's how I'm coming to think of you—as my aurora australis.'

She caught her breath for a moment and looked up at the night sky with a feeling of wonder in her heart but caution prevailed. 'As well as the error of your ways?' she suggested gravely.

'Actually, that's the last thing you feel like at the moment.' He stroked her cheek with his fingertips.

She knew she should resist, but when he drew her closer she found she simply couldn't.

'How does that feel?' he asked.

She shrugged. 'You're rather nice to lean against. You make me feel safe—I mean,' she sought to qualify it immediately, 'say there were wild animals roaming about out there, I'd be much happier to have you around than to be here alone.'

She felt the jolt of laughter that ran through him, then he was quiet for a time. 'Do you often feel unsafe and lonely, Aurora?' he asked at last.

She hesitated.

'One thing that struck me when I skimmed through your diaries, and has been reinforced since I got to know you, is that you've had some long, lonely periods in your life with no mother and your father gone frequently,' he said.

'I...perhaps,' she conceded, 'although I don't usually give it much thought. But it's a bit worse at the moment because my father is away sailing the high seas again, but he's alone this time and he's the only family I've got. Both he and my mother were only children and all my grandparents are gone. I don't know why this has struck me now,' she confessed and tilted her face to his. 'What made you bring it up?'

'It struck me this evening,' he said meditatively, 'that I'd rather have thrown you into the lion's den and, for a slip of a girl for whom, often, her diaries were her lifeline, you were extraordinarily brave—I don't why, but it did. The other thing that occurred to me was—that I would be only too happy to kiss you and make you feel safe.' He bent his head and sought her lips.

Several minutes later, as they drew apart, she was feeling quite different. Trembling with desire and conscious of an electric, physical tension between them as he ran his hands up and down her arms beneath his jacket and handled her in a way she was becoming achingly familiar with. A way that made her pulse-rate soar and filled her with a heady delight because he was strong and powerful, but he made her feel silken, beautiful and desirable.

'This is getting harder and harder to handle,' she breathed.

He cupped her shoulders, then withdrew his hands, closed his jacket up to her chin and took her loosely in his arms. 'But nice?' He rubbed his chin on the top of her head.

'Wonderful. I don't feel so much like the error of your ways any more. Still—'

'You're quite safe from me here at Beltrees,' he broke in quizzically.

'I know, but that's only two nights.'

'Perhaps we could come to a new arrangement after Beltrees.' He tilted her chin and kissed the tip of her nose.

'You know,' she said slowly, 'I'm trying to picture you as a little boy, staring up at the stars.'

'I'll show you my first telescope tomorrow. I made it myself.'

She looked at him wonderingly.

'In the meantime, however, if I'm to stick to my good intentions, perhaps we should go in?' he suggested.

They did, to their separate bedrooms, without speaking except to say goodnight. And it was as if they had an unseen, unspoken link between them, a mental association that was calm and close despite the separate rooms.

But it was a long time before Aurora got to sleep as she contemplated how foolish she'd been to kid herself she only had one goal—getting back her diaries...

The next day, a Saturday, was active.

A tour of the property on horseback, a barbecue for lunch, then tennis. Luke did also show her his first telescope during the afternoon, although it took quite a search through a box-room to find it.

'There.' He dusted it off. 'Pretty primitive! I don't know if it still works—the prisms may have gone haywire.'

'How did you have the knowledge to build it?' she asked, fascinated.

'I got the instructions out of a science magazine. I got a

lot of ideas from science magazines, some that caused me to get my hide tanned. Like the homemade rocket that set fire to the wool-shed roof.'

Aurora burst out laughing.

'Not funny,' he remarked. 'Oh, here's something that should interest you, a crystal radio set. I could actually tune into the flying doctor's frequency—hell, it's broken.'

'Luke, you should keep these properly,' she remonstrated. 'Your kids could be fascinated one day.'

He grimaced. 'It's junk, really. I don't think I've looked at them since I was about…fifteen.'

She closed her hand over his. 'Keep them. You never know. If they were my kids…' She stopped abruptly.

He looked down at her and she felt a tingling sensation down her spine and a rush of colour come to her cheeks. 'I wonder what kind of kids we would have?' he said idly. 'Sassy little girls not above breaking into other people's homes?'

'Or boys that set fire to the wool shed?' she countered, although she was still feeling flustered.

'Perhaps we'd filter out the worst of each other,' he suggested.

'I'm not admitting to any…criminal side that needs filtering out,' she said primly.

'Unless it suits you, Aurora. My father took me aside this morning and asked me if you really broke into my house.'

She looked rueful. 'What did you say?'

'That he should ask you.'

'Thanks! Uh…who knows?'

'What our children would be like? You're right.' He put his hands around her waist and lifted her up to sit her on the edge of a table, then proceeded to study her face enigmatically.

'I know what you're thinking,' she said after a moment. 'I was the one who made sweeping statements fairly recently about not being ready to surrender to marriage, maternity and domesticity—and now I'm talking kids, although it was in the most general way.'

He fiddled with the buttons of her pink blouse, then adjusted some tendrils of hair behind her ears. 'Nope! I wasn't thinking about that at all.'

'Oh. What, then?'

'The lovely sheen of your skin...' he trailed his fingers down her cheek '...the gloss of your lips; the way you hit a tennis ball, as if you'd like to fire it right through your opponent, and how you stick the tip of your tongue out at the same time. Those kind of things.'

'Luke—' she laughed '—I don't!'

'Yes, you do—you certainly are a pocket dynamo, Miss Templeton.'

'I suppose I am competitive,' she conceded.

'But a lot less aggressive on the subject of myself,' he remarked casually, although with an oddly acute little gleam in his eye.

She thought for a bit—with a feeling of being on dangerous ground. 'Perhaps, like your father, I'm reserving judgement.'

'Why?'

'You are still holding two of my diaries,' she pointed out.

'Ah, so this is a "good behaviour" version of Aurora Templeton until you get them back?' he suggested quizzically.

'Wouldn't you...have some plan of action if you were in my shoes?' she countered with some irony.

'Possibly.' He looked wry. 'Was kissing me last night part of your good-behaviour bond?'

She merely gazed at him.

'How about this, then? If there were only you and I at Beltrees, we could go for a swim in the lake without bothering about costumes, we could then make love on the grass, rest and recuperate a bit and have a candlelight supper for two whenever the mood took us.'

Aurora narrowed her eyes. 'I thought I was supposed to be safe from you at Beltrees?'

'We aren't alone,' he pointed out.

'Just as well, Professor,' she said sternly. 'I can see I would be in for a…decadent time otherwise.'

'I wouldn't call that decadent,' he drawled. 'I think it would be rather—delicious.' He kissed her lightly.

She slipped her hands around his neck. 'You're still in that dangerous mood, Mr Kirwan.'

'Could have a lot to do with you, Miss Templeton. Ah—' he paused as a gong sounded '—you're saved by the tea bell.'

Aurora groaned.

'That's highly complimentary,' he remarked, his eyes bright with devilry.

'I was only groaning because the thought of more food after that barbecue is enough to sink me!' she informed him.

'I'm demolished,' he murmured.

She kissed him back. 'No, you're not. In fact, you're still playing games with me, Luke. I haven't quite figured out what they are, but I will!' She removed his hands from her waist and slipped off the table. 'See you at tea,' she said pertly, and left him watching her with a rather wry expression.

But once she was out of sight, she paused to ask herself what kind of games *she* thought she was playing. And groaned inwardly this time.

The rest of their stay at Beltrees passed without incident— until a couple of hours before they were due to leave and Sir David fell off his horse and broke his arm, as well as concussing himself. With the result that he and Luke were flown to the Charleville hospital, and Aurora continued on alone to Brisbane.

She'd assured Luke that she quite understood and he was not to worry about her. He'd kissed her briefly and openly, and told her he'd be in touch as soon as he got back to Brisbane, himself.

She did wonder if he'd instruct Miss Hillier to return her diaries to her, but, when a few days went by and nothing happened, consoled herself with the thought that Luke probably had his safe keys on him. But when a few more days went by with no word from him, she began to feel tense and annoyed and, quite irrationally, not only on the subject of her diaries.

This was a man, after all, who made a habit of either kissing her or thinking about it, then leaving her dangling. Well, it was time she took a stand, she decided. So she rang Miss Hillier, discovered he was due home that day, and informed his secretary that she required an audience with him that evening, come hell or high water.

Miss Hillier demurred, and even protested that she had no control over his movements, but subsided when Aurora threatened to move into her old home.

She chose a severely tailored dark green linen suit for the appointment and wore black accessories. She put her hair up in a no-nonsense pleat and put on the minimum of make-up, then added a bit of blusher because she not only looked but felt a bit pale. Finally, there was nothing left to do but drive up the hill to her old home.

Miss Hillier let her in with an expression of concern on her face. 'He's not in a very good mood,' she said in little more than a whisper.

'Neither am I,' Aurora whispered back. 'All right, lead me into the lion's den.'

'He's just come in and he's on the phone. Take a seat in the lounge and I'll bring you a cup of—'

'Could you make that a brandy and soda?' Aurora requested. 'My moral fibre needs a bit of a boost.'

Surprisingly, Miss Hillier chuckled. 'I might even have one myself.'

*   *   *

Ten minutes later, when Aurora had half finished her brandy and soda, Luke strode into the lounge.

'Aurora,' he said abruptly, 'sorry to keep you waiting. And I'm sorry I haven't been in touch but complications set in—my father developed pneumonia.'

'Oh.' She bit her lip. 'I'm sorry. How—?'

'He's going to be all right, but it was touch and go for a while,' he interrupted, and his gaze fell on the glass beside her, then came back to rest on her face with a tinge of satire in those dark eyes. Nor was his manner of dress any consolation to Aurora. In a charcoal pinstripe suit with a pale grey shirt and dark tie, he was an impressive but distant figure.

He also said, with his gaze on the glass again, 'It would appear you've come on a mission, Aurora. Let me guess—your diaries?'

Aurora took a breath and wondered a little wildly how to proceed. In the light of his father's health he could conceivably be forgiven for forgetting her diaries, and normally she would have forgiven him, but that wasn't all there was between them—or was it? Why else would he not have contacted her? Why else would he be this formal, distant stranger to her now? Why should she be made to feel the last thing he needed on his mind was her and her diaries?

She swallowed, then forced herself to relax. 'I am very sorry to hear about your father, but I'd rather you didn't tower over me like this, Luke.'

He sat down opposite. 'Better?' This time there was a tinge of insolence in his expression.

She eyed him. 'I believe you're not in a very good mood?'

He smiled unamusedly. 'I believe you and Miss Hillier must be in cahoots again.' He looked at his watch. 'Unfortunately I have another appointment shortly, so could we get down to brass tacks?'

Aurora took a very deep breath this time. 'All right. This has gone on long enough. I want my diaries back *now*. I'm about to enter a new era of my life and I need to get this situation sorted out so—'

'All right.'

'So—what did you say?' Her eyes were huge suddenly.

'I'll get them.' He called Miss Hillier, handed over a set of keys to her and requested that she get the two remaining diaries out of his safe.

While they waited, with Aurora feeling slightly shell-shocked, he recommended that she finish her drink. She did so in one large gulp and, when Miss Hillier returned, accepted her diaries dazedly. Miss Hillier hesitated, glanced at her boss, then retreated, taking Aurora's glass with her.

'So—what's this new "era" of your life all about? It seems to have come up pretty suddenly,' he said.

Confusion made Aurora blink several times, then tell him. Once she had, she said hollowly, though, 'I wasn't going to go into the details.'

'Why not? It sounds like quite a coup for you.'

'All the more reason not to want—I mean, now my public profile—'

'I see,' he interrupted. 'You didn't want your diaries floating around out of your control in case I was tempted to— somehow—damage your public profile with them?'

She hesitated, then nodded.

He stood up and went to the terrace doors, where he stood for a while examining the view with his hands shoved into his pockets, then turned back to her. 'Is that the only reason?'

'Of course not,' she answered quietly, and willed herself to keep hold of her composure. 'I hate not knowing where I stand, I hate the thought of anyone reading them—and I don't much like the thought that you could be that kind of man.'

He grimaced. 'I never had the slightest intention of reading them.'

A little well of hope rose in Aurora's heart. She said,

however, 'I wasn't to know that and, even so, it was still a game you were playing with me.'

'And you're not into playing games with men?' he drawled.

Aurora narrowed her eyes. 'Certainly not men on the rebound—or on the prowl.'

He raised his eyebrows thoughtfully. 'Is that how it felt lately?'

'No,' she conceded after a moment, and with a tinge of pink in her cheeks. 'But then the ''you'' of lately is light years away from the ''you'' of now.'

He studied her smart suit and elegant shoes. 'I could say the same of you, Aurora.'

'Have you got back with Leonie—is that what all this is about?'

'Jealous, Aurora?' he queried softly.

She stood up and clenched her fists.

'Before you demolish me or try physically to put me in my place,' he said with patent, hateful amusement, 'if you'd never known about Leonie, what kind of a judgement would you have placed on us?'

She paused. 'How can I? I did know, I still know, so how can I make an unbiased judgement?'

'Surely you must have had some original thoughts into which Leonie didn't intrude? When you were kissing me, for example?' The insolence was right out in the open now.

She clenched her teeth this time. 'You're in an impossible mood! I'll remove my unwanted presence so you can get to your next appointment.'

'Your presence is not unwanted, Aurora. I'd like nothing better than to remove your ''power dressing''—' his gaze roamed up and down her smart but severe suit '—incidentally I preferred your señorita outfit—and make love to you here and now.'

She gasped. 'How can you say that?'

'Easily, because it's true. Making love to you has become

something I think about rather a lot lately.' He smiled slightly. 'Why do you think I didn't come in after we'd been to Point Lookout? Why do you think I took you to Beltrees, amongst so many people, not the least my father?'

She found herself bereft of speech.

'That's why, Aurora,' he drawled with lethal satire.

'You know…you know what?' she said shakily. 'You're the kind of man who wants to have his cake and eat it—'

'More sayings, Aurora?' he mocked. 'You really are a gold mine of them.'

'Oh!' She picked up her bag and diaries. 'That's it. Don't you dare darken my door again, Luke Kirwan, and rest assured I shall take great pleasure in never having to lay eyes on you again!' She all but ran from the room and he didn't move a muscle to stop her.

Three days later as she read her morning news bulletin her mind was still almost as churned up as it had been when she'd run away from Luke. In fact, she was reading automatically until she came to an item that made her pause, stumble, then apologize and continue.

And when the news was finished, Neil, instead of giving her his usual thumbs up, asked her if she was OK because she looked a bit pale and sickly. She told him she was feeling that way, but didn't tell him why, and gratefully accepted his offer of the rest of the day off.

When she got home, she leant back against the front door and marvelled at her stupidity. She had completely forgotten, until she'd come to read an item about a home invasion, that the police still had an open file on her. And now that she'd seen the other side of Luke Kirwan, a side she'd hated, how could she be sure it wouldn't turn out to be the skeleton in her closet Neil had mentioned?

She spent the rest of the day arguing it out with herself but, in the end, there seemed to be only one thing to do.

CHAPTER SIX

THIS time she made no appointment with Miss Hillier.

She drove up the hill, rang the bell, then knocked on the front door. There was no response but there were lights on in the house so she walked round and let herself in through the sliding doors that opened onto the terrace. And she had no intimation that she was about to encounter the scholarly side of Luke Kirwan, but that was what happened.

He'd mentioned to her that he'd had the billiard room converted to a study, and that was where she found him, at his desk, surrounded by a sea of papers with his hair rumpled and blue shadows on his jaw.

He looked up as she appeared in the doorway, and blinked.

'I rang the bell and I knocked,' she said. 'I'm sorry if you were deliberately ignoring them in case it was me, but—'

'I...no,' he broke in. 'I didn't hear them.'

She frowned at him.

'No, I haven't suddenly gone deaf, I just switch off and ignore things like that when I'm working. Sorry.'

'Oh.'

'But I must admit this is a surprise,' he said after a moment and stood up to come round the desk.

It came as something of a shock to Aurora—her inward reaction to the lean, untidy length of him in faded jeans and an old sweatshirt. Nothing detracted from the fact that the way he was put together was sleek, powerful and simply awesome, she thought with a little pulse of panic. Nor did it help her to be subjected to a brief scrutiny up and down her figure and have an eyebrow slightly raised at her conservative attire—khaki cargo pants and a loose check shirt with long sleeves.

'I came because I forgot something,' she said stiffly.

His mouth curved into a wicked grin. 'Not more diaries, Aurora?'

'No. The police file. It's really important to me, because of my new programme that it…that you retract it, or something.' She twisted her hands together.

'Oh, that.' He gestured casually. 'I had it expunged weeks ago. Before our first "date", as a matter of fact.'

Her eyes widened and her mouth dropped open. 'How?'

'I told the police that it was a misunderstanding of a…domestic nature.'

'What?'

He smiled faintly at her incredulous expression. 'A dispute between myself and a…lady friend who had come back to claim some of her property but, on finding the front door open, she decided to dispense with making her presence known to me and just nip in and retrieve her things.'

'You…they *bought* that? In the middle of the night, with a torch, et cetera, et cetera?'

'Lovers who have fallen out are renowned for doing strange things,' he said and looked at her meaningfully.

'So—so—' Aurora had difficulty getting her words out '—I'm now down on the record as being your estranged lover? That's…diabolical!'

'Would you prefer to be down on the record as a burglar?'

'Of course not! No…but…' She trailed off and stared at him, breathing heavily.

'It so happens,' he said after a moment, 'your actual name is not down on any record. They quite understood that my natural gallantry, despite having fallen out with you, precluded me wanting to name you.'

She opened her mouth, shut it, then said feebly, 'Well, thanks. I didn't think you had much natural gallantry, to be honest, but…' She hesitated.

He said nothing, just observed her idly although somehow comprehensively until the heat began to rush beneath her skin again.

'All right!' She closed her eyes. 'That was gallant! But...' She stopped frustratedly.

'Uh—could I offer you a drink?' he suggested and, without waiting for a reply, invited her to sit down while he got it.

She looked around with a frown of concentration while she waited, and a deep feeling of uncertainty because she'd obviously misjudged him, but that didn't explain away their last encounter...

He'd had the billiard room completely redecorated. Two walls were lined floor to ceiling with bookshelves and stuffed with books, and a third had a built-in desk and shelves that housed an impressive display of computer-ware. The main desk was free-standing and massive and situated so he could see the view from the window but, by simply swivelling his chair round, he was able to work on his computer.

She was sitting on a leather couch with a coffee-table in front of it, and in front of the window stood a powerful telescope. All the woodwork was beautifully done, the colour scheme of carpet, curtains and the free wall space was a restful combination of mossy green and copper and the main desk was a beauty, mahogany with many drawers and curved brass handles.

But the aura of the room was much more than tasteful, and not particularly restful. It was very obviously the home of a probing intellect, of a man who had admitted to her that running sheep stations bored him rigid and shown her his first telescope that he'd built when he was ten.

Then he came back with two drinks and sat down beside her.

Aurora took a sip of brandy and soda and said, 'I'm sorry if I—'

'Did you honestly think I'd use that against you, Aurora?'

She closed her mouth, and sighed. 'I didn't know what to think. But, to be honest, after the last time I came here I wasn't, well, I didn't know what to think,' she repeated helplessly.

'Ah. It would be handy if I could expunge that from the record,' he murmured and looked down at her, 'but I was under a bit of pressure, unfortunately.'

'Because of your father? Well, I can see that now, I guess.'

He smiled dryly. 'You're very generous, Aurora. And it was because of my father, but not quite in the way you might imagine. Of course, I was really concerned for his health but…a sudden brush with mortality brought out a strange reaction in him. He told me it was his dearest wish to see me married and settled down before he departed this life.'

Aurora did a doubletake.

'Quite,' he agreed ruefully, then changed the subject. 'Have you eaten yet?'

'Uh…no.' She shook her head.

'Neither have I. How about scrambled eggs on toast?'

'You…could do that? What about all this work you were so deeply engrossed in?' She looked across at the desk.

He grimaced. 'I wasn't getting anywhere with it.' But his gaze returned to his desk as well with something a touch regretful in it.

'Tell you what,' Aurora said, 'why don't I make the scrambled eggs while you capture any last thoughts you may have on whatever it is that's so elusive?'

He turned back to her, took her chin in his fingers, and kissed her lingeringly. 'You are a peach,' he said softly.

But when Aurora had made her escape to the kitchen, she stood for a long moment with her hands on her still-flushed cheeks and a sense of bemusement in her heart because she'd fallen right back under Luke Kirwan's spell without even trying…

*   *   *

'I'm working on a speech,' he told her after they'd eaten from trays on their knees in the den, 'that I've been asked to present as the opening address to an international conference on astrophysics to be held on the Gold Coast in two weeks. I'm trying to…blend the old with the new, I guess. Draw a line from Ptolemy, Copernicus, Galileo, Halley, Newton, et cetera to the modern day.'

'Ah, I know a bit about that,' Aurora said. 'I've just finished a lovely book, *Galileo's Daughter*. I also read another of Dava Sobell's books, *Longitude*, and found it fascinating, as a sailor's daughter. So I'm actually a mine of information, contrary to what you might have suspected, Professor.'

He looked amused, then thoughtful. 'Galileo's daughter…'

'Does that give you inspiration?' she asked.

'Well, it's obviously been done so—and not that I'm suggesting she was humorous—but my speech, because it's the opening address rather than a paper, needs a bit of humour—'

'I'm not sure about Ptolemy. Copernicus was a monk but maybe Isaac Newton or Edmund Halley had a wife that you could draw some humour from?' Aurora broke in to suggest. 'Mind you, it was quite customary in Galileo's days, at least, for scholars not to marry. That's why his daughters ended up in a nunnery—they were illegitimate and didn't have any prospects because of it. You don't—' She broke off and glinted a wicked little look at him. '*You* don't subscribe to that view, do you, Luke?'

'Not at all,' he denied and shrugged. 'I've never thought about it that way.'

'So why did you and Leonie call it quits?' Aurora heard herself ask.

He blinked at her.

Aurora wrinkled her nose. 'Sorry. That just slipped out. Well, it *is* topical, I guess. And I'm reliably informed she's a ten, if not to say an eleven or twelve, Leonie Murdoch.'

'Who by? Don't tell me—Neil and Mandy Pearson.'

Aurora agreed wryly. 'To compound matters, Neil couldn't have been more surprised to hear you and I were walking out together than if I'd told him the…the Aga Khan had taken an interest in me.'

'I think the present one *would* be a little old for you, Aurora.'

She ignored the little glint of irony in his eyes and gestured. 'You know what I mean. He seemed to think we were in different leagues. He also, now I come to think of it, expressed the opinion of you that—no.' Aurora stopped.

'Please don't spare my feelings,' Luke said politely.

'It's not your feelings I'm worried about,' she retorted. 'I just don't feel right about quoting what Neil said in confidence, I guess.'

'Then I'll ask him—you have spilt most of the beans anyway.'

'Luke!' Aurora stood up and put her tray on the coffeetable. 'Don't you dare!'

'There is, actually, no way you could stop me, Aurora,' he murmured. He stood up. 'In fact I might give him a ring right now.'

She looked around a little wildly. 'There's no phone in this room!' And she walked over to the doorway and stood in it with her arms akimbo.

'I know you knocked me out once, but are you seriously suggesting you're capable of barring me into this room?' he queried.

'You knocked yourself out!'

'Aurora—' he came to stand in front of her '—it so happens I was indisposed that night, not to mention wondering whether I was hallucinating. I'm perfectly fit and in my right mind at the moment.'

She looked up at him. 'Is that a threat, Luke?'

'Of a sort,' he said gravely. 'Apart from having something to prove dating back to our first encounter, I can't think of anything I'd rather be doing—than this.' He picked her up and carried her over to a leather settee.

She wriggled in his arms, more from surprise than anything else, but immediately knew she had as much chance of escaping him as getting out of a steel trap. 'I don't propose,' she told him as he sat down with her in his lap, 'to engage in any undignified, not to mention wasted struggles, Luke Kirwan. And I have to point out that you more than avenged yourself for that first night on the very next occasion we met. I also don't intend to succumb to—more blackmail.'

'No? What do you think I have in mind?'

She pretended to consider. 'Kissing me into some kind of submission?'

He grinned at her. 'What a lovely prospect!'

'But you wouldn't—would you, Luke?'

'I certainly had in mind kissing you. If you regard it as a fate worse than death—' his dark eyes glinted '—all you have to do is tell me what Neil said.'

'Try me,' she suggested, a little glint in her own eyes.

'That is throwing down the gauntlet, Aurora.'

She merely composed her features, closed her eyes and clasped her hands at her waist. But he didn't attempt to kiss her immediately. He played with the top button of her shirt, then slid his fingers beneath it and cupped her shoulder.

She resisted the tremors threatening to run through her with an almost Herculean effort of will. She told herself she must be mad—how had she allowed herself to fall into this kind of game with him? But when he slipped her bra strap aside and stroked her breast, she had to bite her lip to give her will power a bit of a boost. And when her nipples peaked, when she moved convulsively at the aching delight he was wreaking on her body, she had to admit she was unequal to the gauntlet she'd thrown down.

Her lashes flew up and she said raggedly, 'He thought, because you've always had women chasing after you, that the concept of monogamy might be a little foreign to you. Luke—' she sat up '—if you ever tell him I told you or let it interfere with your friendship, I'll never forgive you! He was only theorizing because—' she gestured helplessly '—no one could understand why you and Leonie had parted, I guess. You've never made me feel quite like that before, not even at Beltrees,' she added.

'I'm glad it rated a mention.'

Some colour ran beneath her skin as he adjusted her shirt and kissed her chastely. Then she lay back against his arm, which was propped along the armrest of the settee, and studied him. 'You may not be the devil in disguise I took you for, over my diaries and the police file, but there's still so much I don't know or understand.'

'Such as, not being at all sure you want to go down this road with a man to whom the concept of monogamy may be foreign?' he suggested.

She stared into his dark eyes, her own suddenly wide. 'Is it?'

'Of course not.' He lifted his head and looked across the room.

'So—what did go wrong with Leonie?' she asked.

It was a long moment before he brought his gaze back to her. 'Does this indicate a renewed interest in getting to know me, Aurora?'

She chewed her lip for a moment, then looked at him sideways to a quizzical little glint in his eyes. 'After what has just occurred, it may be a little difficult for you to grasp that I still have reservations about that, Luke,' she replied formally, 'but I do.'

'I quite understand,' he said gravely.

She clicked her teeth shut, then said through them, 'No, you don't!

In fact, that is a prime example of a male chauvinist at his worst—what you just said.'

His lips twitched, but before he could respond she went

on intensely, 'Everyone, and I do mean *everyone*, who knows us has exhibited either intense surprise that I should be putting myself in Leonie's shoes, or intense concern for her. What the hell am I to think?' she asked. 'Apart from the obvious—that we must be as different as chalk from cheese.'

'You are,' he murmured, trailing the tips of his fingers down her cheek.

'How so?' she asked, a little stunned.

He moved restlessly and Aurora sat up and slipped off his lap so she was sitting beside him.

And she said quietly, when he didn't answer, 'Maybe not such a threat to your independence as Leonie was?'

'You're actually a considerable threat to my peace of mind, Aurora,' he replied with a trace of humour. 'But I wasn't intending to do anything about it until—' his lips quirked '—you walked into my trap over the matter of Neil.'

She said crossly, 'I should have known better.' Then a lightening smile lit her eyes, but she sobered suddenly. 'It doesn't get me any further forward, though.'

Luke stood up and walked over to his desk, where he pushed some papers around for a moment, then he turned to her. 'I don't know what went wrong,' he said. 'I had the greatest admiration for Leonie, I thought I was in love with her, I went along with her plans for the future in so much as—in the fullness of time we would get married. I even...' he paused and looked around '...bought this house with an eye to that kind of future. Then I got cold feet. For some reason it was like looking down the barrel of a gun.'

Aurora blinked.

He shrugged. 'Perhaps I should rephrase: there was something niggling away at me that I could only identify as a disinclination to change our—*modus operandi*.'

'So you would have been happy to go on as before but

not marry her?' Aurora asked. 'That's...' She couldn't continue.

He smiled briefly. 'Diabolical? She thought so too and I can't blame her. But that's what happened, Aurora. Perhaps you'd like to make a judgement? Although, believe me, it has nothing to do with requiring more than one wife.'

'Just a disinclination to be tied down by any one woman for the rest of your life,' Aurora said more to herself than him, then she looked at him penetratingly. 'You could be more like Galileo and the scholars of his time than you know. Wedded to your science, kind of thing, so that any woman could only take second place.'

'Only time will tell, I imagine,' he replied, a touch dryly.

'You object to me doing this? You did invite me to make a judgement, Luke. And you did, or do, seem to have a rather personal interest in me despite coming close to getting your fingers burnt with Leonie Murdoch—darn it,' she said. 'Does she know about me?'

'If Mandy Pearson or Julia have anything to do with it, I'm quite sure Leonie does—' his tone was even dryer than earlier '—but I haven't tried to hide you—why would I?'

'There's a difference between being open and above board—and flaunting a new girlfriend,' Aurora said distractedly. 'I keep getting back to how soon—'

'Aurora, the reason it happened so soon is because you precipitated it.'

'I *didn't*, I—'

But he broke in again, 'You certainly came to my notice in a rather dramatic way. You certainly made sure it wouldn't be a forgettable encounter—the first one or the second one.'

She gasped. 'I didn't do any of that deliberately! I was desperately trying to avoid you, Luke Kirwan!'

'I know, I know. What I'm trying to say is—things just happened that way. Whereas you seem to feel it was all part of some devious plot on my part—to what? That's where you lose me.'

'Perhaps you should have waited a while,' she said helplessly at last. 'And now this. Your father's worried about you, Leonie wants a reconciliation—is that true, by the way?'

He looked at her but didn't answer for a long moment. 'Leonie seems to think we've thrown three good years away for no real reason,' he said at last. 'I'm not so sure. Aurora, could we talk about you for a change?'

'Why? I mean…what do you want to know?' She held his dark gaze steadily although she was reeling inwardly from his honesty.

He leant against the edge of the desk, crossed his long legs and folded his arms. 'How experienced are you, Aurora?'

She sat down on the settee rather abruptly and clasped her hands together. Then she said slowly, 'I see what you mean—how my expectations and previous experience of men might colour my dealings with you? I'm much less complicated than you are, Luke.' She smiled briefly. 'Several teenage infatuations, then a serious crush, but he was a married man so—he never even knew about it. That's one reason I was so determined to get my diaries back unread—as you probably know,' she said ruefully.

He put his head to one side. 'I must have missed that bit. I didn't read them in detail, I told you.'

'Enough to know…' She stopped and looked away.

'To sense they were a lifeline—yes. Go on,' he said gently after a moment.

'At twenty-three, I took the plunge. In retrospect, I think I was beginning to feel like the last spinster on the planet because it all seemed to blow up out of the blue. At the time I thought This Was It, in capitals, but six months later— well—' she raised her eyebrows '—maybe I'm not so unlike you after all. I began to feel stifled, he became possessive and jealous—over nothing—and I found myself in the uncomfortable position of asking myself what I had ever seen in him. Strange,' she mused.

He was watching her narrowly. 'Perhaps even frightening?'

'Yes, even frightening. I had to hide behind my father, in fact, to extricate myself.'

He smiled faintly. 'That would have gone against the grain.'

She looked wry. 'I do like to fight my own battles, but I was extremely grateful to have Dad do it for me.'

'And do you think any residue of it has coloured your dealings with men since?'

'Yes, it has,' she said honestly, then glinted him a wicked little look. 'As you know, I have strong feelings about being smitten on first encounters and I'm always on the lookout against...'

'Being led down the garden path,' he finished for her. 'Is that all?'

She said serenely, 'It hasn't turned me off men, as you might have noticed, but it would be fair to say I'm older and quite a bit wiser because of it. There hasn't been anyone serious since then.'

He straightened. 'So, how do *you* see us?'

'Ah. I really don't know. Isn't that why this all came up?'

'How would it be,' he suggested slowly, 'if we carried on as before until some clarification comes to us?'

Aurora took her time in answering as a little voice inside her said, Don't do this, Aurora. He may not be the devil in disguise but there's no guarantee you wouldn't get hurt... When was there any guarantee of that, though? she asked herself and looked around—a mistake, as it turned out. Because she encountered the other side of Luke Kirwan that was starting to fascinate her: his scholarly side.

'You mean, more as friends?' she asked uncertainly. 'If

that's what you mean, we'd have to draw the line at what went on in here earlier,' she added with more spirit.

'As in—I'm not allowed to lay a finger on you?' he queried with a wicked little glint.

'Mae West,' she said tartly, 'was of this opinion—Give a man a free hand and he'll try to put it all over you.'

He came over and sat down beside her laughing quietly. But after a moment, he said, 'We could stop here and now, Aurora, if you really wanted to.'

'Is that…how little it means to you?' she asked with a quiver in her voice that she couldn't hide.

He put an arm around her. 'No. It means a lot to me. You may not realize this but I feel a lot more relaxed, a lot less—' his lips twisted '—*dangerous* since getting to know you.'

She leant back against him. 'Really?'

'Really. But—'

'No, don't go on,' she said. 'I think I understand and I feel quite complimented—I probably shouldn't,' she mused. 'I probably should even feel like a pair of carpet slippers—'

'There is not the slightest comparison,' he drawled. 'You are…like a breath of fresh air in my life.'

'Thanks. I guess I have to say that in between making my life a misery, there have been one or two bright spots—but perhaps we should leave it there, for the time being, Professor.'

'May I humbly be allowed to make one last observation?'

'Only one!'

'It's going to be awfully hard to break the habit of kissing you, Aurora.'

'OK, I'll agree to certain concessions.' Her green eyes were sparkling with amusement.

'You mean you'll dole them out when and where you see fit?'

'Luke, I'll do more. I'll kiss you goodnight and take myself home to bed.' And she suited actions to words.

But it ended quite differently from how she'd planned it. It became, once again, a sensory delight that left her trembling in his arms, more physically moved by a man than she ever remembered.

'She was right,' she said huskily, when she could cope with talking.

He drew his finger around the outline of her mouth, and studied her vivid, heart-shaped little face cupped in the curve of his elbow, and ran his fingers through her tangle of curls. 'Mae West?'

'Mmm…'

'Do you mind?'

'How could I? I didn't actually resist—I didn't resist at all.' But she licked her lips cautiously.

He smiled. 'Do you remember something else you once accused me of? Men will be men?'

She nodded after a moment.

'You were so right. That was very much a "men will be men" reaction. In other words, I couldn't help myself.'

'Because I was being bossy?'

He looked rueful. 'Not only that, because you're gorgeous.'

She hesitated, then slid her hands around his neck. 'So are you. Quite the nicest tiger to cross my path, in fact.' And she drew his head down, kissed him lingeringly, then slipped off the settee. 'Goodnight, sweet prince,' she said softly, but with laughter dancing in her eyes, and added, as he moved, 'No, I let myself in, I can let myself out—you get back to Newton's wife!'

The laughing look she tossed him over her shoulder as she slipped out of the room told him that she was perfectly alive to the fact that Newton's bloody wife, he thought darkly, was going to be extremely cold comfort.

He got up and walked over to the window to find himself suddenly pondering where, exactly, Aurora Templeton fitted into his scheme of things. The view over the lit pool did not vouchsafe any answers. He rubbed his jaw restlessly and contemplated the fact that, above all, he didn't seem to have a scheme of things any more.

As his father had been at pains to point out to him, he'd walked away from one woman into the arms of another—why? Not because Leonie had changed in any way, which was what was making it so hard for her to understand... He moved his shoulders restlessly and recalled that his father had even gone further and confessed that he'd almost got cold feet as the altar had approached, but his marriage to Luke's mother had been as strong and enduring as they came so if it was marriage Luke was afraid of—who was to say Aurora would be a better candidate than Leonie?

He had a point, Luke conceded to himself. Unless Aurora had read him better than any of them and he was wedded to his science?

But if that were so and all else aside, was it fair to keep pursuing Aurora? A girl, he reminded himself, who had fought almost tooth and nail to retrieve her diaries because not only had they been intimate memoirs but her mainstay in a life with no mother and a father gone a lot of the time. A girl who talked to her goldfish... And fair to keep pursuing her for no reason other than that he simply didn't seem able to help himself?

CHAPTER SEVEN

A WEEK later Aurora got to meet Leonie Murdoch.

It happened by accident, literally.

Aurora was at a junction in her car, not far from Luke's house as it happened, on her way home from work for lunch. It was a busy intersection and she was turning across the traffic. She'd been waiting a couple of minutes when the car behind her, also there for a couple of minutes, suddenly accelerated and crashed into the back of her. Fortunately her car was not propelled forward far enough to be thrust into the stream of traffic, but it was enough to give her quite a fright.

So she was fuming when she got out of her car, and more so to see the crumpled back of it with a sapphire-blue BMW nose buried in it.

'Where did you get your licence—out of a cornflake packet?' she yelled at the BMW driver, a tall, elegant woman with red hair.

'Where did you get yours?' the woman responded coldly. 'I could have driven six buses across the road by now!'

'If you were at Le Mans,' Aurora shot back, 'driving a Formula One car, but this is suburban Le Manly! So, what were you planning, you dangerous idiot? To drive over the top of me?'

'Not at all.' The other woman closed her eyes in supreme frustration. 'I'm late for a meeting, I don't have time to sit behind dawdling suburban drivers and I...well, I was concentrating on the traffic, I saw a gap I could have got through and I just put my foot down.' She shrugged her silk-clad shoulders. 'It was one of those unfortunate lapses.'

Aurora studied her. Fabulous skin, gentian-blue eyes,

smooth silky hair expertly cut to curve beneath her chin plus
a dream outfit of a wild rice silk suit, but one very uptight,
superior woman inside it, she decided. And said, 'This ''unfortunate lapse'', which could have been fatal, incidentally,
is going to cost you and your insurance company, lady!
Name and address, please?'

'Naturally,' the woman replied, and reached through the
window of the BMW for her purse. 'I have full insurance
so there'll be no problem at all.'

'Thank you! Your lack of apology has been noted too.'
Aurora accepted a business card but didn't read it. 'Got a
pen?' And when that was produced, a gold one, she wrote
the registration number on the back of it and asked for the
name of the insurance company. 'What happens if my car
is not drivable?' she enquired then.

'For heaven's sake—let's see!'

'Your concern has also been noted, Ms—' Aurora said
acidly, and flipped the card over, only to stiffen.

'Look, I am sorry but this has been a really bad day,'
Leonie Murdoch said, a little wildly, 'and I do need to get
going, but if your car won't go, I could call a tow truck for
you on my mobile phone, and I'd be more than happy to
pay compensation or whatever while it's being fixed. Could
we try it now?' she asked intensely.

Aurora hesitated for a moment and looked up the hill towards her old home, only a couple of blocks away. Then
she studied the card again, but all it had was a business
address on it. She said, at last, in a different manner, 'OK.
You reverse a bit and I'll see what happens.'

As it happened the damage to her car was only superficial
and the BMW had a couple of minor dents. So when they'd
established this, Aurora drew one of her cards out of her
purse and handed it over. But Leonie Murdoch didn't even
glance at it before they parted company.

And whether Leonie, when she'd calmed down, would
associate the name of the girl she'd bumped into with her

ex-lover, Luke Kirwan, Aurora had no way of knowing. But she couldn't shake the strong feeling that Luke might have contributed to Leonie's bad day. Why else would she be so close to his home—unless she lived in Manly herself? But even then—why else would she make a basic driving error of the kind she had unless she really was distraught about something?

'Neil,' Aurora said later that day, 'does Leonie Murdoch live around these parts?'

Neil blinked. 'No, she has a unit at Kangaroo Point, right on the river. Why?'

'Just wondered. How's it going with Mandy?'

Ten minutes later, she had the latest, detailed account of Neil's turbulent affair with Mandy Pearson, and Neil had forgotten about her earlier question.

But that evening, before Aurora could make up her mind whether to tell Luke about what had happened, he called to see her unexpectedly. Her car was parked in the drive because she'd been planning to go out again, and he came in with a quizzical little smile on his lips and an attitude that annoyed her and provoked her into revealing it.

'Did you reverse into something, Aurora?'

'Why would you immediately assume that?' she asked exasperatedly.

He smiled crookedly, taking in her hot pink bike shorts and tiny knit top with narrow pink and green diagonal stripes that tied behind her neck and around her waist. Her hair was gathered back with a bright green plastic grip and her feet were bare. 'Women drivers have a reputation for it.'

'I've never reversed into anything in my life! I got *run* into, as it happens, and by your ex-mistress…' She stopped and looked heavenwards.

Luke had already got his hands around her waist and they tightened unexpectedly. Aurora winced and he said immediately, 'Sorry,' and released her. 'You surprised me,' he added. 'Are you serious?'

She shrugged, 'I wasn't going to tell you, well, I don't think I was but—yes, one Leonie Murdoch, stockbroker, did drive her sapphire BMW into the back of me, although I don't think she had any idea who I was.'

He frowned. 'Why weren't you going to tell me?'

Aurora sat down on the settee and curled her legs up beneath her. 'I'm not sure, Luke.'

He stood quite still for a moment, then came to sit beside her. 'You must have some reason.'

She pulled a cushion into her arms, then raised her eyes to his. 'I could be quite wrong, but she was coming from the direction of your house—it was at that intersection just down the hill. She was in a state otherwise it would never have happened, she said as much herself, so I couldn't help wondering if you were the cause of her distraction.'

'Would this have been around lunch-time today?'

'Yes, Luke.' She hesitated. 'Another attempt to patch things up?'

He sat forward with his hands clasped between his knees. 'She came to see me with something like that on her mind, yes.'

'So it's not all over for her?'

'Aurora—' he turned his head to look at her and his eyes were sombre '—no. But there's not a lot I can do about it.'

'Except, perhaps, never having let it get to the stage it did before you decided to run for cover?'

'I didn't—' he paused '—I don't think this will blight Leonie's life, although it's obviously going to take some adjustment. Would you rather I'd married her and then conceded that it wasn't going to work?'

'How do you know that?'

He glinted her an ironic little look.

Aurora moved restlessly. 'I just...feel, I don't know. Uneasy!'

'What did you think of her?'

'Not much at first,' she said ruefully. 'I called her a dangerous idiot and asked her if she'd got her driver's licence out of a cornflake packet, but I did get a fright and she was quite...snooty. At first. Then...kind of desperate. But extremely beautiful.'

'Beauty can be in the eye of the beholder,' he observed.

'It can,' Aurora agreed tartly, 'but no beholder would quibble with her beauty!'

'I meant, I guess, beauty is not the only thing to take into consideration, nor are brains, which she has plenty of, but there are other things that count.'

'Of course.' She shrugged after a long moment. 'How are you getting on with Newton's wife?'

He blinked. 'He didn't appear to have one...'

'I know. I looked him up. His mother abandoned him to his grandmother until he was about nine, he was always cantankerous by the sound of it and had at least two nervous breakdowns. I can't find any reference to Halley having a wife, or Ptolemy, either. No one's even sure when he was born or died!'

'You have done a bit of research,' he commented. 'But Marie Curie was both a wife and a physicist.'

'Her husband was a physicist too,' she said a shade bleakly.

'Aurora, are you trying to tell me again that I'm wedded to my science? If so, may I point out that I'm in no way comparable to Newton, Galileo, Halley or any of those wifeless wonders? If, indeed, they all were. And there must be many more who weren't.'

Aurora chewed her lip. 'I think, though, I need a bit of breathing space, Luke. But more than that, I think *you* should have some.'

'Breathing space?'

She nodded. 'Three years is a long time to be cast off so...so—' she shrugged '—precipitately.'

'Only a week or so ago, you were of the opinion that we should continue to get to know each other,' he pointed out dryly.

'I hadn't bumped into the woman then, I hadn't seen her—distress,' she said intensely.

'All right.' He stood up. 'How long did you have in mind?'

Aurora stared up at him a little nervously, as, by some mysterious process, the man she'd first laid eyes on beside the piano in her old home came into play. He was nowhere near as formally dressed as on that occasion—cargo pants, a sky-blue polo shirt and trainers—and his sleeked-back hair was falling in his eyes, but all the bored arrogance she'd seen that night was suddenly back.

'Until you—I don't know,' she said helplessly.

'Do you remember walking out on me the other night?' he asked abruptly.

'I...I remember leaving you,' she said. 'Why? Did I do something wrong?'

He looked at her with a tinge of mockery. 'Yes and no. You left me to meditate on a lovely slim body, you left me with the feel of the curves of your breasts and hips beneath my hands, the silk of your skin under my fingers and the delicious taste of you on my lips—what's more you knew it, Aurora.'

'I...perhaps,' she conceded with her eyes wide and her own memories flooding her, 'but....'

'Did you—' he indicated the fish tank '—confide some thoughts on the subject to Annie and Ralph? Your diary perhaps? Or did you fall immediately into a deep and dreamless sleep?'

She got up slowly and walked towards the kitchen, feeling hot and uncomfortable all over.

He trapped her against the two-way counter that served as a breakfast bar on the lounge side. He simply rested his hands on it around her. She looked down at their lean strength on either side of her, then concentrated on a brightly painted china bowl laden with apples, oranges and grapes in a bid to control the wave of desire just the sight of his hands and the remembered feel of them on her breasts did to her. But when that little battle was over, she turned to him. 'If you must know,' she said evenly, 'I felt so good, I did just that.'

He still had her pinned against the counter, and the impact of the rest of him so close to her was even worse than the sight of his hands. His polo shirt moulded the lines of those wide shoulders and the sleek muscles beneath. She knew his chest was hard and powerful but that to nestle against it was unique for her. She knew that she loved to lay her lips on the strong column of his throat and that she sometimes felt as if she were drowning in a sea of lovely sensation when he handled her and drew her into his arms.

His gaze roamed from her serious expression to a little pulse hammering away at the base of her throat. 'Well, I didn't feel so good,' he murmured. 'I tore up three speeches, although there was nothing wrong with them. I would have given anything for a couple of goldfish to…say a few choice words to.'

She swallowed, although there was a flicker of humour in his eyes. 'I'm not sure what this is leading up to, Luke,' she said at last, 'although I apologise for inconveniencing you. It wasn't an intentional…leading-you-down-the-garden-path-then-slamming-the-door-in-your-face kind of thing. It was…' She broke off frustratedly.

'I know it wasn't deliberate. It was the pure *joie de vivre* of Aurora Templeton, it was delightful and it was my problem that it—made life a little difficult for me for a few hours. It also, surely—' he gazed down at her '—demonstrates that you're in command, Aurora.'

She raised her eyebrows. 'Why do I get the feeling that's a real trap for the unwary?'

'How so?'

'Never mind.' She looked distracted for a moment, then frowned. 'Why did you come tonight?'

'To ask you to come to the opening of the astrophysics conference.'

Her lips parted.

'Next weekend,' he went on, 'at the Mirage, on the Gold Coast. It's a dinner dance kind of thing. I thought you might like to spend the weekend down there, in your own room...' he paused as if to emphasize it '...but I guess not.'

'Luke...' she hesitated, then went on a little desperately '...don't you have any understanding of how I feel?'

He straightened and studied her. 'A sense of solidarity with your sex which countermands going to bed on the night in question *without* having to talk to your fish or your diary because you felt so good?' he suggested.

She looked exasperated, then wry, and in the end could only shrug.

He smiled slightly and traced the frown lines on her brow. 'I must tell you I don't think Leonie would reciprocate your sentiments were your positions reversed,' he remarked, however.

'Why not? I mean, that's not *all* it's about, but—' She stopped.

'Because Leonie, my dear Miss Templeton,' he said satirically, 'has no sense of solidarity with her own sex. She's fond of claiming she much prefers the company of men to women. And, in relationship to yourself, for example, she—' He broke off. 'No.'

'*What?*' Aurora insisted. 'She doesn't know me from a bar of soap—until yesterday—do you mean, she knows *about* me?' Aurora blinked several times as her mind spun. 'Through Mandy Pearson?'

'The same,' he agreed tonelessly.

'Who I've met *once*,' Aurora stated through her teeth.

Luke shrugged.

'But I know Neil a lot better,' Aurora went on as if talking to herself. 'OK,' she commanded imperiously, 'spill the beans. Leonie has obviously formed some opinion of me... Let me even guess! That you'd get bored with me in no time at all?'

For some reason he smiled briefly. 'To give her credit, she hadn't met you herself, then, so she was talking second hand.'

'All the same... Would you and Leonie have some mutual friends going to this astrophysics bash on the Coast, by any chance?'

'Aurora, yes, there may well be, but—'

'All the better,' Aurora said, with that certain glitter in her green eyes. 'So thank you for the invitation, Prof, I will come! Mind you...' She stopped and studied him suspiciously. 'Have I been set up?'

'How so?'

'I have to ask myself this—why, when only moments ago I was seriously concerned about Leonie Murdoch, am I now, following some well-planted insinuations from you, all set to give her a run for her money?'

'You can still change your mind.' His eyes laughed at her and he put his fingers beneath her chin and tilted it gently.

'Don't kiss me,' she warned. 'I'm not in the mood.'

'All right.' But he stroked her cheek.

'I don't think you should do that either,' she said after a moment. 'It's counterproductive to my state of extreme annoyance with you.'

He laughed softly. 'What can I do? How about this?' he went on before she could speak. 'In answer to your question, perhaps you've agreed to come because you can never resist a challenge? But, the real reason I asked you to this bash—' he looked rueful '—is because you're a constant source of delight to me.'

'Luke,' she whispered and licked her lips, 'am I really?'

'Believe it, Aurora.' He bent his head and kissed her very lightly.

'But I'll take no further liberties. Goodnight. I'll be in touch.'

They didn't see much of each other until the day before the conference.

Aurora was flat out herself and extremely relieved when the first session of her talk-back programme went smoothly and it got plenty of calls. Her interviewee for this occasion was an author who lived on Lamb Island in Moreton Bay and, between calls, they chatted comfortably about his tastes in music and food, his muse, as he put it, and the preservation of Moreton Bay and its islands, about which he was passionate.

The next morning a large bouquet of flowers arrived for her from Luke. The card said simply, 'Well done, Miss Sparky! Luke.'

'He listened to it,' she marvelled with the card in her hands and the flowers on her desk.

'Luke Kirwan?' Neil responded, having squinted at the card over her shoulder. 'Why wouldn't he?'

'Compared to Ptolemy, Galileo, Copernicus, Halley and Isaac Newton, not to mention stockbroking, what I do for a living is small potatoes, Neil,' she said solemnly. She waved the card. 'And this is a professor who can be—extremely scholarly and forgetful at times.'

'Didn't think that was how you saw him, Aurora,' Neil teased.

'Well, I do now. Although, that isn't all there is to him, I will concede.'

Neil laughed. 'Don't we all know it? Leonie is…in a state of contained frenzy, apparently,' he added more soberly.

'So I gather.' Aurora sighed. 'Does she know it was me she ran into?'

Neil did a double take. 'You didn't tell me that's what happened to your car!'

'I know. I just wondered whether, seeing as she and Mandy are such bosom pals, she'd connected it up.'

'Don't think so. Mandy hasn't mentioned it. Leonie would probably have just handed all the details over to her PA. It has been fixed, hasn't it?'

'Yep. Oh, well…do me a favour, Neil, and don't tell Mandy about it.'

Neil looked a little embarrassed. 'Sorry,' he said. 'I…Mandy, damn it—' he swore '—there are times when I don't know why I put up with Mandy Pearson. She's a born gossip.'

Aurora looked amused. 'But great in bed?' she suggested. Neil looked away and the back of his neck reddened.

'Sorry,' she said, and meant it for she liked Neil, 'strike that! And getting back to these flowers…' she looked at the colourful bouquet '…it's fair to say they've made my day!'

'It's fair to say you've made mine too,' Neil responded. 'The feedback to yesterday's programme has been excellent. I've even had a request from the local paper to interview you complete with pics. Which has put me in a cleft stick.'

'Oh?' Aurora frowned at him.

He drummed his fingers on the desk. 'Only because you sound more mature than you look, Aurora. Which is not to say you look girlish but, well, you are young. Young and gorgeous. No problem with the gorgeous bit, but listeners could be surprised at how young you are.'

'Do I have any say in the matter?'

'Well—yes.' He looked at her warily, however.

Aurora grinned. 'I think I'd like to be known for my golden voice and maturity rather than my image at the moment. Let's see if it wasn't just a flash in the pan first and, anyway, a little bit of mystery goes a long way. It's one of the things I've always found so fascinating about radio, trying to put a face to the voice.'

'There, I told you you were mature, didn't I?' Neil said relievedly.

'Thanks, pal,' she laughed. 'I just wish…' She stopped and when he looked at her enquiringly, shook her head.

But later in the day, when she was home alone, she examined the thought again… I just wish Luke had the same, mature view of me…was what she'd been about to say.

Because it was impossible for her to know exactly how Luke saw her. Youthful and immature? she wondered. A girl with a core of inner loneliness—he'd got that right and he did appear to be holding back to an extent. Why?

Then it dawned on her why she was thinking these thoughts—because there was nothing immature about her feelings for Luke Kirwan. There was, instead, a conviction that she'd fallen in love with him, in fact. Why else would she love his company, and feel so lonely without it? Even when she hadn't been at all sure what kind of man he was, she reminded herself. Why else would she be starting to confide more and more intimately to her diary about him? Why else would she worry about his kids not getting an insight into his own childhood or yearn to understand him completely?

Why else was she still concerned about the way he and Leonie had parted?

All in all, it was enough to make her feel edgy, tense and heartily wishing she hadn't agreed, in a moment of madness, to the astrophysics conference. And it manifested itself when he picked her up for the drive down to the Gold Coast in the yellow Saab.

'I'm really not sure I should be doing this,' she said as she watched him place her bags in the boot.

He paused before closing the boot and looked at her searchingly.

It was four o'clock on a Friday afternoon, a clear, lovely afternoon, and the thought of a weekend with the wonderful beaches of the Gold Coast, not to mention the wonders of the Sheraton and Marina Mirage at her disposal, should have been enough to fill her with a pleasurable sense of antici-pation.

Also, the hood of the Saab was down and Luke was enough to make any woman's mouth water, she thought gloomily, in light grey jeans and a charcoal shirt.

She wore a straight pale jade linen dress with dark green suede shoes. She'd had her hair cut a bit shorter so that it curled to just below shoulder-length and she had a marvell-ous Paisley shawl with splashes of ruby and jade to wind around her. Her make-up was light but she was perfectly groomed and deliciously perfumed.

Luke Kirwan took all this in and smiled inwardly—her expression did not quite fit with this glossy, beautifully pre-sented Aurora Templeton who looked good enough to eat. Her beautiful green eyes were distinctly troubled.

'And here I was thinking you might be looking forward to this little break. Especially in light of all your hard work and very successful week on the airwaves! I know I am. I like your new hairstyle, by the way. Very much.' His dark eyes lingered on her shorter hair.

Aurora blinked.

He closed the boot and took her hand. 'If you don't want to come to the dinner tonight, don't—and I mean that. I can take care of myself.' He looked at her humorously. 'There's no reason why we shouldn't enjoy the weekend, though.'

She chewed her lip as she debated this with herself. 'You know that garment bag you just put into the boot?' she said at last.

'Yes. Why?'

'There's a dress inside there that I would hate to tell you the cost of, but it's the most perfect, peachy dress I think I've ever owned.'

Amusement started to gather again in his eyes. 'Go on.'

'I've never worn it, it's new and its guaranteed to slay every last astrophysicist on the planet, not to mention the

Sheraton Mirage. And last but not least anyone who might be…scouting on behalf of Leonie Murdoch.'

'So?'

She gestured. 'I just don't think I'd have the willpower, once I got there, not to don that dress and…see what happens,' she said sadly. 'In other words, I need to make a decision here and now about whether to come or not.'

'It's too late,' he said, and opened her door, still holding her hand.

'No, Luke, it's not! I—'

But he ignored her and picked her up to sit her on the bonnet of the Saab.

'Luke,' she protested, 'this is becoming a habit and, anyway, you should ask first before you manhandle me.'

'Manhandle you?' His eyes were dark and wicked.

'You know what I mean—'

'No.'

Aurora sighed. 'I'm not feeling playful, Professor,' she warned severely.

'Who said I was?' He folded his arms and contemplated her troubled expression. 'You shouldn't have mentioned the dress,' he added gravely.

Her lips parted and she narrowed her green eyes. 'Why…not?'

'I won't be able to rest until I see you in it. Does it have a Spanish flavour, by any chance?'

'No-o,' she said slowly.

'Ah. I only ask because we know all too well what happened with that outfit. Worse, this one, do you think? I just hope I'm able to concentrate on my speech, if that's the case, because—'

'Stop,' she said, trying not to laugh.

'Not until you say you'll come, Aurora.' He looked around innocently.

She did the same and saw her neighbour's lace kitchen curtain suddenly twitch closed. 'You…you're impossible!'

'I know,' he agreed. 'Especially once I've got the bit between my teeth, there's just no stopping me. I checked the
weather forecast, incidentally. It's going to be a beautiful
weekend on the beach. Did you pack any sensational, guar-
anteed-to-slay-all-the-astrophysicists-on-the-Coast bikinis,
by any chance?'

'No. I need a new one. I thought I might buy one down
there—oh, what the hell? Let's go, Luke.' She looked long-
suffering.

'I need a bit more enthusiasm than that, I think,' he tem-
porised.

'What you really need is not to be big enough to get your
own way so frequently,' she returned bitterly. 'How did
Leonie do it?'

'Stop me from getting my own way?'

'Yes!'

'She—deliberately—used certain feminine wiles that you
probably would not approve of, Aurora,' he drawled.

Her lips parted and she started to colour. 'You mean...do
you mean sex?'

'They generally go together, feminine wiles and sex.'

'Not—well...' Several expressions chased through her
eyes, which he observed with a sense of inward laughter as
he waited for what was to come, knowing that, whatever it
was, it would surprise him.

It did.

Aurora slid off the bonnet unaided. 'As a matter of fact,
I'm dying to go down to the Coast with you, Luke,' she
said, and slipped neatly into the passenger seat.

He had to bend almost double to see her. 'I'm delighted,
Aurora,' he said wryly. 'But what changed your mind?'

'Any girl who operates that way deserves what's coming
to her, I guess,' she said serenely. 'I just hope you weren't
concocting that because it's put me on my mettle, you see!'

'I do see and there's something irresistible about it, I must
tell you.'

'Will you get in and drive this car down to the Coast?' she recommended tartly. 'I've also been known to change my mind.'

He laughed and closed her door. 'Yes, ma'am!'

The opening dinner was scheduled for eight o'clock.

That gave them plenty of time after they arrived for a lovely long walk down the beach, something they did in complete accord. Although Manly was a seaside suburb, the protected waters of Moreton Bay lapped its shores, whereas the surf beaches of the Gold Coast faced the might of the Pacific Ocean.

The air was salty as the surf pounded the beach, the sky was huge and it was all quite invigorating.

'Right,' Aurora commented as they wended their way through the beach gate, lovely gardens and around the huge pools of the Mirage resort, 'that's blown away any cobwebs and put me in the mood for the big production. Would you care to call for me at about a quarter to eight, Professor?'

'Whatever you say, Aurora.'

She cast him a suspicious look from beneath her lashes.

'What have I done now?' he enquired as they strolled along side by side.

'That meek and mild air never deceives me, Luke,' she replied. 'It generally means you're laughing at me.'

'Why would I do that?' he countered, stopping and looking down at her.

She put her head on one side. 'Because I'm a novelty?'

'You certainly are.'

She wrinkled her nose. 'Now I feel as if I should reside in a funfair.'

'Not at all—but you said it. There is another scenario that comes to mind rather than a funfair,' he added before she could respond. 'I'm sure I'd enjoy being involved in all aspects of this big production.'

Aurora opened her mouth, then closed it a little uncertainly.

'Yes,' he murmured, surveying her comprehensively in the shorts and knit top she'd donned for their walk, from her riotous hair to her bare toes. 'Were we together, we could shower together, then indulge in a glass of champagne together as we relaxed for a little while and—after that, I could help you to dress. Those kind of to-die-for dresses often need a man's hand to zip you into them and I'm quite sure I'd love to be the one to do it.'

She stared up into his eyes, then blinked a couple of times at the images running through her mind—of herself dressing in front of this man, of his hands on her bare skin, of them showering together. And it took quite an effort to say, although huskily, 'Not today, Luke.'

A shadow of a smile touched his mouth. 'Maybe not. But think about it if you're tempted to feel like a sideshow, not to mention the error of my ways. I know I will be...'

Her room had an ocean view, was beautifully appointed with wooden shutters at the windows and was spacious.

So spacious, she was able to roam around it, thinking deeply for quite a few minutes without feeling caged in. Strange sentiments, she mused. Did it mean he still thought of her as the error of his ways? Did she...? Why had she got this feeling things had come to some kind of a pass between them?

Because of the imminent confrontation with so many people who could compare her with Leonie Murdoch, she answered herself dryly.

Because she was deeply unsure in her heart of hearts of what she was doing here, and what the future held for her in relation to Luke Kirwan, she added to herself, and sat down rather suddenly on the bed, to wonder intensely—why now?

Yet it wasn't such a poser, she discovered. She knew,

even if he did not, that she was in love with him. She knew instinctively and always had that there were two sides to him, just as she knew she was engaging the lighter side of that hawk-amongst-the-sparrows persona she'd seen in him—lovely though it was for her. How long it would appeal to him was another matter, though.

She sighed, then shook out her hair and went to have a shower. It was while the water was streaming down her body that she decided she wouldn't be making any statement tonight, to anyone. Yes, she'd be there, but it would be very restrained Aurora Australis, she thought, and closed her eyes...

An hour later she was almost ready.

All that remained was to step into her dress. Her hair and make-up were perfect—the new length was lighter and easier to handle besides being essentially chic, she felt. Her lashes were carefully darkened so that her eyes were even more stunning, her lips were a glossy berry-red with her nails painted to match, and her underwear was flesh-coloured; briefs, suspender belt and the sheerest of nylons. And her skin gleamed peachy pale and satiny, anointed with a light body lotion that matched her perfume.

She picked her dress up from the bed and stepped into it. As she reached for the zip, she slid her feet into glorious high strappy sandals.

Five minutes later, after a repeated knock at her door, she went to answer it with sheer frustration written all over her face.

Despite this, Luke Kirwan in a black tuxedo with a blinding white pleated shirt-front, a hand-tied tie and silver-rimmed onyx buttons down the front of his shirt, with his hair brushed back sleekly, caused her to catch her breath.

'Aurora,' he said, skimming a dark, quizzical gaze up and down her, 'you're right, that dress is something else—but what's the matter?'

The dress was made of a very fine raspberry velvet, cut low at the back with the front gathered at the throat to a narrow neck band. From the hips, matching raspberry silk georgette was gathered to form a billowing skirt dotted with delicate gold roses. She loved the sleek, fitted feel of the bodice that also exposed her shoulders and back, then the extravagance of the skirt.

But as she held it up in front of her, she said exasperatedly, 'What's wrong? You've jinxed me once again, Luke! I can't do up the neck band!'

'Hey—' he smiled crookedly and put a fingertip on the point of her chin '—no need to get into a state. I have some experience in these matters, as I mentioned.'

She let the dress go, then grabbed the front just before it fell down to reveal her bra-less breasts. 'That's another thing I object to—how very experienced you are, Luke! I...I...' She couldn't go on as no suitable explanation came to mind, then one did and she added, 'I feel as if I'm standing in a long *line* of women you've...either dressed or undressed!'

'Aurora—' he was suddenly quite sober '—not a long line, but there have been some. Nor was I intimating anything of the kind—it's just...' he shrugged '...one of those humorous things. Turn around.'

She eyed him mutinously.

'Look,' he drawled, 'surely you would feel more comfortable continuing this debate fully dressed rather than having to clutch at yourself to remain decent—if that's how you see it? I wouldn't see it as indecent, personally, but it's up to you.'

She nearly bit her tongue as she snapped her teeth closed and swung on her heel.

He said nothing more, not even when she trembled at the feel of his cool fingers on the back of her neck. And finally the little hooks and eyes yielded to his ministrations and she was done up.

'Thank you,' she said expressionlessly over her shoulder.

He merely nodded and walked away from her to the mini-bar where he drew a half-bottle of champagne from the fridge and dislodged the foil cap. He poured two glasses and brought them over to where she was still standing.

'Take a deep breath, Aurora.'

'Why?' She reached out a hand for the glass but he withheld it from her.

'Just do it,' he ordered. 'Square your shoulders and tilt your chin.'

She hesitated, then did it all.

'Perfect,' he said softly. 'Small but regal. It is a peach of a dress, one of the nicest I've ever seen—and positively exquisite down to your fingertips. There.' He put the glass into her hand. 'Now you can tell me to go to hell if you want to.'

'Luke...' she clutched the glass, then took a sudden sip, and started to smile '...how could I after that? Thank you.'

He smiled back at her, then pushed a hand into the pocket of his trousers and studied her narrowly. 'You could tell me if it was only the dress you were so worked up about?'

'I...what else could it have been? It's lovely here.' She moved at last and went to the windows, but night had claimed the view, although she stared out at it for a moment before turning back to him.

'Deep and philosophical thoughts on the nature of life and love?' he suggested.

Her lashes fluttered, giving her away, but she wasn't ready to admit anything in the spoken word. 'Not an appropriate time to be having those, I—'

'I was,' he interrupted.

Her lips parted. 'You were?' she said barely audibly, with surprise written large in her expression. 'But you've been so...so playful today.'

He smiled unamusedly. 'All the same, it's finally come home to me that perhaps I'm not being—quite fair to you.'

'In what way?'

'I'm actually starting to feel—less playful and more and more deeply attracted to you, Aurora. But I have no idea where it might lead.'

She swallowed a lump in her throat and sipped some champagne. 'At least that's honest. I might have preferred it if you'd told me this before you brought me down here, but at least it's honest. Come to that, I don't suppose you've ever been any different, and it's something I guess I've always known…'

She paused as he moved abruptly, then she said with a wry little gesture, 'I know you think I'm a bit of a babe in the woods, but I'm not stupid and—I still don't understand—why tell me this now?' She stared at him with a frown of incomprehension.

He stared down at his glass for a long moment and the lines of his face were suddenly harsh. Then he looked up at her. 'Because it's getting harder and harder not to seduce you, Aurora.'

CHAPTER EIGHT

'WHAT makes you think I'd be so easy to seduce?'

Luke studied Aurora pointedly. From her glamorous new hairstyle to the smooth, creamy skin of her shoulders, the curves of her breasts beneath the raspberry velvet, the slim line of her figure to her toes. Then his gaze came back to rest on her vivid little face and wide green eyes with their fringe of exotic lashes. Lastly, it moved to her glossy, berry-red lips.

Aurora stirred, unable to be unmoved by this silent catalogue of what he found attractive about her. Unable to stem the rising tide of desire within—a response to his dark gaze on her, almost as if his hands were on her as well. And the knowledge that it was getting harder and harder for her not to want to be seduced with every fibre of her being.

She swallowed and moved a couple of restless steps to put her glass down on a table. Then she said abruptly, 'That still doesn't mean to say I would...succumb, Luke.'

Something flickered in his eyes—admiration, perhaps, because she'd chosen not to ignore what had flowed between them. 'No. But it mightn't stop me trying.' He shrugged. 'And despite the playfulness of today, I can see that it's beginning to loom large for you—what road we're going down. Also,' he added, looking around, 'these kind of holiday surroundings are notorious for causing people to let down their guards, which is why I felt—honour-bound, I guess, to bring it up now.'

'But none of this occurred to you before we got here?' she asked huskily.

'The only thing...' he paused '...no, not quite—but it

137

occurred to me before we got here how much I would enjoy spending this weekend with you, Aurora.'

'Then how about letting me be the guardian of your morals for this weekend, Professor?' she suggested. 'I always knew I might be the error of your ways.' She gestured with both hands. 'Nothing's changed.'

'Aurora,' he said dryly, 'I know you can never resist a challenge, but I have to point out that I gave my…morals, for want of a better word…into your keeping quite a few weeks ago.'

She looked at him expressionlessly for a long moment, then, 'Luke, do you want me to go or stay?'

'It's not as simple as that,' he replied impatiently.

'Yes, it is. You worry about yourself and allow me to do the same. But I'm not ready to sleep with you, if that's what you're asking me obliquely. So, if you can't stand the heat, you'd better get out of the kitchen.'

'You…' he started to say with supreme frustration, then began to laugh.

Aurora waited with as much cool as she could muster.

'I wasn't asking you that obliquely,' he said at last, still looking amused. 'I was merely trying to point out that things could get to a mutual stage, a point of no return because we *both* might find we can't help ourselves. But—'

'I shouldn't rely on becoming Mrs Newton at the other end of it? Who says I want to?' she answered, and wondered if a bolt of lightning might strike her down there and then.

It didn't, but her comment did sober Luke Kirwan up. 'Very well, Miss Templeton,' he said at last, after studying her intently. 'Shall we go?'

'One last thing, Luke. I'm not throwing down any gauntlets. Don't *you* suddenly start taking this up as a challenge.'

He came towards her and tilted her chin as he was so often wont to do. 'Isn't that a little like the kettle calling the pot black, Aurora?'

'No.' Her lips quivered in anticipation of one of his light, chaste kisses but it didn't come.

'Then I shall try to be on my best behaviour. Dresses like this one make it difficult, however.' He traced the bare skin of her shoulder.

She shivered but forced herself to rally. 'Point taken—I'll opt for sackcloth and tents from tomorrow, but there's nothing to be done about tonight.'

'Not a thing,' he responded gravely, and did kiss her briefly this time before presenting her his arm formally.

'Luke…' She stopped uncertainly.

He raised an eyebrow and all the dangers signals she'd ever seen in him were back.

So, despite many inward qualms, she straightened her shoulders and tilted her chin again. 'Nothing.' She put her arm through his.

He smiled, but it did nothing to reassure her because it was just about the most enigmatic smile she'd ever seen.

The ballroom at the Mirage was dimly lit and decorated in silver and gold; stars, moons and planets were suspended from a midnight-blue ceiling by invisible thread. It was like stepping into the night sky. In fact Aurora was so enchanted, she forgot to be annoyed with or intimidated by Luke for a while.

It was also a large gathering, at least five hundred guests, she surmised, which had to make it easier to be anonymous. But there was another surprise waiting for Aurora on what turned out to be a never-to-be-forgotten night. She should have expected it. There was ample evidence that Luke was very much sought out by delegates to this conference even before he made his speech.

That he alone amongst the speakers would get a standing ovation had not occurred to her, although just to see him on the dais looking so tall and distinguished wreaked a bit of havoc with her already uncertain peace of mind. But he was also a consummate speaker, entirely at ease, and she suddenly found herself feeling some sympathy for the army of groupies he had to guard against.

It was one of the cleverest speeches she'd ever heard. He got his audience in stitches as, throughout a blending of the old and new in astrophysics, he wove in Isaac Newton's imaginary and long-suffering wife in the form of plaintive asides addressed to ''Mr Newton'', as she called him, about all the trials and tribulations of living with a scientist—and her sad conclusion was that it was the apple falling on his head that had done it because he'd never been the same since.

'That was brilliant!' she said, looking at him a little wonderingly, when he finally got back to her side. 'I didn't know.'

He stared into her eyes and she could see devilry in his quite clearly. 'You suggested it.'

'But I didn't think you were going to go with it and— what I meant was—I didn't know you were so good at that kind of thing.'

'Could I have redeemed myself somewhat, Aurora?' he enquired with his lips twisting.

She laughed a bit dazedly.

'For example,' he went on, 'now all that is out of the way as well as dinner, might you consent to dancing with me?'

'I...' she looked around to see that quite a few couples had drifted onto the floor '...yes, thank you. That would— probably be nice.'

He grinned wickedly and said no more. But he gathered her slim body in its beautiful red dress close to him and, with the aid of the music, wove another kind of magic around her. The sheer magnetism and sensuality of being in his arms was impossible to resist... She even thought once, with an inward little shiver, that she was trapped and held spellbound by this man, and nothing seemed to have the power to change the fact that he was the dazzling centre of her universe.

They sat down after about half an hour and she was introduced to a number of intellectuals and academics, and formed the impression that they played as well as any other kind of people. There were also plenty of wives in evidence, although many of them laughingly commented to Luke that he'd got it so right—scientists were sheer hell to live with!

Causing Aurora to shiver again and cast a swift glance at Luke by her side. He was listening to a grey-haired, venerable-looking man who was inviting him to America to do a lecture series. Despite sounding grateful for the invitation, his reply was noncommittal...

'Don't you want to go to America?' she asked as they drifted back onto the floor.

'I love America but I'm not into lecture tours.'

'You should be—you could make a fortune, I'm sure.'

He looked down at her with clear laughter in his eyes.

'You don't need another fortune—silly me,' she murmured.

'It's not that. There are times when disseminating information goes against the grain with me.'

She blinked. 'Why?'

'Well, of course one needs universities and their research facilities and it wouldn't be fair not to pass on knowledge, but...' he paused, then went on a little dryly '...there are times when I'd like to go and live in a mud hut on the Amazon and just keep it all to myself.'

'That's not,' Aurora said bemusedly, 'the image you projected tonight, Luke.'

'I only let that guy out once or twice a year. It's not the real me.' He looked down at her in an oddly sombre way. 'And, since this has been topical between us lately, Leonie would die rather than live in a mud hut.'

She missed a step and he gathered her close, then stopped dancing abruptly as he stared over her shoulder. Aurora turned after a moment, and there was Leonie Murdoch behind her on the arm of a man who looked distinctly embarrassed.

But Leonie herself looked stunning in a strapless sequined black dress that clung to every inch of her superb figure. Her skin was lightly tanned, her hair was intricately put up, she wore diamonds in her ears and on her wrist, and her whole presence was enough to make most men, as they danced by, take a second, lingering look.

But it was the contact, almost like an electric current, between her and Luke as they exchanged glances that struck Aurora like a blow to the heart, and convinced her that, whatever there was between Luke and his ex-mistress, it wasn't over...

Then Leonie switched her gentian gaze to Aurora, and she blinked as recognition came to her. 'So,' she drawled, 'you're not only the girl who's stepped into my shoes but the girl I ran into!'

'I am the girl you ran into,' Aurora agreed, 'but I haven't stepped into anyone's shoes yet.'

The faintest smile played over Leonie Murdoch's exquisite mouth, causing Aurora to feel, amongst other things, quite insignificant. Then the other girl looked back at Luke and there was so much quizzical humour in her eyes, from feeling insignificant Aurora went to feeling like scratching Leonie's beautiful eyes out...

She was saved by the bell—in a manner of speaking. The band stopped playing and announced a short break. Aurora turned to Luke and said beneath her breath, 'Get me out of here!'

He did.

Without asking, he led her not to her room but through the gardens to the beach, then stopped frustratedly and looked down at her sandals.

'I can take them off.' She did so and put them under the

hedge. 'Don't worry about my stockings. Did you *know* she was going to be here tonight?'

'No, of course not. That was her brother she was with, incidentally. He's a lecturer in my department, that's how we met in the first place—are you all right?'

'Absolutely on top of the world—what do you *think*?' Aurora said intensely. 'I would never have come if I'd known.'

'Aurora, I did not know,' he said harshly. 'The last person I would have expected her to come with was her brother.'

'I take your point, but, if she had to fall back on her brother, how desperate must she be to get you back, Luke?'

He turned away and stared out to sea.

Aurora closed her eyes and counted to ten. Then she took his hand and they started to walk, skirting the tracery left by the tide, Aurora holding her skirt up with one hand. The moon, a full one, was heading for the western horizon behind them, but its glow was giving an other-worldly look to the beach and the surf, bright yet seen through a glass darkly.

She mentioned it.

He agreed and added, 'It's the autumn equinox tonight—the days start to get shorter, the nights get longer.'

They walked for a while in silence, then she said, 'Tell me about a mud hut on the Amazon.'

He considered, then sighed suddenly. 'That's a bit extreme, but there's a call, there always has been to places like Patagonia, the Russian steppes, the Antarctic, the Dead Sea and, closer to home, the Simpson Desert, et cetera. A call to slough off...everything for a couple of months and just do my own thing. I always assumed, with Leonie, that when the call came she'd be content to stay here and do her own thing.'

'She wouldn't have been?'

'At first it was no problem but, funnily enough, it was the closest to home call that began to create problems. This may surprise you but for a while now I've been thinking of going back to Beltrees.'

Aurora stopped walking in supreme surprise. 'To...to grow wool?'

'No. To potter for a while. Years ago I came across some evidence that suggested a meteor strike on the property. I don't know if you remember, but some months ago something fell out of the heavens?'

Aurora blinked, then nodded. 'Something about the size of a golf ball that left a huge dent in the earth?'

'Yes.' He looked amused. 'Anyway, it reactivated my interest in Beltrees from that point of view, but I was too tied up at the time to be able to do anything about it. And Leonie suggested that, since I'd always have Beltrees and any trace of meteor activity wasn't going to go away, perhaps we could fit it around a more suitable time for both of us.'

'That seems a fairly reasonable suggestion.'

'I know. I kept telling myself it was entirely sensible, in fact, but...' He stopped and sighed.

'That's when you started to feel you were looking down the barrel of a gun?' Aurora suggested.

'In hindsight, again,' he said dryly, 'yes. And, selfish as it sounds, that's when a lurking sense of... I don't want to have to fit in with anyone else's timetable'' started to rise to the surface.'

'This is not, though,' she said cautiously, 'a problem with Leonie so much as a problem with yourself.'

He stopped walking and looked down at her sardonically. 'You're determined to side with Leonie for reasons that escape me.'

'That's because you're not a woman,' she replied with a trace of her own irony. 'And I'm not saying I side with her, but that doesn't mean to say that I can't see the problem loud and clear—you don't really want a wife.'

He swore beneath his breath. 'I don't want a wife who is going to resent having to give up her career for me or feel slighted when I go away or make me feel unreasonable when I know damn well I *am* being unreasonable but I can't…help it. The other thing is, Leonie thought she had a tame professor in tow, and that life would be…like this.' He looked around. 'Plenty of social intercourse—'

'She must be very naïve, which I doubt,' Aurora broke in to observe, 'if she ever thought you were "tame".'

He shrugged. 'I meant from the point of view that, while she tried to be all sweet reason at times, she thought she was humouring me. She didn't really understand…what drives me and always will.' He made a frustrated gesture. 'But I'm extremely regretful on her behalf that it took me so long to work it all out.'

They were standing facing each other on that long silvery strip of sand with the lights of Surfers Paradise pricking the dark sky and the waves beside them showing fascinating glimpses of phosphorus glowing as they curled over.

He could probably explain that phenomenon to me, Aurora thought as she stared past him out to sea, and I'd love him to do so. Why don't I just ignore all the rest of it, all the tortured complexities of his relationship with Leonie, all the things that would make any relationship with a woman difficult for him and…deadly for her if she wanted to make it permanent?

Because I can't guarantee I could stand it any better than Leonie Murdoch, she thought with chilling clarity. I can't guarantee that at all…

'Luke—' she moved her hand in his '—let's go back. I'm getting tired of holding my skirt up, for one thing!'

He looked down at her intently, then shrugged. But at the beach gate there was a bench and she sat down on it with her sandals in her hand. He stood in front of her with his hands shoved into his pockets, tall and dark.

'I'm going home first thing tomorrow morning, Luke,' she said quietly, gazing up at him and hoping desperately she was able to contain the tears that were threatening. 'Please don't say anything to try to make me change my mind. It's not Leonie, it's me. You were right when you said earlier that things could get out of hand down here—actually, I think we've got to a stage where things could get out of hand anywhere. But I'm not ready to take that step. I took it once with disastrous consequences, well—' she gestured and her sandals fell onto the sand '—that's how it seemed at the time, anyway.'

He bent down to pick them up and put them on the bench beside her. 'Are you suggesting I'd go all jealous and possessive on you?'

'No.' A stray tear did fall as she smiled at the irony of that, and licked it from her lip. 'The opposite, if anything, but just as bad, I guess—*I* might.'

'Aurora—'

'Luke—' she leant forward and rested her head on his waist '—I'd hate it if you became the error of *my* ways, but that's what it could easily become because I know very well I could be making a mistake. I like you too much for that and I think, in your heart of hearts, you might feel the same.'

He said nothing for a long time, although he started to stroke her hair. 'If,' he said at last, 'I agree with you, it's only because…I would hate to hurt you, Aurora.'

'I know,' she said huskily. 'And I thank you. Look…' she tilted her head to see his eyes '…this is difficult, but I'm sure it's for the best for both of us. Will you let me just get myself home tomorrow? They could arrange a car for me.'

His fingers slid down the curve of her cheek. 'If it gets too difficult, I—'

'No, Luke.' She stood up with her throat working but no tears in her eyes now. 'I know what I'm doing and there's no point in dragging it out. I'll be fine.' Her lips curved into the faintest smile. 'It all started with my diaries; that's where it will end.'

'And when you're an old lady with grandchildren at your

feet, you might read them over and smile a sort of smile no one will understand?' he suggested roughly.

'Maybe—but I'll still know I did the right thing. Goodbye…'

He said her name and caught her wrist. But she kissed his fingers then looked up at him steadily. And the pressure on her wrist relaxed gradually until he released her. 'Goodbye,' he said, with an effort. 'Don't go invading people's houses or doing anything crazy.'

'I won't,' she promised. 'You look after yourself too.' She picked up her sandals and slipped away from him through the gate.

He stared after her until all he could see were the little gold roses of her skirt and the pale skin of her back picking up the reflected glow of the flares that lit the path, then nothing. And he turned towards the sea and told himself it *was* for the best. He'd been a fool to let it get this far anyway; she'd be much better off without him…

So why did he have the feeling he'd let something rare and more valuable than rubies and pearls slip through his fingers like an exquisite butterfly?

CHAPTER NINE

ABOUT two months later Jack Barnard was having dinner with Luke Kirwan at the house on the hill.

Summer had slid into a so far mild winter and they were able to eat outside on the terrace with the night view spread beneath their feet. Chinese take-away was what they were indulging in, with a fine bottle of chardonnay. Jack had brought the wine in anticipation of one of Miss Hillier's delicious concoctions that she often left for Luke to warm up; Luke had rung up for the food after explaining that Miss Hillier was on holiday for a week.

'How on earth will you cope?' Jack asked of his friend. 'I may not like the woman, but in most respects she's a gem. Fancy finding a secretary who also cooks!'

Luke looked at him wryly. 'I can cook some basics when I feel like it, Jack. I'm not completely useless.'

'Never said you were.' Jack partook of the delicious sweet and sour pork. 'But you must admit she runs things down to the smallest detail. Is that why you're off to Beltrees for a while?'

Luke lifted his glass and studied the golden green contents. 'Not necessarily. Barry and Julia are off overseas for a couple of months and my father needs a hand. I also want to search for meteorite fragments.'

'This wouldn't have anything to do with the fact that Leonie has been seen out and about with a new man?' Jack enquired.

Luke grimaced. 'Has she? I didn't know.'

'Question answered,' Jack murmured. 'Are you at all interested?'

148

'I'm quite sure you're going to tell me whether I am or not.' Luke regarded his friend quizzically.

'A media magnate, twice divorced but very wealthy. Something of a playboy, I gather. Of course we're all wondering whether it's designed to make you jealous, but you don't seem to be in circulation much these days—by the way, I believe you've put this house on the market?'

Luke looked around. 'Yes,' he said pensively.

'Why? Because of Leonie?'

'Not because of Leonie. I've never felt the same about it since I...suffered a home invasion one night.'

Jack blinked through his glasses. 'You never told me that!'

'Probably because I came out of it looking a bit of a fool. I left the front door open, not that sh—'. He stopped. 'And I actually got knocked out briefly in the encounter. Nothing was stolen, though.'

'Well, I don't blame you in that case, but...' Jack paused '...it's a funny thing—the bloke you bought it from has gone missing. I remembered the name because I did the conveyancing and I don't think there'd be too many Ambrose Templetons around—what's the matter?'

'Gone missing how?'

'Um...he was sailing round the world single-handed but he seems to have disappeared somewhere between the Cook Islands and Tahiti. I heard it on the news this morning— Luke, I didn't think you ever met him, but you look quite strange!'

'I'm sorry about this, Jack, but I have to go out... Please finish your dinner, though, and if you wouldn't mind locking up for me when you leave—there's a Yale on the front door now, you just have to pull it closed.'

'Well—' Jack half rose as Luke Kirwan was about to step inside '—I...I...'

'I'll call you, Jack!' He disappeared. Two minutes later the Saab, parked in the driveway, roared to life.

Jack sat back and sipped his wine dazedly. 'He hasn't been the same since he bought this damn house,' he commented to himself. 'I'd love to know what the hell is going on!'

Aurora was at home alone, huddled on her settee, staring at her fish.

She heard the knock and her heart started to race—news, surely! But in her haste to get to the door she tripped on the edge of a rug, and she must have left the door unlocked anyway because it opened before she got there—and Luke was standing in her hall.

She stared at him wordlessly as if he were an apparition, then, when he came to her and put his arms around her, all her pent-up emotion burst the banks she'd so rigidly erected and she collapsed against him with her eyes streaming and sobs shaking her.

Five minutes later she was sitting on his lap on the settee and taking sips of brandy from the glass he held for her. Nor did he allow her to speak until she'd finished the small tot and stopped shuddering.

He put the glass on the elephant table and eased her more comfortably against him. 'Tell me what happened?'

She sighed desolately. 'No one knows. He'd arranged a regular sked—radio schedule with an HF station in New Zealand that was also to be relayed here to Manly, and he called me once a week on his satellite phone. But the call is five days overdue now and no one's been able to raise him by radio.'

'That doesn't mean—'

'I know,' she broke in intensely, 'I know it all. It could just be battery problems; radios, phones, they all need some kind of power and he did have a hiccup with the phone about a month ago. But he does have a solar pack on board... He also has an EPIRB, an emergency position indicating radio beacon, that is...'

'I know how they work,' Luke said quietly. 'So no signal's been picked up?'

'No. Which either means he hasn't had to use it or...' she swallowed '...he went down before he could use it. There are so many things...whales, containers, storms.' She stopped helplessly.

'Has a search been mounted?'

'Yes,' she whispered. 'I wanted to go but they said wait a while. They don't really know where to start.'

'I'm not into boats myself, but Barry and Julia are, as you know, and one of their favourite catch cries is when one thing goes wrong you can bet your bottom dollar it won't be the only one, so it could well be batteries, or loose wires in a radio and another hiccup with the phone.'

Aurora smiled shakily. 'I've worked at the Coastguard long enough not to be amazed at all the things that can go wrong on boats, but this is different. It's not only my father—it's the South Pacific out there, not Moreton Bay.'

'Of course,' he said quietly and frowned. 'Why are you here on your own?'

'I...I wanted to be,' she whispered.

'Or because there's no one close enough to care?' he suggested.

She shook her head. 'It's not that. I've got friends, colleagues, mates at the Coastguard, they've all been so wonderful, but...' She stopped and sighed. 'I just wanted to be alone.'

He moved, but her eyes widened and her hands clenched. Damp tendrils of hair were clinging to her face from the storm of tears and he studied that little face, thinking it seemed to have fined down so her green eyes were even more stunning with their wet lashes sticking together in clumps. She wore a lightweight track suit the colour of lemon grass with green sand shoes but he could feel the fine, delicate lines of her body beneath it. Her heavy hair had grown again and was tied back loosely.

'I…was going to suggest,' he said slowly, 'that I made us some of your Arusha coffee—have you eaten lately?'

'No, but coffee would be lovely.'

'Have you got any bread and cheese?'

'Um—yes but—'

'Do you like toasted cheese?' he interrupted.

'Luke—' she paused '—can you make toasted cheese?'

'I don't know why everyone assumes I'm quite useless,' he remarked bitterly. 'I make the best toasted cheese this side of the black stump!'

'Who else has been trying to make you feel useless?' she queried with a smile trembling on her lips.

'My friend Jack Barnard,' he explained. 'That's how I heard about your father. Jack heard it on the radio and re-membered the name because he did the conveyancing on the house. In fact Jack, for all I know, is still sitting on the terrace finishing off the Chinese dinner.'

'Thank you for rushing over,' she said softly. 'And, yes, I do like toasted cheese.'

Half an hour later, she'd finished her toasted cheese and was inhaling the delicious aroma of the Arusha coffee. Luke had pulled up an armchair to the coffee-table and was sitting opposite her.

'Tell me about your experiences of Arusha?' he invited. 'You said you'd been there.'

Aurora laid her head back. 'Ah, Arusha. Yes, my father was captaining a freighter that took a few passengers. There was stuff to be unloaded at Dar-es-Salaam and when some-thing went wrong with the freezers on board we had about a week to kill so we hired a Land Rover and drove up.' She smiled. 'I'll never forget the mad traffic or the state of the roads in Dar. Then this good, long straight highway up coun-try and as we got closer to Moshe we started to look for Kilimanjaro.' She stopped and her eyes were far away.

'It's quite a sight, when it reveals itself,' he commented.

'I couldn't believe it. We were looking too low, then I just happened to look up and there was this snow-clad peak rising out of a blue horizon way up in the sky. I'll never forget it.' She looked across at Luke. 'And Arusha,' she said affectionately. 'We stayed at this lovely place called Mountain Village, it's in the middle of a coffee plantation on Lake Duluti—you could see Kili from there too, as well as Mount Meru. It looked really mysterious. And we went to Ngorongoro, the Serengeti—I did a balloon safari over the Serengeti at dawn.'

'So did I. And I stayed at Mountain Village, saw the lions of Ngorongoro, the wildebeest migration across the plains of the Serengeti to the Masai Mara, saw Olduvai Gorge—in fact I climbed Kilimanjaro.'

Aurora sat up, her eyes wide and wondering. 'Oh! Tell me about it! I wanted to but we didn't have the time.'

Two hours later, they'd shared not only Tanzania but many travel experiences and Aurora was feeling more relaxed than she had for days, even sleepy. She yawned, then apologized. 'It's not that I'm bored, but I haven't had much sleep lately.

His eyes softened. 'Why don't you go to bed?' He stood up.

She hesitated and he saw some of the ghosts come back to her eyes.

'I could stay if you liked. I could doss down there.' He nodded at the settee. 'Just give me a pillow and a rug.'

'That's very kind but—' she began.

'I wouldn't be tempted to take advantage of you,' he said quietly.

Aurora coloured. 'I didn't mean that.'

He looked at her with a sombre question in his eyes.

She swallowed. 'It's just come rushing back to me that we…well—'

'Broke up before we'd barely started?' he suggested.

If only that were true or you knew how tough these two

months have been, Luke, she thought, with her lashes lowered so her eyes were hidden from him.

Then he moved abruptly and her lashes flew up to see that the sombreness had been replaced by a slight smile as he said, 'But we did like each other, didn't we, Aurora? And that's what friends are for at times like these. So don't bother your head with all sorts of complications that don't exist. Just…' he paused, then said humorously '…throw me down a pillow and a rug and go to bed.'

After she'd done that, Aurora took a shower, donned her pyjamas and curled up in her bed with a spare pillow in her arms. She knew she should be thinking of her father—she was, but she was also thinking about Luke; she couldn't help herself. And thinking specifically about what regrets he might have—was that why he'd come? Why he'd said something about breaking up before they'd barely started? Or was he only being a good friend in need?

In which case, how much harder was it going to be for her after two months of still being sure she'd been right to walk away from him but finding absolutely no comfort in it? Despite her flourishing career—she'd made a hit on the airwaves and now had a devoted band of listeners to her talk-back session—she'd felt incredibly lost and lonely. Despite her friends and colleagues and filling her life with interests—she was rarely home—despite it all, the pain of not having Luke in her life was still with her. And now this…

Just the sight of him in khaki moleskins and a blue linen shirt she remembered well, the feel of his arms around her, the way she could talk to him was enough to…what? she mused.

Wonder if it would ever go away, that bereft feeling? Wonder how she could possibly be worse off as Newton's mistress even if she couldn't aspire to be his wife?

Her tired, overwrought mind gave up at this stage and she fell into a deep, dreamless sleep. So deep, she didn't hear the phone ringing downstairs and had no idea she'd forgotten to bring her remote phone upstairs with her.

It was his hand on her shoulder that woke her finally. She sat up brushing her hair out of her eyes and blinking like an owl. 'Who...*Luke*...what?'

He put the phone into her hand. 'Your father.'

She tensed convulsively but Luke smiled at her. 'Talk to him.'

She put the phone to her ear. 'Dad? Is that you? *Dad!*'

Twenty minutes later she ended the call and lay back against the pillows. 'I can't believe it,' she whispered, then sat up jubilantly. 'He's quite OK. It was a battery problem! Well, batteries, bilges and a storm that blew him off course—it was a long story and a bit hard to take in,' she said ruefully. 'And the satellite phone just gave up the ghost! Would you believe it?'

He sat down on the side of the bed and said gently, 'I would. And I'm so very happy for you, Aurora.'

She burst into tears.

He took her in his arms. 'I'm so happy myself,' she wept. 'I really thought I'd lost him. He managed to signal a passing freighter eventually and they came to his rescue. They let him use their equipment and he reckons he'll be able to sail back to the Rarotonga.'

'And you're going to fly over tomorrow if you can arrange it and be there on the dock to meet him.'

'Yes! Perhaps I can even persuade him to give up this round-the-world idea, but, anyway, I can at least spend some time with him. I've got some leave coming up. With a bit of juggling I can get away early.'

He brushed her wet cheeks with his fingers and cupped her face in his hands. 'I've missed doing this.'

She stared up into his dark eyes. 'I've missed it too...'

He smiled briefly. 'I never did get to kiss you goodbye.'

'Is…is that what you're going to do now?'

'Just between friends, Aurora.'

The next day she was winging her way to Rarotonga via New Zealand where she had a joyful reunion with her father but was unable to talk him out of his round-the-world voyage. It was one of the subjects they discussed in their last conversation on board the *Aurora*, before she flew back home a week later.

'I know you worry, I know the last little contretemps took its toll,' Ambrose Templeton said, 'but I'm only sixty, Aurora, and retirement, sitting at home wondering what to do with myself, frightened the life out of me. Also, I'm a sailor at heart and I've dreamt of doing this all my life. Would you, could you be generous enough to allow me to continue with my dream?'

She regarded him wistfully. He looked wonderfully well, tanned and fit, keen-eyed and not the least deterred by his brush with fate. 'Of course,' she said with a sigh. 'Just try to minimize the frights you give me!'

Ambrose hesitated. 'Are you OK?'

'Fine! Why?'

'I…I don't know, can't quite put my finger on it, but it's just occurred to me you're not quite the same. Could there be something—some reason you need me home, darling?'

'None at all,' Aurora reassured him with a grin. 'I'm probably still a bit shell-shocked, that's all. But I would hate the thought of you sitting at home twiddling your thumbs and, although I got such a fright, in my heart of hearts I know you're a consummate sailor. So you have my blessing.' She leant across and kissed his cheek.

An hour later he put her on the plane that took her home. Luke was at the airport to meet her.

She stopped as if she'd been shot as soon as she saw him. He was wearing the same clothes as he had the first time she'd ever seen him. Indigo jeans, a navy jacket, dark blue shirt, although today it was open at the neck.

'This...this wasn't what we decided, Luke,' she said barely audibly as he came up to her and took her bag from her nerveless fingers.

He looked down at her with a glint of mockery plain to be seen in his dark eyes. 'I didn't decide anything, Aurora. I merely went along with your bossiness because it wasn't the time or place to take issue with you.'

'Bossiness?' she repeated blankly. 'How can you *say* that?'

'What else would you call it?' he enquired. 'You chose to sleep with me, you even did it ecstatically.' He looked down her slender figure in a long straight charcoal cashmere skirt with a matching tunic top, red patent shoes on her feet and a scarlet scrunchie holding her hair back, then raised a wry eyebrow. 'You were wonderful in bed, Aurora,' he said *quite* audibly. 'Like a lovely, delicate nymph, all ivory and rose—'

'Stop it, Luke!' she whispered, looking around and nearly dying to see that several people had tuned in with various expressions of amusement or surprise.

'Only if you accept my lift home.'

'No! I...'

'All right. Do you remember when we got to a certain stage how we stopped and sang the Skye Boat song and then—'

'Where's your car?' she said wildly. 'I'll *never* forgive you for this!'

'We'll see. This way.'

She didn't say any more until she was installed in the Saab with the roof closed. Then she turned her furious green gaze on him. 'That was unbelievable! How could you?'

His long fingers played with the keys but he didn't switch the engine on. 'To tell you the truth, Aurora, I found it unbelievable you could sleep with me the way you did then issue a stilted little statement to the effect that nothing had changed and we should regard it as a "ships passing in the night" experience.' He looked at her dryly.

'Why...why didn't you say so at the time?' she stammered.

'You were flying out to Rarotonga the next day. You hadn't recovered from thinking you'd lost your father. You were on an emotional roundabout, that's why.'

She wet her lips. 'But nothing has changed...'

'Apart from the obvious—how would you know?' he shot back.

Several moments later when she hadn't replied, he did switch the engine on and they drove off in silence.

It was a twenty-minute drive home from the airport as darkness fell and that silence lay like a brick wall between them as Aurora recalled so many details of their lovemaking a week ago—including breaking into spontaneous song at one point because she'd felt so very good on all fronts, and her father's safety had still been on her mind, thus the Skye Boat song... She flinched inwardly.

It was she who broke the silence at last, but only to say, 'You took the wrong turning.'

'No, I didn't. You can come and have dinner with me tonight.'

'Luke...'

'Why don't you liken it to your initial experience of me?' he suggested.

'What do you mean?'

'Well, you told me you felt so frustrated you decided to take things into your own hands and it was my fault you felt that way—over the matter of getting your diaries back, Aurora,' he elucidated with an undercurrent of sarcasm.

She cleared her throat. 'I see,' she said in a voice devoid of all expression. 'All right. Just don't count on anything else happening, Luke.'

'You mean you don't see yourself as issuing any invitations tonight, Miss Templeton?'

She gasped, then said fiercely, 'We both got carried away! We...' She broke off frustratedly.

'So we did,' he drawled and drove into his driveway. 'Surely—' he cut the engine and switched his dark gaze to her '—that begs a question if nothing else?'

They ate inside; it was too chilly for the terrace.

It was all prepared and just needed heating up—lasagne and a salad, but it was delicious and bore all the hallmarks of being one of Miss Hillier's concoctions.

'I thought she was away on holiday,' Aurora remarked as they sat opposite each other across a round table in the den, where, as had been in her day, there were some deep, comfortable chairs, a television and this table for informal meals. The chairs were covered in apricot linen with navy piping, the walls were a matt wheat colour with white trim, and the curved window that looked out over the garden gave the room a conservatory feel. There was an extremely fine collection of water-colour landscapes on the walls and a wonderful bowl of gerberas from white to yellow to apricot, orange and deep pink on the coffee-table.

It wasn't an essentially masculine room, but he'd told her that he'd left most of the decorating of the house to Miss Hillier. Aurora had had the feeling ever since that Miss Hillier might have indulged herself in this one room.

Luke had not required any conversation from her until he'd served up dinner. He'd made her a drink and switched on the television so she could watch the evening news. When dinner was on the table, he switched the television off and put Vivaldi on the CD player.

'She was,' he said. 'She came back today. How did you find your father?'

Aurora told him. 'He's having the time of his life and I didn't have the heart to make a fuss,' she finished.

'Did you tell him about me?'

She lifted her gaze to his with a forkful of lasagne halfway to her mouth. 'No. There was nothing to tell.' She ate the mouthful but found it hard to swallow.

'Nothing?' He lay back in his chair and watched her idly until she started to colour.

'Luke—'

'Did it make it into your diary, Aurora? To read over when you're an old lady and—wonder what might have been if you hadn't been so stubborn.'

She stopped eating and sipped her wine. 'No, it didn't.'

'Too painful?' he suggested. 'Too many regrets, perhaps, but you don't know how to handle things since you were the one who laid down the law?'

She looked away with her cheeks now burning and wishing she could press the cool of her wineglass to them. 'Why are you doing this?' she said huskily.

'Because I'm contemplating asking you to marry me and I thought the passage of a week might have made you see things differently. If you've been able to forget that wonderful lovemaking as if it never happened, I haven't. Nor did I think you were the kind of girl to whom those things were…easy come, easy go,' he murmured with a satirical little gesture. 'Do you often sing songs in the middle of sex?'

Aurora pushed her plate away and stood up. 'If your real reason for bringing me here was to insult me, Luke, you've succeeded! Don't bother to see me out, I'll get myself home.'

'Sit down, Aurora,' he ordered.

'You can't make me!'

'I can and I will—and this time I'm serious about it,' he added with a certain rough impatience that left her in no doubt he was.

He watched her react to this, saw the way her fingers whitened on the back of the chair, and suddenly could have kicked himself. 'Please, Aurora,' he said quietly. 'I know you're trying to do what you perceive as the right thing for us, but we need to talk.'

She hesitated, then sank down in her chair.

'We don't need to make such terribly heavy weather of it, however,' he added with a faint smile. 'Tell me about Rarotonga—I've never been there.'

Aurora spread her napkin on her lap and picked up her fork. 'I can't tell you that much about Rarotonga because...' she blinked '...I could have been anywhere in the world.' She dropped her fork and put her fingers to her eyes. 'But it still wouldn't work, Luke.'

'I've done it again,' she said helplessly.

'And just as beautifully,' he agreed as he ran his fingers through her dishevelled hair. 'Mind you, we didn't sing sea shanties this time, but you have a way of making love to me that's—I don't know how to describe it, but it's like capturing a will-o'-the-wisp, a gossamer spirit, the soul of a butterfly in the guise of an exquisite girl.'

She smiled against his chest. 'Thanks, but—how fanciful is that, Professor?'

'It's true.' He drew his long fingers down her spine, then cupped her hip. 'Sleepy?'

'Yes,' she murmured.

'Be my guest.' He drew her head onto his shoulder and pulled the covers over them.

Aurora relaxed with a sigh, revelling in the warmth and the closeness, as well as the feeling of security. Five minutes later she was asleep. And the next morning she flew to Beltrees with Luke Kirwan to spend the second week of her holiday with him.

They had the house to themselves for the first four days. Sir David had taken advantage of Luke's arrival to have some time off—and this time there was no question of separate rooms.

On their first night, after a delicious dinner prepared by the housekeeper and some time spent in front of the huge log fire in the lounge, Luke led her to a double bedroom with a vast bed and its own fireplace with a three piece chintz-covered suite in front of the fire.

He didn't turn any lights on but undressed her slowly in front of the flickering flames.

'Very romantic,' she commented as he unbuttoned her blouse.

'Very,' he agreed, 'but also warm. Just think what it's like outside, clear with a million stars but distinctly cold.'

Aurora shivered. 'I'm glad I'm not out there.'

He removed her blouse, then her bra.

'Would you like me to stand on a footstool, seeing as there's no bonnet of a car handy?' she murmured mischievously.

He cupped her shoulders in his palms and stared down at her high, small breasts. 'I think I can manage. Do I—' he lifted his dark gaze to her eyes '—detect a spirit of playfulness in you, Ms Templeton?'

'Not at all, Professor Kirwan,' she denied. 'I wouldn't presume to mar the solemnity of the moment in any way.'

'Oh, yes, you would, Aurora.' He slid his hands down her arms and stroked her nipples. 'In fact, I get the feeling you specialize in a brand of lovemaking that's far from solemn.'

Her lips twitched. 'I don't happen to be a specialist at it, Professor. I just do, and say, what feels right.'

'So...' he looked down at her nipples as they started to unfurl beneath his thumbs '...at this point in time it feels right for you to point out that I could get a crick in my neck? Is that all you've got on your mind at the moment?' Once again that dark gaze sought hers.

'Not entirely,' Aurora said airily as a tremor ran through her. 'It would be fair to say my mind is on other things as well. Do you know what that does to me?'

'This?' He stroked her nipples again.

Aurora took a breath, but said very gravely, 'It's so nice I'm not sure I could stand what's still to come. It also,' she continued as he started to smile, 'doesn't seem quite fair that I should be the only recipient of this kind of…heaven.'

His smile grew. 'What would you like to do about it?'

'Oh—help you out of your clothes and—show you a thing or two, Luke Kirwan. That's all.'

'All? I don't think *I* could stand that,' he said frankly.

'Well, I think you could stand a lot more than I could,' she replied just as frankly.

'What makes you say that?' he asked curiously.

She stood on her toes and kissed him lightly. 'I just get the feeling I'm in the hands of a master. For your information, I have never sung during sex, before it or after it. And last night I went from vowing to hate you for the rest of my life to—well, being the proverbial putty in your hands.'

'There was no resemblance to putty,' he said softly. 'You were gorgeous.' His hands roamed her upper body at will.

'I think you'd better lead on,' she teased, 'before I die here on the spot.'

But later she wasn't able to tease or be playful as he drew a response from her that left her shuddering with rapture in his arms.

They had a cup of tea and toast very early next morning, then went for a ride.

Aurora wasn't that experienced with horses, but the one Luke chose for her was sure-footed and easy to handle. And he led her to an old opal mine on the property, not much more than a hole in the ground beside a mound of pebbles.

When they dismounted, Aurora looked around at the early morning sky streaked with pink and the vast red-soil country dotted with low sage-green bush that was, apparently, favourite fare for sheep. 'Wow.' She pulled off her hat, threw it into the air and swung her arms joyfully. 'This is wonderful. This is real Australia!'

He laughed. 'You're actually looking quite wonderful yourself, Aurora.'

'Ah, well, I think I might know who to thank for that!'

'I'm feeling exceptionally well myself, as it happens,' he said whimsically. 'But I happen to know exactly who to thank for it.' He reached for her and kissed her. 'You.'

She looked into his eyes and was shaken by the memories of their lovemaking. 'I...' she hesitated '...I felt as if I was flying to the moon.'

'Now who's being fanciful?' he teased. 'But I couldn't fly you to the moon unless it was something we did to each other.'

I'm not so sure about that, Aurora thought, but decided against putting it into words because she didn't think she could explain adequately...

'What is going through those beautiful green eyes at this moment, Ms Templeton?' he enquired.

'Uh—are we looking for opals or meteorite fragments, Mr Newton?' she enquired, with her hands on her hips.

He frowned faintly as if aware of the evasion, then, 'Both. But watch your step,' he warned. 'Those mounds of pebbles are extremely slippery.'

'Romeo!' she responded, causing him to raise an eyebrow at her.

'Mariner's speak,' she explained. 'In the nautical alphabet Romeo stands for R and also means ''yes, will do''!'

'I gather you're an expert on mariner's speak?'

'Oh, yes. Your name would be spelled out—lima, uniform, kilo, echo...and mine is alpha, uniform, romeo, oscar, romeo, alpha—for example.'

He smiled at her crookedly. 'I've often meant to ask you why you volunteer your services to the Coastguard, alpha, uniform, romeo, oscar, romeo, alpha.'

'You picked that up pretty quickly, Professor! Um...I've always been fascinated by radio, I don't really know why. I suppose my father had something to do with it—it's such an integral part of boating. Whenever I was on board with him, I used to spend hours listening to the HF radio. Yachts talking to each other from so far away, weather skeds and the like. Then he suggested I get a radio operator's licence— anyone can take the course, so I took it at the Coastguard and enjoyed it so much I decided to volunteer—what's wrong?'

'I was just thinking...' he paused and ruffled his dark hair, looking momentarily frustrated '...that you're like no one else I know.'

Aurora eyed him in his bush shirt, khaki trousers and boots. 'I should hope so, but I don't see what's so unusual about that.'

'It's not only that. You just...continually surprise me. OK, you look for opals, I'll look for meteorite fragments.'

'I don't like to display my ignorance,' Aurora said, 'but would I know a rough opal if I found one?'

He grinned. 'Probably not. I'll show you what to look for.'

They spent a couple of hours searching and he actually found a small milky-blue opal for her. Then they rode back to the homestead like the wind and tucked into a huge break-fast. And the next couple of days were spent in similar fash-ion. Out and about exploring or helping work the sheep dur-ing the day and spending the nights together.

It was exhilarating by day and Aurora's skin started to glow pale gold, her green eyes shone and she knew she not only looked full of health and vitality but felt it, even in spite of some saddle stiffness she suffered. She also got ex-tremely interested in the subject of meteorites and became as keen as Luke was for the subject.

By night, they talked, listened to music, read—he even got out his old crystal radio set and started to repair it. And they made love whenever the mood took them...

Such as the evening she looked up from her book to see him staring at her with a frown.

'Luke?' she said huskily. 'Have I done something wrong?'

He shook his head and continued to study her.

She'd changed for dinner into her charcoal cashmere skirt and tunic top—the same outfit she'd had on when he'd met her at the airport, even to her red shoes and scarlet scrunchie. They were sitting in front of the fire in their bedroom.

'What is it, then?' she asked.

The firelight played on his dark hair and those fascinating hollows beneath his cheekbones. He'd also freshened up and wore clean jeans and a thin green jumper. 'I was just wondering how to ask you to take your clothes off here and now.'

She raised a wry eyebrow. 'Is that all? You had me worried for a moment.'

'It's not that simple at all. I've been sitting here for the last ten minutes asking myself how you could serenely go on reading your book while I was beset by these fantasies.'

She closed her book and put it aside with a faint, wise little smile curving her lips. 'Who's to say I was so serene?'

'You…weren't?'

'I've just read the same page six times and didn't make any sense of it once.'

'Aurora…' He grimaced. 'I wouldn't have known.'

'That's because I didn't want you to know, just in case our minds weren't running along the same lines. But if they are…' She shrugged and stood up.

Beneath her charcoal top she wore a black bra dotted with tiny strawberries, and when she stepped out of her skirt it was to reveal matching briefs. She heard Luke take an unsteady breath as she straightened, released her hair and shook it out. Then, with her skin touched with the glow of the fire, she took her bra off and slid her briefs down. And she stood before him with her hand outstretched.

He studied the lovely curves of her body, all the slim, petite length of her, then he said rather harshly as his gaze clashed with hers, 'I might not be able to take my time over this.'

'I might not want you to,' she replied barely audibly.

'All the same…' He stopped abruptly.

'Luke, I can cope,' she said gently. 'I'm not breakable. I can even help. Take my hand.'

He got up slowly and put his hand in hers.

She raised it to her mouth and kissed it. 'Come, sweet prince, let's go to bed.'

He hesitated a moment longer, then swept her into his arms and buried his head in her hair.

When she woke the next morning, it was to see that Luke was still fast asleep. She moved cautiously, then sighed voluptuously and stared at the old-fashioned, pressed iron, intricately designed ceiling with a feeling of extreme satisfaction. Not only because of how thoroughly and marvellously sated she felt, but because, for the first time, she had been the one to bestow the fulfilment Luke had been desperate for.

It made her feel like the cat that had got the cream, she reflected ruefully. It made her feel an equal now, rather than a pupil in the hands of a master; it made her feel as if she might have taken him to the moon—instead of the other way around.

Then he stirred, sat up, running his fingers through his hair, and turned to her with sudden, obvious concern. 'How…Aurora? Are you OK?'

'Fine, Luke,' she said complacently. 'Quite fine!'

He threw back the blankets and sheet and examined her minutely.

'Luke,' she protested. 'It's cold!'

He ran his hands down her body, then pulled the covers

up so they were buried beneath them to their chins. 'Thank heavens. I thought I might have been a bit heavy-handed.'

'You were awesome.'

He gathered her close and breathed deeply. 'I certainly got a bit carried away.'

She kissed him lightly. 'It would be fair to say I loved it.'

He smiled at her. 'Sure?'

'Oh, yes,' she said a little dreamily. 'I was thinking only moments ago that I felt like the cat who got the cream. Positively smug, Professor!'

This time he laughed. 'Then how about agreeing to marry me, Aurora?'

Her expression changed slowly. 'I…' she said uncertainly '…I don't know about that, Luke.'

CHAPTER TEN

THERE was a breakfast room leading off the kitchen in the Beltrees homestead. It overlooked the lake and, unlike the rather grand decor of the rest of the house, was country cottagey with a pine dresser laden with blue and white crockery. There was a hatstand laden with Akubras and other hats and a rack for coats, as well as baskets, and on a side-table lay the odds and ends of a riding family: whips, bits and the like.

Aurora was sitting at the breakfast table contemplating bacon, a poached egg and a fried tomato. It was a chilly, overcast day with the lake reflecting the leaden sky above. The swans, which she had seen engaging in a love dance that had made her think of the ballet, *Swan Lake*, were tucked into the reeds on the far bank.

She wore a forest-green pullover with navy track-suit trousers and her hair was tied back severely. Her green eyes mirrored the chaotic emotions that had claimed her since Luke had reacted so savagely to *her* uncertain reaction on the subject of marrying him.

For a moment she'd wondered whether she might break when his arms had tightened around her like a steel trap. Then he'd sworn ferociously and, if you could slam out of a bed, that was what he'd done, leaving her entirely to her own devices.

She'd tried to think about it for some time, then got up and had a shower and dressed. She'd found him in the break-fast room, also showered, from the damp look of his hair, shaved and dressed in jeans and a navy sweater. But the look he'd cast her as she'd come in had been so damning and dangerous, she'd paused in the doorway and contemplated flight.

Causing him to say caustically that he wasn't going to eat *her*, but breakfast was served.

Now, she picked up her knife and fork and started on her meal.

'Would you care to enlarge on your earlier statement, Aurora?' he drawled as he pushed his plate away and reached for the marmalade.

'If you didn't know what was on the cards, why did you come here with me? I did tell you, though. Coffee?'

'Yes, thank you. Uh…' She looked pointedly at the open door leading to the kitchen where she could hear the housekeeper, a voluble, friendly matron, clattering about. 'I don't think this is the right time or place—'

'There's never going to be a better time,' he interrupted, but got up to close the door, not gently.

Aurora grimaced. 'You actually said you were contemplating asking me to marry you, Luke, but in the four days since then you haven't mentioned it again. All right…' she shrugged '…semantics, perhaps, but—why did I come? I couldn't help myself.' She returned his gaze directly. 'That doesn't mean to say marriage is the answer for us.'

'If you're about to cite Leonie, I have it on good authority that she has a new man in her life,' he said coolly. 'If you're about to cite how you came into my life virtually on her heels, we've now known each for something like five months, the last two of which we've spent apart. Time, don't you think,' he said sardonically, 'for me to have sorted myself out?'

Aurora finished her bacon and eggs and reached for her coffee-cup. 'And yet, Luke,' she said steadily, 'if my father hadn't got himself lost, we would still be apart. You've put the house on the market—'

'How did you know that? It hasn't been advertised.'

'Remember Mrs Bunnings? She used to be our housekeeper and Miss Hillier employed her as a cleaner—until a month or so ago when she went to Adelaide to look after her sick sister. We keep in touch.'

He digested this, all the while allowing that dark, arrogant gaze to play over her. 'All right, let's take another tack. Do you usually sleep with men in the uninhibited way you sleep with me, then walk out on them? Or—are you offering to be my mistress?'

Aurora took an unsteady breath and a glint of anger lit her eyes. 'I'm offering you nothing at the moment, Luke. This all happened because I was under extreme pressure one way or another, and because you came to my rescue when I never felt more alone or bereft in my life. I—'

'Only because of your father, Aurora? Or because you were missing me as well?'

She swallowed some coffee, then tilted her chin at him. 'Both. That's my problem, however. But I walked away from you once, Luke, when I wasn't sure you wanted a wife, when I was *quite* sure things weren't over between you and Leonie—and I'm quite capable of doing it again.'

'I haven't seen Leonie from that day to this,' he said.

Her eyes widened.

He smiled satanically. 'What exactly do I have to do to prove to you I want not only a wife but *you*?' he asked lethally. 'Who took whom to the moon last night, incidentally?' His eyes were suddenly mocking.

Her hands trembled around her coffee-cup.

'Don't you think that proves anything?' He eyed her satirically. 'I rather thought it proved something to you when you woke up this morning looking, anyway, so gloriously serene. You could almost say the joke was on me.'

'It's still no reason to rush to the altar, Luke,' she said barely audibly.

'How long would you like, then? A couple of months? Three? That might be a bit hard to arrange because I'm moving up here for the next three months, but I guess we could commute.'

Aurora stood up carefully and for a moment, before she blinked, tears glittered in her eyes. They were gone, however, when she said crisply, 'I'd like to go home today, please. Because I'm now quite sure we wouldn't suit, Luke.'

His mouth was hard. 'I hesitate to repeat your often-spoken phrase, Aurora, but is that all you've got to say?'

'No, it isn't. You should never confuse lust with love, Luke. I would have thought, to be honest, you wouldn't need that explained to you.'

'*Lust?*' he said softly and incredulously.

She clenched her hands. 'As well as friendship, of course—I'll always be grateful for the way you came to me that night. But since there's no way I can prove to *myself* it wasn't a bit of both for a girl who also tugged a chord of pity in you, I think we should leave it there.'

'Lust,' he said again, and this time there was so much sardonic irony in his eyes, she flinched. But he stood up too and came round the table to be directly in front of her, so she was literally being towered over. 'If that's how it came across, Aurora, if that's what you feel you yourself were indulging in...' he paused and waited while her eyes flickered beneath the insult, then went on '...I think you should go home this morning. The plane is going down to Brisbane to pick Dad up, leaving in half an hour. Would that suit you?'

He'd spoken quite mildly but Aurora knew she was on the receiving end of the full force of Luke Kirwan at his most bored and dismissive.

'It would suit me fine,' she whispered, so hurt but also so angry, she was amazed she could speak at all. 'Please don't wait around to see me off. I'm sure someone could run me to the airstrip.'

'Why not,' he murmured, 'if that's what you want?'

'It is.'

He smiled, taking in the strained lines of her face, the sudden pallor, but the fire in her eyes. 'Well, goodbye, Aurora. You've been a few things to me, a cat burglar, a pocket señorita, an unusual lover, a girl who could never resist a challenge—until it came to this. Or perhaps you meant it when you said you intended to stay into "fun" for a good while to come?'

She refused to speak.

He drew the outline of her face with his fingers, then formed a fist to rest it beneath her chin. 'Stay safe, little one.' And he turned away to stroll out of the room.

Aurora was able to hold onto her anger as a means of keeping her composure until she got home. Then it fled away from her as she stared at her goldfish—her neighbour had fed them while she'd been away—and it came home to her that, even while she hated Luke Kirwan, her life seemed to stretch before her in a succession of long, lonely days with only two fish to confide in...

How could he not have understood that, if nothing else, she needed time to think? He was the one who had stepped back from marriage at almost the last moment. He was the one who got these 'calls' to go off and do his own thing, and hadn't been able to see how a wife could understand without feeling slighted. He was the one who *had* accepted her reasoning the last time and rearranged his life accordingly—until her father had got himself lost.

She dumped her bag down at her feet and went to make herself a cup of tea. It was no nicer a day on the coast than up beyond Charleville. Grey, cold and miserable, which was exactly how she felt, she mused as she curled up on the settee with her cup in her hands.

But why did she also feel as if she'd done something wrong?

The thought came to her from nowhere and the word 'lust'

followed straight on its heels. She swallowed a mouthful of tea. She hadn't really meant that, she reflected. It had been a jibe uttered out of anger as well as despair because he had not even attempted to understand how she felt. Yet it had never felt like lust between them…

It had been too wonderful to describe in that term, but she had, and had it turned lethally back on her. Deservedly? Perhaps. Did it make much difference though? she asked herself sadly. Did it alter her conviction that circumstance and pity, rather than real love, had caused Luke to offer her marriage? Or, even if it was real love, could it survive between them?

She finished her tea and contemplated the fact that she had three more days before she started work—and had it to sustain her. And knew suddenly that she couldn't bear three days home alone brooding, she couldn't bear the thought of going to bed alone upstairs because the last time she'd slept in her bed had been the first time she'd slept with Luke Kirwan.

It was so strange, she thought. Once she'd got to know him that arrogant, damningly bored man had become someone quite different, someone she adored—she couldn't deny it as, at last, the tears began to fall. But that dangerous side had come back and she'd run headlong into it.

She put her cup down, wiped her streaming eyes with her fingers and came to a sudden decision. Ten minutes later, after having asked her neighbour to feed the fish again, she was in her car driving north to the Sunshine Coast, hoping to find some sun and solace for the next three days.

'Welcome back! You're looking well, Aurora,' Neil said the next Monday morning. 'All set and rarin' to go? Did you have fun with your father?'

'Thanks, thanks, yes and yes in that order, Neil,' she replied jauntily. 'But I didn't persuade him to come home.'

Neil grimaced. 'Let's hope he's got all the bad luck behind him, then. You have been missed, Miss Templeton! Lots of calls bemoaning the lack of your golden voice on the airwaves.'

'That's…gratifying!'

'There is another piece of news I thought might be of interest to you.' Neil watched her thoughtfully for a moment.

Aurora raised an eyebrow at him.

'Leonie Murdoch has got herself engaged. When she began to be seen in the company of a new man we all thought she was giving Luke the old sauce for the gander, sauce for the goose routine. But Mandy reckons she's really fallen for this bloke.'

'Good,' Aurora said slowly.

'You don't sound too sure,' Neil commented.

Aurora had been staring unseeingly at the console. She shrugged. 'It's none of my business.'

Neil stared at her penetratingly, opened his mouth, then apparently decided against commenting. 'How would you like to interview the Leader of the State Opposition?'

Aurora blinked. 'As in talking politics?'

Neil shook his head. 'As in discussing her pet hobby—growing native Australian bush tucker. Which is not to say the coverage won't provide some political coverage for her, but all you have to be is strictly neutral. When I say ''all'', it's a bit of a challenge, actually,' he added, casting Aurora a fleeting glance. 'If you were to have any strong political leanings one way or the other, for example.'

But Aurora intercepted that fleeting glance and got the uncomfortable feeling that Neil had seen through her carefully erected defences on the subject of Luke Kirwan, and was offering this as bait to help her over it.

Which was just what she needed, she reminded herself. 'OK! How long have I got to prepare for it?'

'That's my girl,' Neil said quietly. 'Three days.'

Two weeks later, on her way home from work, Aurora saw a yellow Saab turn the corner ahead of her, the corner that led up the hill to her old home.

Perhaps Luke was back for a quick visit before the house was sold, she told herself. Or perhaps it was one of any number of yellow Saabs there might be around. But they were not that common, she knew...

That same night she got a phone call from Bunny, back from visiting her sister in Adelaide and full of the news that she'd got her old job back.

'The dragon lady told me the woman they hired to replace me was a disaster and there've been two more since,' she said triumphantly down the line. 'Mind you, you have to be something special to put up with her, but I can't help feeling as pleased as punch.'

'That's great, Bunny,' Aurora said slowly, 'but I thought the house was up for sale?'

'It was for a while but the professor has changed his mind, it seems. And he's spending a lot more time at home these days. Actually, he's a lovely man, not at all what I first thought he was, but then I didn't get to meet him for ages, did I?'

'I...I thought he was spending three months or... thereabouts out west on the family sheep station,' Aurora said raggedly.

'Miss Hillier reckons he's had a change of plan, but how's my little girl going?' Bunny asked breezily.

Aurora stared at the phone for ages after she put it down.

Then she wrapped her arms around her and closed her eyes. What did it mean? What did this tense, jumpy feeling that had invaded her mean for her? That she hadn't given up hope?

She couldn't sleep that night and was incredibly restless for the next couple of days, but nothing happened. No yellow Saab pulling up in front of her house, no phone call, no nothing. And she couldn't believe the pain it caused her to put her hopes to rest once again. Her life reminded her of the autumn equinox: short, desperately busy days, long cold nights and the chill feeling it would be like this for the rest of her life…

Then she got a cold, lost her voice, and had to take a few days off work. At the same time Neil decided to cut her workload so she could concentrate on her music and talk-back programmes. She was in two minds about it—not having to get up at five-thirty in the morning to read the news would be a relief in normal circumstances, but pushing herself to the limits in these circumstances seemed to be about the only way she could cope with life without Luke.

It was a Friday and she was due back at work on Monday, when a lovely basket of fruit and flowers was delivered.

She answered the door and the delivery man said cheerfully, 'Mrs Newton? These are for you.'

'I think you've got the wrong address, I'm not Mrs Newton—' She stopped abruptly.

The man scratched his head and consulted his clipboard. 'Nope, this is the address I've got here.'

'Is there a message?'

They inspected the basket together but there was nothing. 'OK, I'll check back with the shop,' the delivery man said, and pulled out his mobile phone.

Two minutes later he switched it off and pushed it into his pocket. 'The address is right and it was ordered by a man who came in and paid cash for it but he didn't want to send a message—said you'd know what it was all about. He did give his name, though—Isaac Newton.' It was his turn to stop abruptly and look at her acutely. 'Got to be some kind of a joke, right? Even if they didn't twig at the shop, I'm pretty damn sure Isaac Newton isn't wandering round Manly!' He laughed.

'No. Yes. Um…I mean, thanks. I think I know who must have sent them.'

*   *   *

She set the basket on her elephant coffee-table, sat down on the settee and stared at it with her chin in her hands for ages. It had to be a peace-offering—or did it? Perhaps Luke had simply heard via Neil that she was off sick? But…Mrs Newton?

She nearly jumped out of her skin when the phone rang. And she dropped the remote and seemed to be all fingers and thumbs before she got it to her ear.

'Hello…'

'Mrs Newton? This is Carla from the Sheraton Mirage on the Gold Coast. How are you?'

'I…I'm not…I'm…fine,' Aurora said dazedly.

'Mrs Newton, Mr Newton presents his compliments and we have a room reserved for you for tonight and instructions to book a limo to pick you up, should you feel like taking this reservation up—Mr Newton asked me to tell you it was entirely up to you. But, if so, we wondered what time you'd like to be collected?'

Aurora's mouth fell open.

'Ma'am?' Carla of the Sheraton Mirage prompted discreetly after the silence had stretched. 'I believe you're in Brisbane—Manly, actually. It would take about an hour to get down here,' she added helpfully.

Aurora tried to collect herself and looked at her watch. It was two o'clock in the afternoon but… 'Around four?' she heard herself say tentatively. 'Would that…?' She couldn't go on.

'I'll arrange for the limo to be at your door at four, Mrs Newton, and may I say that we look forward to welcoming you to the Mirage!'

'What have I done?' Aurora said to the phone as it went dead in her hands. 'What does this *mean*?' She jumped up agitatedly. More pressure to marry him—but why? Surely she'd let him off the hook… And why wasn't he at Beltrees seeking meteorite fragments?

*　　*　　*

She was still in a state of shock and confusion when the limousine drew up outside the Sheraton Mirage. Then it dawned on her she was going to have to masquerade as 'Mrs Newton' unless Luke was there to meet her, but as she got out of the car and looked around anxiously there was no sign of him.

But as she stood poised, as if for flight, a staff member with a name tag pinned to her jacket bustled forward. It was Carla and she greeted Aurora profusely and offered to lead her to her room. All the check-in formalities had been completed, she confided as they walked through the foyer.

'Is…is Mr Newton around?' Aurora asked hesitantly.

'I'm sure he will be, ma'am,' Carla said serenely.

An hour later there was no sign of Luke so Aurora decided to go for a walk.

It was a wild, overcast day with a strong breeze whipping up the surf and the odd squall passing through. Aurora wore a fleecy-lined track suit and a yellow raincoat as she battled up the beach, head down in the teeth of a minor gale, and battled with the unreality of things.

What was going on? Why had he invited her down, then not even been there to meet her? Was she in the middle of some kind of dream?

She stopped at last, breathless and worried about her voice—it was the last thing she should be doing, braving the elements on top of a recent cold, but she hadn't stopped to think. She *couldn't* think.

She turned around and at least the wind was behind her—then she saw him. A lone, tall figure quite a way from her, but there was no mistaking Luke Kirwan—at least, not for her.

It was a spontaneous reaction, what happened next. She started to run towards him, stumbling in the sand, and he quickened his pace. And she ran right into his arms, crying with frustration and despair…

'Why are you doing this, Luke? I don't know what's going on, I don't know what to think, I don't know why I came—I'm a mess!' she wept.

His arms closed around her. 'Aurora.' He held her closer than he ever had. 'I'm sorry! But I couldn't convince myself you'd really come.'

'I'm sorry,' he said again, this time in the warmth of her room with the shutters closed against the wild weather and lamps on giving the room a gentle glow.

He'd insisted she change into dry clothes and poured them each a brandy. He'd insisted she dry her hair properly and asked her several times if she was warm enough.

Now, as she sat on the settee with her legs curled up beneath her, with no more to be done but feel the warmth of the brandy slip through her veins, he stood in front of her, looking down at her sombrely. Nothing, in the bustle of getting her back to the room, dry and changed, had transpired between them to explain anything, although the way he'd held her in that moment on the beach had given her a slender, delicate little ray of hope. But it flickered beneath this sombre regard and a sense of dread began to take its place.

'Luke,' she said as the words built up in her head and wouldn't be denied, 'I've tried so hard to forget you and convince myself I was right, but it's not working. I know you don't really want a wife but I couldn't be worse off than I am without you, so—'

She stopped as a shudder ran through his tall frame and he sat down in front of her on a padded stool. His hair was still damp and hanging in his eyes. The hollows beneath his cheekbones that she'd always found so fascinating were more pronounced and he looked as if he'd lost weight beneath his navy jumper and bone cord trousers.

'Aurora,' he said with quiet intensity, 'in the space of

getting to know you, I've gone from not really wanting a wife to knowing that I shan't rest until I get one—you.'

She gasped, her green eyes huge.

'I feel like a ship without a rudder. I can't settle to anything, I've lost all interest in meteorites, I couldn't care less how it may have worked for Galileo, living without *you*—is not going to work for me.'

'Luke…'

But he held up a hand. 'This is not something I'm proud of, but I can only say I didn't understand. What love really was, I mean. Yes, Leonie was my companion and my bedmate for three years, but it never filled me with a kind of terror to wake up in the night and think I might have lost her for good. That's what it does to me to think I've lost you. That's why you'd be no good as my mistress, Aurora, if that's what you were going to say—I should spend my life petrified I was going to lose you. I'm sorry, but that's how it is.'

'So it really has nothing to do with…a girl with only two goldfish and a diary to confide in?' she asked tremulously.

'None whatsoever—it's the opposite, if anything. I don't even have a diary or some fish to sustain me. The first time you walked away from me…' he paused and closed his eyes briefly '…I told myself you were better off without a man like me. At the same time, though, I asked myself why I felt as if I was letting something more precious than ruby and pearls slip through my fingers.'

Her lips parted in soundless incredulity.

He smiled, but it was strained. 'The second time you walked away from me I was being entirely unreasonable and I damn well knew it, but I couldn't help myself because I just didn't know how to get through to you.' He shrugged. 'My male ego took an awful hammering that morning.'

Two tears slid down Aurora's cheeks and she sniffed.

He pulled a large blue hanky from his pocket and handed it to her.

She wiped her nose.

'Please,' he said softly, 'don't tell me you still believe it was lust between us. I couldn't stand it. I love everything about you, Aurora. I'm lost without you. I need you more than you may ever know.'

She stared at him wordlessly and read the unflinching honesty in his eyes. Then she put her glass down and leant forward to cup his face in her hands. 'Mr Newton,' she said huskily, 'I need *you* more than I ever dreamt I'd need anyone.'

'You've done it again,' he said, in a teasing paraphrase of what she'd once said to him.

She stirred drowsily in his arms. The night was dark outside and it was still blowing a minor gale, but beneath the covers of her bed they were naked and sated after a glorious lovemaking. 'Tell me.'

'You've bestowed that sheer joyful spirit like a beautiful butterfly in the guise of a gorgeous girl on me, Aurora. I love you.'

She snuggled against him, revelling in the planes and angles of his body and how soft and silky she felt against him, how he'd transported her to the moon again, although this time they'd gone together and matched each other every step of the way.

'Mind you...' he stroked her back, then buried his head briefly in her hair '...I can't help having qualms about repeating myself. Will you marry me, Aurora? There, it's out,' he said humorously, looking into her eyes.

'Luke, I would love to marry you,' she said. 'It's quite simple, really—I adore you.'

'Aurora—' He stopped, then went on, 'Is that really true?'

'Oh, yes,' she assured him, and he could see it in her eyes in a way that took his breath away. He buried his head between her breasts and she stroked his hair.

Then he looked up reluctantly. 'Even...the absent-minded

professor in me, the guy who gets strange calls to do strange things and all the rest?' There was a question mark in his dark eyes.

'Well, there may be times when I'll blame the apple too,' she said gravely, 'but—what we feel for each other will find a way, don't you think?'

'I always knew you were wise as well as gorgeous,' he said a little unsteadily.

'Actually, you started off thinking I was a groupie, Professor,' she reminded him.

'I learnt that lesson the hard way,' he said wryly. 'But there are several things you didn't take into consideration about me. What good husband material I would make, how romantic I could be—'

'Luke—' she started to laugh, then kissed him back '—you're right, I certainly didn't expect…this.' She gestured with a wondering expression on her face, to take it all in: the hotel, the limo, the plans he'd made, Mrs Newton…

'And you haven't seen this yet.' He sat up and reached for his trousers flung across the bottom of the bed.

Aurora traced the long line of his back and felt the muscles flow beneath the skin. 'This' was a black velvet box drawn from the pocket of his trousers. She sat up, brushing her hair back, and stared at it.

'Open it,' he said quietly, putting it into her hand.

She flicked the lid up and went absolutely still. It was a pearl engagement ring exquisitely set in a circlet of tiny rubies and diamonds.

'You…meant it,' she whispered at last, looking up into his dark eyes.

'Every last word of it, Aurora. I hope that every time you look at it, you'll know just how much you do mean to me.'

'Luke…' she rested her head on his shoulder and her voice shook '…thank you, but I've got nothing for you in return.'

'Darling—' he took her in his arms and kissed her lingeringly '—every time you feel like singing when we make love is a priceless gift for me.'

Her lips quivered. 'I knew you'd never let me forget that—' She stopped suddenly. 'Actually, I do have something for you—where did I put my bag? Oh, there it is.'

It was on the bedside table. She opened it and drew out a tiny suede drawstring bag. She undid the ties and poured the contents into the palm of her hand—a very fine gold chain with a milky-blue opal mounted in gold and hanging from it. 'Do you remember this?'

He nodded, staring down at the opal.

'I got it set and put on the chain and, right up until this afternoon, I've worn it next to my heart—I felt if I couldn't have you, I could have this little part of you as a good luck charm and something to remind me of the only man in the world I wanted to love.'

He took it from her and put it over her head, and he settled the stone between her breasts. Then he held her very close. 'Thanks,' he said unevenly into her hair. 'I don't know what to say.'

'Don't say anything,' she suggested, and she slipped her arms round his neck and started to croon against the corner of his mouth, an old song… 'Fly me to the moon…' She broke off and there were tears of joy in her eyes, although she said whimsically, 'How appropriate is that, Professor?'

He lay back with her and murmured wryly, 'Singularly appropriate and—request granted, ma'am.' He did just that.

MILLS & BOON®
By Request

RELIVE THE ROMANCE WITH THE BEST OF THE BEST